# Cowboy Desire

Zia Westfield
Callie Carmen
Virginia Wallace
Jan Selbourne
Alice Renaud
Estelle Pettersen
Eileen Troemel
Nancy Golinski
Patricia Elliott
Dee S. Knight
R.M. Olivia
Starla Kaye
Alan Souter
Suzanne Smith

ISBN 978-1-914301-05-6

Published 2021

Published by Black Velvet Seductions Publishing

Cowboy Desire Copyright 2021 Zia Westfield Callie Carmen Virginia Wallace Jan Selbourne Alice Renaud Estelle Pettersen Eileen Troemel Nancy Golinski Patricia Elliott Dee S. Knight R.M. Olivia Starla Kaye Alan Souter Suzanne Smith
Cover design Copyright 2021 Jessica Greeley

# Table of contents

# Introduction

An eclectic collection of short stories exploring the topic of cowboys, and western themed love. The collection is as diverse as the authors writing them. I love the variety of stories you get when you ask fourteen authors to write on a given topic. The result surprised and delighted me.

I love anthologies, I always have. From the reader's point of view, they give you the chance to read the work of authors you might not have read before. For writers, it gives us the chance to explore a subject we might not usually write about.

The stories within these pages mix soft and tender, often moving and thought provoking, to sexier raunchy pieces. I hope you will enjoy reading them as much as I have.

Richard Savage
CEO, Black Velvet Seductions

# Wild Thunder
## Zia Westfield

## Chapter One

The chill started at the base of her spine and traveled upward, causing her to scoot towards the seductive warmth in front of her. Emmaline came up against something hard, hairy, and radiating enough heat to make her relax. Somewhere in the back of her mind, she knew she wasn't exactly sleeping, but she couldn't seem to forge through the layers of fog to wakefulness.

A spicy scent penetrated the fog. She liked it and snuggled further into the heat. Really, it was most odd. Had she left her bedroom window open?

She tried to think, but her temples throbbed. In fact, it was more like a pounding.

"Hold your horses." The voice slid along her nerve endings like her favorite flavor of chocolate fudge ice cream.

Instead of giving her a sense of peace, the thought acted like a jolt of electricity. Emmaline opened her eyes and groaned at the light streaming through the window, then covered her eyes with her arm. Beside her, she heard a masculine voice swear and felt a shifting that caused her to roll towards the center of the bed and into the very warm body that accompanied that voice. She felt muscles and a sprinkling of hair against her cheek.

None of this made sense. There was a man in her bed. She had no idea who he was or how he'd gotten there. Not good. Her brain could work out that much.

She pried her eyelids open, but that only left her with an eyeful of chest muscles. She took a deep breath to calm her unsettled stomach.

The spicy scent she'd inhaled earlier tickled her nostrils.

At least the stranger in her bed smelled nice. Though what a stranger was doing in her bed was a point of confusion she couldn't quite hold onto.

The pounding she'd thought was her head, seemed to be coming from the door. "Who could that be?" she managed to croak out.

"Hell if I know," the male voice replied with a rumble that reverberated through her body.

She gulped, rolled over and raised herself up on one elbow.

Before she could lift her gaze enough to see her guest, the door burst open and she lunged for the sheet to make sure all bits were covered.

"Room service," a man said as he pushed a cart in.

Room service? Emmaline blinked and took in the decor. This wasn't her bedroom. She wasn't in her house. She wasn't in her bed.

A bright flash blinded her, followed by another and then another, along with the familiar click of a camera.

"What the—?" her companion growled, as he thrust the bed covers aside and stood up.

She got an eyeful of broad shoulder muscles, brown skin and a tapered waist that led to a pair of nicely-fitting boxer shorts. A combination of relief and disappointment swept through her. It was certainly better that he was partially clothed, or she'd have to really face the fact that she'd had her first one-night stand.

The pressure in her head beat a nice little tattoo against her temples. She rubbed them, and that's when she noticed her blouse. She was wearing it. She peeked under the comforter and saw she was still wearing her jeans.

Vaguely, she was aware of the door slamming shut. Her mind scrambled to find an explanation. She squeezed her eyes shut and tried to recall the previous evening. She'd meant to meet her friend Helen for a night out. They'd been drinking. Emmaline was usually careful about how much she drank, but last night she'd decided to cut herself some slack. She recalled some guy sending over drinks and flirting with Helen. After that, not so much.

That spicy scent announced his presence as surely as a bullhorn. Opening her eyes, she found herself looking at crotch-level. Hastily, she raised her gaze, skimming over a hard chest, a stubborn jaw, thick lips and flashing brown eyes. *Oh boy.*

He bent over, his hands fisted on his hips. "Were you in on this? Who put you up to it? Daniels?"

She took a steadying breath. "You're scaring me."

His gaze narrowed, and then he swore under his breath and turned around to march over to the wall. He leaned back, crossing his arms over his chest. "Talk." That was better, but felt rather like a guard interrogating a prisoner.

Emmaline tucked a strand of hair that was falling in her face behind her ear and tried to think of an explanation. She had none. "I was hoping you could tell me how I ended up here." She looked down at herself. "I'm still wearing my clothes. Thank you, I think."

"You said your name was Emmaline Winslow. That true?" The rise at the end of his question told her clearly what he thought.

"Of course, it's true," she said indignantly, swinging her feet over the side of the bed.

He didn't relax the prison guard image. "And you really work at the Rocosa Ridge Sunset Village?"

So she'd told him that much. She wished she could remember what he'd told her, but right now her stomach was staging a rebellion and the drum in her head was going to make her brain leak. She spied the door to her interrogator's right. "I'll be happy to answer your questions in a few minutes, but right now, I think I have an appointment with a porcelain bowl."

She stood, pleased that she didn't wobble too much, and then ran for the bathroom door, closing it firmly behind her.

When she emerged from the bathroom eons later, she gazed longingly at the bed and contemplated the number of steps it would take her to get there. She stepped forward and stopped. The room was empty. She caught the lingering spicy scent of her stranger, but he was gone.

She took a few more steps and grabbed the desk chair. A piece of notepaper fluttered, held down by a pen. She picked it up and read the brief message telling her the room was paid for until one o'clock and that he'd be in touch. He'd scratched a signature at the bottom, but she couldn't make heads or tails of the scrawl. She read the words again. He'd be in touch. What the heck did that mean?

She dropped the paper back on the desk and made her way to the bed. Later. She'd make sense of this mess after she could see the world without a permanent tilt.

## Chapter Two

Gabriel Santos pulled into the parking lot of the Rocosa Ridge Sunset Village and found a spot not too far from the glass front doors. He got out of his truck and shut the door. He angled his cowboy hat against the strong New Mexican sunshine and considered his best approach.

He'd already figured out that Emmaline Winslow was as much a victim of that photographic assault as he was—maybe more. The damage was already done. The photos were out there, and even though Emmaline had been dressed, the photographer had done a nice editing job to make it look a whole lot more sleazy.

Gabriel's fists clenched at his sides and he had to breathe out slowly to release the anger roiling inside him.

He stared out over the craggy landscape, searching for peace in the trees and bluffs that stretched out across the skyline. Slowly, his muscles relaxed.

Somehow, he had to get Emmaline to agree to his plan.

He strode towards the entrance, determination in every step. At the reception desk he flashed a smile at the middle-aged, slightly plump blonde manning the desk. "I'd like to speak to Emmaline Winslow, please."

Her eyes widened the more she stared at him. She opened her mouth and then glanced over her shoulder to an office with the word *Manager* on a sign plate attached to the wall beside the door. Through the glass, he saw Emmaline. She sat stiffly, while a woman with short gray hair spoke to her. Emmaline stood up and exited the room.

"Um," the blonde said, "I think you can talk to her now." She swiveled her seat. "Emmaline, you have a visitor."

Emmaline walked forward, her head bowed. She wore a long yellow skirt and a white blouse that hid her body, but he remembered the way her jeans had clung to her legs and bottom. It took time for the receptionist's words to penetrate and for Emmaline's head to come up. Gabriel's mouth hardened when he saw the suspicious shine in her blue eyes. *Damn!* She looked ready to cry. From the color surging in her cheeks, she clearly recognized him.

She marched past him, saying "I don't have anything to say to you."

"Well, I have something to say to you. And I can do it here, where everyone can hear me, or we can go somewhere more private."

That made her stop. She glared at him over her shoulder. "This way," she ground out.

He followed her into a cubicle of an office, standing at the doorway to give her room. She took a small box, removed pamphlets from it and put them on a shelf. She then picked up a small potted plant and put it in the box. A few bits of stationery followed and a photo in which she was surrounded by old people. He supposed they lived at the facility, but there were no other photos. No parents. No boyfriend. Given what'd happened the other night, he'd assumed she was unattached, but nowadays, you never knew.

Her shoulders sagged and she turned to exit the room, only to seem to recall that he was standing there. He plucked the box from her hands. "We'll talk outside."

She nodded, and whatever fight she'd had in her before whooshed from her like a deflated balloon.

Outside she pulled on a pair of sunglasses and headed to a dark blue sedan. Crossing her arms over her chest, she faced him, her eyes hidden behind the dark lenses.

"Talk," she said, but before he could begin, she let loose. "I was just let go from my job—a job I love, I might add—all because of you and those horrid photos. They're all over social media." She raised her glasses and swiped at her eyes with one arm before lowering them again. "And I don't even know you!"

A cool breeze blew in from the mountains, causing the hem of her long skirt to flutter and her to rub her arms up and down. The scent of lemon wafted to him.

"Gabriel Santos. I followed the rodeo circuit for many years. I grew up in Rocosa Ridge but left after high school. I only came back when my brother and his wife settled here."

She brushed a strand of hair away from her face. "All right, Mr. Santos. That's who you are, but that still doesn't explain what happened."

A few cars had pulled in and doors slammed as people got out. Gabriel noticed some of the people observing them.

"Look, why don't we go someplace more private to talk."

She turned her head, noticing their audience. "I don't think I can walk into a restaurant right now." Her voice dropped. "The gossip." She shuddered.

"How about the Pink Cow?" The local fast-food restaurant sat on the edge of town. "It's early, so there won't be many people there, and we can sit outside on one of the picnic benches."

"All right." She held her hands out for her box and he placed it in them. He studied her, uncertain what more to say. In the end, he said nothing, pivoting and going back to his truck.

The entire way to the Pink Cow, he checked his rearview mirror to see that she was following and hadn't bailed on him. Somehow, he had to persuade her to help him. His fingers tightened around the steering wheel as he recognized she had little reason to since she might view him as responsible for costing her her job. He'd find a way to repay her or help get her a new position. He'd do about anything if she'd agree to his plan.

After they arrived, he ordered coffees for them both and a breakfast burrito for himself and then led the way to a picnic table set on a grassy area. He passed the coffee with milk and sugar to Emmaline and sat across from her.

"Thanks," she said. She still wore her sunglasses, though she'd added a sweater to her outfit.

He unwrapped his burrito and wondered why his hands itched to remove her glasses. He told himself it was because he wanted to look into her eyes to see how she took his request, and not because that shade of cornflower blue was the prettiest shade of blue he'd seen in a while.

He took a bite of his burrito and slowly chewed, looking out at the mountains, letting the silence settle over them. Emmaline sipped from her coffee and by degrees appeared to relax in the late morning sun.

Gabriel finished off his burrito and wiped his mouth. "I told you that I only came back to Rocosa Ridge because my brother and his wife settled here. A few months back they died when the road they were driving on was washed out by mud." He paused and cleared his throat. He still couldn't believe his older brother Francisco was gone. "Their son, my nephew, Alex, managed to survive. He's four years old."

"I heard about that accident. It was terrible," Emmaline said. She reached across the table and laid her hand on his arm. Her hand was warm, her skin a lighter color than his, and he noticed that she kept her nails short and devoid of polish. "I'm so sorry for your loss." She pulled her hand back and he wanted to protest.

Instead, he continued. "I'm in a custody battle with Alex's grandfather, my sister-in-law's father. Neither my brother nor his wife left a will, at least none we can find. The ranch is in my name and Francisco's, as it was passed down through our father. But Alex is also the only heir to his grandfather, who is a wealthy landowner."

"It sounds like Alex is caught between you," she said quietly. "But what does this have to do with the photographs?"

Gabriel rubbed the back of his neck. He'd known this was coming and he would have to lay it all on the line, but he needed to see her reaction when he did so. "Would you mind taking off your sunglasses?"

"My glasses?" Her hand came up, she paused and then removed them, laying them beside her coffee.

Cornflower blue. He'd ridden his horse, Thunder, through a field of cornflowers that exact color. The beauty of it was etched in his memory.

But Thunder was gone, having disappeared the night of his brother's accident. And this woman sitting across from him held his fate in her hands. He had to forge ahead.

"Thank you." He pushed aside the tray that held his burrito wrapper and his coffee and leaned his elbows on the table. "Alex's grandfather was behind that dirty trick with the photographer. I'm sure of it."

He watched her for signs of what she was thinking, but her expression remained closed.

"Do you have any proof?"

Gabriel lifted his head and blew out a breath. "No, I don't have any proof, but I'm sure of it. The court-assigned social worker is coming on Saturday to check out the ranch. It's pretty convenient that my face was plastered all over social media to make me look like an irresponsible playboy out for a good time just before that visit."

"My face, too," Emmaline added.

Gabriel winced. "I know, and I'm sorry. You'd had too much to drink. I couldn't let you drive home, but I couldn't leave you in that bar either. You would've been easy prey for some of the guys there. I'd intended to sleep on the chair or the floor. I think I moved during the night." He shrugged. "Next thing I knew, we were in bed together and there was a knock at the door."

"I don't usually drink very much," Emmaline admitted. "I'm not sure what got into me that night." Her eyes dropped, and he had a feeling she wasn't revealing the entire truth but let it go.

"I need your help. My lawyer tells me that I'm in a bad spot right now. Those photos could knock the legs out from under my case."

A wrinkle creased Emmaline's brow. He wanted to reach across and smooth it out. She was nothing like the flirty, out-for-a-good-time women he usually dated. There was a quiet dignity and strength about this woman, overshadowed by the "No Trespassing" vibe she gave off.

"What exactly are you asking for?" she finally asked.

Gabriel sucked in a breath. Here it was. Time to lay it all on the line. "I want you to be my fiancée."

## Chapter Three

For the thousandth time Emmaline questioned her reason for being in the foyer of Gabriel Santos' ranch house. But she knew why she was there. The idea of Alex being a pawn caught between two adults tugged at her heartstrings.

It really wasn't her business. Maybe Alex was better off with his grandfather. But she simply couldn't ignore the situation.

It hit too close to home, to the little girl caught between two indifferent parents that she'd been.

She'd arrived less than an hour ago. Gabriel had given her a quick tour and had disappeared, leaving her in the foyer as they waited for Alex and the social worker to arrive.

The white two-story house with its wrap-around porch and green trim would welcome the visitor. Inside colorful throws and pillows lightened the dark leather furniture. Instinctively, Emmaline knew it was Gabriel's sister-in-law who had added the feminine touches. A photo of the couple sat prominently on the stone mantelpiece. There were other photos, some clearly from more than a century past. History peeked out from every corner, from the hand-carved staircase to the second floor, to the antique bootjack that had been placed near the front dooShe heard the sound of an approaching engine. Gabriel bounded down the stairs. "They're here."

He stood before her, looking impossibly handsome. He was a rodeo star. She'd looked him up and knew he'd won at least two championship titles for bronc riding. So, okay, he was currently a former rodeo star. But she was not the kind of woman to hook up with a cowboy. Gabriel had to have had women falling all over him. He was way out of her league.

He shifted his feet, his expression serious. Reaching into his jeans pocket, he pulled out a diamond ring. "This was my mother's. I'd like you to wear it."

Emmaline's heart pounded, blood rushing to her head. She couldn't think. He took her hand, his skin rough from working on the ranch. He slid the ring on her finger. It was a little big and she curled her fingers to keep it from falling off.

"I'll get it sized properly next time we're in town." He grabbed the front doorknob and pulled the door open. Dirt spewed up as a small car pulled into the circular drive.

Emmaline's head was in a whirl. She hadn't expected a ring. But how could she back out now?

Gabriel placed his hand on her lower back and ushered her forward. The heat from his hand seeped through her clothing, warming her from the inside out. Gabriel exuded strength and a deep sense of family. She could admire it even as she told herself that she was playing a role. If Gabriel really had Alex's welfare in mind, she'd help him, but if he was looking to use Alex for some agenda of his own, she'd walk away.

A middle-aged woman emerged from the small silver compact. She opened the rear passenger door and a moment later a little boy emerged. He wore jeans and a red superhero sweatshirt.

"Uncle Gabriel!" he yelled and ran to Gabriel, wrapping his arms around his leg. Gabriel reached down and lifted the boy onto his shoulders. Alex squealed in delight.

The social worker came up and introduced herself. Gabriel led the way into the house and lowered Alex to the ground. Alex looked around and it was painful to see the transformation as a shroud of grief weighed the boy's shoulders down.

Emmaline dropped to her knees beside him and spoke softly. "Alex, I'm Emmaline, your Uncle Gabriel's fiancée. That means we're going to get married." The words tripped off her tongue. A part of her was appalled at what she was doing, while another part wanted to do whatever it took to help Alex. "Why don't you show me your bedroom while your uncle talks to Ms. Tillman?"

Gabriel tousled Alex's hair. "Go with Emmaline. Show her your horse collection. We're going to spend the day together, so think about what you want to do after lunch."

Alex gave a shy smile. "'Kay. Let's go," he said to Emmaline.

In his bedroom, Alex proceeded to drag out all his possessions, the most beloved of which was a stallion he claimed was just like Thunder.

"Uncle Gabriel says Thunder is gone like Mom and Dad. Do you think he's up in heaven, too?"

Emmaline's breath caught in her throat. Big brown eyes looked at her with too serious an expression. "I bet that wherever Thunder is, he's watching out for you, and your mom and dad."

The answer seemed to satisfy Alex because he returned to his toys, keeping up a running commentary. He handed her a pony and then returned to building his western town. The white pony with head up and one foot raised looked ready to tackle anything, despite its size. Emmaline smiled and slid to the floor where she joined in the play.

"You both look like you're having fun." Gabriel stood in the doorway, his casual strength making her heart flutter. She forced her gaze on Alex instead.

He ran to his uncle and grabbed his hand. "Come play with us."

Gabriel snatched his nephew up and swung up, making Alex squeal. "Time for lunch, but tell you what, how about we go riding this afternoon."

Alex hugged his uncle around the neck. "Yes, please!"

"Go wash your hands, buddy" Gabriel ordered. As Alex rushed off to the bathroom, Gabriel reached down and offered her a hand up. "Thanks. I really appreciate that you kept Alex occupied while I talked to the social worker."

Emmaline felt herself flushing. "No problem. Did everything go okay?"

Gabriel shrugged. "She's satisfied that Alex enjoys being with me, but beyond that, who knows?"

After lunch they saddled horses and took a ride to a creek on the property. Alex rode with his uncle, sitting in front of Gabriel, his face alight with curiosity. For Emmaline, it'd been a while since she'd been on a horse and it felt exhilarating.

She sat on a blanket enjoying the afternoon sun, while Gabriel skipped rocks across the creek with Alex. The diamond on her finger sparkled in the sunshine. It was an old-fashioned setting and she thought it was beautiful. Once more she wondered what she'd gotten herself into, a pretend engagement with a man she barely knew.

Gabriel dropped down beside her and tipped his head back so that she got a better view of the hard planes of his face, the skin darkened from years outdoors, and those impossibly long lashes that made her heart beat too fast.

"Alex is a great kid," she said.

"Yeah, he is. It's just the two of us now. I can't lose him." His voice roughened and there was a wealth of emotion captured there. "Thank you for being here today."

She was far too susceptible to this man. Desperate to change the topic, she said, "Alex mentioned a horse named Thunder. What happened to him?"

A shadow crossed Gabriel's features as if the sun had hidden behind a cloud. "Thunder was mine, a stallion I raised and trained myself. When I was in town, I'd stable Thunder here with my brother. The night of the accident, I was in Santa Fe and I'd left Thunder here, like usual." He paused and stared out towards the horizon. "I got a phone call in the morning. They'd found my brother's truck half-buried in mud. There'd been a bad storm that night. It looked like the road had washed out and the truck had gone into a gully. He'd gotten Alex out and then he went back for Katherine when they were hit by a mudslide."

Emmaline placed a hand on his leg, the diamond winking in the light. "I'm really sorry. I can see how much you love Alex."

His hand came up and covered hers, the feel of his calloused skin sending goosebumps along her skin. She was responsive to this man and it unnerved her.

"The social worker will pick Alex up this afternoon. She's agreed to bring him to visits each weekend until the court decides custody." His thumb caressed her skin creating tingles of heat.

Emmaline strove to keep her voice steady. "So he lives with his grandfather now?"

"Oh yeah, Big James Daniels, owner of the largest spread around here. He wasn't happy when his daughter fell for a local rancher with a mixed heritage of Mexican and Native American. But that hasn't stopped him from demanding complete control over Alex." His brows slashed downward and his features tightened.

Emmaline turned her hand so that their hands were palm to palm. The need to comfort this man seemed to rise up from deep inside her. "Alex loves you. I'm sure you'll find a way to have him in your life."

He tightened his hold on her hand and studied her. She glimpsed a vulnerability in his gaze that speared straight to her heart. "Maybe," he said, "but my lawyer says it will be difficult without you. Will you continue to be my fiancée? Will you help me?"

She glanced over at Alex, his freckled nose wrinkled as he watched a bug crawl along his hand. He deserved to be happy and loved. He'd lost so much in his short life. And then there was this man beside her who took her breath away even as he touched on something she didn't recognize in herself.

"Yes, I will."

## Chapter Four

Gabriel patted the head of Cleopatra, a dark chestnut mare with a black mark in the center of her forehead, who was in the early stages of her pregnancy. "Looking good, old girl. I'll have the vet come out next week to check on you." Cleo was one of several horses he and his brother had purchased over the years. They'd planned to build a horse breeding and training ranch. Now there was only Gabriel to carry it on, and maybe one day, Alex.

He gave one last pat and stepped outside the barn door, closing things up for the night. Thunder rumbled in the distance. They were in for some storms over the next several days.

Gabriel pulled off his hat and swiped his arm across his brow. Sweat stained the back of his shirt and plastered his hair to his scalp. He stunk like horses and a day of working in the fields.

The first thing he was going to do was shower off the stink and then he was going to grill a steak and drink a cold beer. After that, he'd call Emmaline.

Nearly three weeks had passed since he'd asked her to be his fiancée. She'd been with him for a second visit with Alex and he'd also taken her out to lunch and dinner. He liked her company. She was refreshing in her honesty and lack of pretense. She took pleasure in simple things like the wildflowers along the side of the road or a butterfly landing on his arm.

He'd never met anyone like her before and he didn't know what to do about it.

In two weeks, he was scheduled to go to court for a custody hearing. He didn't have the money Big James Daniels did, but he wasn't going down without a fight.

Later in the evening, with a beer in hand, he went out on the front porch and sat on the rocker Katherine had placed there. She and

Francisco would sit there in the evenings and talk about their day. They'd so been in love.

He rubbed his chest as he recalled the memory. Now it seemed quiet and empty, despite the light fall of rain, the chirps of the night insects, and the occasional whinny of one of the horses.

He pulled his cell phone out of his shirt pocket and pressed Emmaline's number. She answered on the second ring rather breathlessly.

"Did I catch you at a bad time?" he asked.

"No, not at all. I'd left my phone in the kitchen. I was on the back porch trying to coax that kitten to come eat. It gets close and then runs away." She laughed a bell-like tinkle that called to his blood.

"It'll come around." He didn't doubt that she'd win the feline over. She'd won him and he was a lot tougher to take down.

"We'll see. How was your day?"

He told her about the never-ending chores and repairs he'd done about the place. He found himself confiding more and more with her about his plans. Emmaline listened and asked practical questions that had helped him refine some of his plans.

"How about you?" he asked in return. "How's the job hunting going?" He felt bad that she'd lost her job because of what'd happened. And yet, he probably wouldn't have met her if it hadn't. The idea of not having her brightness in his life squeezed his chest tight.

"I've applied for a few things. We'll see." She paused, and he could imagine her tucking a strand of hair behind her ear. "I've got some savings, so I'll be fine. Don't worry."

A beep sounded and Gabriel pulled away to see that he had an incoming call. He recognized the local number for the Daniels spread. Had something happened to Alex?

"Hang on, Emmaline. I've got another call."

He didn't wait to hear her reply; he switched lines. "Santos."

"Uncle Gabriel?" The young, frightened voice filled the line.

Gabriel shot up from the rocker. "Alex? What's going on, buddy? You okay?"

Sniffles filled the line. Gabriel hurried back inside and grabbed his key. He was halfway to his truck when Alex replied. "Grandpa won't get up."

Relief coursed through Gabriel. Alex was okay. It was Big James who was in trouble. "Alex, is there anyone else in the house with you?"

"No. Jus' me and Grandpa."

"Stay on the line, Alex. I'm coming. I'll be there soon."

Not wanting to chance losing the connection, Gabriel sent a quick text to Emmaline explaining the situation and asking her to send an ambulance. He put his truck in gear, hit the windshield wipers and headlights, and peeled down the drive. The Flying S had been in the Santos family well before the Daniels family had settled in Rocosa Ridge, but there was no doubt that the Daniels ranch, the Triple D, covered more acreage and ran a much bigger operation. As he drove, he kept a running dialogue with his nephew, fear for Alex clawing at his throat.

Gabriel barreled under the Triple D arch, noting that the gates were standing open. He pulled to a stop in front of the ranch house, flung the gear into park and turned off the engine. He hopped down from the cab and ran to the front door, his boot heels clacking against the cement drive. Before he could climb the porch steps, a wrangler rounded the corner. He had a hitch in his step, which was about all Gabriel could distinguish in the darkness.

"Who're you?" a gravelly voice asked.

"Gabriel Santos. Alex's uncle," he added impatiently. "He called me to say Big James had fallen. I drove over and I'm going in."

He saw that the front door was partially open. Heart pounding, he pushed the door open the rest of the way and stepped inside. Behind him, he heard the old cowboy following him, but the man didn't protest.

Gabriel had never been inside the Daniels' place, neither had Francisco. Big James had cut his daughter off when she'd eloped with Gabriel's brother. Yet, after the accident, Big James had been determined to hold onto his grandson.

"Alex!" he shouted.

"Uncle Gabriel," Alex called back.

"Sounds like he's in the family room," the old cowboy said, brushing past Gabriel and leading the way forward.

They found Alex sitting by his grandfather in a large recreation room, a telephone in his hand. Big James lay sprawled on the floor, unconscious. There was a small trickle of blood near his hairline. The old cowboy leaned over, checking for a pulse. Gabriel scooped up his nephew and hugged him. He closed his eyes and winged a prayer of thanks to every religious entity he could think of.

An ambulance siren penetrated the silence. "I called them when I got Alex's call," Gabriel explained, blessing Emmaline for doing as he'd asked.

"Best to wait for the medics." The old cowboy rocked back on his heels and observed Alex. "I'm Toby Gwynne. Was the foreman. Retiring. Me and the missus are heading south tomorrow to be with our daughter. She's expecting our first grandbaby." He scratched his chin. "Must've tripped or something. He's stubborn as a mule and too damn hard-headed to die over something like this."

Gabriel wasn't sure if it was a warning for himself or reassurance for Gwynne. It didn't matter. As long as Alex was safe, that was all he cared about.

The paramedics entered and took over. Gabriel moved out of the way, ensuring Alex didn't see or hear too much. He knew that he'd have to go to the hospital and follow up on the old man. As big as the gulf that lay between himself and Big James, the man was still Alex's grandfather, and Katherine's father. Gabriel had always believed in family and had always done his duty.

The paramedics lifted Big James onto a stretcher and strapped him in. Gabriel and Alex watched them wheel the stretcher out the front door.

"You all right, Alex? I'm proud of you for calling me to help your grandfather." Gabriel didn't want to think of Alex being alone with his grandfather on the floor for the entire night.

Alex pulled his thumb out of his mouth, a habit that Katherine had worked hard to break him of, and that he clearly had returned to due to everything happening to him. "Is Grandpa goin' to be okay?"

"They're going to do everything they can. Would you like to go to the hospital?"

Alex nodded slowly. "Why'd the bad man hit Grandpa?"

Gabriel nearly stopped breathing. "Bad man? What bad man?"

Alex shrugged, and clung tighter to Gabriel. "I woke up. Grandpa was shoutin'. So I came downstairs. It was dark down here. A big man hit Grandpa and he fell. The bad man ran away."

Gabriel didn't know who the bad man was, but he'd have to report it to the Sheriff. "Let's go pack a bag, buddy. We'll go visit the hospital, and then you'll stay with me for a while."

"Will Emmaline be there?" Alex asked, his head tucked against Gabriel's shoulder. "I like her."

"Me, too, buddy. Me, too."

## Chapter Five

Emmaline pushed through the doors into the waiting room of Rocosa Ridge's only hospital. It was more a clinic than a full-fledged hospital. Anything serious was usually treated in Taos. Her pulse beat at a rapid tempo. She spied Gabriel speaking to a uniformed deputy.

"Emmaline!" Alex slid off the chair he'd been sitting on and ran to her, throwing his arms around her thighs and nearly knocking her over. Her arms wrapped around him and she held on.

"Grandpa's hurt," he said through muffled tears. "A bad man did it."

"I see," she said, though she didn't see at all. She looked up and caught Gabriel's attention.

"They think it's a guy named Dooley," Gabriel explained. "Big James fired him, and it looks like Dooley came back to settle the score. Some petty cash is missing, too."

Emmaline nodded and continued to caress the top of Alex's head, offering what comfort she could.

Two large doors opened and a doctor in a white lab coat with a stethoscope hanging around his neck came out. "Are you here for Mr. Daniels? I'll be keeping him overnight. At his age, it's better to play it safe. He's asking for his grandson and someone named Santos."

Gabriel reached for Alex, but the little boy shook his head, clinging to Emmaline's legs. "We'll go together, Alex. You and me with your Uncle Gabriel. That okay?" She was asking the doctor as much as the little boy.

Alex brought his arm across his face to wipe the tears. " 'Kay," he said on a hiccup. She took his hand and they trooped to a room halfway down the hall where a nurse stood in the doorway, beckoning them in.

"We have another gentleman in the next bed, so please keep it down," the nurse said.

The curtain was partially pulled around the first bed. The nurse led them to the second bed next to the window. "A few minutes only. The doctor gave him a sedative and it's likely to kick in soon." The nurse exited, leaving them at the foot of the bed.

Emmaline had heard of Big James Daniels. Rocosa Ridge wasn't a very large town and, as the wealthiest landowner, he was a matter of local interest. The white bandage around his head, combined with his pale features and gray hair, diminished the man who was reputed to be larger than life.

Alex shrunk against Emmaline. Giving his hand an encouraging squeeze, she led him closer to his grandfather. "It looks much worse than it is. Your grandfather is going to stay here a day or two, so that the doctor can keep an eye on him."

Blue-gray eyes stared at her under bushy brows. "Come over here, Alex." He sounded scratchy and cleared his throat. Alex stepped closer. "That blasted Dooley hit me. I wouldn't need to be here if Santos had minded his own business. I'll have one of the men stay with you in the house tonight."

She sensed Gabriel bristling and he pushed forward to stand next to him. "Look, old man, if it weren't for Alex, you might've spent the night on the floor and who knows what would've happened. Alex is coming home with me."

"I've got custody. Don't be thinking you can steal him away." Daniels' voice rose and he tried to lift himself up, only to fall back on the pillows.

Alex leaned against Emmaline and she hugged him to her side. "Both of you stop it, right now," she said firmly. "You are frightening Alex for no reason. Mr. Daniels, you are going to stay in this hospital bed and do what the doctor says so that you can get better and be with your grandson. And you," she said pointedly to Gabriel, "are going to give Alex the safe space he needs, because you love him. Alex is not a bone to fight over. Now, I'm going to take him down the hall to the vending machine for some milk." She didn't know if it had milk and she didn't care. "Come on, Alex."

She took Alex's hand and marched towards the door but stopped short when a voice called out from the other bed. "That you, Miss Emmaline?"

Surprised, Emmaline halted and pulled the curtain further back to reveal an elderly man with silver hair and mustache propped up against a pillow, the bedside light on. "Mr. Fuentes, what're you doing in here?" He was one of the residents at the Rocosa Ridge Sunset Village.

"Just a touch of indigestion, but they shipped me here. When are you coming back? Place isn't the same since you left. They put some battle-axe in charge who thinks fun is a dirty word." He looked so disgusted that she couldn't help laughing.

"I'm sure that's not true at all." She sighed. "I can't come back to work. But I promise to drop by tomorrow or the next day to check on you."

She did in fact find a carton of milk in the vending machine and got it for Alex. It wasn't long before Gabriel joined them, his booted heels announcing his arrival. She expected him to blast her for interfering as she had, but other than a swift appraisal, he didn't say a word.

"Let's go home, champ," Gabriel said.

"Is Grandpa going to be okay?" Alex asked solemnly.

Gabriel squatted down to be at eye level with his nephew. "Your grandfather has got a hard head. He'll be fine."

Alex nodded and slipped his hand into Gabriel's and they proceeded to the truck. Emmaline pointed to her car. "I'll say goodnight then."

Alex released his grip on Gabriel's hand and ran to her. "You can't. I want you to come." His head whipped around. "Uncle Gabriel, please tell Emmaline to come. She has to." He grabbed her hand and tugged her towards the truck. "Please."

Gabriel pushed his hat back and looked at her. The rain had stopped and the moon was out, which, along with the parking lot lights, highlighted the planes and angles of his face. Fatigue was etched into the lines around his mouth.

"I know it's a lot to ask, but would you? Stay with us, I mean. I think Alex needs you."

*What about you?* The words formed on her lips, but she bit them back. "Of course. I'll follow you to the ranch."

Alex was fast asleep by the time Gabriel pulled up in front of the ranch house. Gabriel carried Alex into the house, directing Emmaline to light the way up to his bedroom. She pulled back the bedclothes, and working efficiently with Gabriel, the two of them put Alex into his pajamas, and left him sound asleep under the blankets.

The moonlight bathed his face and her heart ached at the sight. He was becoming all too dear to her, when all of this would end as soon as the court hearing took place.

"Let's go downstairs," Gabriel suggested. He paused long enough to hang up his hat by the door, and then led the way into the family room. Gesturing for her to sit, he said, "I don't know about you, but I'd like something to drink."

Feeling edgy herself, Emmaline nodded. "Do you have a glass of white wine?"

Gabriel moved behind a bar and she heard a refrigerator open. He came up with a bottle and, snagging a wine glass, he poured a small amount into the glass. He returned the bottle, and when he straightened, she saw he had a bottle of beer in his hand.

He brought the drinks over and sat down on the sofa next to her, careful to keep distance between them.

He handed her the wine. As she took it, her fingers brushed his, and heat swirled low in her abdomen. She took a shaky breath. "Thank you."

He leaned back against the leather and drank from his beer, his eyes half-closed in exhaustion. She wanted to go to him, to offer whatever solace she could. Instead, she cradled the wine glass in her hand and sipped slowly from it. They weren't a real couple.

She startled when his hand touched her arm. She shifted to see him better, butterflies fluttering in her stomach.

Those impossibly long lashes of his shielded the look in his gaze. "I need to thank you. You're wonderful with Alex. I don't think I could have dealt with everything tonight on my own."

"You would have," she said.

The air thickened between them and her heart rate sped up. He moved with delicious slow precision as he took the wine glass from her hand and placed it on the coffee table along with his beer. "Emmaline, I badly want to kiss you."

She couldn't speak, so she nodded. She badly wanted to kiss him, too.

Her breath hitched as he leaned forward, and her eyes lowered. His lips were warm and she tasted the beer. His tongue traced the seam of her lips, sending a shiver along every nerve ending and lighting a fire in her nether regions.

She opened her mouth on a sigh and he dove in. Their tongues tangled in a dance as old as time. He speared his hands into her hair, which kept her head at an angle that seemed to give him as much pleasure as it did her.

Her fingers clenched around his shoulders. It was wonderful. Heady. Better than any champagne she'd ever had. But Emmaline Winslow had a practical soul. A rodeo champion had no reason to chase after a woman who had spent her days working with the elderly. Emmaline wasn't exciting or flashy. Her life was simple.

She was not the woman for Gabriel Santos, and if she wasn't careful she was going to lose her heart and it would be all her fault.

As the thoughts tumbled in her head, a small boy's voice called out from upstairs. "Uncle Gabriel, Emmaline! It's Thunder! He's here! I saw him!"

## Chapter Six

"I saw him! I really did!" Alex said to Gabriel, before pressing his face against his bedroom window.

Gabriel placed a hand on Alex's shoulder as he stared out into the darkness. Moonlight cast shadows and he had to wonder if his nephew's imagination had been working overtime. "Maybe you dreamed it, buddy."

Alex shook off his hand. "I didn't dream it. I saw him!"

Gabriel glanced helplessly at Emmaline, who hovered near the doorway. She moved in further and dropped to her knees. She picked up one of Alex's toy horses that looked a heck of a lot like Thunder and held it up.

"Thunder is a special horse, isn't he?"

Alex nodded, his bottom lip quivering.

Emmaline passed the toy to Alex, who grabbed it and hugged it to his chest. "Why do you think Thunder visited you tonight? He must have had a good reason to want to see you."

Alex sniffed, wiping a sleeve across his nose. "He wants to come home. We have to go find him and bring him home."

"All right, then. Tomorrow, let's make a plan to bring Thunder home." Emmaline said.

Alex's face transformed from despair to hope, his eyes bright. "Promise?"

Emmaline nodded. "Promise." She crossed her heart. "Now, how about I read you a story and then you have to promise to go to sleep."

"I will," Alex said, racing to his bookshelf where he pulled out a dogeared picture book. "Read this one. Mommy always read this to me before bedtime."

Emmaline shot Gabriel a quick look before moving to sit on the side of the bed. Alex clambered under the covers and stared up at her expectantly. Emmaline began to read.

Gabriel watched the two of them for a few minutes, something heavy settling in his chest. Abruptly, he turned away. In the living room, he poured a drink and stalked to the bay window that overlooked the front of the house, the same view Alex had from his bedroom. The boy had to have been dreaming. Thunder was gone, just like Alex's mom and dad.

His hand tightened around the glass and he swallowed the last of the whiskey. He heard a sound behind him and whirled.

Emmaline hesitated at the entrance of the living room. "He's asleep."

She eyed him warily, which ticked him off. It didn't help that he wanted her. This was not the time or the place.

Emotions battered his insides. "Why'd you do it?" He lowered his glass to a table and faced her. "Why'd you make a promise you can't keep?" She flinched at his accusatory tone, but he couldn't stop himself. "Do you have any idea what you've done? How the hell are we supposed to bring Thunder home? I've searched all over Rocosa Ridge. The damn horse is gone!"

Emmaline lifted her chin, her face pale. "He needs to believe that Thunder can find his way home. He's lost his mom and dad. His grandfather is in the hospital. He's clinging to Thunder for a reason. You can't take that from him."

"Damn it, I'm not taking anything." He'd seen Alex's face and knew the boy would be crushed when nothing came of it. "How could you make a promise you couldn't keep like that? What right did you have to raise his hopes that way?" She appeared stricken, but never wavered her gaze.

"None. I had no right." She said the words softly, but he heard them. He also heard the underlying hurt.

He turned his back to her and strode to the fireplace where the photos of his family stared back at him. It was his job to keep Alex safe. To protect him. Love him.

Why did he feel like he was falling down on the job?

The sound of a door closing reached his ears. A motor started and the lights of a vehicle swept past the living room windows. Emmaline was leaving.

Gabriel continued to stare at the cold ashes in the fireplace, his insides raw from feelings he couldn't name nor wanted to face. Somehow he would fix things with Alex.

\*\*\*

The next morning stomped those intentions flatter than a mud pie. When he went out to the barn to feed the horses, he discovered one of them had thrown a shoe. He left a message for the farrier and then returned to the house to make breakfast and get Alex up. Coming down the stairs after waking Alex, he caught sight of something winking from the table by the front door. He stepped closer and swore when he realized it was the ring he'd given Emmaline. She must've left it when she'd walked out on him last night. It felt like he'd been kicked in the chest as he picked up the ring. He pocketed the ring and headed to the kitchen where he found he'd forgotten to pick up eggs. Breakfast would be cereal and toast. Footsteps clattered down the stairs and Alex burst into the kitchen, skidding to a stop.

"Where's Emmaline?" His gaze fell on the two bowls on the table.

"She went home," Gabriel said gruffly, as he carried milk to the table.

Alex didn't move from his spot. "When's she coming back?"

Gabriel reached into the cabinet to grab Alex's favorite cereal brand and reminded himself to tread cautiously. "I don't know, buddy. She's busy and might not have time for us."

"But she promised," Alex insisted.

Gabriel winced, the ring burning a hole in his pocket. "Listen, why don't we go into town. I need to do some shopping."

"Can we see Emmaline?" Alex asked solemnly.

Gabriel rubbed his jaw. "I don't think that's such a good idea. Come on, sit down and eat your breakfast."

"I don't want to. I want Emmaline." Alex whirled and ran out of the room, running up the stairs and slamming the door to his bedroom.

"Alex!" Gabriel followed to the foot of the stairs when his cellphone rang. Thinking it was the farrier calling him back he took the call. "Santos."

"Make sure my grandson is back home this afternoon where he belongs," a familiar voice demanded.

"Big James, is that you?" Gabriel asked.

"I'm getting out of this damn hospital and I want my grandson under my roof. See he's there." The phone disconnected.

Gabriel held his phone, tempted to hurl it across the room. The day couldn't get any worse.

## Chapter Seven

Emmaline held the cursor over the Send button and read her reply for the umpteenth time. She'd been asked to a job interview in Albuquerque. If she got the job, it would mean relocating.

Thoughts of Gabriel and Alex filled her mind. She missed them. As crazy as the fake engagement idea had been, she had really enjoyed her time with them.

Gabriel's accusations rang in her ear and she rubbed her chest at the imaginary pain there. She hadn't intended to make things more difficult for Alex. But what did she know about raising children? She shouldn't have interfered.

Shaking her head to rid herself of her thoughts, she forced herself to hit send.

She stood up and thought about her plans for the rest of the day. They didn't amount to much other than shopping and dropping by the hospital.

The vibrating tone of her cell phone buzzed against her desktop. She reached for it and checked the name. Gabriel. Her heart took off at a gallop and the room temperature rose several degrees

Taking in a deep breath, she hit Accept. "Hello."

"It's Alex. I can't find him." Gabriel said quickly, an edge to his tone.

"What do you mean you can't find him?" Emmaline gripped the phone, aware that a great deal could happen to a little boy on his own on a ranch.

"I mean I went up to his room so that we could go into town and he's not there. I've checked the house, the barn, and the bunkhouse. His backpack is gone." He paused. "And the toy he calls Thunder."

Guilt swamped her. "This is my fault. I never should have encouraged him."

"We can talk about that later," Gabriel said impatiently. "I'm going to saddle up and search the back of the property. Call the Sheriff for me and ask for help. Then drive out to the ranch and keep your eyes peeled for Alex along the route. For all I know, he could be trying to head back to his grandfather's." A wealth of pain came through the line, and Emmaline bit down on her lip to keep from saying anything. It wasn't the time. "Thanks." The line disconnected.

Emmaline wasted no time contacting the Sheriff's Office and then, snatching up her keys, she ran out to her car. A few miles outside of town, a light rain pattered against her windshield. She leaned forward, fearing she'd miss Alex in the worsening weather. Had the little boy dressed properly? Upon passing the Triple D, she slowed down. This section of road lay between Gabriel's ranch and Big James Daniels' and contained a number of treacherous curves.

Briefly, she thought of the custody battle between the two men. Would Big James use Alex's disappearance against Gabriel? Then she chastised herself. The only thing that mattered was finding the little boy and bringing him home safely. She sent a prayer up to Alex's parents, asking them to protect their son.

The sky darkened and the clouds opened up, dumping heavy rain on the road. Emmaline slowed down even more as she approached one of the blind curves.

As she came around the bend, something huge bolted across the road. Emmaline slammed her foot on the break. Her small sedan slid across the wet, slick pavement. She tried to compensate by turning the wheel, but it was too late.

Her car shot over the edge of the road and landed in a ditch. Shaken from the impact, Emmaline sat back to catch her breath. She scanned the front windshield for a sign of what she had seen.

Unhooking her seatbelt, she climbed out of her car, which listed at an awkward angle. Rain poured down on her, soaking her instantly. A quick examination told her she needed a tow truck to haul her car out of the ditch. She reached into her jacket pocket for her phone, when a horse's whinny sounded above the pounding rain.

Emmaline stared in disbelief as a horse that looked remarkably like Thunder rose up on its hind legs, before plunging into the woods.

"Wait!" Emmaline hesitated a second and then chased after the horse. She couldn't explain it, other than a need to follow. The horse she mentally called Thunder raced up the hillside, pausing now and then to look back as if to check she was there. It all seemed too fantastical, but Emmaline determinedly charged up the well-worn trail that wove in and out of the trees and brush.

She slapped a tree branch out of her way only to find she couldn't see Thunder anywhere. Where had he gone?

She rushed forward, hoping to see him, when a flash of red caught her attention. She moved forward cautiously and then let out a cry at the sight of the small boy huddled against a tree trunk. "Alex!"

Emmaline checked the boy over for injuries and then hugged him, relief pouring through her.

"Did you see Thunder?" Alex asked, his voice muffled against her shoulder. "Where'd he go?"

"I don't know. I'm sure he'll be back. Now, let's go home."

Of course, when they got back to the car, she remembered that she couldn't drive anywhere, so she and Alex got in and she cranked up the heat to take the chill out. Immediately, she dug her cell phone out and called Gabriel to let him know she'd found Alex.

Twenty minutes later Gabriel rode into a view, looking like a cowboy from the old west with his Stetson and poncho. Emmaline got out, protesting when Alex joined her, getting wet all over again.

"Uncle Gabriel! I found Thunder! I really did!" Alex launched himself at his uncle. "But he's gone again. And I got lost, but Emmaline found me." He wrapped his arms around his uncle's neck and clung there like a monkey.

"That's great, buddy. I promise we won't give up looking for Thunder, but let's get you dry and warmed up." Above Alex's head, Gabriel's gaze met hers. "Thank you."

Words failed her, so she nodded. Somehow, somewhere, she had fallen hard for this rodeo cowboy. It wouldn't do. He had already made his feelings clear. She was glad she'd been able to help him find Alex, but it was time to move on and close this chapter in her life and pray the pain ripping through her would dull to an ache over time.

"You two go on. I'll wait for a tow truck." Emmaline said.

"Both of you are going to get checked out by the doctor," Gabriel ordered.

Before she could argue, a Sheriff's department vehicle showed up, and an hour later, she and Alex were being checked by a friendly elderly doctor who dressed up their scratches and told them that they needed a hot bowl of soup, which sounded perfect. He then told them they could go home. Since Gabriel had excused himself a moment ago to take a phone call, Emmaline and Alex waited side by side.

Raised voices came from outside the room and then the door burst open. Gabriel and Big James crowded in the doorway.

"I'm taking my grandson home where he belongs. My lawyers will make sure you never see him again." Big James poked a big finger in Gabriel's chest.

"Listen, old man," Gabriel began, but Emmaline interrupted them.

"Stop it! Both of you! You're upsetting Alex." She wrapped an arm around his shoulders, hugging him to her side.

Both men fell silent, though they stalked forward like two rival bulls ready to tear into one another at the slightest provocation. Emmaline sighed in exasperation.

Alex tugged on her arm. "I want to live with you and Thunder. Can I?"

Emmaline swallowed the lump in her throat and tried to come up with an answer.

"Don't be ridiculous, Alex." Big James snapped. "You're coming home with me."

"We'll see what the judge says," Gabriel interjected.

Emmaline slid off the hospital bed. "Both of you, outside now!" Brooking no arguments, she took each by the arm and marched them out the door, which she left open so they could keep an eye on Alex.

"Alex is not a bone for you to fight over." She recalled her own parents fighting and the scars she still carried. "He's a little boy who is going to grow up into a fine young man with his own opinions, wants and needs. And if you keep tearing him apart like this, he isn't going to need either one of you. He's going to walk away and carve his own path." She knew she was talking of her own experience, but it didn't matter. They would destroy Alex if they didn't come to some kind of understanding. "Both of you are the only family he has left. Do not make him choose between you." She pointed at Big James. "Your daughter," she swung her finger to Gabriel, "and your brother deserve better in honor of their short lives." She dropped her hand and swiped her suddenly sweaty palm against her thigh. "That's all I have to say." She stepped back in the room and shut the door on their stunned faces.

## Chapter Eight

### Two weeks later

Gabriel once more checked the roast he had going in the oven. Ten more minutes and it should be perfect.

He glanced at the clock above the stove. Six o'clock. She'd promised she'd come. She'd also told him that she'd been offered a job in Albuquerque and had to give an answer by Monday.

He was hoping he could give her reason to turn it down.

The sound of a car door shutting sent him hurrying to the front door. Relief coursed through him. She'd come.

He ran his hand over his hair and, with a deep breath, opened the front door. Emmaline approached slowly.

"Hi," she said shyly.

"Thanks for coming tonight," he said. She'd refused his invitations the past two weeks for one reason or another, though she'd talked to him on the phone. He'd taken heart from that fact. If she'd really wanted him out of her life, she'd have hung up without thought.

He led her into the house and said, "Dinner is almost ready. Can I get you a drink?"

"Water is fine," she said. "I have to drive."

Gabriel nodded, though he recognized the gambit for what it was—a warning that her time was limited. Well, he'd never given up when it came to riding broncos. He wasn't giving up now.

"Today was the custody hearing," Gabriel said. "I thought you deserved to hear the result." He handed her a glass of water, their fingers brushing momentarily.

Emmaline sucked in a breath. "I know. I mean, I was hoping you would tell me what happened."

"We won," he said.

Her brow creased. "You mean, you got custody of Alex?"

Gabriel shook his head. "We both did. Big James and I will share custody. And we owe it all to you."

Emmaline put the glass on the dining table and took a step back. "I don't understand. I didn't do anything."

Gabriel moved closer. "Yes, you did. You saved us from hurting Alex. He doesn't need to be choosing between us. Family is family."

Emmaline brought her fingertips up to her mouth, emotions swelling inside her. "So what will you do?"

The oven bell dinged. Gabriel smiled. "Let's eat, and then I'll tell you what we decided."

Gabriel kept dinner conversation light. He talked about his rodeo days and asked Emmaline to talk about her time at the care facility. She'd been reluctant at first, but with encouragement she'd matched his amusing stories of recalcitrant livestock with stories of the two-legged kind.

When they reached dessert, he invited her to take it in the living room where he had a fire going in the fireplace. Wariness flitted in her gaze, but she accepted. Her reaction reminded him that he hadn't won the trust of this particular filly just yet.

They sat in front of the fire, drinking coffee and eating the apple crumb pie that he'd picked up in town in a comfortable silence.

Gabriel put his empty plate on the coffee table, and twisting in his seat, faced Emmaline. He wanted to reach out and touch the silky strands of her hair, brush his hand across her smooth skin and touch those sweet lips with his own. He willed his body and his thoughts under control and began to speak.

"You were right when you took Big James and me to the woodshed over Alex. We were ripping him apart and didn't even know it." He rubbed the back of his neck. "In our defense, we always wanted the best for Alex."

"I know that," Emmaline said with a soft smile. "The thing is, kids are smart and sensitive. He might not understand completely, but he understood enough."

Gabriel nodded. "That hospital stay was a wake-up for Big James. I think he realized that Alex needs both of us in his life. In fact, he offered me a job."

"What?" Emmaline's mouth practically hung open.

Gabriel chuckled. "Seems he needs a foreman. Since we'd probably be at each other's throats, I agreed to do it temporarily until he can hire a new foreman."

"What about this place?" Emmaline made a sweeping gesture with her hand. "Don't you need to run it?"

"I've got a friend who's willing to come down and help run this place. Eventually, Alex is going to own the Triple D. By helping Big James, I'll be in a better position to guide Alex in the years to come, and I'll still be able to keep an eye on things here."

"I see," Emmaline said. "Does Alex understand?"

"We explained it to him. Big James and I aren't always going to see eye to eye, but we made sure Alex understood that it was two bulls snorting at one another and had nothing to do with him."

Emmaline laughed at that, the sound a caress to his soul. "And what did Alex say?"

Gabriel paused a beat. This was the moment he'd been preparing for all day. "He said that he was okay with it as long as Emmaline came to live with us too."

Emmaline's face drained of color. Not the reaction he'd hoped for. "That's silly. I mean, he's a little boy. He doesn't know what he's saying." With a trembling hand she returned her plate to the coffee table. "It's late. I should get going." She stood up.

Gabriel stood as well. "Don't go. This isn't about Alex. It's about me."

Her eyes grew wide. "I don't understand," she whispered.

Gabriel took a step closer. "I lived life on my own terms, never giving a lot of thought beyond the next rodeo. Then I lost my brother, and my world went dark. I didn't know how much my family meant to me until they were gone." The photos on the mantelpiece reminded him of all that had been ripped from him. Taking courage from his big brother, Gabriel took another step forward. "Alex became everything to me. I guess it was the same for Big James."

"That's understandable," Emmaline said, as she reached out to lay a comforting hand on his arm.

Gabriel covered her hand, needing the connection. "Maybe. But neither of us realized what we were doing to Alex until you came into our lives." He brought his hand up to cradle her cheek. "Alex isn't the only one who needs you. I need you. You make me want to be a better man. You make me wish I could offer you more than just a beat-up cowboy. But I guarantee this cowboy will love you forever."

Tears spilled over Emmaline's cheek and onto his hand. Gabriel took that as a good sign and pulled her into his embrace. He pressed tiny kisses against her eyelids, the corner of her mouth and any place he could reach. It wasn't long before the tears turned to laughter and then to passion.

Gabriel spent the night taking Emmaline to the heights of passion, but if he'd been asked who'd mastered her, he'd have to say the shy brunette had placed her brand on him for all time.

***

The rosy fingers of dawn left a trail across the bedroom. Gabriel smiled down at the woman snuggled up against him. He could get used to this.

A commotion outside caught his ear. Moving quietly, yet swiftly, he tugged on a pair of jeans and went to the window, pulling back the curtains. His bedroom looked out on the back of the house and the fenced paddock.

"What the—" Gabriel murmured in disbelief.

The rustling of bedclothes sounded behind him and then Emmaline came up beside him, wearing his shirt. "What is it?" she asked. "Is that Thunder?"

Gabriel pulled her under his arm, relishing the feel of her there. "Yeah, I think Thunder came home." He swallowed the lump that had lodged in his throat.

"He's not alone," she said, pointing out the window.

Gabriel peered out again. "Well, I'll be." He hadn't seen the chestnut when he'd first spied Thunder tossing his head and prancing in the paddock.

"Looks like Thunder has a friend," Emmaline said.

Gabriel dropped a kiss on Emmaline's head, a smile starting in his heart and working its way upward. "I think he met his match. I know the feeling."

He turned Emmaline in his arms and kissed her with all the love and longing that he'd built up over a lifetime.

This cowboy was ready to settle down with his forever woman, and her name was Emmaline.

The End

# Ava
## Callie Carmen

## Chapter One

### Ava

I'd been a fool pining over Joshua. I'd been in love with the man since I was twelve years old. I had barely dated in college, knowing it was Josh I wanted when the time was right. After I'd graduated, I had even followed him to Michigan. When he'd told me he had fallen in love with another woman, I had been sick to my stomach for days. I'd quit my job and moved back home to Kentucky where my heart belonged. I'd promised myself I'd never fall for another man. Dating, sure. But love – no way. There would be no more wasted time and heartache in my life.

At least something good had come out of my friendship with Josh. I'd banked away over forty thousand dollars while I had house sat for him when he was overseas on an ex-pat assignment. I'd used it as a down payment for the home my contractor, Ryan, was building. I now had a mortgage to worry about, and I was counting on my full-time art business to cover expenses. I prayed that it would be enough so I wouldn't have to go back to being a bookkeeper part-time.

A truck was coming up the long gravel driveway as I stepped out of the barn. Ryan was in the driver's seat, but who was the black-haired hunk riding shotgun? Ryan parked, got out of the truck and we gave each other a hug. "How are you, Ms. Ava?"

"I'm right as rain and more than ready to get this show on the road." I smiled.

"Glad to hear it. As promised, we are finishing the upstairs of your art studio in the barn today."

The other door shut, and I peeked around Ryan's shoulder. A tall man holding a cowboy hat stared at me with steely, cold gray eyes that made me shiver. I crossed my arms to warm myself.

## Colton

Throughout high school, I had done the framing for our family art gallery and framing business with my father. Since graduating, I'd only been helping once in a while when I stopped home for a visit during rodeo breaks. When Ma had called about Dad falling and getting an arm bone bruise, I'd been concerned. Being a ProRodeo cowboy, I had known what that meant. Dad's arm would be in a brace, and he wouldn't be able to do any framing for at least a month because he had to rest his arm. So, I had temporarily stopped competing and had come home to help.

I needed to get back on the road as soon as possible if I was to become one of the top breadwinners in the ProRodeo circuit. Only the top fifteen cowboys could be part of the Wrangler National Finals Rodeo in Las Vegas come December. It was already the start of May and I'd only earned a little over a hundred thousand. Only a third of what I needed to finish the year at the top.

If I made it again this year, I'd have enough saved to hang up my rodeo hat and start my performance horse ranch. I'd raise and train quarter horses with bloodlines that dominated in steer wrestling, team roping, tie-down roping and cutting. Horses with those bloodlines were larger, faster and more muscled and had more stamina than the average quarter horse. They would be like the ones I already owned. They'd proved themselves champions in the ring time and time again. These quarter horses could also be used to do typical ranch chores for those clients who wanted them for ranch work. I already owned and trained with a Heel-O-Matic which was a steer-like machine that had the motion and mobility of a real steer. It would be perfect for my clinics and summer camp training. With each sale, I planned to give the new owner a five-day training clinic, so the horse and human could each learn the language, personality, and skill of the other.

The last thing I needed was to take on a new art client. Especially a spoiled rancher's daughter with too much money and too much free time who thought she could paint. Sure, she was hot, but so were some of the buckle bunnies that followed the rodeos and cowboys. Those females were around pretty much whenever a cowboy needed some lovin'. That wasn't my thing, but now and then I'd meet one that wasn't all starry-eyed. I'd spend some time with her, and if we hit it off, we'd end the night in bed.

## Ava

I bobbed my head to the left, and Ryan turned.

"Who's your friend?" I asked.

"Colton, this is Ava Kinkaid. Ava, this is my brother, Colton Maples."

He tipped his hat but didn't say a word.

"You said you were looking for a professional to take over the framing of your artwork, since you had to leave the other one behind in Michigan. Colton's your man."

He was gorgeous, but his contemptuous snort let me know there was a coolness to him. It was nice of Ryan to help me out. However, I didn't think I could work with someone as aloof as his brother seemed. Have sex with? Yes. I'd been in a dry spell for over a year and it had gotten so bad that I'd named my vibrators. There was Griffin the mythological beast; he rocked my G-spot every time. And Dante the broody inferno; he always rubbed my clit until I couldn't breathe. My body heated.

But business was business, and the framing of art could make or break a painting. If this guy sucked, there was no way I would work with him. There was too much at stake. He could impact my income. Colton would have to prove he could come through with the goods. I didn't care how hot he was, I'd find someone else who-

He took a few aggressive steps forward and put out his hand.

I drew in his masculine earthy scent, and desire stirred through me. I crushed my lips together to stop the moan trying to flow out of me as our hands touched.

He shamelessly held tight as his eyes admired the contours of my breasts, hips, and legs. When our eyes met, a powerful sensual heat passed between us. Sparks flew through my stomach. God, I needed to get laid. The burning ended all too quickly when Ryan cleared his throat.

I yanked my hand away and wiped it on my hip to rid myself of the raw power of attraction to Colton.

An amused smile played across his mouth.

I squinted. *Beast.* "I'll be the judge of your work."

## Chapter Two

### Colton

I had to admit, I'd felt a twinge in my gut when I'd touched the blonde beauty. Her dilated eyes had told me she'd felt it too. A roll in the hay with her now and then might make this month tolerable. I gave her my standard I-know-what-you-want-from-me smile. The glare she had given me let me know she didn't like that one bit. A buckle bunny would have taken my hand and said, "What are you waiting for? Take me to your trailer."

Ava could hide behind her disgusted look, but she couldn't fool me. She was interested. I found it comical when she said she'd give me a chance to prove that I could frame her pictures. Like I needed to be tested. I'd been doing this kind of work for ten years, and I'd made some pretty poor art look like masterpieces with my gorgeous frames. My frames were works of art themselves.

The three of us went upstairs to her studio above the barn and hot damn it was huge. The lighting from the row of raised windows was so good that there was no need for any additional lighting during the day. Ryan was one hell of a contractor.

When she finished going over all the building details for Ryan, he got right to work giving instructions to his staff.

She turned to me with a smile and said, "Can you ride a horse?"

I laughed, and she looked at me with sparks in her eyes. She tapped her foot and waited for me to answer.

Damn, she was adorable. "I'm a professional rodeo cowboy. So, yes."

She looked me up and down, and the sparks disappeared and her eyes darkened. She twirled blonde strands around her finger. "What events do you enter?"

"I compete in as many bull riding, saddle bronc riding, bareback riding and roping events as I can. Why? Are you into rodeos? I thought that would be beneath a family like yours, with all your champion racehorses."

She crossed her arms, stuck up her nose and let me have it. "Yes, well in high school I had lower standards and attended a rodeo now and then with my friends." She started to walk down the stairs but turned back, "Then I got on with my college degree in fine arts and minored in business. So there was no longer time for such childish things."

Hot damn. She was a little spitfire.

## Ava

We saddled up Thunder and Blue Bell then rode to my parent's barn about a mile away. Colton's hips rotated, following the motion of his horse forward and back with a nice stable thigh. His form was perfect, but his rotating hips were making my vagina twitch. Maybe it was just the motion making me think about making love because of my sex dry spell, and it wasn't Colton that was turning me on. *Yeah, right.*

When we stepped into my makeshift workspace in my parents' barn, he whistled. "Hot damn. That is one hell of a sculpture. It looks just like your horse." He lifted a brow. "Where did you have it made?"

His praise flowed over me like a warm wave. "Right here." I pointed to my chest. "I made it."

He pulled back his lips and shook his head.

"Were you thinking I wouldn't be good enough to sculpt a piece like this?"

He took off his hat and wove his fingers through the sheen of his lustrous hair. I couldn't help myself. I wanted to entwine my fingers in his locks and pull him down for a kiss. My stomach muscles tightened. *Control yourself.*

"No. It's just that I expected paintings, not this." He lay his hand on the crest of Thunder's sculpture then stroked down the contours to the withers, back, loin, croup, thigh, gaskin, hock, cannon bone, fetlock joint, and finally the hoof.

I pictured his big, strong hands doing the same thing to my body. I felt my panties dampen.

He continued to study my work. "This sculpture is stunning. It belongs in an art gallery."

His compliment had joy running through my veins. "Too late. A local museum commissioned it."

He gazed at me, and for the first time I saw the smile lines around the sides of his mouth. The steel-gray eyes that had given me a chill earlier looked at me with a warm glow. It almost looked like affection, or maybe admiration.

It took my breath away. The man had me yearning to touch, kiss, and even jump his bones one minute, and had me making snarky barbs at him the next. I'd already decided that if I was attracted to someone, I would have fun with him, some wild sex, and then send him on his way. Perhaps Colton would be the one to put Griffin and Dante into temporary retirement.

I turned away from him and flipped through my paintings while he talked about his horse, ironically called Lightning. How in God's name was a weekend warrior going to be good at framing works of art? I decided I'd give him two pieces of art to test his work. Especially since I now knew that he was a roughie making a living eight seconds at a time.

I trusted Ryan. He had already shown he was a fantastic contractor and had a staff that excelled in skills and efficiency. So I should be able to trust his brother to do a good job too. But time would tell.

Colton stuck around and helped Ryan put some cabinets in my studio. Before they left, everything in the studio was completed, which pleased me no end. As Colton got into the truck, I handed him the one wrapped watercolor painting and one photo that I'd selected to test his framing skills.

His smirk was maddening, and before the door closed all the way I thought I heard, "Chickenshit."

My body heated, and I wanted to slap his face. I was the customer. Who did this cowboy think he was?

Fortunately, after Ryan started the truck, he swatted his brother in the shoulder. Colton had the audacity to turn back to me and wink as they pulled away.

I couldn't believe it. I stuck my tongue out at him. The beast threw his head back and laughed as they drove away.

***

The truck from the museum had come by and picked up the sculpture first thing the next morning. I moved all my supplies over to my new studio, and one of Dad's ranch hands helped me move my art. With everything settled I was off to visit two of the finest art galleries in Lexington. I had a portfolio of all my art in hand and references from my dealers in Michigan.

The first gallery owner said he loved my work and would think about the possibility of doing a show with me. I left there hopeful.

It was noon when I arrived at the Maples Art & Framing Gallery.

The bell above the door rang as I stepped into a huge showroom. This was much larger than the establishment that I'd just left.

A distinguished older gentleman with a lovely smile stepped out from behind the counter. "Hello. How are you?"

"Well, thank you. And you?"

"Well. Except for this confounded thing." With the help of his left hand, he lifted his right arm that was in a brace and had a sling around it.

Oh, my God. Maples. Was this Ryan's father? Shoot. I had stuck my tongue out at Colton. He could mess up my chances of working with his father. His gallery had the best reputation in all of Lexington. My stomach gurgled. "My name is Ava Kinkaid. You wouldn't be the parent of Ryan and Colton Maples, would you?"

"Hmm. Kinkaid." He rubbed his chin. "Are you Buck Kinkaid's daughter?"

I bobbed my head. "Yes, sir."

"Any daughter of Buck's may call me Winston. Your father has purchased several paintings from us over the years. As well as the horse statue out in front of your family's home."Thank you, Winston. My father is a big supporter of the arts. He even encouraged me to enter a fine arts program in college. I combined it with a minor in business, so I would understand both ends of the industry."

"Wait. Are you the young lady that my son has talked nonstop about since yesterday?"

"Why, yes. Ryan has been doing extensive work for me. And he is doing a wonderful job. You must be so proud of him."

"I am, thank you. But no, I was talking about Colton."

My stomach rolled over, and I thought I would lose my breakfast. What the heck had he said about me? If he ruined this for me, I'd-

From way in the back of the gallery, the voice of my worst nightmare called out. "Dad, look at the framing I did on the blonde beauty's painting."

I'd kill him. Blonde beauty. So unprofessional. Winston would never work with me.

"It does her work of art justice. Don't you th-"

He stopped dead.

He was holding my watercolor painting of old worn silos being swallowed up on three sides by trees and with unruly grass in the front. It was titled "Better Times." I'd used all warm, darker tones. He had chosen the dominant green color of rockwood jade from the painting as the top mat. For the accent mat, the narrow inner edge, he'd chosen the rain worn gray of the weathered wood on the silo. The bottom of the mat was deeper than the sides and top, which provided a visual balance. The matting was wider than the beautiful, cherrywood frame, which was how it should be. They drew the eye to the art rather than to the frame. It was excellent workmanship.

I was about to compliment him, but he had to open his big mouth. "So, you missed me so much that you had to ask Ryan where I worked?"

I had to remain professional in front of his father, but the look I gave him made Colton flinch.

I turned back to his father. Actually, I'm here to see you, Winston. I was hoping you'd have time to go through my portfolio and to let me tell you a bit about my experience. Then I wanted to discuss the possibility of a partnership that will be beneficial to both of us.

He looked over at Colton. I was too afraid to do the same. I couldn't have stood it if I'd seen him shake his head no. If he did, it would be my fault. He pushed all my buttons, forcing me to give him snarky comments and disgusted faces. He probably thought I was a drama queen. One not even able to take a bit of teasing.

Mr. Maples gazed at me. "If the rest of your work is anything like this one"—he swooshed his hand towards my "Better Times" painting—"then I'd be happy to look at your portfolio."

I puffed out the breath I'd been holding. He pulled out the seat in front of his desk and I sat. "Wonderful," I squeaked.

"While I study your creations, tell me about your career as an artist so far and your plans for the future."

I calmed my racing heart and dove right into telling him about my education, then the successes I'd had while in Michigan. I even gave him a list of business references. He didn't give me any signs of how he felt about my work as he flipped the pages and studied it. I put my hand in my sweater pocket and felt the business card I had placed there. I rolled it over and over again. It helped a bit with my nerves.

"Very interesting. Now tell me about your overall game plan, your vision for the future. What motivates and inspires your creative process?"

I gazed over at Colton, who seemed to be taking an interest in our discussion. My stomach tightened.

I told Winston about my new studio.

"It's beautiful, Dad. The natural lighting is killer."

He was helping me. I felt tingles run up my spine, but then he ruined it with a wink, and his father saw it. Ugh.

"He's right; it is wonderful. Since I've gotten back to Kentucky, I've devoted myself full-time to art, and I plan to do so going forward."

He closed my book and slid it in front of me. "Do you have a significant body of current work that hasn't been exhibited elsewhere?" He shook his finger at me. "That includes other galleries or online."

I explained that I'd been working nonstop for the past six months on a wonderful collection, some of which were in my portfolio. They included photos, watercolor and oil paintings and a few sculptures.

At the mention of my sculptures, Colton piped in, "Hoo, doggie. Her horse sculpture is–"

His cell phone went off playing "Hillbilly Bone" with Trace Adkins and Blake Shelton.

It made me giggle inside. I'd seen them perform that song in concert and it had been a blast!

He looked at the screen and gave me a half-smile. "I'm sorry, I have to take this call. It's from my whiskey company rodeo team sponsor."

He combed his fingers through his hair and paced while I answered Winston's questions. I did, however, snoop and listen in on Colton's conversation at the same time. It was an old trick I'd mastered while eating with the ranch hands. There were always at least three conversations going on at once and I could chime in on all of them.

"Brian, how are you? Thanks. He'll be fine in about a month." He stopped dead. "I know. Yeah, I get it. You're not paying me to sit on my ass." He looked at me and cringed.

I grew up on a ranch. Did he seriously think I'd never heard a man swear before? It was kind of sweet of him to worry that I'd be offended. Maybe there was hope for him yet.

"Brian, it's not like I'm dropping off the face of the earth. Next weekend I'm competing in Franklin, Tennessee and then running up to Clarkston. A couple of weeks later I'm off to Farmington, Missouri. Two weeks later I'm at the New Berlin event and then home for the Lexington Rodeo the second week of June. After that, I plan to get back on the road full-time. Good. I'm glad you approve. Yes, I'll let you know if anything changes. Thanks, man. I owe you one."

Hmm, he had sponsors. That meant he was one of the best rodeo cowboys. I knew from my high school days of attending rodeos and even dating a few cowboys how hard those men worked to get to the top. Colton had to be motivated, brave, and dedicated to the craft. And here he was putting all of that aside to help his parents. My heart fluttered.

It sounded like he could get his sponsor off his back by participating in some local rodeos. This man was not just a pretty face. I bet he'd been a bit cold yesterday because he was thinking that he needed to get back on the road, not be messing around at my place. And here I'd thought he was kind of a prick. A sexy prick that I had wanted to boff, but now I knew there was much more to him. Sigh.

Winston cleared his throat.

Shoot, I hadn't heard what he said. "I'm sorry. I got distracted."

"Yes, I noticed," he looked over at Colton and grinned. "What I said was, I'd like to do an exhibit with your collection."

Colton was by my side again, and he squeezed my shoulder.

"Congratulations." I looked up, and it was as if he was elated for me, his smile was ear to ear.

Be still, my heart. *Stop. Stop. Stop. No caring too much. You'll get hurt again.* Especially with a roughie. The ones that do it full-time like him have seventy to a hundred rodeos a year and have to travel all over the US. They're barely ever home. I mouthed thank you and he ran his fingers back and forth across my shoulder blades. Tingles ran down my spine.

Winston slid my portfolio in front of me. "Would your collection be ready a month from now?"

Oh my God. I couldn't help myself. I bounced up and plopped back onto my seat. The two of them chuckled. I felt my body heat, but embarrassed or not it was pretty funny, so I laughed with them. I looked up at Colton. "I guess that depends on you, because as you probably noticed yesterday, I have a lot of art that needs to be framed. Are you up for all that work in such a short amount of time?"

He smirked. "I am if I get a little assistance from you."

"Anything you want from me, it's yours." My vagina clenched as his eyes darkened.

"Well, that's settled. One month from this Saturday. Now, you two have a lot of work to do, so I'll leave you to it. It was lovely meeting you, Ava. I hope we have a long and successful relationship together." He nodded, then left me alone with Colton.

# Chapter Three

## Colton

Working side-by-side with Ava for the past two weeks had been productive. That woman was a damn hard worker. But it had also been torture being so close to her five days a week and not being able to touch her. After all, this was a business arrangement between her and my family. If I screwed it up with casual sex, I wouldn't hear the end of it from my parents or Ryan.

The more I got to know her, the more time I wanted to spend with her. She laughed at the stories I told, and if I said something she didn't like she was all over me in a heartbeat. I loved that about her. The buckle bunnies were usually sickeningly sweet, almost fake the way they fawned over the rodeo cowboys. But Ava was real.

She wasn't the spoiled rich girl that I thought she'd be. Sure, her dad had given her the land her home sat on, but she was paying for the house, stable and studio on her own.

She told me about how, when she was younger, she used to spend a lot of time alone. Just her and Thunder. She'd often ridden him to that very spot on the highest hill that overlooked rolling hills, trees, and a stream below where her new home was being completed. She'd loved sitting there for hours, drawing and painting. It had been her little slice of heaven that she said had filled her with joy. I had to agree with her. It was the most beautiful view I'd ever seen.

Unfortunately, today being Friday, I couldn't work. I had to leave for the Franklin Rodeo. So yesterday I had told her not to bother coming in, and the disappointed look on her face had hit me right in the gut. We still had a lot of framing to do, but I hoped that her disappointment was about more than work. I hoped that she would miss me. I would sure miss her. And I kind of fancied more than a roll in the hay with her.

I couldn't wait until my life as a traveling nomad was over. I was getting too old for this way of life. I had enough money saved for the livestock, buildings, indoor and outdoor training facilities and ten acres, but I needed to purchase at least twenty acres to make my plans work. If things didn't get any more screwed up this year, I should have enough by the end of this rodeo season.

Right now, I needed to get on the road to keep my sponsors happy, because they covered my gas and expenses. Those always came in between forty and fifty thousand dollars a year. There was no way I could lose that kind of backing. It had taken me too long to become good enough to earn those coveted sponsors.

As if that wasn't enough to worry about, when I got to the barn to pick up two of my horses for the tie-down roping event, I ran into the owner. She told me she was selling the place. I needed to find a new location to board Lightning and the other horses before next weekend. That was a tall order, since I'd be gone all weekend and busy framing during the week. I'd have to ask around at the rodeo.

On Monday, I might have to ask Ava if I could temporarily keep my horses in some of her empty stable stalls. That way I could spend time with her on the weekends when I wasn't away. I believed that I was falling in love with her but knew it would be too much to ask of her to take on a man that wasn't around often. I'd seen my friends try to make their relationships work and it had almost always ended in them crying in their beer.

## Ava

I was nervous about showing up at the rodeo to surprise Colton. We'd become friends over the past couple of weeks, so I wanted to give him some support. After all, he had been working his tail off for my art exhibit. I told myself that was the reason, and it had nothing to do with the tingles I felt when we were together. Each day before I entered the workstation at the back of the gallery I chanted, *Don't fall in love. Don't fall in love.*

After he'd told me he hoped this would be his last year on the road, I couldn't resist seeing him in all his glory on a bucking bronco or bull. He'd explained his plans to breed quarter horses that would be well-trained and could be used for calf, breakaway, and team roping as well as cutting and ranching. Or for someone that was willing to pay top dollar for a well-trained riding horse. He had saved up a small fortune from his winnings over the past years and had made some excellent investments on the side too. I was proud of this strong, motivated, intelligent man who made me laugh. And, yes, sometimes he pissed me off, but even then, he filled me with warmth.

He'd told me about his youth training camp plans. He wanted to teach kids interested in rodeo all the basics, and a few tricks he'd learned along the way. One that surprised me had to do with balance and him standing on a hard ball about the size of a soccer ball. Sometimes for up to an hour a day. I couldn't imagine trying to balance myself on something that moved and was so small for even a minute, let alone sixty minutes. His core strength had to be phenomenal.

The camp would run the month of June, and if a student couldn't afford to attend, he would give them a scholarship. As a kid, his best friend had lived with his mom and they hadn't been able to pay for the lessons. The owner had let his friend attend class for free. It had made an impression on Colton, so he wanted to do the same thing for other children in need.

It had melted my heart.

For years he'd traveled the professional rodeo circuit with his buddy, until his friend got injured. His eyes had misted when he'd talked about it.

I'd hugged him in that moment and had felt flutters in my stomach and a sense of being home. I'd never felt that with another man. I had become self-conscious and quickly got back to work on the frame I'd been making. I'd felt his eyes on me, but I hadn't dared to look his way.

The announcer came over the loudspeaker. "Up next is Colton Maples. The three-time bull riding champion of the Franklin Rodeo. Let's see if he still has what it takes."

Oh my God, he was up next, and the bull was already kicking inside the bucket chute. This would be a vicious ride. I inhaled deeply.

The gate blasted open, and Colton held on with one hand while the other arm swung in the air to the rhythm of the furious beast's thrusts.

Colton was spurring. It wasn't required, but when the rider lifted his legs away from the bull and brought them back again, it added points to his score. It made it more difficult and harder to control. It scared me to death. The bull kicked his hind legs over his head. When the bull dropped back down, I saw Colton lock his knees, then set his feet back down as the buzzer rang.

I was up on my feet with everybody else, screaming his name and cheering. I had to roll my shoulders and neck to relax. It had been the longest eight seconds of my life. When a score of ninety-one was announced, the crowd went wild. He ended up finishing the day in first place, as well as first in bareback, second place for saddle bronc riding and first place in tie-down roping.

After his last event, I ran over to see him and tried to get behind the shoots. I got stopped by two large security guards wearing cowboy hats. I lied and said I was Colton Maple's girlfriend. In that moment, my body lit on fire. I knew then it was what I wanted. Never getting close to another man, like I'd vowed after Joshua, wasn't good enough for me. I deserved true love too. And I would try my best to have that with Colton.

"You and about ten other girls," they said in unison.

I wasn't going to be able to see him. I felt nauseous.

One of the younger cowboys overheard them and called out to Colton. "Hey, Maples, there's another buckle bunny here to see you."

He swooshed his arm at the kid letting me know he wasn't interested in any bunnies.

My heart soared. I pulled a twenty out of my pocket. "Hey, kid. There's a twenty here with your name on it if you tell Maples that Ava Kinkaid is here to see him."

"Do ya mean it?"

"I sure do." I winked at him.

"Damn. I'm on it."

The guards just shook their heads.

The young cowboy ran over to Colton and tapped him on the shoulder and pointed in my direction.

He practically ran to me. I hugged him with all my strength as he lifted me off the ground and spun me around. I sang in his ear, "I wanna be a cowgirl. And you can be my cowboy." He put his head back and roared. Seeing him so happy made me laugh along with him.

"I can't believe you're here. I missed you."

He missed me. It felt like sparklers were lit inside me.

"I wanted to tell you how the competition was going. But you weren't here."

He hadn't put me down yet. My lips were in a giant grin, but they slowly came back together when he lay his forehead on mine. Staring directly into his eyes was an intimate sensation, and it felt like he agreed with me and wanted to explore our relationship more deeply.

He softly pressed his lips to my mouth and spread my lips with his tongue. I tasted his mint flavor and drew in his musky scent. The combination sent my libido into a passionate need for privacy so I could explore more of him.

# Chapter Four

## Colton

When I saw her smiling at me between the two guards it literally lit up my world. She radiated happiness when she saw me look in her direction. Until that moment, I had never realized how powerful a smile could be. I beamed inside, knowing that she had made a five-hour drive to be here. When the kid told me my girlfriend Ava was waiting for me, it had sent as much adrenaline through me as the bull ride that I'd just gotten off.

There was no better time for a first kiss than now, while she was in my arms giving me the warmest hug ever. I slowed everything down except my pulse and gazed into her eyes. They twinkled, then turned to affection when our foreheads touched. That was my signal to lean in for our first kiss. I had been dreaming of that moment all week long. When our lips pressed together, the sounds of the crowd disappeared, and an insatiable pleasure spiked through my body. I craved more.

I put her down and entwined our fingers together. It felt like energy flowed between us, giving me an emotional connection with her. Holding hands was something I had never done with any woman at the rodeo. I wanted all my friends and everyone else there to know that Ava was special to me and that we were a couple. God, I prayed we'd be a couple after this. I'd only be on the road another seven months. If she would hold on until then, I'd be hers.

I had to attend an event at the sponsor tent. I hated those things, but with Ava at my side, it wasn't the chore that it usually was. She charmed all of my backers, and some that didn't back me. When they found out she was the daughter of Buck Kinkaid they all wanted to talk about the horse racing industry.

I didn't know if she knew how important today was for me. I wasn't only worried about keeping my sponsors while I was taking time off to help my family, I hoped to pick up a few more benefactors too.

She was wonderful. Every time someone brought up horse racing, she would bring the conversation back to me and the big wins I'd had at the rodeo that day. By the time we left the tent, I had two more business cards in my hand. They wanted to meet with me the following week to discuss sponsorship.

It was pretty late, and she had a five-hour drive ahead of her. There was no way I was going to let her drive home tonight. A breeze blew strands of her hair onto her face. I brushed them behind her ear, cupped her cheek, and kissed her forehead.

She quivered.

It was all I could do not to throw her over my shoulder and take her to my trailer to make love with her. "I'm sorry I kept you so late at the sponsor tent. You impressed me in there. The way you handle business sponsors is nothing short of amazing."

She smiled. "Thank you. I get that naturally from working around my father and his clients all these years."

God, she was constantly surprising me. A phenomenal artist, fantastic with finances, hardworking, and it turned out, a good friend. She'd supported me by coming today and by helping with the sponsors. If I hadn't been falling hard for this woman before, I sure was now. "Do you have a hotel room for the night?"

She shook her head. "The ones closest to here were booked, so I was going to sleep in my car." She grinned. "I even brought my pillow."

Dang, she was adorable and beautiful. "It's not safe for you to stay in your car. Some of these yahoos get rowdy and drunk. How about we go grab that pillow of yours and you stay in my trailer tonight?"

She smirked, took off my cowboy hat, and combed her fingers through my hair. "Why Mr. Maples, I thought you'd never ask."

"Hot damn!" I scooped her up in my arms and carried her over to my trailer and up the two steps to the inside.

She giggled all the way there, until I carried her to the back of the trailer to my bed. She kicked off her cowboy boots and grinned. "But will you respect me in the morning?"

I laughed, put her down onto her stockinged feet, turned her around, and gave her a spank on the bottom. She turned back pouting, rubbed her butt cheek, and pretended that it hurt. But I saw the glow of desire in her eyes become a fire of lust.

I grew hard as I watched her eyes caress every inch of my body as I undressed. I would finally have the woman that I had ached to touch for the past two weeks. My pulse raced faster as I unbuttoned my shirt and Wrangler jeans. I almost swallowed my tongue when she started fondling her breasts. I couldn't wait to get her naked. This would be a night I'd never forget.

## Ava

He ripped off his shirt, and I saw bruises on his washboard abs from his rides today. I wanted to kiss every one of his injuries away. He tugged off his briefs and jeans, making his championship belt buckle clink when it hit the floor. Wetness seeped between my thighs at the sight of his swelled shaft.

"Come here."

I trembled at the need in his guttural command.

I stepped closer, and he lowered his mouth to mine. His hungry kisses sent shivers down my spine. Slowly, he unbuttoned my top and brushed his thumbs over my hardened nipples.

I moaned.

He unsnapped my bra and tugged the straps and blouse over my shoulders. Coolness from the air conditioner made me shiver as the clothes plunged to the floor. I moaned and arched my back as he cupped my breasts, begging him to suck them.

He kissed both nipples. "Pretty," he growled.

I whimpered.

The beast ignored my need to be sucked, dropped to his knees, and dragged my shorts and panties to the floor. He licked my clit and my heat clenched. "Mmm, you taste like heaven."

I forgot all about my breasts.

He stood and lay me back on the bed. "Spread your thighs for me, I want a better view of your beautiful pink pussy." I did as he wished and gasped when he stroked his shaft twice while watching wetness drip from my heat. "Good girl," he groaned.

He leaned down and pinched the tips of my nipples while spreading my folds with his tongue.

"More," I cried.

He flicked my bud, and I thrusted to get tighter to his mouth. He released my breasts and pressed down on my thighs giving me little if any control of my movements. He sucked my clitoris out of my clitoral hood, and I screamed.

I grasped his hair between my fingers and held on for dear life.

His warm, wet suction had me panting and crying for him not to stop. He released my thighs and scooped my butt cheeks with his strong, callused hands, adding pressure and friction with his tongue.

My entire body was on fire with pleasure. The sensations of his groans and growls sizzled through my nerve endings. His gifted mouth sent me into a soul-shattering, heart-pounding orgasm. Blasts of brightly colored lights flashed behind my closed eyelids, and quivering waves of bliss flowed over me.

## Chapter Five

### Colton

I rushed to my nightstand, pulled a condom out of my wallet and rolled it onto my throbbing member. There was no way I wanted to miss her spasms clenching my cock. I lifted her by the waist, lay back on the bed and had her straddle me with her beautiful backside facing me. She took hold of me and guided my aching hard-on into her warm, wet pussy. She complained because I held her still for a few moments until her walls clamped around me.

"Hot damn. Babe, I love that sensation." I growled and released her.

She took hold of my calves and surged up and down my erection. Each time her luscious bottom bounced against me sent vibrations to my groin. Being in this position enabled me to watch my sex enter her gorgeous body, and it added to the pleasure, making it more intense. I shuddered.

I glided my fingers up both sides of her spine, to the tiny hairs on the nape of her neck. She quivered.

She seemed free, like she had no inhibitions with me. She ground back and forth, up and down, or in circles, whatever made her feel good, until she grabbed hold of my thighs and flexed her back. It must have pressed my length against her most sensitive spot. "Colton," she cried.

I took hold of her hips and control of the pace, making sure I pressed against her inner wall with each lunge. I stimulated her clit as I ground her nub against me. She gasped, and I knew she was close.

The buildup of tension through my midsection let me know I wasn't far behind her. I was desperate to see her face when she came. I lifted her off me, turned her around, and marveled at the look of pleasure on her face.

I slid back into her wetness and the same feelings built again, only quicker this time. With every stroke the sensitivity increased.

She screamed and the walls of her heat compressed around my overly sensitive dick. Cum gushed out onto my balls. A tingling sensation started in my groin, built slowly around the head, and down my shaft. My entire body shuddered into uncontrolled bursts of blissful ejaculation. It was pure ecstasy.

Ava collapsed onto my chest, and together we slowly quieted. It had been an exhausting day, and I was spent, but I didn't want to crash on her. I wanted her to know how special she was to me.

Before I could get a word out, she rolled to my side and looked up. She was flushed and her skin glowed. Stunning. "Colton."

"Yes, babe?"

"I overheard you talking with some cowboys in the tent about needing a place to keep your horses. A couple of them had room for them at their ranches, but they were not from Kentucky."

I bobbed my head. "That's true."

She drew her brows together and her lips pulled back into a straight line. "Well, I don't want you to have to move away."

My heart burst with joy that she might be falling for me too.

"I have plenty of room in my stables, and I thought you might like to keep them with me instead of having to leave home."

God, she was wonderful. I cleared my throat and kissed her forehead. "Under one condition?"

"Anything," she whispered.

"In seven months, I'm hanging up my hat. I want you in my life when that time comes, because I'm crazy about you. Do you think you can handle being just mine? Even with me being away so often, but with my promise to stay true to you while I'm on the road?"

Her body did a little jolt, then she wiggled up and kissed me. "I can't think of anything I want more than that." The twinkle in her eyes and her giant smile let me know her words were true. I felt like the champion of the National Final Rodeo. "Yeehaw!"

She laughed.

"Then the answer is yes. You'll be helping me out so much, and now I won't worry about Lightning and my other horses when I leave some of them behind. I'll let the kid that cleans their stalls and feeds them know where he'll be working. He's dependable, so you won't have to lift a finger. He even exercises them for me.

"With that settled, do you mind if I close my eyes and nod off to sleep. It's been a long but fantastic day."

She kissed the tip of my nose and said, "Goodnight, cowboy."

I closed my eyes with a smile on my face and never even felt her move to her own pillow. I was out in seconds.

## Chapter Six

### Ava

I had been flying high ever since the night of the rodeo two weeks ago, when Colton told me he was crazy about me. I hoped that meant he was falling in love, because I had already fallen hard. I'd never felt this kind of desire, passion, and love for anyone.

The two of us had spent the last two weeks finishing up all the framing for my art collection. Colton had really come through for me, and tonight was the event. My parents were in attendance, and Winston and Dad had been busy discussing how talented I was. That's what Dads are for. Cheering on their kids. It made me smile inside.

But then they got to talking about Colton and me as a couple and how they felt about it. I didn't stick around to hear their conversation. Our fathers' approvals or not, I wasn't changing how I felt about Colton. I loved the man with all my heart.

He was dressed in a navy suit tonight and looked like a million bucks. I had seen some ladies at my show eyeing him more than my art. He came up to me and gave me a kiss just as I finished talking with a small group of customers.

"Congratulations! Your collection was a huge hit. I'm so proud of you, baby."

I beamed up at him. "I couldn't have done it without you."

He chuckled. "Honey, if the kid that takes care of my horses had framed your work they still would have sold. They're wonderful."

My stomach fluttered. He gave me a squeeze and scurried off as the last of the folks came over to say goodbye to me. Out of the corner of my eye, I saw him go into the back room with my father. I hoped Daddy wasn't going to give him some lecture about how to treat his daughter or ask him his intentions. Ugh.

Winston locked the gallery door after the last patrons. Daddy and Ma came over to say goodbye. I asked where Colton had run off to. Daddy cleared his throat. "The boy had to attend to his horses. He asked me to tell you he'd see you back at your place."

I couldn't help it, my lips turned down.

"Now don't you give that boy a hard time. He's a good man and I like him."

"Well then, that's all that matters. My dad likes him." I laughed.

"That's right, and don't you forget it, little lady." He chuckled and kissed me goodbye.

Mr. Maples gave me a hug and told me I'd been a star. That I'd charmed the wallets off quite a few customers. We laughed and stepped out into the warm summer evening.

Right in front of the gallery was a white carriage with my gorgeous black stallion, Thunder, and Colton standing next to his beautiful white mare, Lightning. It was like a fairytale come to life. Colton stepped over to me and took hold of my hand.

My pulse quickened.

"Babe, tonight I received your father's blessing to marry you."

He filled my heart with joy.

Colton got down on one knee and pulled a velvet box from his pocket. He opened it and a beautiful diamond ring sparkled up at me.

My eyes filled with tears.

"Babe, I need you to be mine forever. I love you. Will you marry me?"

Lightning and Thunder whinnied and bobbed their heads.

We laughed.

"I've loved you since the moment you ran your hand over my horse sculpture and looked at me with affection and admiration. Yes, I'll be yours."

He put the ring on my finger, lifted me into the carriage, and kissed me sweetly as we rode off into the moonlit night.

## The End

# Orion
## Virginia Wallace

Perhaps, thought Daisy, she should have thrown on something to wear besides what she was *already* wearing, and her riding boots. Her thigh-length nightgown wasn't exactly the ideal outfit for a night ride...

But she didn't have a moment to spare.

Daisy gave Buster a slap on the flank as she swung into the saddle and stood up in the stirrups.

"*Go*, boy!" she whispered, tightening her grip on the reins.

Daisy had chosen the chestnut stallion because, out of all her father's horses, Buster loved nothing more than to run.

And run he did.

Daisy leaned forward, grateful that no one was following her; the bright moonlight was almost certainly illuminating her panties as her nightie blew up in the breeze. She should also, she thought, have taken a moment to tie back her fiery red tresses; her hair was *way* too long to leave flying about!

"*Faster!*" hissed Daisy, leaning low over the stallion's neck as he thundered across the pasture. Buster obeyed eagerly, doubling his speed as he approached the electric fence which bordered the sprawling O'Reilly Ranch.

The fence was meant to contain cattle, not horses, and Daisy locked her legs as Buster leapt easily over it. The ranch was behind her now; ahead lay the foothills of Montana's Absaroka mountain range.

Daisy moaned as a peal of thunder echoed in the distance. *Please don't start raining*, she thought desperately.

A bolt of lightning split the night as though it meant to mock her unspoken prayer, leaving Daisy to blink away the spots in her eyes.

There was but a single trail through the foothills, at least one that was passable to horses. Daisy knew the trail by heart, and so did Buster;

the trees were blocking the moonlight now, but the horse ignored the darkness as he charged into the woods.

*This is insane*, thought Daisy. *I don't even know what I'm doing, or why I'm doing it.*

She flexed her back and knees, easily moving in sync with her horse. She had learned to ride nearly as soon as she'd learned to walk; her lithe, lean form reflected her years of practice.

The trees thinned out a little, and Daisy looked anxiously skyward as she shook her tangled hair from her pale gray eyes.

*Oh no*, she moaned internally. *No, not again.*

The Montana sky was spattered with stars and dotted with silver-edged clouds as far as the eye could see; even the full, silver moon couldn't overwhelm their grandeur. But there was a strange anomaly in the sky, too, one that Daisy had only ever seen once.

A swirling circle of lights hovered just below the cloud line. The lights looked like stars, but Daisy was certain that they were *not* stars; they were too low, and too distinct.

Daisy could smell Buster's sweat as he galloped through the trees, but even the scent of over-worked horseflesh couldn't mask another odor: the ozone-laden aroma of an approaching rainstorm.

"Please, *no*," groaned Daisy.

The rain began pouring down as though God himself had wrung out the sky, instantly drenching horse and rider both. At the selfsame moment the deluge splattered onto the waiting earth, a brilliant flash of light split the night.

Daisy was nearly thrown from Buster's back as he skidded to a stop, cavorting sideways as he whinnied in panic.

"*Easy*, boy!" she cooed, laying a gentle hand on the stallion's neck as she dismounted. "It's okay, big guy. We're here."

Buster snorted indignantly, shaking his head in irritation.

Daisy dropped Buster's reins and walked slowly ahead. Her hair was hanging in sodden tendrils, and her gown clung to her slender body as though she'd just been baptized. The rain was almost too dense to see through, but Daisy ignored the deluge as she squelched through the mud.

She stopped at the edge of a large pool; she'd often come here to fish for trout as a girl. This place was lovely by day and even more so by moonlight, but the picturesque nature of the scenery was now brutally suppressed by the punishing rain.

Perhaps the beauty of this spot had somehow been mere illusion all along.

Daisy looked sharply to her right as a loud snort caught her attention. "*Jasper?*" she whispered.

The silhouette of another horse appeared through the curtains of rain, saddled and bridled. Daisy took his reins gently and patted his nose.

"We'll get you home, bud," she said, rather loudly over the pounding rain. "Where's… Where's…"

She couldn't finish the sentence.

Jasper turned his black head toward the pond and snorted again. Daisy dropped his reins and walked slowly through the mud, approaching the water's edge with hesitant steps.

"*No!*" she cried.

She fell to her knees, choking back a sob as she reached for something. That 'something' was a discarded Stetson hat, which meant there was no more hope. There was no point in looking skyward; the celestial anomaly was certainly gone by now.

Daisy stumbled to her feet and turned around. There was a rocky outcropping near here, she knew; it would keep both her and the horses dry until the rain stopped. Her gown and panties she could simply strip off and hang up to dry.

It wasn't like there was anyone to see her, anyway.

And Daisy hated *that* most of all!

"WHERE *ARE* YOU?!" she screamed at the sky. "WHERE DID YOU GO!? WHERE DID YOU *COME* FROM?!"

A bolt of lightning flashed overhead, but alas it offered no answers.

Daisy took a deep, deep breath…

And then she screamed at the top of her lungs. But her cry was not inarticulate, or without purpose. No, Daisy did not simply scream. She screamed out a *name*. A name that she'd once loved, had once murmured with something akin to worship on her pretty lips.

A peal of thunder, louder than any she'd ever heard in her life, drowned out her agonized wail. Choking, crying, and too hoarse to unleash another tirade at the sky, she fell to her knees and wept into the mud.

\*\*\*

## The Day Before

Daisy wiped the ultrasound gel off her abdomen with a paper towel, and modestly pulled the waistband of her skirt back up.

"The doctor will be with you shortly," smiled the nurse, rolling away the cart.

As she took a seat on the edge of the exam-room bed, Daisy found herself wishing that the lights weren't so bright in here. Truth be told, she disliked doctor's offices in general; doctors had a habit of telling her things that she didn't want to hear.

*I'm only twenty-four,* she thought miserably, wiping her eyes. *I shouldn't be going through something like this.*

It seemed to take forever for the doctor to arrive...

Daisy straightened up as he entered, feeling her heart beginning to pound.

"What did you find?" she asked breathlessly.

"Well," said the aging doctor, flipping over the top page of Daisy's chart, "It could be worse."

"That means it could be *better*, too," moaned Daisy, adjusting the tie on her ponytail just to give her shaking hands something to do.

"I know," said the doctor sympathetically. "But endometriosis isn't exactly a curable condition; it's just something that you treat as best you can. I don't think the scarring on your ovaries requires another surgery at this point, if that helps."

Daisy nodded, only feeling but so relieved by the doctor's reassurance. She'd already had two laparoscopic surgeries to remove the excess tissue from her body, and she wasn't looking forward to another.

"What does this mean for... for... How will this affect me in the future?" she asked, scarcely able to form the question.

"Your birth control pills will help manage the symptoms. But other than that..."

"What?!" demanded Daisy anxiously, looking at the 'sharp disposal' box on the wall to avoid meeting the doctor's eyes.

"Miss O'Reilly," said the doctor evenly, "I'm going to give it to you straight. If you don't have children soon, you may never have them at all. If that isn't something you're ready for right now, you may want to consider having some of your eggs frozen."

Daisy looked as though she'd been slapped; she just stared at the doctor with her mouth open.

"I'm sorry, Daisy," said the doctor gently. "I know that's not what you wanted to hear, but that's all I can tell you at this point. I've been treating you for this since you were fourteen, and that's my diagnosis. I won't be offended if you seek a second opinion."

"No, thank you," said Daisy dully. "I don't think there's any point."

"Well, call me if there's anything else I can do for you," said the doctor kindly. "Try to enjoy your summer, okay?"

"Thank you," said Daisy, sliding off the bed.

Walking outside into the bright sunshine, she took a seat on a bench and pulled out her cell phone. Unlocking the opening screen, she smiled wanly as she looked at her desktop photo. It was a picture of herself, sporting a dazzling smile. Standing next to her, holding her securely in his affectionate embrace, was someone who'd completely, utterly rocked her world: Orion.

Such a funny name he had, Daisy thought when she'd first met him.

A funny name, perhaps, but he certainly didn't have funny *looks*; it had taken Daisy weeks to get over blushing in his presence. Orion was tall, chiseled, with dark hair, and eyes as blue as the Montana sky itself. He could ride just as well as Daisy, and he'd proven a godsend to the ranch. Old Willie O'Reilly, Daisy's father, was just that: old, and getting a bit too elderly to easily run such a large spread. Orion was proving himself as a manager as well as a ranch hand, and father and daughter both were grateful for his expertise.Daisy tapped the Contact icon to call Orion.

"Hey, you!" he answered immediately. "Ready to go?"

"Yes," said Daisy simply, unwilling to elaborate.

"I'll just be a minute," said Orion. "I'm here with Louie, down at the supply house. We're going over the volume we ordered last year, to see if we can't cut a better deal on the sweet feed for the horses."

"Take your time," sighed Daisy.

"I won't be long," promised Orion. "Would you like to catch a movie before we head back?"

"No, thank you," said Daisy. "I'll see you soon."

After saying goodbye, she disconnected the call and put the phone back into her purse.

Daisy leaned back on the bench, trying to clear her head. She was silly, she knew, to have insisted on making Orion drive today; she was perfectly capable of driving herself. But driving in Livingston always made her nervous. She hated parallel parking her Jeep, and having to negotiate stop signs and traffic signals. Livingston was a tiny town, for sure—barely seven thousand people—but it was nevertheless more crowded than the open fields over which she was used to driving.

Besides, Daisy kind of *enjoyed* having Orion chauffeur her around.

Opening an e-book on her phone, she tried to lose herself in a story while she waited for her boyfriend to pick her up. But her panicky thoughts proved to be stubborn things; they were unwilling to lie dormant and refused to surrender to the tale beneath which Daisy was trying to bury them.

*What if I never have children?* Daisy wondered against her will.

She scrolled down a page, trying to force herself to read.

*Why is Orion not making a move?* she thought unwillingly. *It's been almost two years, and he knows damn well that I love him.*

Daisy scrolled down another page, even though she'd not read the one before it.

*Is he gay?* she wondered. *Some kind of eunuch? Can't he see that I'm tired of being a 'maiden', and I want to become a wife? Doesn't he want ME the way I want HIM?!*

Daisy finally surrendered to her feverish wonderings and closed the e-book. She returned the phone to her purse, and leaned back on the bench. If she couldn't force herself to read, she realized dully, then she'd have to settle for simply watching the cars pass by the clinic. She was wishing, for the thousandth time, that she had a mother with whom to discuss these matters. Sadly, her mother had perished from a stroke during childbirth; as Daisy O'Reilly came screaming *into* the world, Susan O'Reilly faded *out* of it. Willie was left to raise his daughter alone, and he'd never remarried.

She found at least some relief in the mundane, in idly watching Livingston's sorry excuse for 'traffic' passing her by.

It seemed like forever before Orion pulled up, skidding to a stop as he always did. Daisy privately thought that Orion drove like he was flying an airplane, or maybe a fighter jet. She managed a thin smile as she rose from her seat and smoothed out her flouncy skirt.

Orion climbed out of the Jeep and opened the door for her, as he always did. "Hey, Daffodil!" he chirped. "Did everything go okay?"

"I suppose so," said Daisy, climbing into the Jeep as Orion closed the door behind her. She used to feel shy whenever Orion used his pet name for her. She didn't anymore, but she still found it childishly cute.

What a strange creature Orion was, thought Daisy as he shifted gears and pulled onto the road. When she'd first met him, he never used any kind of slang at all. No "hey", no "okay", or "alright". He used to speak *so* carefully, like he was measuring his words, almost as though he were a foreigner trying to figure out the local lingo.

*What did the doctor tell you?*

"About what?" asked Daisy evasively.

"Huh?" said Orion as he shifted gears. "I didn't say anything."

"Didn't you just ask me what the doctor told me?" said Daisy, wrinkling her nose.

"No, I didn't. But since it's on your mind…"

Daisy could never quite say why she always heard things around Orion. Was she simply anticipating his statements, his questions, and formulating them in her head? If so, the problem lay with her, not him. But there *were* moments in which she felt her thoughts were being violated.

Daisy took a deep breath and fixed her eyes on Orion's ring to calm herself.

It was a beautiful thing, Orion's ring, forged of some metal that Daisy could never quite identify. But the ornately wrought metal was not nearly as breathtaking as the stone set in its center; it was the oddest color imaginable, a color that she couldn't name if her life depended on it. Orion always wore it, on the ring finger of his right hand.

"So," ventured Daisy slowly, "the doctor says I don't need another surgery right now, but the scarring is still pretty bad."

*What else did he say?*

"I'm *getting* to that!" snapped Daisy.

"I didn't say anything," said Orion mildly.

*Of course, you didn't,* thought Daisy. "I'm sorry," she said aloud. "I didn't mean to bark at you."

"It's okay, Daffodil," said Orion gently.

"He said," continued Daisy, hoping that she wouldn't cry, "that my time is running out to have children. He even suggested that I have some of my eggs frozen."

Orion tightened his grip on the steering wheel as he fixed his eyes on the road.

"Orion," said Daisy, blinking away tears, "what do you have to say?"

"I'm sorry to hear that," he said, in a carefully neutral tone.

"Sorry to HEAR that?!" wailed Daisy. "Orion, this is *me* we're talking about! The woman you *love!* In case you missed my point, I need to get *on* with my life!"

*You want me to marry you and give you a child?*

"Now *that* seemed a little abrupt!"

"*What* seemed abrupt? I don't understand."

"You didn't say anything, did you?" moaned Daisy, holding her head in her hands.

"No."

*Dear God, I really am going crazy*, thought Daisy. "I'm just saying, Orion, that if you *really* love me—"

"You know I do," said Orion firmly.

"Then *please* tell me you have something in mind for our future," said Daisy.

Orion went quiet for a moment.

"Maybe I have to figure out my own first," said Orion. "My future, I mean."

"What's *that* supposed to mean?"

"It means I need to think," said Orion.

"Great!" said Daisy. "The clock is ticking on *me*, and *you* need to think!"

Orion said nothing.

Daisy rode in silence back to the ranch. She didn't wait for Orion to open the door for her this time; she simply jumped out of the Jeep and ran inside her father's house. As she slammed the front door furiously behind her, she could hear the Jeep pulling away. Orion lived in a furnished apartment over the main barn, and that was likely where he was heading.

Daisy ran to her loft and threw herself into bed.

*Don't cry*, she told herself.

Refraining from tears, she realized, would be easier said than done.

\*\*\*

Daisy climbed out of bed that night, feeling groggy and somewhat bloated. Perhaps, she thought, she'd gone a little overboard with the pasta. But then, her father always had been an excellent cook. It was good, she thought as she stretched, that she got so much exercise; otherwise, her trim figure might not stay trim for very long.

Daisy opened the sliding glass doors of her loft and adjusted the oversized men's tee shirt that she was wearing as a nightie. She'd bought it in Billings years before, at a concert. Appalled that the merchandising crew had run out of petite-sized shirts, she'd improvised and bought herself a Guns n' Roses *nightgown* instead.

Daisy took a step onto the wooden widow's walk, the deck that adjoined the top story of the house. She never failed to smile whenever she stepped outside thus; a widow's walk was a typical feature on oceanfront houses, so named because wives would anxiously pace them as they waited for their husbands to return from sea.

The ocean was hundreds of miles from here, but Daisy was nevertheless fond of her widow's walk. Satisfied that the evening temperatures weren't particularly chilly, she closed the glass door to keep the bugs out of her room.

The night sky was clear, as it usually was. Daisy looked upwards, letting the breeze gently tousle her shining hair as she gazed at the stars.

Daisy *loved* the stars!

They never failed to instill in her a sense of eternity, a breathtaking glimpse into the utter vastness of the universe. Countless were the stars, most of them untold light-years away; Daisy knew that she was seeing the stars not as they *were*, but rather as how they *had been*. By the time the light they emitted tonight reached her world, she would be long gone… and others would go on to see the night as it was in *her* day.

Stars serve as a mute treatise on immortality, and Daisy cherished them for the same.

She scanned the night sky, seeking her favorite constellation.

As always, her sparkling eyes zeroed in on the three twinkling dots that made up the center of the constellation. Daisy widened her gaze, letting the mythical image slowly take shape in her mind's eye.

The Hunter: the ancients had called the constellation by that name. Daisy shivered, imagining the towering form of the Hunter raising his mighty weapon across the night sky as he claimed his latest kill. If he were real— if the Hunter really *were* a being that spanned the entire sky—then he would surely be the largest entity in all of creation.

Daisy lowered her gaze, eyeing the sprawling ranch before her. The horses were stabled now, and the cattle asleep. The hustle and bustle would begin again tomorrow, as it always did, but tonight there was a profound blanket of peace spread across the O'Reilly ranch.

She still remembered her upsetting conversation from earlier. But even the memory of the doctor's grim news could not undo the sense of calm that she felt right now. Closing her eyes, Daisy returned to the memory of another night, one in the more recent past, a night much like *this* one...

*** 

## Two years before

One of the horses, an older, cranky mare, whinnied softly in protest as Daisy slid open the barn door.

"Sorry, Trixie," said Daisy apologetically, turning her flashlight away from the irritated horse. "I didn't mean to disturb you."

The chaff from the hay blew softly across the plank floor as the breeze meandered curiously inside. Daisy walked softly through the stalls, careful that her riding boots didn't make too much noise. This was only a barn, after all, but it seemed nevertheless respectful not to make too much noise.

"Buster?" whispered Daisy. "You awake, boy?"

A casual snort betrayed Buster's wakeful state, and Daisy was careful not to shine the flashlight in his eyes as she unlatched the stall door. "Wanna go for a run, boy?" she asked playfully.

Buster willingly followed Daisy outside and stood patiently while she fetched a bit, bridle, and saddle. Buster, thought Daisy in amusement, would be better garbed for this night's ride than she was; she'd taken off on impulse, only pausing long enough to don her riding boots.

But tonight was *perfect* in every way, absolutely idyllic. Her Guns n' Roses nightie would be just as comfortable outside as it was in her bed, and she could always throw a blanket across the saddle for padding. Setting the required tackle outside, Daisy slid the barn door shut.

Buster stood obediently still as Daisy saddled and bridled him and hoisted herself into the saddle. He seemed eager tonight, and full of anticipation for his unplanned outing.

Daisy ducked low over Buster's back as he began to run through the open field, guiding him gently toward the fence. Buster quickened his thunderous pace, stretching out his neck as he raised his plumed tail.

Locking her knees as Buster sailed over the fence, Daisy shook her hair from her face and set her gaze upon the foothills beyond. Ahead lay the usually darkened trail, but it was not dark on *this* moonlit, magical night. No, tonight the woods were *alive!* They danced with merry shadows gifted by the smiling moon. Daisy guided Buster carefully toward the woodland trail, enjoying the flitting shadows as she did.

Buster slowed down a little as he turned down the trail; this path had a lot of twists and turns, and he knew it. He settled into a medium canter as he bore his pretty mistress through the trees, flicking his ears with contentment.

Daisy could only vaguely see the stars through the dense tree line now, but they sparkled at her here and there as if to assure her that yes, they were watching over her still.

It is a comforting feeling, thought Daisy, to be watched over by the stars.

She lost all sense of time as Buster carried her along, but at last her reveries were broken as Buster came to a slow stop. He was stopping to drink; he always stopped here for a drink.

Daisy dismounted and slipped off her riding boots. She buried her toes in the soft, lush grass, admiring the sparkling pool from which Buster was slaking his thirst.

The tinkling mountain stream which fed the pool was barely audible tonight, and the pool itself was as smooth as glass. Despite being so small, barely fifty feet in diameter, the shimmering pond was kept absolutely pristine by the constant influx and exit of clean mountain water. The water reflected the starlit sky like a mirror, almost making it hard to tell which way was up.

Daisy walked to the edge and dipped a toe in the water.

She felt no sensation of cold, nor one of heat. It was as though this night—this place—was a dream; thus the Elements had been stripped of their usual power.

Without even thinking, Daisy pulled her makeshift nightie over her head and dropped it into the grass.

"What are *you* looking at?" she giggled as Buster eyed her topless body curiously. "You're a *horse*. You aren't supposed to be interested in me!"

Buster snorted as Daisy peeled off her cotton bikini panties and dropped them beside her discarded t-shirt. She took a few steps into the water and leaned backward, submerging her naked body. She kept her eyes open, looking up at the night sky through the distorted lens of water. The stars sparkled just as brightly but they were fuzzy now, and indistinct.

Rising for air, Daisy brushed her wet hair back and blinked the water from her eyes.

That's when she saw... *it.*

A sudden light appeared in the sky, swirling in circles like an angry storm cloud. But the circle of light was too bright to be a cloud; it looked more like a small galaxy, or nebula, composed of the selfsame stars that illuminated the sky above.

But the apparition was too low to consist of stars; it looked like it was hanging even lower than the usual cloud line.

As Daisy stared, wide-eyed, the swirling un-cloud of not-quite-stars flashed brightly, as brilliantly as a bolt of lightning...

And then it was gone.

Daisy ducked low in the water. She wasn't afraid so much as curious. What *was* that thing? Some sort of electrical phenomenon, born of heat or pressure?

She swam idly about for a while, forgetting what she'd seen. She almost wanted to stay here forever, in this perfect place, but the weather would change, of course, spoiling the effect. Perhaps, she thought, this was precisely why such moments are priceless: because they are fleeting, and only find lasting existence in memories.

Daisy rose from the pool and climbed ashore on the opposite bank from which she'd undressed, wringing out her hair as she did. Buster was walking lazily about, munching on the grass and paying his mistress little heed. She could simply sit here awhile and air-dry before heading home.

Smiling, Daisy threw one more longing, wistful gaze at the stars.

*Truly, you are a sight for weary eyes.*

Daisy screamed, and immediately covered herself: One hand over her underwear zone, and an arm across her bare breasts.

"WHO'S THERE?!" she screeched, feeling her heart starting to pound.

"I apologize," said a gentle, soothing voice from the trees. "I meant no offense."

Daisy's eyes darted to the far side of the pond, where she'd left her shirt and panties. But something told her to stand her ground, to not run just yet.

"Come out where I can *see* you!" ordered Daisy, trying to sound assertive.

Slowly, a figure emerged from the shadows of the tree line.

Daisy was tempted to run for her clothes again, but she felt no desire to flash her un-clothed derrière at this stranger.

*You are lovely beyond words, young lady.*

"Don't *say* things like that!" snapped Daisy. "You CREEP!"

"I don't understand," said the intruder, in a deep, calm voice. "I said nothing."

"You *didn't?*"

"I did not," said the stranger, stepping forward.

"Stay away from me!" warned Daisy, wanting to run but feeling as though her feet were shoed in cement. "Leave me *alone!*"

The stranger stopped within an arm's length of Daisy, smiling. He was a handsome fellow, Daisy realized against her will. His dark hair was long, shining beneath the moonlight, and his eyes sparkled in a luminescent shade of blue.

He was clad in a long robe, woven in white with silvery threads around the edging. Daisy noted the details of his clothing and looked back up at his face... his very, *very* handsome face.

*Allow me.*

Daisy closed her eyes, wondering why she felt so utterly mesmerized. She should be running, she knew; this man could have been—and probably was—*stalking* her.

But she couldn't run. Even afterward, she couldn't explain why she didn't run.

Daisy shivered as she felt folds of soft cloth enveloping her naked body. The stranger was careful not to touch her as he pulled the robe closed around her trembling form and tied the belt.

"Thank you," she murmured, opening her eyes.

"Now it is *I* who must blush," said the stranger.

He was clad only in a loincloth now, and Daisy quailed as she stared at his muscular body.

"What's your name?" she whispered.

The stranger hesitated, looking pointedly into her eyes... and in that moment, Daisy looked to the stars, unable to meet his piercing gaze.

She eyed her favorite constellation as she waited for the stranger to give his name. *There* shone the three stars that made up the Hunter's belt, and *there* shimmered the stars that constituted his mighty weapon.

"My name," said the stranger softly, "is Orion."

Daisy gave him an odd look, cocking her head in curiosity.

"Your name is Orion?" she said slowly. "How did you know I—?"

Daisy didn't finish the sentence, because her unspoken question suddenly struck her as absurd. The stranger couldn't *possibly* have known that she was looking at Orion, the mighty celestial hunter.

"What is *your* name?" asked Orion gently.

"My name is… it's…" began Daisy.

*Don't give him your name!* she thought.

"My name," she said at last, flushing because she wasn't used to lying, "is… Daffodil."

Daisy was tempted to smack herself in the forehead. What a *cheesy* moniker to offer! If she needed another flower name, she could have at least chosen Rose!

"Daffodil," repeated the stranger gravely. "I am honored to have met you."

"Um… thanks," said Daisy, backing away as though some spell had just been broken.

The stranger watched in silence as Daisy slipped her panties on underneath the robe and climbed onto Buster again.

"Will you be all right?" asked Daisy awkwardly. "Out here, I mean. You can keep my nightgown if you'd like."

"I will be… all right," said Orion, raising his hand in farewell. Only then did Daisy notice the ornate, strange ring on his right hand. "May peace follow you wherever you go… Daisy."

Daisy kicked Buster into a canter, frightened that the stranger had used her name. Who was he? Where did he come from? If he'd been stalking her, then why didn't he just go ahead and…

That thought was too awful to articulate, even mentally, so Daisy tried not to think at all as she rode home.

\*\*\*

Today

Daisy awoke early and after she'd dressed she made a beeline for the kitchen. She made a habit of never doing *anything* before she'd had her morning coffee!

The prior evening's journey down Memory Lane had resurrected a nagging set of questions, questions that she had always entertained and yet never dared to voice. Where was Orion from? Who were his people? Why did he first appear in the middle of the woods, only to reappear the next week with a haircut, wearing proper ranch-hand clothes and holding Daisy's folded nightie? Why was he so smart, and such an able manager?

Hell, what was his last *name?!*

Daisy slugged her coffee as quickly as she could without scalding her mouth, disturbed by her sense of growing unease. She was in love with Orion, and certain that he loved her just as deeply. Perhaps they could have forged a life together. But *now* her body was proving itself to be a ticking time bomb, threatening to sabotage her hope of a family.

Why was Orion acting so casual about all of this?! *Maybe I have to figure my own out first… my future, I mean.*

Those words made Daisy see red.

Setting down her coffee mug, Daisy left the house and walked toward the main stable. Orion would be there, she knew; he always was this time of the morning. Already the air was growing humid, and uncomfortably hot; she could feel beads of sweat forming beneath her tank top and jean shorts.

She found him at last, dragging a bale of hay out of the barn. She smiled wistfully, remembering her teenage fantasies of sexy, sweaty cowboys. She'd always imagined them gallivanting about on their trusty steeds, boldly engaging in brave deeds of derring-do… But alas the cowboy realities often proved far less glamorous than her lustful, adolescent daydreams.

All but the sexy and sweaty part, that is. Orion was shirtless, prompting Daisy to look awkwardly away. His sculpted, glistening body conjured desires in her that didn't quite fit the moment's agenda.

"We'll have to let these bales sit for a while," said Orion, wiping the perspiration from his face as he fanned himself with his hat. "They were cut a bit green, I think."

"May we talk?" asked Daisy primly as Orion donned his shirt.

"Of course," said Orion, taking a gulp from his water bottle as he took a seat upon one of the hay bales. "What's on your mind?"

"You *know* what's on my mind!" she said, taking a seat beside him. "The same thing that was on my mind yesterday."

"I see," said Orion, staring straight ahead. "You're worried about what the doctor told you."

"Aren't *you?*" demanded Daisy heatedly. "I wouldn't be so worried if I already had a home of my own, and a… a…"

"A husband?" asked Orion mildly.

"*Yes*, a husband!" snapped Daisy. "What's wrong with you? Don't you *want* me?"

"Like nothing else in this universe," said Orion sincerely. "But things are more… complicated than you know."

"Are you running from the law?" asked Daisy bluntly.

"What?! No!" snapped Orion. "What makes you ask such a thing?"

"What's your last name?"

Orion looked surprised at that. "My… My last name?"

"Yes, your last name. You know, the one they put on your driver's license. The one you use when you pay taxes. *That* last name!"

"It's not pronounceable in your tongue," said Orion dully. "But it means 'explorer' in English."

"What kind of answer is that? I mean, what name did you *put* on your license?"

*Maybe I have ways of keeping others from asking to see my license.*

Daisy wasn't even aware that the subject had suddenly vanished from her mind.

"What are we going to do?" she whimpered. "I mean… my medical issues *are* an 'us' problem, aren't they?"

"Of course they are. But…"

"But what?!"

"I may have to… *go* somewhere. Perhaps tonight, if conditions are right."

"What? When will you be coming back?" asked Daisy, feeling an icy stab of fear.

"I can never return," said Orion, lowering his head. "Not once I decide to leave."

"WHAT?!" screeched Daisy. "You've strung me along for nearly two years, and now you're… you're *leaving?*"

"I don't have a choice, I'm afraid," said Orion, tracing the engravings on his ring with a trembling finger. "Maybe I'm obeying an arbitrary set of rules. Or maybe… maybe I'm just homesick."

"You… You can't be *serious*," protested Daisy, shocked.

"I'm afraid I am. I wish that it weren't so."

And that was the end of it. Daisy couldn't recall exactly what she'd screamed at Orion after that, but she remembered that her words consisted of declarations of hatred and frivolous, venomous accusations.

But that's what spurned love does.

It makes one a little crazy.

***

The hour was late, and it was dark outside. Daisy stood on her widow's walk yet again, wrapping her arms around herself.

It felt like rain.

Daisy silently welcomed the oncoming storm; the deafening sound of water pounding on the roof would help quiet her thoughts and soothe her pain.

Smiling perversely, Daisy spread her arms wide and subconsciously wished that a bolt of pre-storm lighting would strike her.

A breeze rose from the west, ominously foreshadowing the coming storm.

Daisy smiled grimly, waiting for a crack of thunder.

But she didn't hear a crack of thunder.

Instead she heard a truck door, slamming off in the distance.

Daisy opened her eyes and lowered her arms, squinting as she looked toward the barn.

One of the Jeeps had skidded to a stop before the main stable entrance, and someone was climbing out. Orion, Daisy knew instinctively. She watched as he opened the door and disappeared inside.

What on *earth* was he doing?!

Daisy waited with bated breath as the breeze ceased; even the oncoming storm itself seemed to be on hold.

Orion emerged from the barn at last, mounted on a horse that, even from that distance, Daisy could easily identify as Jasper. The black stallion emerged from the stable at a dead gallop, charging across the field toward the outer fence.

Daisy turned and ran into her bedroom, leaving the sliding glass door open as she threw on her riding boots. She was in too much of a hurry to don jeans, or a shirt; her trusty Guns n' Roses nightie would have to do.

The following ride was fast, and quickly became wet as the harbinger breeze fulfilled its dark promise. But at last, the frantic ride came to an end, leaving Daisy naked and sodden. She crouched miserably underneath the rock outcropping while her clothes dried out, and her horses stood sheltered beside her.

Daisy wiped her eyes, holding the muddy Stetson hat in her trembling hands.

Orion had arrived with the low-hanging nebula, and Daisy knew instinctively that he'd departed with the same. The skies were dead now, blanketed with a dreary shade of gray and bereft even of rain clouds.

"Where did you *go?*" she whimpered.

The still night air offered no solace, and no answers.

"*Fuck!*" snarled Daisy. "Where did you even *come* from?"

Answer there came none.

"Well?!" snapped Daisy, vaguely aware that she was slowly coming undone. "WHERE THE HELL DID YOU *COME* FROM?!"

*I came from your dreams, the ones that you so wistfully linked with mine. They crossed the entire universe, our dreams, and they bore with them our unspoken longings.*

"Who's *there?!*" shrieked Daisy, scooting back in alarm.

*Someone you know. Someone you loved... once. But I fear that I have disappointed you.*

Daisy pressed her back against the rock wall behind her, covering her naked form with her arms. "GET OUT OF MY HEAD!!!" she wailed. "WHY ARE YOU *ALWAYS* IN MY HEAD?!"

*I cannot help that you sense my thoughts, my love. It was never my intention to intrude upon your mind, and I was never offended that you so often traversed in mine.*

"Who *are* you, Orion?" whimpered Daisy. "Where did you *come* from, and where did you *go?*"

*Before the Great Flood, before history even began, mankind became too powerful for his own good. The technology he possessed made him mad with power and overwhelmed even his basic sense of decency.*

"What does that have to do with ANYTHING?!" demanded Daisy.

*Before Babel, the fateful day upon which God became disgusted with mankind and crushed his every marvelous advance underfoot, my people grew weary of human depravity. So we gathered our families and took to the stars.*

"You came with... *that?*" whispered Daisy. "That weird circle of stars?"

*I did. Conditions had to be perfect in order for me to come to you... You, whom I have watched for so very, very long.*

"You... you've been *watching* me?"

*You fascinated me. Your beauty, your kindness, and your devotion to home and family. I risked everything to meet you, Daffodil.*

"And then you went *back*, didn't you?" moaned Daisy, shamelessly forsaking modesty as she held her head in her hands.

*The conditions were right this night, yes. And they will never be so again, at least not during my lifetime, or yours. I missed my planet, and yearned to return to it.*

"So I'll never *see* you again?" sobbed Daisy.

*Stand up, Daffodil. Close your eyes, and face to the east.*

Daisy rose and faced east. She closed her eyes meekly, not understanding why she felt the need to obey such an order.

*Do you trust me, Daffodil?*

"Yes," whispered Daisy.

She trembled as she felt a pair of strong hands reaching around her bare waist from behind.

*You are afraid, are you not? You are worried that motherhood will forever be denied you.*

"Yes," replied Daisy dully, blinking away a tear.

*Allow me, my love, to give you the life for which you hope.*

Daisy shook as she felt a hand rest firmly on her taut stomach. The hand slid down, down until it rested upon her lower abdomen, a mere pinky's width away from her clean-shaven womanhood.

*I ask again: Do you trust me?*

"Yes."

Daisy screamed as a searing pain tore through her insides. She fell backward, convulsing as a pair of strong arms caught her.

She regained her feet only slowly, and it took her a moment to realize that the pain was quickly fading away.

"What did you just do?" she asked shakily.

*I gave you your life back, in the most beautiful form possible: hope.*

"What exactly should I be hoping for?" asked Daisy.

Daisy felt the hands pulling away from her waist. She just stood awkwardly still, naked and more than a little bashful, with an expression of confusion flickering in her slate-gray eyes.

*May I have the honor of becoming your husband? I forfeited my only chance to return home because I love you more than anything else that I have ever loved. Please tell me that I did not make a mistake.*

"No," said Daisy tremulously. "No, you didn't make a mistake. And *yes*, I… I accept your proposal."

She closed her eyes as she felt something being slipped onto the ring finger of her left hand.

She raised her hand, pressing her fingers tightly together to keep Orion's ring from falling off. "It's *beautiful!*" she breathed. "A bit oversized, I'm afraid, but maybe I can put it on a cha—"

Daisy had been about to say 'chain' as Orion's ring was too big for her finger…

And then, suddenly, it wasn't.

"So what do we do now?" asked Daisy, admiring her newly-fitted ring without feeling the need to ask further questions about it. "I'm naked, you know. Do… do you *want* me?"

*Soon. We will make a covenant, you and I, and after that we will consummate our union with a merging of flesh. Consider that my way of honoring your purity, as well as upholding the traditions of my people.*

Daisy flushed, feeling an unaccustomed warmth growing between her thighs.

*Shall we go home?*

"I thought you *missed* your chance to go home?"

*I declined to return to my planet because I didn't want to leave the one thing that now represents home to me: the woman I love. Get dressed, and let us ride away to our shared life.*

Daisy dressed slowly, and then turned around.

"Do you like the ring?" asked Orion, winking. He looked oddly ordinary now, clad in his usual jeans and a plaid shirt.

Daisy wiped away a tear, eyeing Orion's handsome face. "It's out of this world," she replied, reaching down and picking up Orion's hat. "*Thank* you. Should we… shall we go?"

Orion smiled as he reclaimed his trademark Stetson; he placed it upon his head as he planted a long, tender kiss upon Daisy's eager lips.

Daisy reeled as the kiss lingered on, suddenly stricken by a vision: the image of a small boy, with dark hair and eyes as blue as the sky. The vision overwhelmed her senses, and it took a moment for her to regain the power of speech.

"What the hell was that?!" she blurted. "What did I just *see?!*"

*Perhaps it was me, as I was long ago. Maybe it was the more distant past, a glimpse of one of my ancestors. Or could it possibly be the future, the one for which you hoped? Do not spoil destiny, my love, by trying to understand it.*

"I'll never get you out of my head, will I?" grinned Daisy, reaching for Buster's bridle.

*Almost certainly not, Daffodil. Your mind is no longer your own, and neither is mine. Let us both be grateful that it is so.*

Daisy O'Reilly had counted on riding one horse home tonight, while guiding another.

But she'd been blessedly wrong in her assumption.

This night the pair of horses bore *two* riders home, carrying them towards a bright future…

Together.

## The End

# The Long Paddock
## Jan Selbourne

## Chapter One

Shelley put the key into the ignition and raised her eyebrows at the young woman beside her.

"Are you feeling okay, Gina?"

A shy smile. "Yes, I am, and thank you again."

"Happy to help, I couldn't leave you there." Shelley reversed out of the car bay and drove onto the highway. "The road's as flat as a tack so it shouldn't take us more than an hour." Her foot pressed the accelerator and in minutes the car was humming smoothly at 100 kph.

"It's a big country and I'm lucky to have seen so much."

Shelley glanced at her fair-haired passenger with soft English skin. "Holidays?"

"No, I'm here on a work visa which ends in December. My first trip away from England and I've had a wonderful time, well, up until today."

"What the hell happened?"

"The two friends I was travelling with had a huge fight at that roadhouse. It was very embarrassing, so I went into the ladies' room, and when I came out, they weren't there. I must have looked like a lost rabbit because a waitress pointed to the door. 'Your friends went outside,' she said. I raced out to see them arguing beside the car, really yelling at each other. Mary threw Mark's luggage at him, nearly knocking him over. My luggage was thrown onto the ground and she drove off."

"That's a real fight," Shelley said dryly. "You said you were stranded. What happened to him?"

"I ran over to get my backpack, saying something stupid like 'Where has she gone? What will we do?'" Her voice caught in her throat. "Mark went over to the group of men standing beside their trucks, then told me he was hitching a lift with one of them. He was furious and humiliated and—"

"He was a complete arsehole to leave you there." Shelley said flatly. "I am glad I walked in for that cup of coffee."

She nearly hadn't stopped for that cup of coffee, but it was another one hundred and twenty kilometres and she needed to stretch her legs. She hadn't noticed the woman huddled in the corner of the restaurant until she'd carried her coffee and sandwich to a table close by. Young, hair pulled back in a ponytail, bulky backpack beside her, and crying. When she'd said, "Hey, what's wrong?" the girl had shaken her head, then blubbered that her friends had driven off without her, there were no direct coach services to Victoria, and she didn't know what to do. For the first time, the rule of never picking up anyone was broken.

"Look, I'm on my way to Deniliquin," she'd said. "Coaches go from there to Melbourne every day."

Shelley glanced again at her companion. "Why were the three of you driving on this road to Victoria?"

Gina made a face. "Mark said we should see more of the outback. I'd looked at the map, it seemed a good idea, but I had no idea it would take hours to get this far."

Shelley grinned. "Hay is flat and open and not much to see. However, this road has a history. It was called the Long Paddock and it's still known by that name."

"I'm not sure what you mean, where's the paddock?"

Shelley laughed out loud. "This is it, over six hundred kilometres. What we are driving on now follows a part of the open unfenced stock routes and tracks linking inland Queensland and New South Wales to Victoria and their greener pastures. Graziers up north and west would send their stock on this route to the Victorian markets. Even now, during droughts, and there are plenty of them, when there's no feed on the land, farmers put their stock on the road, trusting the drovers to follow this old stock route. They'd be away for months." She rolled her eyes. "I sound like a boring old schoolteacher."

Gina shook her head. "No, you don't. How on earth did these people live for months away from home?"

Shelley shrugged. "Part of life in the outback. Years ago, depending on the size of the mob—maybe a thousand or more cattle or sheep—

there'd be three, four or five stockmen, their horses and dogs, and the camp cook. Those men were more at home on the back of a horse than on the ground. They'd take shifts to keep watch over the stock at night in case something spooked them. I've heard stories of them stampeding right over the drovers asleep in their swags." She smiled at Gina's wide eyes. "Not my idea of camping out."

She cleared her throat. "Now, there are still sheep and cattle on the road, and horses and dogs, but the drovers travel with a car and caravan and often a water tanker. Watching the dogs work is something else, they can outthink us. Still, it's a damned hard life."

"A very hard life," Gina agreed. "Do you live in Deniliquin?"

"No, I'm originally from Warwick on the Darling Downs in Queensland."

"I worked at Warwick hospital for three months."

Surprised, Shelley looked at her. "Really?"

"There was a shortage of physiotherapists in rural areas and I was willing to go anywhere and see the country."

"Oh, okay." Shelley touched the accelerator to 110 kph. "Nothing exciting about me. I moved west for a while, then travelled a bit. Now I'm on my way to spend a week with my close friend from school days. Four years since we've seen each other."

Gina smiled at her. "A lot of catching up?"

Shelley chuckled. "Definitely. Emails and phone calls are great, but a bottle of wine and talking until midnight is much better. Enough of me, where are you from?"

"I grew up in Kent, my dad now lives in Canterbury. I studied physiotherapy and worked in London for a year. A friend was applying for a work visa to Australia and talked me into joining her. At the last minute she backed out and I came here on my own."

"Where did you meet the fighting losers?"

"In Queensland. I feel a real fool now."

Shelley's foot eased off the accelerator. "See that moving blur ahead of us, probably two or three k's away?"

Gina peered through the windscreen. "Yes."

"A mob of sheep." Shelley smiled at Gina. "Do you want to take photos of action on the Long Paddock?"

The car slowed to 60 kph, then 40 then 20, and stopped as a milling sea of sheep surrounded them.

Gina held her tablet up to video them. "Do we sit here until they move away?"

Shelley pointed to two men on horses at the back of the mob. "It'll take a while, but they'll move. You can watch the dogs at work while I check my phone for any messages."

One from a friend saying hi, one from Bob—she'd read that later; one from Liz:

>Where are you?

She replied:

>Stock on road, will text when on my way.

Shelley looked up to see one of the stockmen approaching. When he dismounted, she wound down the window and her heart missed a beat.

"Christ, what's that famous line from the old movie? Of all the gin joints, in all the towns in all the world, she walks into mine."

Gina frowned at her. "What did you say?"

Shelley closed her eyes. "Never mind."

The stockman leaned down to the window. "You're the last person I expected to see."

"You took the words out of my mouth." She would not let him rattle her. "How long must we wait?"

"Until they are off the road, unless you can do better." He remounted with the ease of a man born in the saddle, whistled an order to a dog. and they moved away from the car.

Gina's voice was hushed. "Who was that?"

Shelley let her breath out. "My ex-husband."

## Chapter Two

Shelley pulled into the parking bay and pointed across the road. "The Information Centre will give you timetables and a list of accommodation. Are you sure you have enough money?"

"Yes, thanks. I managed to save a bit, and my dad put one hundred pounds in my account." Gina's eyes dampened. "I am very grateful to you."

Shelley hugged her. "I enjoyed your company. You have my number, text me when you are leaving and when you get to Melbourne, or I'll worry." Gina picked up her backpack. "I will, and I'll email all the sheep photos to Dad and my friends at home. How lucky was I?"

"See one, see them all." Shelley grinned at her. "Take care."

She watched Gina walk across the road to the coach terminal, waved and reached for her phone to text Liz.

>See u in 15.

She drove away, took two wrong turns, crossed the river again and finally made it onto the right road. "After 10 k's you'll see the Stock Crossing sign, another half a k on the left is our road. You can't miss it," Liz had told her. *Yeah right, Liz. Say that and I'll miss it.* Shelley smiled to herself. Liz Carter, best friend since boarding school, had met her sheep grazier hunk when he and fifteen other Australian farmers had attended an agricultural gabfest in Canada. Liz, on a working holiday there, more holiday than working, had claimed him, and six months later they'd married in Sydney. And what a bash that was. Liz had taken to life on the land like a duck to water while she—

"Shit!" Shelley hit the brakes and reversed back. "Stupid idiot," she muttered as she changed gears, turned left and drove along the dirt road to Yarrabah. Down to 15 k's over the cattle grid, past fenced paddocks and—

"Oh wow."

At the end of the driveway was a large, red brick homestead with verandas on three sides. Gardens and a small gazebo spread out in front like fans. Behind the house were outbuildings of some sort. As Shelley got out of the car, the front door opened, and Liz was running towards her.

"I can't believe you are really here!" Liz's dark blue eyes sparkled. "You don't look any different either." She peered closer. "Well, I don't think you do."

Shelley swallowed the lump in her throat. "It's been too long, Liz, and—"

She stood back. "You look fantastic!"

Liz's cheeks coloured. "I am in that first glow."

"What? You mean you are...?"

Liz nodded. "We wanted time together first and a family was put on hold while we worked hard to get Yarrabah back in the black. Now I'm finally expanding."

Shelley hugged her again. "Congratulations. I am so pleased for you both." She stood back. "Where's Ross?"

"We've leased some land for agistment and there's work to be done there. He'll be home before dark. Where's your luggage?"

"I'll carry it."

"I'm pregnant, not crippled, now give me a bag."

Shelley stopped inside the cool tiled hallway. "Your home is beautiful and has such character."

"Ross's grandparents built it. We updated the kitchen and bathrooms, but the rest is original. We kept the open fires because they're part of the heritage of the place. The next big expense will be replacing the electrical wiring. Come on, I'll show you your room and we'll have coffee, or would you like wine? I'm not drinking, but you can."

"Wine. It's been a long day. Liz, I am so glad to be here."

***

Shelley deliberately studied her wine glass. "No crystal ball could have predicted Miss Dance Until Dawn would join the squattocracy."

Liz laughed out loud. 'Not quite the squattocracy, my friend." Her face became serious. "It's been a lot of hard work and worry. You know the mess Ross inherited."

"His father died leaving Ross and..." Shelley hesitated. "I can't remember his brother's name."

"Paul."

"Leaving Ross and Paul this and another property mortgaged to the hilt. If I remember correctly, Paul wanted to sell the lot. Ross asked the bank for mercy."

"Minnimar was sold, and what was left after the bank cleared the mortgage was given to Paul, on the condition we take Yarrabah. Ross said his grandparents would turn in their graves if the bank foreclosed. It was touch and go, and thank God for the good seasons and good markets." Liz smiled. "Our dams are full, our water tanks full, and one more payment to the bank and Yarrabah will be ours."

"I am very happy for you both," Shelley said quietly.

"What about you, Shell? Tell me more about your job and what you've been doing since you moved to Bathurst. I'm trying to say I hope you are settled now. I worried about you after—"

"After I walked out? It took six months of moving around and feeling sorry for myself to get a grip. I went from one job to another, and, as you know, I got this one at the veterinary hospital and leased the perfect flat the same week. A message to me to get on with life." She felt her cheeks redden. "And I've met someone."

Liz leaned forward. "Ooh, do tell. Is he tall, dark and handsome?"

"No, medium height, fair and, believe it or not, a banker."

"Hah, a cheap home loan?"

Shelley chuckled. "We aren't that serious. He's nice and considerate, although a bit set in his ways."

Liz nodded. "Probably what you need. Do you have any regrets?"

"About being on my own while Mack was away droving? The boozing nights with his mates at the pub when he was home?" Shelley said bitterly. "No regrets at all."

"Good. Well, I'm glad you are here for another reason. I need help in the kitchen. Paul will be here tomorrow. He's staying the night and going on to Adelaide next day. Ross has asked the neighbours over for a get-together barbecue." She screwed up her face. "I don't like Paul at all but he's Ross's brother."

"If I remember, they look alike."

"That's where it ends, they are as different as chalk and cheese." She looked up at the sound of car wheels outside. "That'll be Ross."

The front door opened and closed and a tall, well-built man with dark eyes and a wide smile walked into the living room. Shelley felt a pang of envy when he tenderly kissed Liz, then he was giving her a hug with, "So good to see you again, Shelley. Did you have a good trip?"

"I did, Ross, and it's wonderful to be here."

"I'll get a beer and join you both."

## Chapter Three

Liz grated cheese over the top of the huge dish of sweet potato bake and placed it in the oven. "It should be enough with the onions and the breadsticks."

"I can make another bowl of salad," Shelley offered.

"No need, none of the men eat salad." Liz's voice deepened. "Not eating bloody rabbit food."

Shelley grinned at her. "Just like *real* men don't eat quiche?"

Liz pushed her hair out of her eyes. "Yep." Her voice dropped to a growl. "Feed the man meat!"

"You love it here, don't you?"

"I really do, and you'll love our neighbours. Knowing Ross, he'll have asked half the district."

She swung around at a voice behind her.

"Hello, Liz, I've just learned I'm to be an uncle. Wonderful news."

"Thanks, Paul." She kissed him on the cheek. "Do you remember my best friend, Shelley? She was at our wedding."

Shelley held out her hand. "Hello Paul, it's really nice to see you again."

Paul shook her hand while his eyes undressed her. "Of course I remember you."

Withdrawing her hand, Shelley moved over to the fridge. "Do you want me to put the meat on the trays, Liz?"

"Yes please." Liz cocked her head and grinned at Shelley. "Someone's arriving. Come and meet the locals."

The next thirty minutes were a blur of faces and handshaking and laughter. The "bring a plate" that accompanied every invitation for get-togethers like this were placed on the trestle tables set up under the trees. There were potato salads, king prawns and seafood sauce, curried eggs, beef sausages, garlic bread, sauces and dips, and waiting beside the smoking barbecue were marinated T-bone steaks, lamb cutlets and pork ribs.

Another car was coming up the driveway. Ross strode towards it with, "Glad you could make it."

Shelley almost dropped the tray of plates when a grizzled old man with bowlegs got out of the car, followed by Mack.

Hands shaken, a g'day here and a g'day there. It seemed everyone knew the old bowlegs, while Ross casually introduced Mack. When they came closer, Shelley forced herself to look at David McIntyre, the man she'd married and divorced.

"This is Liz's good friend, Shelley Taylor," Ross said jovially.

Her eyes pleaded with him as she held out her hand. "I'm very pleased to meet you."

"Yeah, good to meet you," Mack replied neutrally, and thank God, they moved on to someone else.

*Breathe, breathe.* Shelley walked unsteadily into the house. *Go to the kitchen for something. Anything. Carry it all the way to the barbecue without dropping it. Breathe.* She almost jumped out of her skin at the voice behind her.

"Liz tells me you are a veterinary nurse?" Sally, from a nearby farm, smiled at her. "Can I help carry anything out?"

"Yes, I've been a registered vet nurse for a few years now." Shelley handed her one of the hot potato bake dishes. "Thanks. I don't think I can juggle two."

Enough food to feed an army, more laughing, and a verbal encyclopedia on sheep breeding and last month's rainfall. The recycle bin was filling rapidly with empty beer cans and, picking up her glass of wine, Shelley eased her way back to the old seat under a tree.

"So that's Liz," a voice said quietly. "Never did get to meet her."

Shelley looked up the man beside her. Five feet ten inches, not an ounce of fat on him, face weathered by years in the sun, clear hazel eyes. "Thanks, Mack. I couldn't tell her, she'd be embarrassed and upset that I'd been thrown into this." Another deep breath. "Why are you here?"

"Barney offered me the job. Good money, and I took it. He's still living in the fifties, but he's one of the best stockmen I know." He leaned against the tree. "Why are *you* here?"

"Isn't it obvious? She's my friend, she invited me, I am here. And no, you never did meet her because you were either away droving or drunk at home."

When Mack didn't reply, Shelley glared at him. "You've brought Ross's sheep to the agistment, now go away and do what you do best, drink yourself stupid."

"I stopped drinking a year ago."

"Pull the other leg."

He held up the can of Coke in his hand. "Grandad died last year and—"

"I'm sorry," Shelley said softly. "He was a lovely man."

"I was with him that last week, and it got to me that..."

He hesitated. "He did a lot for me and I had bugger all to show for it."

Shelley stood up. "I think Liz wants me." She walked back to where Liz stood with several women. "I'll take those plates and whatever else inside, Liz. Sit down, for heaven's sake."

A grateful smile. "Thanks, Shell."

\*\*\*

Mack watched Shelley carry a loaded tray back into the house. He shouldn't have come here, but Christ, he had no idea where she was living or what she was doing. She hadn't changed—lush figure, high cheekbones, dark hair and olive skin inherited from her Italian mother. Honest, brutally honest, with dark eyes that hardened like pebbles when angry. And she'd been angry with him plenty of times, until the day he came home to find her gone. If there was ever a time to get drunk, it was now.

"Nope," he muttered. "Not now, not ever." He wandered back to the group of men as Ross's brother moved away, picked up another tray of dirty dishes and headed towards the house. Expensive clothes, not a hair out of place, full of himself. What had he said to Barney and a couple of men whose names he'd already forgotten? Something about Yarrabah was a family inheritance. Mack shrugged, picked up one of the few meatballs left on the table and forced himself to listen to whatever they were laughing about.

A mobile phone rang, and its owner moved away to take the call, giving Mack a clear view of Paul striding away from the house. Bored, he strolled over to the fence dividing the house from the home paddock as Shelley, holding a bucket, walked along a back pathway to the chicken pen. She heaved the contents to the waiting hens, dropped the bucket to the ground and kicked it viciously. Then she burst into tears. In seconds he was beside her.

"What the hell is wrong?"

She turned away from him. "Go away and leave me alone."

"Shell, I'm sorry, I wouldn't have come here if I'd known. Look, I'll drive Barney's car back to the caravan and he can get a lift with someone later."

"It's not you." She wiped her eyes on her sleeve. "Just leave me alone."

Mack stared at her wet, distraught face and the penny dropped. "Ross's brother just came out of the house. What did he do?"

A choked sob. "What you men do best, hit on anything with boobs! I can't stay here, and I can't tell Liz." Tears ran down her cheeks. "She's pregnant and doesn't need this."

Mack gripped her shoulders. "You can tell me. What did he do?"

Shelley shook her head, then the words tumbled over each other. "I knew as soon as he walked into the kitchen. He said, 'my room or yours?'

When I tried to get past him, he pushed me up against the fridge. He was all over me. I tried to yell out but his hand—I—"

She shook her head. "It doesn't matter."

"Tell me," Mack said softly.

Shelley wiped her face again. "I think I bit his fingers because he moved back. When I tried to knee him, he banged my head against the fridge, called me a dago dyke and walked out. Now I have to leave while he gets away with it."

Mack felt the blood pounding in his veins. "Go inside, wash your face and fill your wine glass to the top. You aren't leaving."

Shelley pulled away from him. "Don't you do anything stupid. For God's sake, don't make it any worse."

"I won't." He glanced around. "It sounds like some of them are leaving. Go inside. I won't say a word."

Mack walked back to the group of people who were making half-hearted moves to leave. As usual, the women would be driving home. He looked around. Paul was talking to Ross, who looked like he'd been kicked in the guts. A couple of neighbours interrupted them to say farewell, Liz was kissing someone's cheeks. Paul was now walking towards the gazebo while talking on his mobile phone. Mack waved goodbye to the family with three kids, strolled towards the gazebo and waited until Paul had finished his call.

"Paul, glad I've got you on your own. You said you were in real estate?"

Paul's wine-glazed eyes looked him up and down. "Sydney real estate chum, a bit above *your* price tag. Talk to the local property yokels. They'll—"

He gave a sickening whoop as the air was punched out of him and he doubled over to collapse on the gazebo floor.

## Chapter Four

Mack watched the car approach and come to an abrupt halt. Taking a deep breath, he waited until Shelley got out and walked over to meet her.

Her face was stiff with anger. "What did you do?"

"What are you talking about?"

"You know what I'm talking about." She threw her hands in the air. "Ross found Paul out the back, moaning and throwing up."

"Must have been the fish."

"We didn't have fish!" she said furiously.

"There was a plate of king prawns, bloody nice too."

"You were at someone else's home. You had no right to get drunk and pick a fight."

"I didn't pick a fight, and I was cold sober."

Uncertainty crossed her face. "That's not all."

"Don't tell me he dropped dead."

Shelley's mouth tightened. "It's not funny, Mack. Last night he and Ross had a terrible argument—I think it came to blows—and Paul was gone. Liz was crying. This morning she told me they are driving to Wagga to see their lawyer."

Mack frowned at her. "It's Saturday."

"I know. He's been the family lawyer for years and agreed to see them at his house as a favour. I think Liz said he'll be in Sydney all next week. Paul told Ross he's disputing their father's will." She pushed her hair away from her face. "I don't know the details because Liz was really upset. Something about an agreement after the old man died. He wants a share of Yarrabah."

"So that's why Ross called Barney."

Shelley blinked at him. "Pardon?"

"All he said was urgent business that couldn't have come at a worse time. He's worried about the lambs and predators and asked Barney and me to stay on for a couple of days."

"I told Liz I'd go home, they don't need me hanging around at a time like this. But she wants me to stay, the dogs and chooks must be fed." Her eyes narrowed. "You hit him, didn't you?"

Mack shrugged. "The pompous prick told me I couldn't afford a place in Sydney."

"You hate Sydney!" Shelley spluttered.

"Yeah, I do. Barney and I've got a full day ahead, so I might see you later at the house." He turned and walked back to the caravan. Christ, what a bloody tangle.

***

The car bumped slowly over the cattle grid, Shelley touched the accelerator and drove towards the empty homestead. Turning off the ignition, she leaned back against the headrest and closed her eyes. The best laid plans of mice and men had nothing on this. Her first two full weeks off work in over a year and Liz had emailed, "Come down here!" She'd been looking forward to it so much, and what happens? On the same road, on the same bloody day, Mack's driving sheep to Ross's agistment. Then everyone comes together for a peachy-pie barbecue, she gets assaulted, and the laughing gods haven't finished with her. Oh no, she's on her own in this old home while a huge family disaster unfolds.

The loud jangle of her mobile phone made her jump. Bob. "Hi, Bob. I am sorry I couldn't talk earlier. Liz and Ross left about an hour ago, and I've just got back to the house."

His voice, always calm and reassuring. "I've been thinking over what you told me last night. A lot of wills are being contested now, and this isn't a house in the suburbs, this is over a thousand acres of prime land. It could be a long and dirty business. And expensive."

"I know, and what upsets me is how happy Liz was telling me they are almost out of debt." Shelley opened the car door. "Liz asked me to stay here while they're gone, but I won't stay any longer. They'll have enough to worry about without me under their feet."

"Good. I'm missing you already."

*And I can't wait to get away from here.* "I'm missing you, Bob. I'll call you tonight."

Shelley opened the front door and stopped. The old house felt empty and gloomy and grim. She shouldn't have agreed to stay here, not after what happened yesterday. Where was Paul now? *Shit, does he have a key?* She'd wait until late afternoon, feed the dogs and chooks, make sure the doors and windows are locked, and stay at a motel in Deniliquin. *No, stupid, how will you get back in tomorrow?*

"I'll think of something," she muttered, and she walked through the house to her room. She'd change her shoes and go for a good long walk.

\*\*\*

The stabbing blister on her heel told her she'd walked too damned far. Pulling off the offending boot, she hobbled over the gravel driveway and entered the house. Cold as charity inside. Shelley limped into the bathroom, found a Band-Aid, and went to the kitchen. Coffee and—

She stopped dead. A car outside. Please, not Paul. She ran back to the living room to peer through the window. Mack and a dog? Gritting her teeth, she went into the hall and opened the door.

"What do you want, Mack?"

"Nice to see you too," Mack said evenly. "I'm not here for me. Would you look at Milly?"

Shelley's eyes widened at the dog standing behind him. "Milly?" She bent down and spoke softly. "Hi Milly, do you remember me?"

A lump rose in her throat when Milly came towards her, tail wagging. "Dear girl, I remember you too." She stroked the soft head and looked up at Mack. "What's wrong?"

"I don't know. She's good for days, then she's tired and wants to lie down." His voice caught in his throat. "It's in her eyes, like she's in pain, then an hour later she's working again."

"Is she eating?"

"Not much, not like she used to. She was her old self the last few days, working like a Trojan, then today she lay down by my feet. It's not a tick, I checked."

"Why didn't you take her to a vet here?"

"It's Saturday, they wouldn't do any tests until Monday. I won't leave her there all weekend."

"You never worried about leaving me alone all weekend," Shelley threw back at him, then wished she'd kept her mouth shut. "Sorry. It's in the past, damage done."

"I know I was a lousy husband," Mack said quietly. "You had every right to walk out. As you say, damage done."

Shelley couldn't look at him. "Bring her into the living room. I'm not sure I can do anything. I doubt Ross would have a stethoscope."

She knelt beside Milly and gently pressed her chest and ribs and stomach. "You say she looks in pain, then seems to pick up?"

"It wasn't that noticeable, until the last few days. We hadn't worked the week before Barney called me for this job, so she was lazing around like I was."

"Coughing?"

"No," Mack sat on the floor beside them. "She's only four."

"I know." A tiny smile. "I gave her to you. What about her bladder and bowels?"

"She usually does what she has to do on her own, I don't watch." He hesitated. "I thought she threw up yesterday, but Barney had just fed his dogs. She might have gobbled something down too fast."

"From now on watch her bladder and bowels and how much she eats." Shelley's hand fondled Milly's ears.

"What do you think?"

"You know I can't say anything without proper tests. She might have picked up a bug or a virus." Shelley kept her eyes on Milly. "Or it might be more serious. She's not to work tomorrow, and get her to the vet on Monday."

"She's the best dog I've had, Shell. She loves working, bloody well knows what to do before I do."

A litter of squirming playful border collie pups, their dad a prize-winning sheep dog, their mum given three months off work to produce the litter. When one fat puppy had crawled into Shelley's lap she'd told the breeder, "I've just found my husband's birthday present."

Mack's voice cut into her memories. "It's damned cold in here."

Shelley got to her feet. "I'm not staying here on my own. I'm going to a motel."

"You'll be lucky to find a room. There's an open-air concert in town tonight to raise money for something or other. The only reason I know is that Barney was grouching about roads closed off around the football oval."

"This house gives me the creeps."

"Do you want me and Milly to stay?" He held up his hands. "Before you bite my head off, we'll sleep here in the living room."

"Don't even think about free sex, Mack."

"I just said I'd sleep in the living room."

"Because I've met someone else."

A pin dropping would have woken the dead, until Mack said, "You deserve someone better than me, Shell."

"I think I've found him."

Another silence before Mack spoke again. "I'll camp on the floor here tonight, and Liz and Ross should be home sometime tomorrow afternoon. I'll be honest, I wouldn't trust Paul an inch."

Shelley felt huge relief. "Thank you."

"Why don't you find some leftovers to eat while I light the fire?"

## Chapter Five

Shelley stared into the flickering flames. She'd put a pile of blankets on the sofa. They'd eaten leftovers, drunk coffee and talked for more than an hour about everything except themselves. She stole a glance at Mack in the armchair with Milly at his feet. She had to ask.

"Why did you stop drinking?"

"Do you want the short answer or the long answer?"

"Whatever's the easiest."

Mack let the air whistle through his teeth. "I woke up to myself. Long answer, after Granddad died, I had no one, and no one cared a shit about me. You'd gone, and then he got sick. It was cancer, and within six weeks he was dead. All I had was my share from the divorce and next week's hangover. Before you say it, I have no one to blame but myself."

"Did you find giving up hard?"

"No, which surprised me. I just stopped, and funnily enough my drinking mates soon lost interest in me as well."

The room was quiet for several minutes. "Why are you down here, Mack? I mean, you always worked up north."

"I worked for the Caseys at their merino stud. We took a lot of their stock onto the road when it was dry. As you know they have agistments all over, and we were on the Long Paddock for a while. I had a chance to look at a property for sale about 20 k's from here, the bank had foreclosed on the poor buggers. I liked it here, so I took the plunge and bought it."

Shelley felt her mouth drop open. "You *bought* a property around here? How many banks did you rob?"

Mack grinned at her. "The look on your face is priceless. Where does a drunken bum from the bush get that sort of money? I had what Granddad left me, I worked non-stop at the stud for over a year and hardly touched my wages."

"I'm lost for words."

"Don't think I had the full amount—hell no, far from it. I had to borrow, but my job with the Caseys was my reference. That's why I took this job with Barney, so I could go there and check out what's needed before I move down."

"Move down?" she repeated faintly.

"Hey, it's nothing like Yarrabah, the old squatters got the best pastures. Mine is a bit over three hundred acres. I'll put some stock on it and I can find work anywhere." His face grew serious. "What about you?"

"I'm fine, thanks. I'm working at a wonderful veterinary hospital."

"Where?"

"Bathurst."

"Does the someone else live there?"

"Yes. I'm glad you've done well, Mack."

"Why don't you come with me to look at Cooinda, my new pastoral empire?"

"No, I'll be going home as soon as Liz returns. You should be finding someone else."

Mack shook his head. "Nah, I'm a one-woman bloke, Shell."

"A new lady will appreciate the sober man, Mack," she said lightly and stood up. "I'll leave a few lights on, this place is like a tomb at night."

Mack looked directly into her eyes. "You know how I feel about you. I stuffed it up, but my door is always open."

"Take Milly out, and watch her pee. I want to know if she has trouble."

Shelley closed the living room behind her, turned on the hall lamp, and the kitchen light, in case he wanted to leave early. *Please, leave early.*

***

The loud bang woke her from a deep sleep.

Another bang on the door and it opened. "Get up."

Fear lanced through her. "Who is it?"

"It's me. Get up, there's a fire somewhere."

Shelley pushed the bedcovers aside and groped around for her dressing gown. A hand clasped her arm. "Outside now, and we'll find it."

"How do you know?"

"Jesus, Shelley, I know smoke when I smell it. Outside!"

Heart thumping like drums, she ran out the front door. Nothing, but she could smell it. Mack let go of her arm and ran around to the back of the house and yelled, "Here!"

She followed and stopped dead. They could see smoke and flames behind the window of the storeroom next to the kitchen.

"Put Milly in my car and bring me the torch under the seat. The main power switch must be turned off, but I don't know where it is." He ran his hand through his hair. "Christ, is there a hose? Where are the buckets?"

"I think they're in the storeroom." Shelley held her hand out to Milly cowering away from them. "Milly, come here sweetie." But the frightened dog backed away further and Ross's dogs were now barking. The car. Shelley ran to the car, felt for the torch and, holding the door open, yelled, "Milly, get in now!"

Like a bolt of lightning, Milly was in the car and huddled down onto the floor. "Good girl, we'll get you soon." Shelley ran back and the torch was snatched out of her hand.

"Found the power box!" And the kitchen went black.

Shelley pushed her way into the kitchen and felt around the benches for anything that would hold water. Her hands went under the sink—thank God, a bucket. Into the sink, turn on the taps. Woeful pressure, the water pump doesn't work without power. Grope around the shelves for the large salad bowls. Her dressing gown fell open. Throwing it onto the floor, Shelley grabbed the first full bucket and ran outside. Mack took it from her, and from then it was a blur of bowls and saucepans and a five-gallon tin drum filled over and over from the house water tank. Between their efforts, the fire hissed, steamed and died.

Mack leaned against the wall of the house. "Not as bad as it looked, more smoke than fire." He pushed himself upright. "I'll try to shut the dogs up."

Shelley watched him walk over to the dog kennels and, after a few barks and whimpers, it went quiet. Her eyes were gritty from the smoke, her pyjamas were sopping wet, and she wanted to cry.

"If we weren't here the house would have burned down."

Mack peered into the blackened storeroom. "What the hell started it? No electrical gear. No lights on." He shone his torch on a burned hole in the wall. "Might be old wiring, I've seen it happen before. Mice chew through the old insulation and wires. But I can't see any switches in here."

"The fridge switch is on the other side of the wall, in the kitchen."

"You'll have to call the fire brigade first thing in the morning, they'll know what to look for." He shivered. "I'm getting Milly from the car and going inside."

"Mack."

He looked back at her.

"Thank you."

He nodded and walked over to the car.

The embers of the fire were built up until it was blazing, and the tension in the room was thick. Shelley bit her lip; she had to say it.

"How am I going to tell Liz and Ross you were here with me when a fire broke out?"

Mack shrugged. "Tell them whatever you like, I'm too tired to think or care."

"Don't bite my head off. You offered to stay here, and I am glad you did because that saved their home. Okay, I was embarrassed, but telling them you are my ex would have embarrassed them more. Can't you see my predicament?"

"Yeah. We used their house for wild sex and then set fire to it."

"I don't know whether to throw something at you or hit you."

Mack got to his feet. "It's almost dawn. Barney and I have a full day's work ahead of us."

Neither of them moved.

"When are you going to your new place?"

Mack glanced at Milly, now standing beside him. "Most likely Monday, after I take her to the vet."

"If it's okay with you, I would like to look at it. Text me and I can follow in my car, and don't work her today, Mack, I'm worried about her."

"I don't know your number."

"Sorry." She recited while he jabbed the numbers into his phone. A brief nod, the door closed behind him, and there was the sound of his car starting up.

Shelley felt the tears prickling her eyes. The electricity was off—no hot shower, no coffee. *As soon as there's light outside, clean up the kitchen and the mess as best you can. Drive into Deniliquin for breakfast, and while you are there, phone the fire brigade. Then wait for Liz and Ross to come home.*

## Chapter Six

Shelley's throat was dry, and her heart was thumping. She'd been a bundle of nerves all day, and when Liz and Ross arrived home, she'd abruptly ordered them into their own living room with, "I want you to sit down. There was a fire in the storeroom, but it didn't spread. The fire brigade guys were here. The power is back on and they'll contact you with their report. So please, before we talk fires, tell me what your lawyer said."

Liz's wan face turned a shade paler and Ross stood up. "I'll look now."

"Ross!" His eyebrows had shot up at her sharp voice. "Little damage, and I need to talk to you both, but first, your lawyer."

He did sit down, which surprised her, and she tried to absorb what he was saying because her stomach was churning like a washing machine.

"Then he took us into his study and never said a word while we told him what Paul intends doing. We had to sit there like statues while he read Dad's will again, and then the agreement. He didn't say it, but I don't think he was impressed with a one page handwritten agreement signed by Paul and me. We were as tense as fence wire when he looked at us over the top of his glasses. 'This agreement states that the property Minnimar will be sold, and after all debts are cleared the balance, if any, will be paid to Paul. He in return relinquishes any share of Yarrabah. Is that correct, and is that what transpired?' I told him yes, at that time both properties were mortgaged. Paul didn't want the debts, he wanted to offload the lot. I trusted him, but Liz insisted we put it in writing. Well, those eyes over the glasses went to Liz. 'Very wise, and I presume you've kept accurate records of all income and expenses incurred since then?' We assured him we have, and he leaned back in his chair and smiled. 'You could suggest to Paul that if he wants half of Yarrabah, he must reimburse you half of that mortgage you've paid as well as other costs incurred, such as new rams to improve breeding. But I jest. In brief, Paul received money from the sale of Minnimar, and from what you have told me, he has not shown any interest in Yarrabah until now. I'll discuss this with a barrister while I'm in Sydney, however I think a stiff letter to Paul will suffice. He doesn't have a leg to stand on.' "

A tired smile touched Ross's face. "We felt a huge load lift from our shoulders."

"I am so glad," Shelley said sincerely. "You don't need this turmoil after working so hard. Liz, are you feeling alright?"

"I'm feeling better now, but I worry Paul might push it, although our lawyer said he will be prepared if that happens."

Shelley's heart was thumping. "Now, I want to tell you about the fire and yesterday, and I want to apologise."

She told them everything—Mack with the stock on the Cobb Highway, the shock when he arrived for the barbecue, Paul's assault, which had Liz spluttering with fury, Mack's worry over Milly, her fear of being alone in the house, and what followed.

"I know this sounds prim, but Mack stayed in the living room. There's nothing between us now. Sometime in the early morning he smelt the smoke and hauled me out of the house and turned off the power. We used buckets and anything holding water and, thank God, put it out. He left before dawn, because he and Barney are watching your stock. I tried to clean up as best I could and called the fire brigade. I'm sorry I didn't tell you about Mack, we were both embarrassed. Then Paul—"

She stared at the floor. "I might as well tell you it was Mack who punched Paul. I'm sorry, I should not have come here."

The room was silent. *Get up and go home now.* When Shelley looked up, Liz and Ross were staring at her as if she were an alien. Then Liz giggled.

"Oh Shelley, your face! Don't be embarrassed." Her smile widened. "This is almost like a novel, but in reality, if it weren't for you and Mack, we'd have lost our home."

"A novel? Don't talk crap, Liz!" Liz's smile faded at Ross's angry voice. His face was tight with emotion. "I've had a bastard of a weekend. What the hell else will be thrown at us?"

Liz was beside him. "It has been horrible, but we have a good lawyer and we have our home."

His eyes were wet. "I'll look at the damage and go for a walk. I might find something else to kick us in the guts."

Shelley watched him stride out of the room. "I'm so sorry, Liz."

"It's not you, Shell. Nothing to do with you and Mack. In fact, you did us a massive favour being here. It's what Paul has done, and he's worried about me. The fire was the last straw. We knew the wiring needed replacing. It might be as old as the house, maybe our insurance won't cover it." Liz bit her lip. "He'll walk it off. He always does."

"I'll go now."

"You will not. It's late and you are not driving on the highway at night. You'll hit a damned kangaroo." She gave a small smile. "Or run into another ex-husband. Stay tonight and go home tomorrow." Liz stood up and held out her hand. "Come on, let's look at the damage."

Shelley stood up and hugged her. "You are the best friend in the world, and Ross is a lucky man."

## Chapter Seven

Shelley finished her second coffee and looked at her watch for the third time. Any more coffee and she'd be looking for a ladies' room on every corner.

She couldn't tell Liz and Ross she was meeting Mack today. She'd put her luggage in her car and hugged them both, insisting they let her know about any updates with the lawyer and the insurance company. Tears had fallen, another hug, and she'd driven away to wait at McDonalds in Deniliquin for the text message.

Now she was feeling like a gauche teenager waiting for a boy her parents disliked. Mack had no intention of texting her, and to be fair, why should he? She'd made it plain that she'd moved on, and she had. Bob was all Mack wasn't—steady, affectionate, considerate, and with a solid career in finance. Home and sober every night. She'd text Mack that she was on her way home and wish him the best. Damn, she hadn't thought to get his mobile phone number. Time to go, but first the ladies' room, because it was a long drive to Hay.

Shelley turned the ignition, and as she put the car into reverse her mobile buzzed.

>I'll be on the Finlay Rd, B58, near Hyde St.

Muttering, "I'm not s street directory," she went back inside McDonalds. "Can you tell me how to get to the Finlay Road?"

Over the river, along Davidson Street and turn right. Easy. She turned right onto Finlay Road, which was the Riverina Highway, and drove slowly until she saw Mack's car. He gave a brief wave from his window, then pulled away from the kerb, and she followed.

About ten minutes later they turned onto a dirt road and dropped down to 50 kph until Mack pulled over and stopped beside a gate with the faded nameplate *Cooinda*. He opened it and came up to her window.

"Leave your car here," was all he said. She got out and into his passenger seat, and they continued on to a small house and a hayshed. When the car stopped, she looked at his profile.

"What's with Milly?"

"She's at the vet now. He's doing blood tests and x-rays. I'll go back about four." He looked away. "I asked him if it was cancer. He said he'd have to wait for the results."

"She might have eaten something that's stuck in her bowel. She might have picked up a virus. Veterinary medicine and treatments are up there with ours."

Mack looked at her. "She's sick."

"I know, and she's in the best place." Shelley got out of the car and looked around. A full dam, trees around the house, green pastures. "This is nice. Can I look inside the house?"

"Sure." He handed her a keyring. "I need to check a few things."

The second key opened the front door and she walked into a narrow hallway. Ugly, drab wallpaper. Living room on the left with a large combustion wood heater, adjoining glass door to the dining room. On the other side of the hall were two big bedrooms with worn floor coverings, a bathroom and kitchen. Electric stove, sinks, cupboards. It would have to be fifty years old, maybe more. She opened the back door and stepped out onto the porch.

"Oh, my."

In the overgrown garden a profusion of purple wisteria hung from an old wooden frame, which might once have been a garden setting. As she walked closer, she could see the wisteria had grown over wooden seats and a table beneath the frame. Like it was protecting the memories of much happier times in this garden. Shelley made her way to the holding pens and kept going to where Mack was in the hayshed.

"It's lovely here." She pointed behind her. "Don't cut down the wisteria."

Mack's eyes were amused. "Wisteria doesn't feed sheep."

"I know that, you dim-witted man. Walking through the house and seeing that garden, like its frozen in time. The only thing left from happy days a long time ago, maybe when the house was built." She smiled at him. "You did well to buy this place."

"Thanks. It was a big decision for me, and I hope the right one."

Shelley walked back to the house, locked the doors and, not knowing what to do, wandered over to the sheds. Empty. She made her way back to the car and waited until he joined her. They didn't speak until the car stopped and Mack got out to open the gate. Shelley followed him and walked over to her car.

"I'm going on home now."

"Right."

"Thanks for bringing me here. Please let me know Milly's results."

"Yeah, I will." Mack cleared his throat. "The door's always open, Shell. What I'm trying to say…you know how I feel. If things go wrong with Mr Someone Else."

"You will meet someone and—"

"I might, but I told you, I'm a one-woman bloke." He took her hand. "Take it easy on the roads"

She looked down at his hand and impulsively hugged him. They stood holding each other until she stepped back. "I'd better go."

## Chapter Eight

Shelley walked into the staff room, drank a glass of water and checked her phone. Bob had called twice. She hit call and he answered immediately.

"Sorry, Bob, it's been a very busy morning."

"Don't worry. Just wanted to say hi and I'll pick you up at six." A chuckle. "I want you to look especially lovely tonight."

Shelley rolled her eyes. "The second time you've told me, Bob. I'll do my best."

"You are lovely, but you know this is important."

"I do know. Dinner with two bosses from Melbourne, and the possibility of a move up the ladder for you. I promise not to eat with my fingers and belch."

Deep laughter. "And I won't ogle your cleavage. Seriously, it is important for me, and—"

A pause.

"If they or their wives do the usual, 'Where did you grow up? Which school?' questions, you don't have to mention your mother. What I mean—"

Shelley cut him off. "I don't discuss my family or my life with people I've never me before."

"I know, sweetheart. I'm just saying this now, so you won't feel under scrutiny or embarrassed. Last thing I want. See you at six."

"I'll be ready." Shelley put the phone in her pocket. A new dress that cost a fortune. An important dinner at an expensive restaurant. Don't belch in the boss's face and don't talk about your mother's suicide.

She looked up when the door opened. "Hi, Shelley. This came for you in the mail."

"Thanks." She couldn't remember ordering anything. She ripped open the post bag and pulled out a collar and a letter.

Hi Shell,
I knew you worked for a vet hospital in Bathurst but didn't know which one, so I called all of them. When the receptionist asked if she could take a message because you were busy, I hung up. I had the address

and I'm hoping this gets to you.

I didn't text because it's been a hard week, and to be honest, I couldn't talk to anyone. Milly had a cancer in her stomach. The vet and I decided she should be given a chance and he operated. He thought it went well, and she seemed to be recovering but two days later had a seizure. The vet told me she was failing, and I sat with her while he put her to sleep.

I brought her back to Cooinda and buried her under the wisteria you liked so much. I remembered what you said about a nicer time. It was the hardest thing I've done, because she was all I had from our time together. I thought you'd like to know she's in a nice place. I want you to have her collar. You called it her dress-up collar when she wasn't working.

Because Cooinda was empty, the bank and the stock and station agent agreed I could move in and pay a nominal rent until contract settlement. I'm going up north for a few days to finalise a few things, not that I have much to finalise. I guess this is a new start for me as well.

Take care, and like I said, my place is yours.

Mack.


Shelley wiped her wet face. From a man who never put his feelings on paper, hated writing Christmas cards, to this. She put the letter and collar into her bag and wiped her eyes again.

"Keep a grip, girl, keep a grip, Big dinner coming up tonight."

\*\*\*

Shelley closed the door behind her, kicked off her high-heeled shoes and walked into the bathroom. She wriggled out of the tight dress and wiped off the make-up. The face in the mirror said it all. What a god-awful night. Bob had been tense on the way to the restaurant. This dinner was important—first impressions are lasting impressions. The two bosses and their expensive wives were very nice, but each time they spoke to her, Bob would butt in to answer. When one of them attempted to make friendly conversation by asking if she'd grown up here, Bob had answered, "No, Shelley was a student at the Presbyterian Ladies College in Brisbane and studied veterinary science. We hope to move on from Bathurst soon."

*I studied veterinary nursing!* He'd been trying to impress. He'd been keeping her in her place, most likely worrying that her pedigree wasn't up to scratch. She'd become silently angry, drank too much wine, and, thank God, hadn't made a fool of herself.

Driving home, Bob had said, "It was a most successful evening. They were very impressed with you, although"—he'd squeezed her knee—"you did drink a bit too much. Next time you'll feel more comfortable."

Comfortable? She was feeling as miserable as sin. Stuff the whole bloody world.

***

Mack slammed the engine cover back into place and cursed every tractor to hell. Wiping his hands on his trousers, he bent down to look underneath and was reaching for a plug when he heard a car engine. He jerked back, hitting his head, and fell against the tractor wheel. His breath caught in his throat.

Shelley was getting out of her car.

He stood up and wiped his hands again on his trousers. "Hi. I didn't expect you."

She lifted a large box from the passenger seat and walked towards him.

"I brought you a housewarming present, but there's a catch."

She lifted out a border collie pup. "She comes with me, if you want us."

The End

# Space Cowboy Blues
## Alice Renaud

Josh Reynolds opened his eyes and groaned. His brain felt like it was about to spill out of his skull, and his body insisted that it had been turned inside out. He stared at the white ceiling of the spaceship and waited for the pain to recede. Earth experts said that travel in hyperspace got easier with time.

Earth experts knew jack all about flying through wormholes to the other side of the galaxy.

"Coffee, sir?"

He stared at the robot who was presenting him with a steaming cup. "You brought coffee all the way from Earth?"

"Of course, sir." The robot's eyes flashed green. "Anything for your comfort."

The coffee tasted good. Better than good. Like a warm house after a long ride through the snow. Each sip soothed the jagged edges of his space-travel sickness. By the time he handed the cup back to the robot, he almost felt like himself again.

The robot dropped the cup in the trash disintegrator and rolled over to the porthole. "Is sir ready to see Planet 2215?"

"Sure." Josh sat up and unclipped his harness. Anticipation flickered in him. Seeing a new world for the first time never lost its appeal.

The robot pulled up the blind. For a moment all Josh could see was blue. Dark blue below, light blue above. Then his eyes got used to the bright light of the alien sun. The blurry picture became a vast prairie, undulating to the edge of the horizon under a cloudless sky. The effect was eerie, yet vaguely familiar. "Looks almost like my grandpa's ranch. But with blue grass."

Sparks of excitement danced in his veins. His body, confined for weeks, longed to breathe fresh air and walk further than the length of the spaceship. He got up and was pleased to discover that he could stand without wobbling. Maybe he was getting accustomed to hyperspace travel after all. "I'd like to go out."

The robot went out and reappeared seconds later, carrying a hazmat suit, boots, gloves, and a transparent helmet-type mask that would cover Josh's entire head.

Josh's bright anticipation dimmed. "I'd forgotten. The planet's not safe."

The robot helped him into the suit and fastened the gloves to his wrists. "The problem is the radiation, and the micro-organisms that float in the atmosphere. A few seconds out of the suit, and you will get irradiated, or infected, or both. A few minutes, you will become very ill. Any more than that—"

"I get the picture." Josh hadn't meant to snap. He took a breath through the mask. "Sorry," he said, as if the robot had feelings that could be hurt. He spent so much time with these intelligent machines, he couldn't help treating them like humans. "It's a damn shame." He was speaking more to himself than the robot as they walked out of the sleeping pod. "The first planet I see in ten years that looks like Earth, and it's unhabitable."

The robot corrected him politely. "Not quite, sir. Inside the Domes, humans can live freely. The locals, of course, can go anywhere without suits or masks."

Domes. Locals. Josh strove to remember the film he'd watched about Planet 2215 before take-off. Earthmen colonists had built bio-domes to live in, miniature Earths dotted over the surface of the alien planet. Locals looked like humans, but with blue skin, and green or blue hair. That was all he could recall.

He didn't usually spend much time studying the world he was visiting; he rarely stayed more than a couple of weeks on site. He examined the animals that might be used like cattle or horses, took pictures and samples for the science boffins back on Earth, pocketed his fee, then he was off. To the next job… the next planet… the next herd of oddly-shaped creatures. That had been his life for the past ten years, and it was a good one. Plenty of cash in his account and more freedom than any cowboy could hope for. He'd never once wished to learn more, to be more than a visitor.

But this planet was different. With its prairie and vast blue sky, it looked too much like the place he'd once called home. He wanted to find out more about this world.

"Tell me about the locals," he asked the robot. "What are they like?"

The robot was operating the mechanism to open the exit hatch. "You can find out for yourself, sir. The settlers from Earth radioed the ship earlier and told us that a local person called Melynas was coming to greet you."

The panel slid to the side, revealing a square of blue sky, a patch of blue grass, and a drop-dead gorgeous, blue-skinned woman.

The robot gestured at her with his metallic arm. "This is Melynas, sir. She will take good care of you. I will be here on the ship if you need me."

The woman bowed deeply. "I am at your service, sir." Her English was good, flavored with a lilting accent. Her voice was pleasant too, clear and musical like a running stream.

The robot gave Josh a nudge. "You might want to stop staring and get off the ship, sir." Josh realized he'd been gawping at the woman like a dumbass greenhorn. How should he greet her? He'd no idea. He'd rarely come across sentient aliens in his space travels, let alone female ones. He was usually welcomed by robots or Earth colonists. Life-forms were common across the universe, but intelligent life-forms were rare.

Intelligent, smoking hot life-forms were even rarer. The woman's tight-fitting, all-in-one navy suit showcased her slim waist and high, round breasts. A turquoise scarf concealed her hair and framed a smooth and lovely face. He wondered how old she was. She looked in her early twenties, but maybe her species aged slower than humans.

"Have fun, sir." The robot flashed its eyes at him and disappeared into the ship. Josh shook his head and jumped down onto the blue soil of Planet 2215. These machines were getting sassier by the day.

He bowed to the woman and wished he was wearing a hat to tip it off. "Good day to you, ma'am."

Surprise widened her dark eyes. "You are very polite, sir. You do not need to be so respectful, I am only a native female, here to serve you."

*What the hell?* Anger kindled in Josh. Which jackass had told her that? "You deserve as much respect as me. More so, because it's your planet we're standing on."

A slow smile spread over her pretty face. "Not all earthmen feel that way."

"Well they damn well should." Shame tinged Josh's irritation. Humans had spread over the galaxy for the past three hundred years, conquering and colonizing world after world. When they encountered alien species, they didn't treat them as equals. Settlers from Earth saw native people as inferiors.

He had to show this woman that he wasn't like them. He cleared his throat. "I'm sorry if my fellow earthmen haven't always treated you right, ma'am."

She shrugged, as if it didn't matter. "I'm delighted to meet you and welcome you to Albastra, Mr. Reynolds."

"Josh, please. Call me Josh." Albastra. So that was the real name of Planet 2215. A nice name, but not half as nice as her.

Her smile widened, revealing perfect teeth. They were pearly white, like a human woman's. "Then you have to call me Melynas. Come, I will take you to the herd."

Curiosity blazed in him. The settlers hadn't sent him any pictures of the animals. He only knew that they occupied the same ecological niche as cattle and horses on Earth. "Are the creatures wild or semi-domesticated?"

A hint of mischief sparked in her dark eyes. "Very wild. The settlers haven't dared go near them yet." She paused. "That's why they asked you to come, right? They say you're one of the best animal herders on Earth."

Josh could feel his chest expanding with pride. One of the best, eh? "We call ourselves cowboys."

She nodded. "All right, cowboy. Let's go."

Side by side they walked through the tall indigo grass, heading for a hillock in the middle distance. It gave him the perfect opportunity to study her more closely. Her hands were sky-blue, like her face, but the strand of silky hair that had escaped from her scarf was as green as the ocean on Earth. A fragment of a poem surfaced in his memory. "Far and few, far and few, are the lands where the Jumblies live. Their heads are green and their hands are blue, and they went to sea in a sieve." Edward Lear, his grandpa's favorite poet. Gramps would have loved to see this planet and this woman. She was as beautiful as a fairy.

They'd reached the hillock. She bounded up the path with a lithe, otherworldly grace, and he lumbered after her, encumbered by his protective gear. He wished he could cast off his suit and take her hand. He wished he could run with her through the blue prairie, with the sun on his face and the wind in his hair.

But he would die if he so much as removed his mask. Everything on this planet was deadly for him.

Including her.

The thought popped the fantasy bubble that had formed in his mind. He'd come to do a job, not get distracted by local women. He trudged up to the summit. His body felt as though it were encased in lead.

Melynas gestured at the plain below them. He followed her gaze and froze, mute with shock. Surely his eyes were playing tricks on him. Or maybe an alien virus had fought its way through his protective clothing and was messing with his brain. The animals grazing down there couldn't be unicorns. No friggin' way.

"What are these creatures?"

Her face shone with pride. "They're beautiful, aren't they? We call them hunoowins. It translates as 'single horn.'"

So he wasn't dreaming. He gazed at the graceful creatures with the pointy horn on their head, torn between wonder and amusement. "Well, I'll be darned. Blue space unicorns." He had truly landed in a fairy tale, stranger than any of the stories Gramps used to tell him when he was little. "Can they be ridden?"

A wistful expression came over her face. "The males of my species used to long ago, if the paintings in the old city are to be believed. But no one has ridden a hunoowin for a very long time." She gave him an appraising look. "The settlers hope that you can tame one. To see if they can be used like horses on Earth."

Josh studied the unicorns. They looked like horses all right, but the horns were long and sharp. They could easily skewer a man if they wanted to.

"Are you going to get close to them? I'll understand if you don't want to. It could be dangerous." Melynas's voice was soft, but there was a challenge in her dark gaze. And Josh could never resist a challenge.

"I'll have a go. Call the ship if I get injured; there's a medic robot on board. It knows how to patch me up."

Without waiting for her reaction, he strode down the hillock towards the herd. Time to show this local beauty what a real cowboy was made of.

\*\*\*

Anxiety snaked through Melynas's stomach. What had she done? She hadn't really believed that Josh would approach the hunoowins on his own, on foot and unarmed. She'd thought that he'd go back to his ship to get a robot, or a weapon at least. She shouldn't have incited him to go near the herd with no protection other than his flimsy suit. The hunoowins were gentle creatures, but if they took fright, they could easily trample him or gore him with their horns. The fear spread to her legs, turning them into jelly.

"Stop!" she cried, but her shout was carried away by the wind, and Josh clearly didn't hear her through his mask.

He was moving slowly towards the lead hunoowin. Melynas wondered if he knew she was the matriarch, leader of the herd. But he'd never seen the animals in his life; how would he know their habits?

The tall female hunoowin glared at him and lowered her horn. Melynas's breath stuck in her throat. She could only wait, frozen with fear, as Josh stood his ground and stared his blue death in the face.

Seconds passed, which felt like hours. Then the hunoowin lifted her head. Her wary gaze never left Josh, but she didn't bray in alarm or start a stampede. Melynas exhaled. Now, surely, Josh would back off and return to the safety of the hillock.

Instead, he edged closer to the animal, so slowly it seemed he was barely moving at all. When he was but a few inches away, he lifted his right hand and presented it to the hunoowin, palm up.

Melynas's muscles tightened as fresh anxiety squeezed her chest. What on Albastra was he doing? The matriarch's sharp teeth could snap his fingers off.

The hunoowin sniffed Josh's hand. Then she licked it.

Astonishment wiped out all other emotions. Melynas had lived alongside hunoowins for years, watching them and taking pictures. She'd never gotten that close to one, let alone touched it. Now this man, this cowboy, just arrived from Earth, was making friends with the herd leader.

Because the matriarch had accepted him, the rest of the herd did as well. They glanced at him and returned to their grazing, satisfied that the strange creature in the suit wasn't a threat. After a few minutes, the lead hunoowin abandoned Josh's hand and wandered off.

Josh backed off as slowly as he'd approached. At last, he reached the foot of the hillock and turned to Melynas with a grin.

When he was safely back on the summit, she collapsed on the grass, dizzy with relief. "I thought you were in real trouble there. You're the most reckless man I've ever met!"

He sat next to her, chuckling. "That was nothing. I've ridden bulls in rodeos; they have horns as sharp as that, and two of them. And I've ridden mustangs, wild horses, bareback."

Alarmed, she sat up. "You're not thinking of riding a hunoowin, are you?"

Josh's smile made him look younger, full of life and mischief. "Don't worry. I'm not completely mad. I won't try to ride one of them... today."

Her anxiety must have shown on her face, because he burst out laughing. His rich, deep rumble was like a hot spring bubbling around her. "Don't look so scared. I won't attempt it today, or tomorrow. But I'll try before I leave. I'm sure these animals can be tamed. They're gentle, and they like apples."

"Apples?" She wasn't sure she'd heard him correctly. He dug his gloved hand in the pocket of his suit and produced a bag full of small, brown things. "A fruit from Earth. The robot always puts some dried slices in my suit before I go meet creatures from another planet. Works a treat. Even unicorns can't resist apples."

His blue eyes sparkled with humor through the transparent material that shielded his face. It made her want to say something funny, so she'd hear him laugh again. She wished she'd watched more comedies from Earth. She'd focused on studying the customs and language of his people, but she didn't know any of their jokes. So instead she said the first thing that came to her mind.

"Bribery always works."

He nodded. "Bribery and gentleness. I'll have to educate the settlers on how they should treat these hunoowins."

"I won't let anyone hurt them!" Whoops, she hadn't intended to sound so sharp. He might get offended. "I'm sorry, I didn't mean to imply that your fellow earthmen would harm the hunoowins..."

He leaned over and laid his hand on her arm. "I'd never let that happen. I'm glad you care so much about these beautiful animals. We have that in common."

His soft voice soothed away her embarrassment. Talking to him was so easy, as if he had been her friend for years. No male had ever made her feel that way. Then again, the only males of her species left on the planet were either too young or too old for her, and as for the settlers from Earth... when they looked at her with their hard and greedy eyes, she was glad that they couldn't touch her. But Josh was different.

She would have liked to sit next to him all afternoon, but he'd had a long journey and he must be tired and hungry. She was forgetting her duties as a hostess. She stood up. "Come on, I'll take you to your hotel inside the Dome, so you can have a rest and some food."

"Sounds like a good plan." He pocketed the bag of dried apples and got up. On the way to the Dome, he told her a little about his childhood on Earth. "I grew up on my grandfather's ranch. He bred cows and horses." He gazed around him, at the blue grass stretching to the horizon, and the vast, spotless sky above. "This place reminds me of the ranch. Only our grass was green, and our animals brown, white or black. I had a black colt, a young horse, when I was a kid. My granddad swore that I could ride before I could walk."

So that was why he was so good with animals. He had a bond with them. Melynas pictured him riding on his horse across the plains, like the cowboys in the old Earth movies that she'd watched.

"How did you know which hunoowin was the herd leader?"

He grinned. "Lucky guess. She was bigger than the other animals, and I noticed that the rest of the herd watched her and followed her when she moved. She's a splendid creature, with her indigo coat." His face was alive with curiosity. "Why is everything blue here?"

Melynas pointed at the sun above their heads. "It's a natural adaptation that shields us from solar radiation and the micro-organisms in the air. The color blue offers the strongest protection, so most animals and plants on Albastra are blue. Green and purple give some protection too, but not as much as blue. Sufficient for nighttime, but not during the day."

He listened intently to every word she said, as if he thirsted to know everything about her world... and about her. "Is that why you cover your head?"

She patted her scarf. "Yes. I have green hair, so in the daytime, it's prudent to protect it. At night I don't need to."

He seemed about to ask another question, but they'd reached the Dome. The see-through wall stretched in all directions, a seemingly endless barrier between her world and the artificial, Earth-like home that the settlers had created. She gestured at the white decontamination pods lined up against the transparent surface. "We both have to get cleaned up, so we don't bring any radiation or viruses into the Dome. The robots have brought your clothes from the ship. They'll be in this pod, see, the one marked with a pictogram of a hunoowin. I'll see you on the other side of the wall."

He glanced over his shoulder. Was it her imagination, or did he look wistful for a moment? "OK. It will be good to be out of this suit. But I'd like to see more of your planet later. With you... if you want?"

A small wave of happiness lapped over her heart. "Sure! Tonight I can take you to the old city, where my ancestors used to live. It's not far."

He beamed at her. "I'd love that."

She shouldn't get so fired up about showing Josh around, she told herself in the pod's shower. In a few weeks, he'd take off in his rocket and she'd never see him again. She dried herself and turned to the robotic attendant so it could spray her with disinfectant. And even if Josh remained on Albastra for longer, they could never be more than friends. She shouldn't even allow herself to get too close to him. She put on her hazmat suit, gloves and mask.

It would be a toxic relationship. Literally.

That was what her rational brain said. But then she stepped out of the pod and into the clean, antiseptic world inside the Dome, and saw him waiting for her.

Damn, he was hot. Now he was out of his suit, she could fully appreciate what a fine specimen of humanity he was. His checkered shirt and jeans hugged his lean, muscular frame. His blue eyes sparkled under a mop of tousled chestnut curls, and his smile could have floored any female, of any species, at a hundred yards. Excitement bubbled up and washed away the walls she was trying to build around her heart.

He looked her up and down, and a flicker of uncertainty crossed his chiseled features. "Do you really have to wear all that gear?"

His question killed her buzz, yanking her back to reality. What had she been thinking? Even the shortest, most casual fling was out of her reach. She fiddled with her mask so he wouldn't notice her despondency.

"I'm afraid so. You're safe inside the Dome, but I carry my planet's radiation and viruses with me. They don't harm me, but they could kill you. I have to wear personal protective equipment at all times inside the Dome, and we shouldn't stay in close proximity for too long."

His smile was a little forced. "I understand. But surely you can have just the one drink with me at the hotel?"

So he was prepared to take a risk just to be with her. In spite of herself, she felt something in her lift. "One drink will be fine."

The streets inside the Dome were thronged with settlers and a few local women, like her, fully covered up in protective outfits. Most earthmen gave her and Josh a wide berth, but some stared at them and leered. Josh ignored them, but she noticed that he moved closer to her, as if to protect her. A warm, bright feeling spread around her chest. Damn, but if she wasn't careful, she would find herself falling for him. Hard.

The hotel was one of the newest in the Dome, a shiny white building with all the mod cons. A robot welcomed them and took them up to Josh's suite on the top floor.

"Wow." He went up to the floor-to-ceiling window and gazed at the view. "Is that the old city?"

Melynas joined him, taking care to keep two meters away from him, as required by Dome regulations. From their vantage point, they could see the area where the ancient city stood, glimmering in the declining sun. "Yes. It's even more beautiful at night. The buildings glow in the dark."

Josh was about to ask something, but he was interrupted by a robot opening the door. It carried a tray laden with tea for two and Earth-style pastries, which it deposited on the round table in the middle of the room.

"Thanks, buddy." Josh gestured at Melynas to sit down and proceeded to pour the tea and arrange the pastries on the china plates. The robot withdrew to the doorway and stood there watching them.

Melynas pulled her mask down and took a sip of tea. "You really are very polite, even to robots. I like that."

Josh winked. "Well, some of these machines are smarter than me." He bit into a cake. "Yum, cinnamon rolls, my favorite. I never expected to find these here."

Melynas put her cup down and nibbled on a chocolate chip muffin. "The robots have been programmed to produce Earth-style food. The settlers try to make the Dome as much like their home as possible."

Josh wiped his mouth on a napkin. "It would be better if they tried to adapt to this new world, instead of making it into a copy of the old one. And importing their bad habits, like leering at women." He frowned. "I didn't like the way some of these guys looked at you. They should show more respect to a lady."

No earthman had ever called her a lady before. The glow in Melynas's chest spread through her limbs. She took a larger bite of her muffin. It tasted delicious, as delicious as the man sitting opposite her. "I don't want to be too hard on them. They're young men, far from home. Albastra is a fairly recent settlement. There are very few earthwomen and families here. And there isn't much for the young men to do when they have finished work, except drink in the bars and look at women they can't touch."

"Maybe, but that's not an excuse to hassle you or the other local ladies." Josh drained his cup and refilled it. "Don't your men protect you? Don't they stop the settlers from harassing you?"

Melynas swallowed the rest of her muffin. "There aren't many males of our species left. On Albastra, only one boy is born for every nine girls. We're not sure why, but our wise women say it's the reason why our civilization has declined in the past centuries."

Josh's eyes widened. "Only one child in ten is a boy? That's one hell of an imbalance."

The glow in Melynas's chest was fading, replaced by a creeping sadness. Her ancestors had built wonderful cities and tamed the wildest animals. Now her diminished people clung to the remnants of a lost civilization and could only exist by serving the settlers from Earth. No matter how nice Josh was, he couldn't really understand what it was like.

She sighed. "Most boys take a job on a human spaceship as soon as they can. There isn't much for them here. They don't want to do menial jobs for the settlers, who prefer robots anyway for the heavy work. Albastran boys want adventure and the company of other males. They're valued on the spaceships, because they can resist the radiation from outer space."

Josh sat in silence, digesting her words. "I wish there was a way I could help."

The concern in his voice lightened some of her gloom. "I think there might be. My ancestors once tamed the hunoowins. If you show the settlers that these animals can be domesticated, there will be jobs on Albastra for our men and boys. They can herd the hunoowins, collect their milk, and make cheese. The settlers will see the value of local animals, looked after by local people. They will learn to respect us and our planet, instead of pining for Earth."

Josh's smile was like a beam of sunshine, straight into her heart. "I'll do everything I can to make it work."

His gaze held hers. The late afternoon light played in his chestnut curls and gilded his handsome, caring face. Silence thickened between them, until it became something almost tangible… something that bound them together.

"I'll stay as long as I need to," he said, every word heavy with meaning.

The light in his eyes drew her towards him. She was helpless before this gravitational pull. She opened her mouth to tell him that he was welcome to stay. For as long as he wanted. For good—

"Time's up!" the robot announced from the door.

Melynas jumped at the shrill, mechanical voice. The golden afternoon seemed to fade to grey around her. "I have to go."

"Why?" The disappointment on Josh's face tugged at her, but she'd no choice. The robot was right. The robots were always right.

She got up and adjusted her mask over her mouth and nose. "I can't stay more than twenty minutes close to a human indoors. The risk of contamination becomes too high after that. If I don't go now, an alarm will sound and the robots will drag me out."

"Shit." Josh jumped to his feet. "I hadn't realized. Will I see you tonight?"

Her rational brain told her to say no. She liked him too much and she could read in his face that he liked her too. But one touch from her could poison him. She should decline, in a polite but firm tone, and keep their relationship strictly professional.

"Please?" he asked. No one had ever looked at her with such longing. His gaze was like rain falling on parched soil, awakening a yearning that had lain dormant for years. The need to be cared for… valued… cherished. Even if it was only for one evening. Even if they had to keep their distance.

"Yes," she heard herself say. "I'll wait for you at the entrance of the old city, the gate closest to the Dome."

Josh beamed. "Eight o'clock?"

She nodded, not trusting herself to speak. The robot at the door whined. She waved at Josh and walked out. The memory of his smile kept her warm as she walked through the sterile streets of the Dome.

A group of young settlers were hanging out by the gate. They called out to her and made gestures which on Earth were probably obscene, but she ignored them and walked out onto the dusty road with her head held high. She had time to go back to her village, get changed, eat, and come back to the old city. To Josh.

***

The ancient city rose before Josh like a fever dream, its beauty undimmed by the passage of time. The smallest houses had seven levels, and many buildings were higher. The curved walls of the storeys made the towers look like piles of sea-glass pebbles... luminous pebbles, for they glowed in the dark, every shade of blue and green with the occasional flash of purple. He let out a sigh. "It's wonderful. I've never seen anything like it. And I've seen plenty."

Melynas beamed, obviously delighted by his reaction. "Come, I'll show you my favorite spots. There's a lot to see; the city is six thousand years old."

They ambled through the maze of dusty streets. Blue grass grew between the worn stones that had once been a pavement. As they walked, Melynas pointed out buildings and monuments and explained their history to Josh. She was the perfect guide, as cultured and intelligent as she was gorgeous. He listened, entranced, while the wind blew over the deserted towers. He watched her lovely face, while stars glittered overhead and ancient sculptures gazed at him with jewel-bright eyes. Hers was the kind of beauty that seeps into a man's soul and stays there for life.

As the evening wore on, he realized that he hadn't been keeping the required distance from her. In fact, he was walking so close to her that his arm bumped against hers from time to time. But he didn't care. And she didn't tell him off... or step away.

Midnight found them in an elegant square. A statue of a hunoowin stood at the center, shimmering like a giant sapphire amid an expanse of grass.

Josh stroked the statue's nose. "I wonder what makes the stone glow like that."

Melynas's expression was wistful. "No one knows. The city was abandoned centuries ago, and we've forgotten its secrets. We don't know how to maintain it anymore. But it's still here, and still beautiful."

"Not as beautiful as you." The words came out of Josh's mouth without going through his brain first. He swallowed, appalled at his clumsiness. She'd think he was coming on to her, drooling over her, like the dumbass settlers in the Dome.

Melynas laughed. The silvery sound cascaded around them, as if a fountain had burst into life. "You're such a flatterer."

He wanted to say that it was only the truth. She was the most precious treasure in this otherworldly city. Her hair fell in glossy emerald waves onto her shoulders. Her short midnight-blue dress left her arms bare. She stood only inches away from him… he only had to move his hand a little to touch her flawless skin.

She gazed at him from under her dark eyelashes. "What are you thinking?"

His mouth grew as dry as the dust on the cobblestones. He couldn't tell her where his thoughts were wandering… could he? Her perfume wafted towards him, a mix of flowers, ripe fruit and exotic spices. He couldn't help himself. He had to get closer to her, to inhale this bewitching scent. He took one step forward. Now they were almost touching.

She passed her tongue on her lips. The night breeze played in her hair and lifted the hem of her dress. He caught a flash of sky-blue thigh, but she made no effort to pull her skirt down. As if she liked him watching her… as if she wanted him to do more than watch. A tongue of fire licked the root of his belly. He imagined himself sliding a hand under her dress and caressing her flesh… higher and higher… until he reached the secret place at the apex of her legs. He wondered if she had hair down there and what color it would be.

Her gaze caressed him, soft and full of longing. "Josh…" she murmured. His name in her mouth was like a promise. He inclined his head to touch her lips with his… and bumped her nose with his face covering.

She stepped back, shaking her head. "Oh Josh, I'm so sorry. The mask is so thin, for a second I forgot it was there…" The words tumbled out of her, laden with regret.

Acidic frustration burned his chest. "Sod the mask." He raised his hands to remove it.

She gasped and slapped his wrist, a sharp sting that reverberated into his heart. "What are you thinking?" Her voice hissed across the square like an angry wind. "You will die if you remove your mask, Josh! You will die if I touch you!" She clasped her hands and twisted them. "We can never be together. Never."

Her anguish was a cold wave, chilling him to the bone. She was right. He'd gone mad. For one second he'd been ready to throw his mask and his life away, for the sake of a kiss.

Tears shone in Melynas's eyes. "We shouldn't meet again. I'm putting you in danger."

She turned and ran, as light as a hunoowin, across the empty square and into the dark streets. He wanted to shout at her to stop… to follow her… but his limbs had turned to lead and he was having trouble breathing through the damn mask.

He whacked his head against the statue, so hard it hurt. "Why?" he asked the stone animal, the city, the entire universe. He'd found love at the other end of the galaxy, and she could never be his. The knowledge seeped into him like a poison, until he ached all over.

Minutes passed, or maybe hours. Time had stopped in the enchanted city, whose beauty now seemed to mock him. At last he shook himself and began the trek back to the Dome. He knew that he shouldn't stay too long outside. Even with protective gear, there was a risk the radiation and viruses of Albastra would worm their way into his body and cause damage.

Right now, he didn't care. But his feet took him back to the transparent wall that shielded the artificial city. He dragged himself into the nearest decontamination pod and tore off his hazmat suit. He wouldn't think about Melynas. He'd shower and put on fresh clothes, then he'd go back to his hotel and order something strong to drink.

But his brain had other ideas. His gramps used to sing an old George Freeman song when he was sad. Now it surfaced in his memory, attracted by his gloom. It went round and round in his mind, driving him nuts. He turned the shower on, as hot as he could bear it, and scrubbed himself until his skin turned pink and smarted. The damn earworm wouldn't leave him alone. He gave in and sang it, just to get it out of his head.

He stepped out of the shower and turned on the dryers, singing until he ran out of breath.

He leaned his brow against the wall. Right now banging his head against the hard surface seemed like a good idea. Even the strongest liquor wouldn't fill the hole inside him.

A piercing scream tore through the wall of the pod. A woman was shouting outside! Josh froze for one second, then his instinct kicked in and he scrambled back into his clothes, suit and boots. He had to go and help.

"Stop it!"

It was Melynas's voice!

Fear and fury slammed into him like a double hurricane, propelling him towards the door. He stuck his mask on as he yanked the door of the pod open and shot out of the Dome.

Melynas was tussling with two Earth settlers. One of them was holding her by the arms while the other was lifting her dress up to her waist, ignoring her frantic kicks and screams.

"Stay still, blue bitch," he said, his speech slurred by drink or drugs. "I want to see the color of your panties."

Josh pounced on the bastard, caught him in a chokehold and squeezed. Hard. The man let go of Melynas and tried vainly to free himself, gasping for breath through his mask.

"Let her go or I'll kill your mate." Josh's red-hot anger blazed in every word. The other man hesitated. His grip on Melynas slackened. She twisted round and kicked him in the groin.

The man howled in pain and doubled over. Melynas darted to Josh. He tossed the other settler aside. "Run!"

They plunged back into the safety of the pod. The robots, alerted by the commotion, had already swung into action. One of them was speaking in an intercom. "A woman has been attacked outside Gate 8. Send the guards."

Another robot bustled up to Josh and Melynas. "Do you require medical assistance, sir? Madam?"

Melynas shook her head. "I'm fine, thanks. He arrived just in time." She smiled up at Josh. Sweet relief washed over him. She was safe and well, thank God. He took her hand and gave it a squeeze.

Melynas looked down and snatched her hand away. Her eyes were round with horror. "Josh! You forgot your gloves!"

Shock emptied Josh's mind. He stared at his bare, vulnerable hands. He'd rushed out without proper protection, and now Albastra's poisons had penetrated his body. He knew what it meant. His mind switched to survival mode, and he found himself issuing instructions to the robots. "Quick, get me to a medical facility and call the best doctor you have in the Dome. I must get treatment ASAP."

"Find Doctor Jones," Melynas said to the machines. Her voice shook. "I think it will be OK, Josh. You weren't out for more than a few minutes." She said it as if she were trying to convince herself.

A strange calm descended on Josh. It wasn't the numbness of shock. He felt as though his entire life had led to this moment. This was as it should be.

"I'm in the hands of God," he said. He wished he could take away the pain in Melynas's face. "Don't be upset. I always knew this could happen. And I'd do it again in a heartbeat, to keep you safe."

Her eyes shone too bright under the electric lights as she put on a hazmat suit and mask. "You will be all right. I know about the radiation and micro-organisms of Albastra. I can help the doctor fix you."

The robots proved that they'd been well programmed for emergencies. In seconds, a ground vehicle arrived and they bundled Josh and Melynas into it. They sped through the streets to the medical facility, a sterile white building on the other side of the Dome. The doctor was already waiting in the lobby, a tall earthman with cropped silver hair, in full protective gear. He took charge with brisk efficiency. "Get him up to a room and radio the nearest spaceship. I'll do what I can, but if it's not enough, we might have to evacuate him to Earth."

Dismay wrapped Josh in its clammy embrace. He didn't want to return to Earth, poisoned or not. He wanted to protest, but the robots were ushering him into the lift. Minutes later he was sitting on a bed, with Melynas standing a safe distance away.

The doctor knelt in front of him. "OK, let's have a look at you."

Josh extended his hands, palms down. They had acquired a pale blue sheen, like a summer twilight reflected in a dusty mirror. Worry twisted his gut. "Shit. Is that the radiation, doc?"

Shock and wonder passed over the doctor's face. He opened his mouth, but no sound came out. Melynas breathed out a sigh. "It's a miracle."

Confusion clouded Josh's brain. Miracle? Wasn't he supposed to get very ill, or even die? They were both staring at him as if an angel had suddenly appeared. "Why am I turning blue?"

The doctor's eyes were shining. His professional carapace melted away. He looked like a boy on Christmas morning discovering a long-awaited toy. "We knew this could happen, in theory. But in all my time on Albastra, I never saw it. Wow. The paper I will write about this! My colleagues on Earth will go green with envy."

"Or blue." Melynas giggled.

They were driving him nuts. Or perhaps they'd gone nuts. Josh took a deep breath. "OK, you two, can you please calm down and tell me what the hell is going on?"

"It is the radiation, and the micro-organisms. But not in the way you think." The doctor rested his gloved hands on his knees. "The blue color is the external manifestation of a protective mechanism that we still don't fully understand." He paused and seemed to remember he was talking to a cowboy, not a medic. "I mean, the blue color indicates that you have protection from the radiation and viruses of this planet. That's why animals, plants and people on this planet are blue. It's an adaptation that has evolved over years, but we know that sometimes it can develop very quickly, after a short exposure to Albastra's atmosphere. We've seen it in slugs."

"Slugs?" Josh wondered if the doc was taking the mick. But his face was serious. "So slugs can turn blue after a short time on Albastra. But I'm not a slug."

"You most definitely aren't." Melynas's voice was a honeyed purr in his ear.

The doctor smiled. "We knew that in theory it could happen to humans too. But obviously, it's not the sort of thing you can test." He clapped Josh on the shoulder. "You're a very lucky man. Albastra is accepting you. She is turning you blue, so her radiation and organisms won't hurt you anymore. No more hazmat suits for you!"

The clouds were dissipating, and bright hope shone in Josh's brain. "I can live here freely? Like a native?"

"The first human man to do so." Melynas stroked his hand. A shiver of electricity ran over his skin.

The doctor got up and moved towards the door. "Well, it seems my task here is done. I'll go back to my office to prepare my report. I'll be back tomorrow to check on you and see how far the color has spread. The faster you go blue all over, the better."

"Wait!" Josh called. "Is there a way to accelerate the process?"

The doctor didn't stop. "Just expose yourself as much as possible to Albastra's fauna and flora," he said over his shoulder. "Get close to the native life-forms." Then he exited the room, followed by all the robots. The door closed behind them, leaving Josh alone with Melynas.

He turned to her. He wanted to ask her what she thought of all this... but what he saw snatched the breath from his lungs.

She was standing before him, completely naked. From her wavy emerald hair to her dainty toes, she was perfect, the most glorious thing he'd ever seen. The tips of her breasts taunted him, as dark a blue as the tantalizing triangle at the apex of her thighs. A slow, seductive smile lit up her lovely face. She gestured at her luscious curves. "Would you like to get close to *this* native life-form?"

Joy and desire flared up in him. "If you want to, you will make me the happiest man in the universe."

***

Anticipation coiled in Melynas's belly. Josh's gaze raked over her, heating up her skin everywhere it landed.

She wasn't completely without experience. She had dated boys of her own race, when she was a young teenager, before they'd all sailed off into space. Later, she'd had erotic films, her hands, and the electric toys the human settlers brought from Earth. She knew how to pleasure herself… but Josh was real. And he could give her more than pleasure. He could give her what her soul and body had longed for all these years.

She licked her lips. "Take off your clothes."

He bowed. "At your service, ma'am."

He ripped off his suit, boots and shirt faster than she would have thought possible. She sashayed up to him, feasting her eyes on his broad shoulders, his muscled torso, his washboard stomach…

His pupils widened, and his nostrils flared like those of a hunoowin. He was beautiful. He was all male. And he was hers. He smelled so good… wood smoke and freshly mown grass, an earthy, mouth-watering scent. She reached out and traced the V of dark hair that led down to his belt. He inhaled sharply and lifted his hands to stroke her shoulders.

A thrilling giddiness swept over her. She'd been lonely for so long, but now her lover had come to her, from the other side of the universe. And she would savor everything he had to offer. She leaned into his touch and allowed her fingers to glide lower… to brush against the bulge in his jeans.

"Melynas," he said, his voice husky with need. He cupped her breasts and caressed them, circling the hard tips with his thumbs. Currents of awareness zapped her and she pressed herself against him, breathing him in. His scent became deeper, muskier. She laced her hands around his waist and stood on tiptoe to rub against him. His hard cock grazed the hairs of her mound through his jeans, filling her with a sharp, sweet yearning.

He angled his head to brush her lips with his. She opened her mouth, willing him to enter her, taste her… but he only caught her upper lip between his and touched it with the tip of his tongue.

"Tease," she breathed. She dipped her hand inside his jeans and stroked the firm curve of his ass. He made an animal sound deep in his throat and plunged his tongue into her mouth. She sucked it and dug her fingers into the cleft of his buttocks, caressing the soft skin there. She wanted to explore and possess every inch of him. Every night, for the rest of their lives.

His kiss grew rougher, his tongue dueled with hers as he pinched her nipples and rolled them between finger and thumb. Pleasure radiated through her breasts and down to her belly. Against her stomach, his cock felt like it would explode out of his jeans. She had to see it... touch it... She broke off their kiss and fumbled with his belt.

His breath came out in staccato bursts. He helped her open his jeans and at last his freed cock rose to meet her mouth, erect, splendid, a dream come true. She gave the throbbing tip a lick, savoring the salty taste of him.

Josh threw his head back and roared. "You drive me mad, woman!"

She wasn't a woman anymore. She was a female, an animal. She'd surrendered to her wildest instincts. She shoved him back until he fell on the bed and straddled him. She closed her hand around his cock and stroked him. He moaned and cupped her damp mound. His thumb found her slick, swollen nub, and teased it. A new ecstasy pierced her and she cried aloud. No man had ever made her body sing like this. His fingers parted her lips, exploring her. The pressure in her core grew until she felt she would explode with need. She lifted herself up and guided his cock into her wet opening.

Josh groaned. He grabbed her hips and pushed deep inside her. Pleasure ripped through her, so intense that her vision blurred and her nerves hummed with delight. She rose on her knees and slid down, shouting with joy when her mound splayed against his hard stomach, jolting her with bliss. They moved as one... harder... faster... Her walls rippled and pulsed around him, and she lost herself in the sensation. She heard him shout her name, felt warm liquid gush out of him, and her own orgasm exploded at last. She was dissolving... her bones were melting... she was a blistering comet, a shooting star, streaming across the galaxy.

***

Josh opened his eyes. Sunlight streamed through the window and danced in Melynas's hair in a thousand shades of green. She lay on her side, her head cushioned on her arm. Her blue hand rested on Josh's shoulder.

He kissed it, and she stirred. He trailed his lips up to her elbow. Her eyelids fluttered. "Hi, darling," she said, her voice husky with sleep.

She'd called him "darling." Fierce joy leapt in his heart, brighter than the Albastran sun. He twined her silky hair between his fingers. "Hello, my love."

She gazed at him with dark, merry eyes. "Welcome to the first day of the rest of your life." She stroked his chest, smiling like a turquoise Cheshire Cat. "Look at you. Blue all over."

Josh looked down at himself. The pale sheen of the previous night had deepened into an even, azure shade. The hairs on his arms and chest had turned indigo. "I'm truly a local now."

Her hand paused on his stomach. "Are you sure you don't mind?"

They'd talked about it, as night had turned into early morning. He'd assured her that he was delighted to stay on her planet. With her. He was touched that she was asking him again, to make sure it was what he truly wanted. He caught her hand in his. "I haven't changed my mind. I belong here. We belong together."

She glowed with happiness like a living jewel. "I thought maybe you would miss Earth. The ranch you were telling me about."

He gathered her in his arms. "That ranch is long gone, my darling. When my gramps died, Grandma sold it to move closer to my sister. Now there's a freeway in the middle of it." He pressed his lips to her hair. "This is my home now. We'll build a cabin in the blue prairie and domesticate a couple of hunoowins. I look forward to a little blue colt playing by the door." He paused, hesitating to voice his dream.

"And a little baby on the cabin floor?" Melynas's laughter filled the room like a musical stream, flooding his soul with tenderness. But she grew silent when he kissed her and slid his hand down her belly... the belly where their son or daughter would soon grow.

He would never sing the Cowboy Blues again. He had found his woman's loving, and she was no longer far away. She was right here in his arms. Today, tonight, and every night, under the wide Albastran sky.

## The End

# Loving Jack
### Estelle Pettersen

## Chapter One

### Olivia

### Queensland, Australia

I was finally home.

Standing on the side of the empty Warrego Highway, I took off my shoes to feel the red, dusty soil between my toes before gazing up at the cloudless, azure sky. The wave of warm heat subtly hit my face as I breathed in the fresh country air. There was nothing more peaceful than the silence that engulfed the highway, which stretched from the city of Brisbane, on the east coast, to Roma, a western country town in the state of Queensland, Australia. Roma was one of the scattered little places that mapped the vast Australian outback. Cattle Country was what they called the Maranoa region, and Roma was in the middle of it.

An old carcass of a dead red kangaroo decorated by a cluster of flies rested on the side of the road where I'd parked my tiny white Toyota. The kangaroo's death was probably the result of a hit and run. This tended to happen out here, particularly at dusk or dawn when they came out in droves, out of the blue and onto the highway. Putting my flat shoes back on, I hopped into the vehicle and drove further west to Roma. I looked forward to seeing Mum, Dad, and my little sister Josephine—it'd been years since I had seen them in person. The last time we'd hugged was when they'd said bon voyage at Brisbane International Airport on the day I left Australia to live in London five years ago.

About an hour later, I recognized the old gas station on the left side of the road as I was about to turn to the right into town. As I slowly turned, distracted by the dazzling lights of the newly revamped diner by the station, I felt a bump on the car's front left bumper.

*Shit!*

I had turned too widely and bumped into a utility truck standing still at the stop sign. I moved my rental car to the side of the road, and the driver of the truck followed suit. After parking, I felt my hands shake in trepidation when I saw a tall, familiar figure step out. His ocean-blue eyes, hooded by long, dark lashes, were still the same as if it'd only been yesterday when we'd last spoken. His wavy, golden-brown hair blew in the wind as he removed his felt Akubra hat. Ah, that hat. He still wore it after five years. I remembered giving him that hat, which featured a plaited bonded leather band with a brass plate.

Jack McCullen.

He was an irresistible Aussie devil in a simple white t-shirt and a pair of jeans. I should have known trouble was right around the corner when I drove my vehicle into town. Instead of greeting me with the million-dollar smile he gave every woman who caught his eye, his mouth twisted into a contortion of anger and frustration.

"Bloody hell! Watch where ya' driving, mate!" the six-foot-two hunk yelled at me. His open palms were directed at my car.

"Don't get your knickers in a knot. She'll be right!" I shouted back, stepping out of my car. "It's just a small dent, and I'll get that fixed."

"Livvy?" Jack tilted his head, wrinkled his aquiline nose, and squinted. "Is that you?"

"Jack, it's good to see you." I smiled smugly, placing my hands on my hips and crossing my legs.

"Strewth, I nearly didn't recognize you. You've changed your hair!" Jack scratched his head.

"Yeah, I cut most of it off," I replied, remembering that the last time he'd seen me I'd had waist-length coppery red hair, not the messy bob cut I sported these days.

"It's not bad, hey?" Jack revealed a lopsided grin as he swaggered toward me. He still had the playful twinkle in his eyes he used to give me years ago.

"Thanks, Jack. It's not half bad." I grinned, smoothing my hair.

\*\*\*

A short while later, after exchanging phone numbers and writing the details of the damage for my insurance company, we were playing a pool game at the White Bull Tavern. I had apologized for the millionth time for bumping into Jack's truck, and he jokingly replied, "You owe me one."

I stole glimpses of his toned body as he angled and steered it forward against the pool table, aiming for the ball with his stick. I didn't mind losing the game, as long as I could watch the show that came with it. The guy could have been a model, with his broad shoulders, slim waist, narrow hips, and long legs—heck, I didn't mind at all.

"Whoa! Nice shot, Jack. You'll have to teach me that one," I exclaimed as I watched the white ball hit two colored balls, which fell into a corner hole. "You're winning, so let's call it a day, shall we?" I asked, feeling defeated as he made another smooth shot, sending a colored ball down its rabbit hole.

"You don't like to lose, do you? Sore loser," Jack teased, nudging my elbow with his suntanned arm. There it was again, that darn sexy grin that could make a woman wet and pant with want.

"It's just luck, mate," I commented, wickedly sticking my tongue out.

"So, you owe me a cold one," Jack said, eyeing the beer taps at the bar.

"It's only four-o-clock in the afternoon, buddy," I replied. We both stood and did a staredown until I blinked.

"Your shout," Jack said, chuckling as he walked toward the bar counter.

"Fine. I suppose it is Friday, the start of the weekend, eh?" I joked, following my childhood friend. "But after this, I've got to head home. I haven't seen Mum, Dad, and Jo yet."

"No worries, shorty," he hinted, trying to pepper our conversation with humor as we sat on bar stools. His tall frame towered over my slight five-foot-three figure. If he wanted, Jack could lift me with one arm and throw me over his shoulder.

"Sweet Home Alabama" played in the background inside the musty pub. The place had an old, familiar smell of beer blended with the waft of grill smoke coming from the kitchen.

"They play this old song in just about every country pub along the Warrego Highway," I laughed, turning to Jack.

"I'm just stoked that you're back," he declared, placing his hat on my head. He tilted it back slightly, so it wouldn't cover my eyes.

"It's good to see you again, Jack," I said, placing my fingertips on the felt hat. We hadn't parted on good terms the last time we'd seen each other. It was before I left Australia five years ago, and I wasn't in a good place, fresh from a failed marriage to a cheating bastard named Angus Wilson. I didn't want another painful walk down memory lane, so I cast the past aside for a cold glass of beer.

"Two beers, please," I ordered, leaning on the bar counter. "Fourex Light on tap."

"Good to see you're still a Queenslander," Jack remarked a few minutes later, eyeing the two beers that came to us. "You're not drinking any other shit."

"I'm a Queensland girl, you know that. Are you still playing for the Cowboys?" I asked. The Cowboys was one of the state's rugby league football teams.

"Uh, nah. Knee injury," he replied, tapping his right kneecap. "I banged it up real good a year ago, and the doc told me to find a new career."

"Was it Doctor Brewer? Is she still around?"

"Nah, she retired last year. There's a new doc in town. He and his family moved here from Brissy."

"What are you doing these days?" I was curious, wishing I'd kept in touch with Jack. Keeping connected hadn't always easy as we'd had different agendas and had grown apart.

"I'm a different kind of cowboy these days. I'm working on the family farm." The McCullens owned one of the biggest cattle farms in southwest Queensland. Roma had the largest store cattle sale yards in the southern hemisphere, processing more than 400,000 cattle a year with sale days on Tuesdays and Thursdays. "It's just temporary until I move to Brissy," he continued.

"You're moving to Brisbane?" I raised both eyebrows. I never thought Jack would think of moving to the big smoke again.

"Yeah. After my injury I applied for a job with the education department. I finally got a response—they're looking for a maths teacher at a high school in the northern suburbs."

"So, when do you start?" I asked, slicing my eyes in skepticism.

"What's that look that you're pulling, Livvy? Didn't you think I'd put my education degree to good use? I'm good with numbers, if you remember." Jack put one arm around my shoulder, giving me a gentle shake.

"Yeah, that was the one subject you managed to beat me in," I retorted, sticking my pink tongue out, letting loose a little snippet of my competitive nature. We'd gone to the same school up until the seventh grade. After that, we'd attended different boarding schools in Brisbane during our high school years, only to be reunited as friends at the same university. "So, what are you up to these days? Any plans?" Jack asked.

"I applied for a job in Brissy too. They're looking for a media relations officer in the justice department. So, I figured, why not?" I shrugged my shoulders. Jack pulled his arm away from me and drank his beer.

After some small talk and finishing our drinks, we walked out of the pub and said goodbye.

"Hey, what does it take for a friend to get a hug?" Jack smiled, teasing me with his gorgeous eyes that swept me away like a Pacific Ocean wave.

I looked up at him with my dark eyes and stepped a few inches closer. I flinched a little when he touched my hair and worked his fingers to my pale cheekbones before tapping my freckled nose. Placing my arms around Jack's slender waist, I gave him a decent hug, clinging onto him a little longer than friends normally would. I heard his steady heartbeat and breathed in his fresh, masculine scent. I realized this was the closest I had been to a man in a long time. Loving Jack was not hard at all. Telling him that I always loved him was another story.

## Chapter Two

### Olivia

### Later that evening

"So, how does it feel to be back?" my sister Josephine asked in front of Mum and Dad at the dinner table. At twenty-two, she was five years younger than me and eager to travel around the world.

"I'm knackered right now," I replied in a half yawn. I passed a tray of steamed vegetables to Mum after scooping some broccoli, carrots, and potatoes on my plate, which was coated with mouthwatering roast beef and gravy.

"What was London like?" Dad asked in between bites of his meal. He was a bright-eyed man with bushy eyebrows whose middle name was curiosity. He worked as a real estate agent for the Maranoa region, which included towns surrounding Roma.

"London is a city that never sleeps, but I grew tired of being in a rat race," I said.

"Well, London sounded like quite a change from here," Mum commented. She was originally from Brisbane but had moved to Roma to work as a photographer for the local newspaper years ago.

"I missed the fresh Roma air and seeing the stars so vividly at night, especially the Southern Cross." I stabbed my food with a fork and plopped the delicious gravy-soaked roast meat into my mouth.

"What was it like to work in a public relations agency?" Jo asked.

"Honestly? It was madness. I was drained and burned out, to put it lightly." I sighed and ran my fingers through my hair.

"It only took you five years to come home." Dad smiled, patting my shoulder.

"Jack missed you." Jo had to sneak that comment into our family dinner conversation.

I glared at Jo, then hissed, "Jack belongs to Ashley."

"Not anymore, hun," Mum countered. "Ashley married Derek Thompson two years ago."

"*What?*" I nearly choked on a piece of broccoli. "Why didn't you tell me?"

"We thought it was best that Jack told you himself," Mum answered.

"So it's true?" I glanced at Jo.

"Yup, apparently Jack's heart wasn't in the relationship. They broke up shortly after you moved to London," Jo said.

"Wow, okay." Perhaps it was the jetlag or the overwhelming sense of being back home again, but I'd forgotten to ask Jack how things were going with Ashley, his girlfriend during our university years. They'd seemed like a steady couple, and I'd thought he'd propose to her at some point.

Our university days were also when I'd started seeing Angus, one of Jack's friends. Angus proposed to me in my last year, and we were married a week after my graduation. It was a marriage that lasted for only one day, after I caught him screwing one of our guests in the restroom during the wedding reception. Broken-hearted, I'd filed for a divorce, embarked on a trip to London, was eventually offered a job at a PR firm, and the rest was history. Here I was, five years later, back home, eating dinner with my family while coping with the warm summer heat. I should have been feeling tired, but I was energized by the change of circumstances: Jack was single.

*** 

After dinner and catching up on more local gossip with my family, I went for a walk along Miscamble Street to gaze at the stars, before returning home to see the familiar red utility truck parked on our driveway. It had a slight dent to the right front bumper, which I had caused earlier that day. A Christmas beetle crawled over my foot as I stared, open-mouthed, at the truck. I gently kicked it away and went around the house to the backyard, where I heard two men talking.

"Well, here she is." Dad patted his knee and got up from his favorite chair on the veranda.

"Jack, it's a nice surprise to see you twice in a day," I exclaimed, scratching my head. He didn't have his hat on, and he had smoothed out his golden-brown curls, which framed his masculine face. He had changed and now wore a collared shirt, accentuating his broad shoulders. If only I could touch his shoulders and kiss his lips; the way he'd moved his mouth when he'd spoken earlier that day had put me in a trance, wishing we were kissing instead of talking.

"I borrowed your dad's hammer drill last Sunday. Mine was faulty, and the shops were closed," Jack said with a wicked sparkle in his eye, then glanced at the tool that Dad picked up from the table. "I figured that I'd give his drill back since I bought a new one earlier in the week."

"Thanks, Jack. I'm only too glad I could help. Tell your father I'll join him for tennis next week," Dad said, patting Jack's shoulder before making his way inside. Our parents had been friends for years, and our mothers had bonded over Jack and me being born only a day apart in the same year; he was one day older than me.

"How is your dad?" I asked Jack, remembering that the last time I'd seen his father, he'd been diagnosed with skin cancer.

"He's much better these days. Can't go out without sunscreen. Slip, slop, slap, he always says." Jack moved closer to me once Dad was out of sight.

"Ah yes, Mum would always tell me to slip on a shirt, slop on some sunscreen, and slap on a hat," I commented, turning to Jack while leaning my lower back against the veranda's railings. He grabbed the railings by my side, and leaned forward, gazing at the darkness on the grass and the steel clothesline.

"Say, what's news around town?" I asked.

"Ash and I broke up shortly after you left for London. It wasn't working out. Remember Charlene?" Jack's eyebrows knitted, and his lips tightened, looking slightly strained.

"Yeah, I'm meeting Charlie for a cuppa coffee tomorrow," I replied. I was looking forward to catching up with one of my closest friends.

"There's something you need to know about Charlie and me. We dated last year. I just want to be upfront with you on this, so you don't hear it from anyone else." Jack's eyes stared at mine.

I shrugged my shoulders and smirked. "Well, yeah. That's a bit of news for me, but hey, it's your business, not mine."

"I missed you, Livvy." Jack frowned, then looked down at his shoes, before looking up at me again. "Things weren't the same when you left."

"I needed to leave, Jack. I couldn't... I wasn't in the right frame of mind, and staying here would have been worse for my depression," I confessed.

"You know, I don't blame you after what Angus did. He was a bloody ratbag." Jack placed both hands in his pockets and moved one step closer to me. I breathed in his familiar, fresh summer scent, which had the essence of clean laundry and sweet citrus.

"You were friends," I said. "Have you spoken with him in these past five years?"

"Nope. Not after that night." Jack was so close to me that I felt his body heat radiating against mine.

"Jack, I'm sorry I snapped at you then." I touched his bicep and felt the hard muscle through the cotton shirt.

"It wasn't your fault. I was just bloody pissed that my mate cheated on his woman on their wedding night. He was a fucking cunt, doing what he did." Jack bit his lower lip and bowed his head. "Excuse my language. I shouldn't speak like that in front of a lady."

"You're right. Angus was a bloody royal bastard, wasn't he?" I stroked Jack's arm, half-smiling at a memory that was once painful but didn't hurt anymore. "Jack, I've learned to let go of the past. Angus doesn't matter to me anymore. And what you did that night—you were just trying to stick up for a friend. After all, we are friends, right?"

"I still shouldn't have beat the shit out of him. I just lost it."

"I've never seen you lose your temper the way you did that night," I said, tucking a tendril of fallen hair behind my ear. "I reacted badly because I was a mess of all sorts, lashing out my emotions. Seeing Angus with another woman was too much for me, so I snapped. It's so surreal, but it's the past."

"Yeah. I'm glad you let go of that," Jack said. His fresh scent and body heat were enough to make me want to do more than kiss him. Dirty, wild thoughts of Jack naked in my bed flashed in my head, but I needed to know one thing.

I smiled, placing my hands in my jeans pockets like Jack. "So, you and Charlie, huh? Any plans there?"

"Nah, it didn't last long." Jack's eyes studied mine, but with a flash of pain. "Livvy, did you meet anyone while you were over in London?"

"Well, I dated a few guys, but it was never anything serious," I admitted, shaking my head. "I always knew I'd come back home."

"I'm happy that you're back because I missed you," Jack said, revealing a lopsided grin. "Hey, are you free tomorrow night? I'd like to see you then."

"I haven't made any plans. Sure," I agreed, giving a small shrug to my shoulders.

Jack tapped the veranda railing with his finger three times, as if he was making a lucky wish, and grinned. "Great, I'll pick you up at eight. Don't be late."

"I won't." I sighed and tucked more loose hair behind my ears as I watched Jack stroll back to his utility truck. After living in Brisbane and London, I realized I was home. I, Olivia Jane Bertrand, was ready for an erotic adventure, and perhaps a whole lot more, with Jack Ethan McCullen.

### Chapter Three

#### Olivia
#### Eight p.m., the next evening

"Livvy, Jack's here!" Jo's voice sang out from the hallway.
*Shit!*
After trying on a few of my old outfits, I'd resorted to the fact that I had gone up a size in clothes in the past five years. To make matters

worse, my suitcase had been left behind in transit and was now on the way from Singapore's Changi Airport to Brisbane, before being transported on the overnight bus to Roma.

"Bugger this shit, Charlie! I may as well go out in my birthday suit, since nothing seems to fit," I exclaimed, rubbing the side of my face.

"Hey, don't mess up your makeup," my closest friend said. "Relax, you'll be right."

"Alright? The bloody bastards left my suitcase behind at Changi Airport!" I lamented, eyeing my old clothes strewn all over the floor and bed. It was long overdue to donate them to the Salvation Army charity organization. "I'll get this frikkin' mess cleaned up and take it to the Salvos."

"Hey, I've got something for you," Charlie said, smiling coyly. We'd caught up over coffee earlier in the day and talked about life, work, old memories, and everything else we could think of, including Jack. I had admitted to Charlie that Jack had asked me out tonight. Honesty was the key to a fruitful friendship or relationship, after all. In turn, Charlie had confessed that she and Jack had dated last year—a great detail that she'd left out of our messages and phone calls while I was living in London. "I wanted to tell you in person," she'd revealed at the café. "It didn't last long; it was more a fling thing last Christmas when I came home to visit my family."

While Jack and I attended the same university in Brisbane, Charlie had moved to Sydney to study law. She now worked as a solicitor in Canberra, Australia's capital city, and returned home for the holidays. With Christmas around the corner, my homecoming was a timely reunion with close friends like Charlie, who would stay for another week or so before returning to work.

"So, were there any hot, adventurous men in London?" Charlie's dark eyebrows wiggled and her nose twitched as she unzipped her backpack. Her family was indigenous to Roma and belonged to the Mandandanji people.

"Nope, no hot adventures for me. The closest I got to an adventure in London was watching old Harry Potter movies," I admitted. "Believe me, the city life is all hyped up yarn—storytelling. That's all it is."

"I'm glad you and Jack are hanging out again," Charlie said, rummaging through the contents of her backpack. "He felt bad for the way things were between you and him when you left home."

"Angus deserved the punch in the face," I replied, biting my lip.

"Oh, it wasn't that," Charlie commented. "It was when Jack said to you—"

"Forget about it. I don't need to be reminded of the past," I interrupted, eyeing what Charlie was trying to remove from her backpack. She was fair dinkum honest, and that was why I could trust her with a parachute on my back. Charlie was by my side, helping me sort through an outdated wardrobe. Was it awkward knowing that my best friend had slept with the guy I had feelings for? To be honest, I didn't want to think about what they'd done together. That was the past, and we ought to let bygones be bygones.

After all, Jack was a friend of mine too. I had to admit that I'd always had a secret crush on him, and I'd pushed it back into "file number thirteen" over the years. However, the feeling of his presence had grown immensely strong when I'd sat on the plane, miles above the earth, reflecting on life, friends, and family. What had driven me to come home? Was it the mundane dreariness of the busy city life and being boxed in an office? Was it the need to be with my family, friends, and to connect with Jack again? I needed to reunite with my family, my network, my home, and my soil. The warm, red soil I walked on was part of my home. I'd felt a vortex of dark emptiness in my heart after my failed marriage, which had lasted no longer than a simmering bowl of two-minute noodles.

As for Jack, any other man wasn't worth the effort. However, I'd known Jack for most of my life. He'd never taken advantage of me the number of times he'd got me home safely after a drunk night out with our friends. He was neither a cheat nor a liar, and had once said to Angus, "I don't cut anyone's grass." That was when Angus and I were dating, and he'd had the nerve to ask if there was anything between Jack and me.

"Oh, Livvy! Jack is in the living room!" Jo's voice resonated from outside my bedroom.

"Shitty, shitty, shit!" I cursed, shimmying out of an old skirt that was too tight around the waist.

"Here," Charlie said, lifting a garment out of her backpack. "I thought you might need this tonight."

"No way!" I gasped. "It's perfect!"

Charlie smiled and patted my forearm. "It's a Cinderella rescue dress. Put it on, and it'll do the trick." The outfit Charlie was holding was a sleeveless butterfly-print dress that appeared to be my size. Putting it on, I smiled at how it accentuated my curves in all the right places. The hem fell to just below my knees, and there were two hidden pockets!

"I can't believe it's even got pockets! I love pockets," I gushed, feeling at home in Charlie's Cinderella dress.

She tilted her head, observed the dress on me, and nodded in approval. "It really suits you. Do you like it?"

"I love it!" I hugged her. Charlie really was a trooper and a lifesaver.

"Well, you can keep it. Consider it a welcome back gift."

A minute later, I entered the living room with Charlie next to me and glanced at the handsome stud who had shaved. There was something incredibly sexy about a guy who sported a short stubble, but I appreciated that Jack had made an effort to groom and shave for me that night.

"G'day, stranger," Charlie greeted Jack, who gave her a light hug. A tiny sliver of jealousy tested my mood, turning it from rosy pink to begrudging green. However, Jack quickly turned to me, and his eyes lit up with eagerness, sending my envy to run like the clappers, swiftly in the wind.

"You look nice, Livvy," he commented, eyeing me up and down a few times.

"Ah, guys, I'm gonna head home. Catch ya' later in the week, Liv," Charlie cut in, then added, "Enjoy your night out together!"

"So, where are you going?" Jo asked, folding her arms.

"Uhm, I dunno," I replied, shrugging my shoulders. It wasn't as if I was armed and prepared for a date with a handsome country boy.

"I'd like to keep it a surprise. It's nothing fancy, just a simple meal. It's the company that counts most, hey?" Jack grinned, pulling me into a hug. Except it wasn't just any ordinary hug. I felt something stiff pressing against me as I inhaled his delicious, fresh scent. My heart pounded faster, and my vaginal walls clenched, eliciting a sensual feeling of desire—something I hadn't felt for a while. Letting go of our embrace, I looked over at Jo, whose eyes widened with surprise and curiosity. Her face said it all: Jack and I had entered a zone where we were more than just friends.

## Chapter Four
Jack

### Ten p.m.

Fuck, I couldn't stop staring at Livvy. The woman was bloody stunning, charming the socks off my feet with her direct gaze and honest smile. Heck, I was just a simple farm boy in love with a beautiful woman. I'm no wordsmith, but I've never liked the term "fall in love" because it implies that one would descend or lose their position. I'd like to think that we choose to rise or ascend in love. Well, that's enough of my lesson on life. I was never into philosophy or spirituality.

After catching up on five years during dinner at a restaurant in town, we strolled—her arm was linked with mine—down Bungil Street and a little further to a giant bottle tree with a girth of nearly ten meters, or about thirty feet.

"I missed this old tree," Livvy exclaimed, pulling me into her warm embrace. "Do you remember when we were kids?"

"Yep, you tried to kiss me here. You said I was a cane toad who might turn into a prince." I chuckled, tucking a tendril of hair behind Livvy's ear.

"Well, you were my childhood crush," Livvy admitted. "Do you want to know another secret?"

"Secret?" I nudged Livvy's ribs and winked. "I thought I knew all your secrets."

"Not all secrets." My tiny temptress winked back.

"Tell me," I groaned, feeling my cock stiffen—Livvy had that effect on me; the ability to get me aroused and weak in the knees in no time.

"Nope. Not yet." Her lips revealed a coy smile when she shook her head. She refreshed my life like the water down Bungil Creek on a blistering hot day. The thing about the creek is that its flow varies from a little trickle to a raging river after heavy rain. I'd seen Livvy in a rage, and that was on her wedding night when Angus, the bloody root rat, was caught with his pants down, shagging some other bird.

"Bugger it!" I frowned, trying not to think about Livvy's wedding night. I had a bit of baggage to get off my chest, but I didn't want to spoil the night by bringing up the ghosts of the past. This wasn't the night for Dickens' *A Christmas Carol*.

"Are you okay, Jack?" Livvy asked, touching my cheek with the back of her hand.

"I'm fine, just a little tired from a long day of work. I don't get the Saturdays off," I growled.

"I thought your family hires people to help you out on the farm," Livvy remarked.

"There's still plenty of work to do." I glanced sideways, then down to Livvy's bare thighs and calves.

*Ah, her smooth, creamy legs.* If I lifted that dress, I'd get a glimpse of what was in between them. Did she shave? Was she bare? Did she leave a landing strip? I licked my lips, wanting to taste her sweet sex and bury myself inside her.

"Do you want to come over for a cuppa?" I asked, clasping her delicate hands with mine.

Livvy glanced down, fanning her long, curled dark lashes. Slowly gazing up, she bit her lower left lip as her magnetic maroon eyes hypnotized mine. "I'd love that," she huskily replied.

Fuck, the stiffy was back.

\*\*\*

## Olivia

I knew where we were heading when I recognized a large sign on the old road to the McCullens' cattle farm about twenty minutes later. Jack parked in front of a magnificent, high-set Queenslander home. It was built of timber, raised off the ground, with a corrugated iron roof and a spacious veranda. The front lawn was a gardener's delight, with outback flora and an old eucalyptus tree, where Jack and I had carved our initials when we were about nine years old.

"I haven't been to your house for a while," I commented as we walked up the steps. "I'll get a chance to see your mum and dad and say hello."

"They're visiting some relatives in Toowoomba this weekend, so it's just us tonight," Jack replied, then cleared his throat. "Come over for dinner next Sunday arvo. They'd love to see you."

"Sure," I said, stealing a glance at Jack's athletic physique. "Does that crazy bush turkey still visit your backyard?"

Jack released a light chuckle, then tilted his head and flashed his megawatt smile. "Did you miss Fred?"

"He was a real nutter, that one! Fred would've made a good Christmas meal."

"Fred disappeared shortly after you nicked off to the other side of the world. He's never come back."

"Well, good riddance!" I smiled, feeling the warmth of Jack's body as he stepped closer toward me.

"Ah, you miss him," Jack murmured, cupping my face with his rough, warm hands. He was right. I missed that crazy, feathered bundle of insanity, who was part of the McCullen farm. However, it was Jack who I craved—I felt his warm, minty breath on my neck as we stood in front of the door in heated silence.

"Livvy, there's something I've wanted to do with you for a long time," he confessed, pulling me tightly into him.

"I wanted it too," I whispered, inhaling his spiced, woody aftershave. My fingers trembled as they touched his tanned face and traced the tip of his aquiline nose, down to his soft lips.

"Will you kiss me?" Jack's deep ocean eyes begged mine.

"With all my heart," I replied, teasing him with my beguiling smile. I parted my lips, allowing him to taste the sensuality in my soul. If the eyes were the windows to the soul, then the mouth was a doorway.

Then, just then, it happened. Jack's mouth descended on mine, and we were fused in a feverish kiss—slow and passionate with the slip of tongues at first, then greedy and lustful as his tongue lashed mine. I mimicked his every move, absorbing his hot, succulent kiss, which was *oh, so tasty!*

"I missed you, Livvy," Jack groaned. A tingling sensation shot through every artery, sending my heart into a blazing inferno, a raging bushfire, when Jack's hands explored my hips and buttocks.

My fingers massaged his broad shoulders and muscular arms, then worked their way down to his slim hips before hooking his leather belt, pulling his hips and groin into mine. "I've always wanted you," I admitted, lifting the cotton fabric of his shirt.

*Eureka!*

I struck gold when I felt the scorching heat of Jack's naked skin under his clothing. I made the next move—a gutsy one—and unbuttoned his shirt, exposing his bare chest, lightly dusted with curls.

"I've had a thing for you too, but I never thought I stood a chance," Jack's low voice drawled. His lush lips powerfully engulfed mine while he tightened his grip to secure me in his sensual hold.

"You have me," I affirmed, then overtook the kiss while brushing his chest before moving further down south. *One, two, three*, I counted silently, feeling each ripple of his toned stomach. *Four, five, six.* I'd seen him shirtless before when he was training, but I'd never touched him as my lover until now.

His hands skated on my waist and hips before making their way to my round ass cheeks. "You're curvier. Sexier," he mused, pressing his thick arousal harder against my pelvis. His hands found their way under the hem of my dress and caressed my buttocks, feeling the lace trimmings of my panties. I silently thanked Charlie for talking me into buying a new pair of lacy black panties at a lingerie shop earlier that day. I'd had enough time to wash and dry the provocative undergarment so that I could slip into it that evening.

"Mmm, that kiss was delicious," I purred, tasting his silky lips again. Feeling ravenous, I wanted a bigger bite of the sweet, juicy apple.

"Do you want to go inside?" Jack briefly glanced at the door. His assertive hands tickled deeper under my buttocks, dangerously close to my moist sex while he continued rubbing his hard erection against my body.

"That depends," I flirted, toying with the curls on the nape of his neck.

"Tell me what you want," Jack whispered, leisurely enticing me with little nips of love along my neck and décolletage. His every move was seductive, alluring me into a whole new world.

"I think you know what I want," I moaned, tilting my head back as an invitation for my wild country boy to taste more of me. Eager to continue our outback adventure, Jack planted sizzling kisses on my earlobe and jawline before his lips found their way back to mine. This Aussie bloke knew how to tantalize a woman with his body and his mouth. Who would have thought that our first kiss would be hotter than the outback heat in the summer?

## Chapter Five

### Jack

"Your place is still pristine," Livvy commented when we were inside.

Her eyes stared up at the decorated fans and the ornate ceiling roses that suspended Mum's fancy chandeliers in the hallway.

"You know your way around the house," I replied, then whispered into her ear, "You'll learn your way around my body too."

Livvy blushed, then slowly walked around the living room, touching the furniture as if she had just been here yesterday. "You have me," she had declared earlier. *You have me.*

"Come with me," I commanded, opening the door to my bedroom.

"Do you remember this room?" I toyed with Livvy's ribcage, rubbing my thumb just under her left breast.

"It's changed a lot," she said, eyeing the grey walls and the walk-in wardrobe next to the en suite bathroom. Her wide eyes settled on my bed as her pink tongue licked her full, pouty lips.

"You smell delicious," I murmured, aroused by her erotic scent, which had a sweet and sensual undertone.

"It's organic lavender oil. It feels so supple on my skin," Livvy's husky voice replied, tracing the skin from her slender shoulder to the top of her ripe cleavage.

"You're a fucking cocktease," I said, wishing my hard dick were inside her. Burying my face against the smoothness of her neck, I asked, "Are you nervous, Livvy?"

"About ending up in bed with you?" She taunted me with her mischievous eyes. She lowered her lashes, then looked up, revealing a naughty smile as she bit the side of her lower lip.

Blessed with breasts that were more than a handful, she had the sensual curves of a burlesque performer, killing me softly with her wicked teases. For years I'd wanted to lay my hands on her delicate body, suck her nipples, and lick her vaginal lips before dipping my stiff dick into her wet core. I found easy pleasure with other women after breaking it off with Ashley, but I longed for my Livvy. A possessive thought jumped out of my mouth like a roo hopping onto the highway.

"Did you have many men, Livvy? Did you fancy European men?"

"Jack, does it matter to you?" Livvy's face fell, and her eyes chastised mine with the look of "shame on you!"

*You're fucking roadkill, mate,* I thought to myself. I stared back before replying, "I just want to get to know you better. I want to know what you've tried and what you'd like to do with me."

She took my arm and serenaded the pulse below my palm with a kiss from her juicy lips. Her pupils were dilated, pleading for carnal pleasure. "I discovered new things about sex when I stopped over in Amsterdam on the way home. I watched a live sex show and wanted to try the things they did, but only with you. That's my secret."

Throwing her a lopsided grin, I fished a condom foil from my pocket and placed it on the bed. "I might have a few things you'd enjoy. I planned for tonight. Just in case, you know." Pulling Livvy close to me, I pressed her body against mine. "What do you like, sweetheart?" I slowly unzipped her dress, loosening its grip on her feminine frame.

"Restraints," she moaned as her dress fell onto the polished wooden floor. "Feathers, lace, silk, leather, and handcuffs."

"What about the leather paddle? Do you like your bottom spanked?" I gazed at Livvy's buxom curves, which trumpeted that she was all woman. Her sheer bra showed off her protruding pink nipples, which begged to be sucked. My eyes traveled lower to her lovely hips and her tiny lace panties. One tug was all it would take to unveil a hidden oasis of rousing wonder.

"Spanked? Hmm, do you think I need a good spanking?" She stepped closer to me, undoing my belt and unzipping my jeans. Unlatching the back of her bra with one swift clinch of the clasps, I watched her ample breasts jiggle as the bra slipped off her body.

"You came home late. It took ya' five bloody years. Don't you think that deserves a little smack?" My tongue ran across my teeth as I grinned, entranced by her light-pink nipples that were plump and erect on her pale skin. They were mouthwatering strawberries on cream pushed against my bare chest.

"Mmm, I might let you," the pussycat purred, making her way past the elastic band of my cotton boxers and downward to my throbbing cock.

"Oh, fuck!" I gasped as my hard length twitched at her touch. I groaned, burying my face into the smoothness of her neck. "Tell me that you're begging for it."

"I've wanted this fella for years," she cheekily confessed. "Where's the paddle?"

"Undress me first," I grabbed her hand. It was my turn to tease her now. All it took was seconds for my clothes to join her dress on the floor, leaving me naked. "Do you like what you see?" I shifted my stance with an air of dominance.

Arching her left brow, Livvy's eyes smiled with delight, and her lips curved into a salacious grin. "I should've jumped you years ago! I didn't know this pretty boy was packing dynamite!" she blurted, then continued playing with my erection. She knew how to massage the tip of my cock, rubbing the loose foreskin with her two delicate fingers before giving the area a gentle tug, up and down. I guided her with the pace, slowly at first, then quickening as I felt the excitement grow more intense.

"That's it. That's it, sugar," I coaxed, wanting more of the thrill that came with Livvy's tugging. I pushed her onto the bed, and we continued our lovers' play with me on top, licking and suckling her nipples while palming her full breasts. Suddenly, I felt a familiar rush when she applied more pressure and teased the glans with her thumb, eliciting a droplet of clear fluid.

"Slow down, love," I said, releasing her fingers from me. "I'm not ready to come yet."

Livvy nodded her head and tucked her hair behind her ears, exposing her sexy brown eyes. I removed the duvet from under her, revealing a surprise that made her gasp and cover her mouth. "Jack—"

"Lie down." I directed my eyes at one of the straps near the bed restraints. "I think you're going to enjoy this."

"Oh, you're a wild cowboy!" Livvy gushed as I placed the restraints on her hands, spreading her on the mattress like an eagle.

"This Aussie cowboy wants your pussy," I drawled, tracing the trimming of her panties before drawing them down her shapely legs, exposing her cunt. I tilted my head, gazed at her bare mound, and grinned. *She was fully shaven and looked tasty!*

After spreading her legs wide and fastening her ankles with the lower bed restraints, I gave her pussy lips a light tickle. "Are you ready for the ride?" I teased, inserting two fingers inside her hot sex.

"Mmm, I want you to corrupt me," Livvy moaned, closing her eyes.

"You'll enjoy this, then." I took out a burgundy satin blindfold from my bedside table drawer and tied it around her head. "I want you to be aroused with your other senses."

"Oh, Jack!" she panted, touching my head and feeling every muscle of my shoulders. I moved downward, kissing her stomach and her hips before my index and middle fingers found their way back to her pretty pussy. I gave it a teasing rub, causing her to gasp in pleasure, then dipped them into her exposed pinkness.

"You're wet," I groaned, feeling her slick juices flow, thickly coating her silky clit.

I explored the shape, snugness, and angle within her vagina, pleasuring it and delving further until my fingers found something that felt a bit like a mushroom cap. Her breathing hitched, indicating slight discomfort, so I withdrew a little and explored the front wall inside her. In turn, Livvy rocked her pelvis in sync with my finger fucking, which became faster and rougher. She mewled and thrashed her head in pleasured rapture while my fingers greedily plunged in and out of her.

"Jack, I'm going to come," Livvy whimpered, almost incoherently in spellbound mesmerization.

"Not yet," I commanded, kissing her mons. I delicately parted her outer lips then kissed her clit, giving small sucks while my tongue tickled the delicate nub. I enjoyed devouring her, breathing in her feminine scent as I lapped up her swollen slickness. Suddenly, she stiffened, then arched her back and cried out my name, grabbing my hair tightly as a flood of ecstasy washed over her body. I tasted my lover's cream in my mouth, savoring her sex.

"Yes, that's it. Good," I soothed, as her body twitched and shivered, then started to relax from the tightened exhilaration of her orgasm.

"You were amazing," Livvy said breathlessly, stroking my hair with gentleness after I removed the blindfold and restraints.

"This was just foreplay, sweetheart," I replied, shifting off the bed. Standing up, I swept my eyes across her nude form and smiled sinfully. "Are you keen for more?"

"Where's the paddle?" Livvy asked eagerly. I smirked, glancing at a small cupboard that was within an arm's length.

"In there?" Livvy's eyes followed mine, targeting the cupboard.

"Go on, take a look," I invited her to open Pandora's box.

## Chapter Six

### Olivia

I reached out to the cupboard near Jack's bed, only to feel a sharp sting on my wrist. "You forgot to say 'please'," he scolded me, with a tantalizing gleam in his eyes. "Do you like it rough?"

"Yes," I answered, "and I'll tell you if it hurts."

"Good," he replied. His face softened for a moment, and his calm, temperate eyes reminded me of the ocean on a warm, sunny day when the tide was low. However, within a flash, they darkened and stormed into high tide with a ferocious passion. Sitting on the bed, I stared at the man in front of me, and I wondered if I truly knew Jack. I mean, the Jack I knew was a nice guy, albeit hot as fuck. So, who was this dominant sex god with steel arms, muscular legs, and a firm butt?

"Livvy," he commanded, sensually rubbing my shoulders. How easy it was for him to touch me, to make me melt for him.

"Before you open the cupboard, I want you to suck me." He grabbed my hair, bringing my head closer to his manhood's heady scent.

I stared at the round tip of Jack's cock, then down to the light, intricate veins that ran along the thick shaft, which jutted from a nest of dark pubic curls. "It's impressive," I murmured, then lowered my eyes to the testicles that hung between his muscled thighs. I was ready to give him a good, hard suck.

"Take it in your mouth," he ordered, slapping the side of my face with his erection, before teasing my lips with its smooth head. I looked up, allowing his length to slip between my lips and toward my throat.

"Aah, that's it, Livvy. Good girl," Jack moaned as I sucked him while gently rubbing his balls. I continued kissing his length, running my tongue on the veins along the shaft, then wickedly teased the sensitive glans.

"You're such a fucking tease," Jack growled. "Do you know that? You've taunted me for years with that pouty mouth of yours, sweetheart."

I massaged him with my lips, taking as much of him as I could. Hearing his breathing grow heavy, I worked my magic on his balls and applied light pressure on a spot behind them. Just when I felt him grow tense, he commanded me to stop. "Get up," he ordered.

"But why?" I protested. I wanted to give Jack the blowjob of his life.

"Now's not the time to be insolent, sweetheart," he replied, pinching my nipples. "Get up!" I obeyed and stood in front of my lover, allowing him to sweep his gaze down my naked body.

"This belongs to me tonight." Jack inserted two fingers between my vaginal lips with flawless expertise that made me moan in pleasure as he delivered a fulfilling kiss. Our tongues connected like sparks of electricity energetically entwined in breathless passion.

Slowly breaking away from the kiss, I glanced at the cupboard and wondered what Jack was willing to show me tonight. *Please. Say the magic word.* "Please? Please, can I open the cupboard?" I begged, teasing him with my wide eyes and lusty pout. Jack casually removed his fingers, which were slickly coated with my vaginal juices, licked them, then traced them around my pink lips.

"You're delicious. Taste yourself," he insisted, prompting me to open my mouth and take in his fingers. I began to suck on them, licking the saltiness of my juices.

"That's it," he coaxed, rubbing the warmth of his nakedness and the addictive scent of his musk on me. "You're my good girl, aren't you?"

Nodding my head, I looked up at the devilish charmer whose lips curled up while his hand gestured toward Pandora's box. I turned the knob of the cupboard and opened it. Blinking my eyes, I gasped. Then, slowly, I revealed a sly grin. Jack and I had a few things in common in the bedroom—we both liked a bit of kink and a dash of an adventure. I lifted a large, fragrant candle from the top shelf and brought it to my nose. The candle was redolent with the scent of exotic patchouli, evoking the mystery of an oriental harem. Placing the candle back, my fingers moved down to the next shelf and discovered a range of vials. I took one out and opened it, breathing in the scent of jasmine oil.

"There's geranium, juniper, and more oils," Jack remarked. "I'd like to give you a full body massage with a happy ending, perhaps another time."

"Tell me, Jack. Is every night a happy ending with you?" I chuckled, placing the vial back on the shelf after dabbing small drops on both my wrists, then rubbing them against each other for the oil's soothing scent to take effect on my skin. A bendable vibrator, hemp rope, and a flogger with leather fronds lay on the next shelf below.

Jack picked up the vibrator and turned it on. "I want to use it on your clit, vulva, and nipples," he murmured, kissing my neck and collarbone while teasing my nipples with the vibrations.

"Oh," I groaned, feeling a single trickle of wetness run between my legs—a remnant of my last orgasm coupled with a new wave of excitement. Jack continued rubbing each nipple with the vibrator, before teasing my wet clit with it.

"You like that, don't you, love?" he hummed, increasing the vibrator's speed.

"You're going to make me come again soon if you keep doing that," I warned him as he guided the vibrator along my sex, which clenched in response to the titillation. He pinched my nipples with his other hand and enticed each of them with quick, rough flicks of his tongue. After a short while, the buzzing sound of the vibrator disappeared. So had Jack's touch. My aroused nipples hardened even more when they felt a surge of coldness in the absence of his hot handling.

"Jack?" I asked. "Why did you stop?" I stared at the man who stood in smug silence while the moonlight shone through the window, casting a contrast of light against the darkness, accentuating the contours of his firm muscles and tight, masculine jawline.

He caressed the curves of my naked hips. "I want you to keep exploring the shelves until you find what you really want tonight."

"But I just did—" I began to blurt, then stopped dead in my tracks when I eyed a black silicone ball gag, steel handcuffs, a feather tickler, and—

"Take it out," Jack coaxed, nodding at me. "Go on."

There it was—a leather and fur paddle with my name. My fingers traced the words "Olivia Bertrand", which were etched on the leather side of the paddle. The other side was covered with soft, sensual fur for gentle raps on the rear. "I want you to spank me," I confessed, handing the paddle to Jack, who sat on the edge of the bed. He patted his lap and took my hand, signaling that it was time for a little game of spanking.

"I'm going to smack your bottom. Do you know why?" Jack asked as I lay face down on his lap with my bare ass high up in the air.

"Because I've been bad for leaving you alone all these years?"

"Oh, you've been bad for nicking off, but I wasn't alone," he said, rubbing my clit. "I've had plenty of women to keep me company."

I tried to squirm, but he held me tight, refusing to let go. Just as I started to relax, I felt a stinging smack on my right ass cheek. "Ouch!" I cried out, feeling the sharp pain, followed by a wave of pleasure.

"Do you want more?" Jack asked, holding the paddle high in the air.

"Yes, please!" I cried.

"Then count. That was one."

"Two!" I yelped, feeling the sting once again, a little harder than the first. After that, each smack was as stimulating as much as it was punishing, releasing a natural high that led to heightened arousal for more.

By the time I'd counted to ten, Jack had given me one last swat on my sore rear before switching to the paddle's soft, furry side, rubbing it gently on my buttocks and lower back. He ended the punishment with a sensual tap, then announced, "It's time for you to ride me."

I watched Jack position himself on the bed, resting his back in easy comfort. Noticing the Akubra hat on top of his bedside table, I picked it up and placed it on his head. "I'm looking forward to riding my country boy tonight. Can I call you mine, Jack?" I asked.

"You can call me anything you want, sweetheart," he grinned. Damn, he looked sexy with his wavy hair curled under the hat, which was made for all seasons—sun, heat, rain, and storm. I climbed on top of him, feeling slightly giddy at the start. I was already on a wild ride, beyond the point of no return.

"Here, you'll need this," Jack said, taking the condom. "Put it on me."

I quickly glanced at our clothes on the floor when Jack turned my head toward him and locked my eyes with his. "No regrets?"

"No." I shook my head. "No regrets."

"Good," he replied, giving my ass cheek a light spanking.

I removed the latex condom from its wrapper, rolled it onto Jack's hard erection, and slowly pushed myself down, letting him slide in, inch by inch. He placed his hands on my hips as soon as I descended, rubbing them as I adjusted to his size. I leaned forward so I could take more of Jack inside me, grabbing his shoulders as I moaned loudly. "I feel you," I said, staring at his eager eyes. The heat of his thickness inside me was energizing, like a fever burning all up.

"I've wanted this for so long, Livvy," Jack groaned, thrusting deeply into me as I rocked my hips backward and forward, feeling the softness of his thick pubic curls that brushed against my shaven mound.

"Oh, Jack! I want you so much," I cried, sliding up and down him in synchronized rhythm and pace. I yearned for him as the salty soil craved for sweet rain in the dry desert heat.

"You have me, Livvy. Tell me again. Do I have you?" Jack grunted, massaging my buttocks while increasing the speed of our lovemaking.

"Yes," I admitted. "You have me, Jack!" I squeezed my inner wall muscles as I leaned further, rubbing my breasts against his manly chest. We continued fucking hard in swift erotic motion as his hips bucked in forceful rhythm into me. Never in my life had I felt so alive with all the pleasure being injected into my body each time his cock thrust inside me. My breathing sped faster as if I'd run miles and back to come home to my lover.

"I love you, Livvy." Jack's eyes pierced mine as he removed loose strands of hair that flew across my face. "Let me see your eyes. I want to see your eyes when you come."

Suddenly, I felt the urge to shout when his dick stiffened, and its thick knob hit my most sensitive spot, sending volts of pure, intensified ecstasy. "I'm coming!" I screamed, digging my nails into his warm, sweat-soaked skin.

I watched Jack's face tighten then relax as he cried out my name, releasing his orgasm while mine flooded over like waves washing the shore. "Fuck, Livvy! That's it!" His blue eyes lit up like vibrant fireworks that brightened the darkness of the southern sky. He grabbed my body tightly, hugging me as if nothing else mattered while I clung onto his hard muscles.

After I had removed the loaded condom, we lay in each other's arms in serene silence as the fresh scent of sex wafted in the cool night air. I slowly dozed into a peaceful slumber, feeling a release of tranquility when Jack kissed my forehead and said, "Good night."

## Chapter Seven

### Olivia

### Sunday morning

I opened my eyes to the brightness of the morning sun, hoping to find Jack by my side, but he was gone. Staring at the space next to me, I rubbed my ass cheeks and felt the silkiness of a soothing ointment that had been smeared on them while I was asleep. Its scent was eucalyptus, a remedy for aches and pains, among other things. Jack had cared for me.

I got out of bed and noticed that he had placed an old shirt on the bed for me to wear. After putting my panties and Jack's shirt on, I strolled outside to the back and stared at the hectares of property surrounded by bush life. Shielding my eyes from the sun's intense glare, I gazed at a machinery shed and workshop in the distance near a small lake. Jack and I used to swim in that lake when we were younger. Further out was a laneway to the cattle yards. The McCullens hired people mainly to rotational graze their cattle with bikes or muster on horseback. Speaking of horseback, Jack must have gone for a morning ride on Champion, his favorite thoroughbred gelding, who was certainly not for beginners. I preferred Snowy, one of the McCullens' older horses, who didn't buck, bolt, kick, or bite.

Putting on an old pair of sandals, which were probably his mum's, I meandered around the backyard, basking in the afterglow of scorching sex and the sun's hot rays. I was about to take one more step when I heard a rustling sound behind the bushes. Uh, oh.

*Fuck! Fred's back!*

The bloody turkey bolted out of the blue, charging toward my legs with that sharp beak and a mad look in his beady eyes. There was no way I could have missed the old, grey bird, a gift from Jack's uncle Bill in Brisbane when he visited years ago. I sprinted as fast as I could, but Fred was quicker, speeding at me in all his feathered, territorial glory. In my panicked state, I miscalculated my feet's coordination and fell to the ground, clumsily hitting the hard dirt.

"Oww, you vicious bird!" I spat at Fred, who made one painful peck on my foot before turning to a manly figure whose shadow covered me.

"Off! Off you go." Jack's voice growled at Fred, who ran in full flight, disappearing behind the bushes.

He stood naked, wearing only his Akubra hat and an old pair of RM Williams boots. Every sinew and muscle that made him a man was perfect, and there was not an inch of fat on him. He'd been a little on the thin side when we were kids, then athletic and slim in our teens, and even when he'd beefed up for the Cowboys, he'd had those slender hips. He wasn't as bulked up these days, but hot damn, he still had broad shoulders, a firm ass, and sturdy legs.

"Bloody hell, the fucking chook!" I shouted, nursing my sore foot, which had been pecked by the game bird.

"It's a turkey, mate! Not a bloody chicken!" Jack placed his hands on his hips. Every muscle of his body gleamed in the sun. "Here, let me have a look. Are you bleeding?" He bent down and checked my foot.

"No. I'll be fine," I replied, getting up and wiping the soil off my face and arms.

"Here, you missed a spot," Jack said, removing a speck of dirt from under my eye with his thumb. He had always been protective of me, ever since we were kids. Now, he was a different kind of protector—he was a lover who cared for his woman.

"Where were you this morning? Where are the farm staff?" I asked, eyeing Jack's relaxed cock.

"I was fixing a few things in the shed and I've given the staff the day off today." Jack removed his hat and wiped a trickle of sweat above his brow. "Do you want to go for a little swim in the lake? We can have some breakfast after that."

"I wouldn't knock the offer back," I grinned. I took his hand, and together we walked toward the lake.

*** 

About an hour later, Jack and I were naked, refreshed, and revived from the cool, clean water after a good swim. We had a bit of fun on one of the large, smooth rocks, where Jack's mouth decided it was hungry for cunnilingus. I wanted him inside me again, but he refused to venture without protection. "I don't want to knock you up too soon," he said, stroking my wet hair. "I care about you, and I love you more than you know."

"Jack, can I ask you something?" I scratched behind my ear.

"Go ahead. Ask."

"There's just one thing I need to know. Remember what you said on my wedding night?"

"I remember it well."

"Did you mean what you said, Jack?"

"I meant every word I said, but I didn't mean to make you cry," he whispered, nuzzling his cheek against mine.

"The tears were already there," I replied, remembering the bullfight between him and Angus.

"What I said was the truth." Jack's deep ocean eyes penetrated mine as waves of certainty wiped out doubt.

*You should have bloody married me instead!* I closed my eyes and sighed, remembering Jack shouting those words at me before he stormed away that night.

"Honestly, what you said was the catalyst that tore me apart," I confessed. "I left not only because of what Angus did but because I realized, right there and then, that I couldn't have you—you were still with Ashley, and I thought you'd said those words purely out of anger. My heart broke that night because I knew you were right. I should have married you, Jack."

"It's never too late," he suggested, throwing me a slight grin. He inhaled my natural scent and caressed my body with his rough hands while kissing my neck, breasts, and pink peaks.

"I need to tell you something." I inhaled the fresh air, then released the tension tightening in my heart. It was time to tell him the truth.

"What is it?" His eyebrows furrowed with concern as we both sat up. His eyes probed mine, pleading me to love him.

"I've always loved you, Jack." I took his hand, which squeezed mine, indicating his gratitude.

"Be with me," he whispered, then licked his lips before placing them on mine. Everything felt almost perfect then.

*Almost perfect.*

"What about Brisbane?" I asked. "You never answered my question when we were at the pub the other day. When do you start your new job?"

"I'm moving to Brisbane in a few weeks," he replied. "You know, to get settled and stuff at a house I bought before school starts next month."

"So, what happens if I don't get the job I applied for in Brissy?" I asked.

Jack wrinkled his forehead, contemplating an answer. "You can always move in with me and apply for other jobs while you're there."

"Oh," was all I managed to say before walking toward the house. Did he think I'd just pick up my swag and move in with him? I was sure there were women who would just move in with Jack at the drop of a hat if he asked them to leave everything for him. If I moved to Brisbane, would I be moving for him or me? I didn't want to center my life on someone else's goals and plans without a proper goal of my own.

"Hey! Where are ya' going?" I heard Jack call after me as I strode across the red earth patched with dry grass.

"To check your fridge if you've got brekky. I'm starving!" I yelled back, feeling my stomach rumble.

Twenty minutes later, I sat silently across the table from Jack, watching him chew his muesli crunch cereal while I ate my Vegemite-coated toast. The coffee-colored spread, when applied thinly on bread, had a great, salty taste. However, it was an acquired taste that I'd grown up with.

I awkwardly broke the ice. "So, what's our story?"

"Our story?" Jack raised his eyebrows, then zoned in with a thoughtful smile. "It's a story about a boy and a girl who were the best of friends. As they grew up, they ventured off to other lands and kissed a few cane toads along the way."

"Hmm, it sounds like an interesting yarn," I commented.

"They met up again…" Jack paused.

"Then what?"

"The rest is up to you."

Jack

Six months later

I'd have liked to say that Livvy and I had our happily ever after in Brisbane by now, but life isn't always so simple. I moved to the city shortly after our night together on the farm. Livvy didn't get the job there, but she found work as a publicity officer for Roma's town council. She wasn't the type of woman who would move solely for a relationship; she needed her own purpose in life and her independence. We decided it was best for her to try out the council job while applying for more jobs in Brisbane.

She made a short trip to Brissy to return her rental car after fixing the dent. In turn, I visited her and my family during Easter. For us, love wasn't just about sex and attraction. It was a multifaceted intangible that could last for years without any explanation.

So, there I was standing at the city's main bus terminal, holding a mixed bouquet of chrysanthemums, gerberas, and lilies, waiting for the bus to arrive at nine o'clock, and there it came, pulling into its bay. Was Livvy on the bus, as she had promised? It was a long weekend, and she'd decided to take a few extra days off to spend a week with me.

A minute later, I watched the passengers leave the bus while the driver began to unload the luggage onto the pavement. I saw families and friends reunite, no doubt as eager as I was to see Livvy.

Then.

Suddenly.

There she was.

Her copper-red hair blew wildly in the autumn wind before she flicked it from her face, revealing her sunny, brown eyes and her warm smile. My heart pounded with excitement as she stepped off the bus and ran into my arms, hugging me tightly. After a passion-coated kiss, she took the bouquet, inhaled the fresh floral fragrance, then slowly let go of me to grab her gear that the driver placed on the pavement. "Oi! I need a bit of help," she called out, lifting the handle of a suitcase.

"Here, let me take it for you—"

"Nah, darl, take the other one." Livvy pointed at another suitcase.

"Two?" I scratched my head. "That's excessive for the week!"

"Who says I'm staying for a week?" Her lips curved up into a secretive smile.

"Is it two weeks?" I placed my hands on my hips, then picked up the handle and strolled the second suitcase.

"Nope." Livvy maneuvered her suitcase's wheels, walking with me to the car park.

"A month?" I twitched my mouth. One month with Livvy was wishful thinking.

She shook her head, which stopped me in my tracks. I let go of the suitcase handle and turned to her.

"How long, sweetheart?" I asked, massaging her shapely hips, bringing her pelvis into mine.

"Well, do you remember the job I didn't get with the justice department?! Livvy beamed. "They called me a week ago and offered a one-year contract for a similar role with the possibility of becoming a permanent position."

"Fair dinkum?" I needed to know if she was being honest with me.

"Fair dinkum." She nodded, her eyes staring intently into mine. "It's the truth."

"Well, then. Are you up for another adventure?" I pinched her ass cheek.

"How about a lifetime of adventures?" Livvy asked. I noticed that a small travel bag she had tucked in her arm was not fully zipped. The tip of a leather handle poked out from the bag.

"What's that in your bag? Take it out and show me," I ordered, folding my arms. I threw a dirty grin at her. Livvy slowly removed the handle and revealed her favorite toy. Her name was etched on the leather side.

"Let's go home," I said, offering her my hand.

"I'm already home, Jack," she replied, taking my hand to her lips. "I've come home."

## The End

# Mail Order Mate
## Eileen Troemel

## Chapter One

### Mates Arrive

"Up you go," Jack said as she lifted her niece into the large hauler they used to go longer distances.

"Auntie Jack," Molly asked. "Why do we gotta go to town?" She knelt on the seat of the hauler. Her red hair, so like her mother's, fell over her shoulders in twin braids.

"The government's requiring it," Jack said.

"Cause of the sickness that took everyone?" Molly asked.

"Yeah. Probably," Jack said. A year ago, her sister, brother-in-law, parents and fiancé had all worked the land on this new world. It was hard work. Their herd of jumbos provided them with everything they needed. Their manure fertilized their crops. Three times a year, their coats were sheared and the wool used to create blankets and clothing. The milk and the butter it provided were used for drinking and baking. The jumbos' meat filled their stomachs. Once a year they butchered a single jumbo to keep the household in food. Large mammals, the jumbos were native to this planet. On arriving, the explorers had discovered how friendly they were. It had taken people like Jack and the other ranchers to domesticate them. They had four legs, long fur in nearly every color, which was necessary for their short but frigid winters, and a snout to gobble up bugs, spiders, and foliage.

Upon arriving ten years ago, Jack had discovered several eggs. When they hatched, she raised them. The eggs produced one or two chicks each. The sicin birds produced eggs daily. Her family was the first to have fresh eggs and birds to eat. Their flock of sicin spawned most of the local flocks. The land provided the rest. The homestead garden flourished under Jack's mother's attention.

"Scooch over," Jack said. Lifting her work boot, she saw the dust of the land fall away. She had the land and her niece. Six months ago, a sickness had started. It swept through the jumbos, killing half of them. The xenobiologists had no clue what caused it. Then they got sick too.

Once people got sick, the disease swept through like a flash storm in the spring. Her father was the first to go. Fever, puking, and delirium. Rash under the arms and on the stomach. Either the fever broke or the person died in two days having convulsions.

Nothing from the government worked. They brought in doctors in safety suits. They tried a dozen vaccines, but nothing worked. The sickness swept through the whole sector. It had started on Vendar, the planet closest to the small sun. People didn't know they were sick and had traveled.

When they'd heard news of it here on Baila, people had scoffed. It couldn't reach them. They were isolated and far from all the other settlements. They were an agricultural planet. No one visited. But it had reached them.

Jack sighed and stepped up into the hauler. She watched Molly, trying to hide her grief from her. "It's something about mates," Jack said.

"Mail Order Mates like Grandpa used to tease you about?"

"I don't think these are mail order," Jack snorted.

"But all the adults gotta get mates because we're too few here." Molly sounded more adult than she should.

"Maybe," Jack said. Her father had died. She'd got sick at the same time. She remembered being weak and dreaming of strange things. When she woke on the third day, her mother was feverish and her father dead. It swept through the homestead. Her fiancé, her sister, her brother-in-law and Molly's younger sisters had all died. Molly had woken weak and an orphan. Jack felt the sting of tears as she settled in the seat.

"Are you gonna get a mate?" Molly asked.

Jack stared through the windshield. The homestead sat squat on the land, long and spread out to allow the three couples space and privacy. It echoed with loneliness now. "We'll see what the government says."

"I read about the aliens," Molly said as she fastened her harness.

"Yeah?" Jack asked. "Tell me what you know."

"They—the explorer teams out in space—discovered them four sectors over," Molly said.

Jack placed her hand on the starter and the engine hummed. "Yeah. Do they have horns and a tail?"

"You know they don't," Molly laughed. "Their skin is black as night. The men are fierce warriors."

"You sound like you're telling fairytales."

"Some of our people have darker skin," Molly said. "Joey…" Her words faltered. She bit her lip.

"He was a snotty brat," Jack said, just as she always did, but she reached out a hand to hold Molly's. Joey had been Molly's best friend. The same age, they'd played together as often as possible, even though Joey's family ranch was two hours from theirs. No one in the family had survived. "I miss them all." Molly sniffled and leaned on Jack.

"I do too," Jack said, letting her grief show to her eight-year-old niece.

"There's hardly any kids in the classes anymore," Molly whispered.

Jack nodded. "I know, Mol. It's gonna take time."

"But if you have to take a mate, does that mean you don't love Uncle Patrick anymore?"

A lump formed in Jack's throat, like it always did when she thought of Patrick. His blond hair, his laughter, and the way he swept her into his arms to make her feel safe and feminine. "I don't think we stop loving when a person dies," she said softly.

"But you'll take a mate?" Molly asked.

"I don't know. We're listening. We'll see whether we have a choice."

"Because the government people are bastards." Molly bit her lip.

Jack barked out a laugh. "You sound like your dad and grandpa."

"But Mom would scold me," Molly said, giggling a little.

"Yes, because that's a grownup word."

"We're wasting the suns' light sitting here," Molly said, another phrase she'd heard from her grandpa.

"We sure are," Jack said. "Let's go see what the bastards want."

The hauler held six if people didn't mind squishing into the two bench seats in the cab. Molly sat next to Jack. She'd rarely left Jack's side since the rest of their family had died. The first few weeks, Molly screamed for Jack if she was out of sight.

Behind the cab, a flat, low bed allowed jumbos to step into it easily.

It held three or four jumbos, depending on their size. People used big haulers like this to get to the ranch locations. This hauler had carried all their belongings from the port in Caha, the only city in this region. The ranches were scattered around Caha, and all trading and goods came through the city.

Between the ranch and Caha lay land filled with dense forests, rivers, and other ranches. While they drove, Jack looked out over the land. It was hers now. Hers and Molly's, she guessed.

As they were used to move everything, the haulers had worn the track away from the homestead smooth. Once a year, crops and jumbos were shipped off to market to provide food for those in Caha and on other planets in the sector. The Caha region provided the food for eight other planets.

Jack slowed as they approached the first river crossing. This late in the season it should have been low, but it was better to be cautious.

"Look," Molly said, pointing.

Jack looked to her right. A herd of poidhs were gathered in the river, fishing. Jack stopped the hauler and counted. Eight of them. No, there were two smaller cubs. Must be newly out of the den. Poidhs—the one thing which killed the jumbos for food. Her father had never killed them, though other ranchers did. He'd felt they were part of the cycle of nature. So long as they didn't take too many jumbos, her father had never hunted them.

They stood on their hind legs to peer around. One roared on seeing them. Jack didn't move. She waited to see if they would charge or if they were just posturing.

"Are they gonna charge us?" Molly asked.

"Probably not," Jack said.

"They got cubs." Molly pointed to the two little balls of rusty orange fur on the edge of the river. The adult poidhs were more gray than orange. The cubs were always a darker rusty orange. The trees where they hid their dens were the same color. It hid the cubs well, but out in the open like this, their coloring made the cubs vulnerable.

"We'll keep going," Jack said, moving into the river. The hauler jerked as they drove over the rocks. Molly grunted a couple times, like her mother used to do. Jack reached out to squeeze her shoulder.

Molly watched out her window as her grandfather had taught her to. "Do you think grandpa would approve of you getting a mate?" she asked.

Jack grunted but said nothing.

"He didn't like Patrick," Molly said.

"He didn't like me being with anyone," Jack said.

"Because you were his baby girl?" Molly asked, repeating what Jack's father had called her when he was moved.

"Yeah," Jack said, feeling the lump in her throat again. She'd adored her father. She'd shadowed him all day as a child.

"So new men he wouldn't like?" Molly asked.

"Probably not. He got used to Patrick after a bit."

"If you get a new mate…"

Molly trailed off as the track to town got rough. Once it leveled out, she continued.

"What…?"

"You're mine, kiddo," Jack said.

"Even if you get ten mates?"

"Ten men would be a lot of hassle."

"What if you get tons of kids from your new mates?"

Jack reached over and took Molly's chin. "You and me, we're a team. We stick together no matter what. Ten mates, no matter how many kids, no matter what. We stick. Got it?"

"Yes'm," Molly said, grinning.

"No. I'm not taking on ten mates and having tons of kids," Jack said.

"You just said," Molly giggled. "I'd help with all the kids."

"No. Definitely not."

"Isn't that what Mom said?" Molly asked grinning.

"Stop distracting me. I have to drive."

***

Jack reached up to help Molly down. "Everyone's headed into the town hall," Molly said, wrapping her arms around Jack's neck. "Is that where we gotta go for your ten mates?"

"Not ten." Jack smiled up into Molly's grinning face. She watched the people from town and from other ranches wander into the town hall building. This is where they'd gathered to determine how many had lived. It was the building where they'd been told their dead would be collected and disposed of so as not to contaminate the land. No markers. No graves. Jack swallowed and set Molly on the ground. "Don't wander off."

"I'm gonna help you pick your mates." Molly slipped her hand into Jack's hand. Despite the heat, Molly's hand felt icy. Jack knew she was afraid. Her mother had always got cold hands when she was afraid too.

"It's gonna be fine," Jack said but didn't let go of her hand.

"You should take your hair down," Molly said. "It's pretty. How come Mommy had red hair but your hair is almost black?"

"Grandpa's mom had red hair. Grandma had my color hair." Nerves danced in Jack's stomach like a sicin male doing a mating dance. "I'm not sure I want one mate, let alone the ten you think I need."

"But the government people are…"

"Hey," Jack said. "Once."

"'Kay," Molly said. "I wanna see these aliens. Maybe they have horns and are hiding them."

Jack took a deep breath, straightened her back, and tightened her jaw. "Might as well find out."

Molly kept up, skipping along next to her aunt. They crossed the hauler-lined streets. It looked like most of the ranchers made it to town. Jack stepped from the bright outside into the dark interior of the building.

"Jackleen," Olivia said. "We're in the big room."

"Livvie," Jack said, knowing it would annoy the shop owner. Olivia Cambell had wanted Patrick for herself and had been difficult ever since he'd showed his feelings for Jack. Her long blond hair was always perfectly styled. Her clothing was never dirty or torn. She was a proper lady—at least according to Olivia. When the sickness hit, Olivia lost her family like most others.

"I've asked you—" Olivia blurted out.

Jack cut her off. "Ditto."

"You're setting a bad example for Colleen's daughter."

"You start that nonsense again and we won't make it to the big room."

"We're in here," said a man from the government. "You ladies are required to join us." His brow furrowed and his gray hair stuck up.

"Of course, Mr. Ramen," Olivia said, batting her blue eyes at him. "We were catching up."

"Sure." Jack stepped in front of Olivia and through the door to the biggest room in the building. She recognized the people on one side of the room. The other side was filled with people remarkably like the humans.

"Not black as night," Molly said, disappointment a sigh as they walked down the center aisle.

"No horns either," Jack murmured as she took a seat in the front row.

Molly leaned into her until Jack pulled her to sit on her lap. She stared at the crowd of people across from them. "There's a lot," she whispered.

"About the same as we have here," Jack said. Looking across the aisle, she saw men and women looking very human. There was a pattern in their skin whether it was a tattoo or natural markings she didn't know. Their skin tones varied just as those of humans did.

She saw one couple clinging to each other as they leaned towards another man. He was big. Big arms, broad chest, he looked uncomfortable on the chair.

Mr. Ramen strode up the aisle. Waving his hands, he hushed the people in the room. "As you know, the sickness hit this planet hard. More than fifty percent of the population didn't survive. These people have come from a world where they are overpopulated. They are looking for a fresh start."

"Let's just get on with it," Wendall said. His ranch lay on the other side of town. He'd lost his wife and three boys. "I've got jumbos to get back to and more chores than one person can do."

A general agreement went around the room. Mr. Ramen waved for everyone to be quiet again. "We're not forcing you, but almost all of these people are single."

"Look," Wendell said. "We don't need a government man to tell us we're supposed to couple up. It's simple. The women looking for mates should go to the front of the room and we men will pick."

"Hell no," a female voice called from the back.

"Why do the men get to pick?" Jack said.

"Cause there's more of you women," Wendell said. "How do you wanna do it then?"

More grumbling rumbled on both sides of the room.

Jack stood up. She didn't want to be the center of attention. She didn't want to pick. "Like Wendall, I've got responsibilities." Molly stood in front of her, holding both of Jack's hands. "I'm single. I have a ranch north of town. I've got room and plenty of work to fill the day. I don't have time for courting or negotiating or anything. I've got to look after my place and my niece." She turned to face the newcomers. "I lost everyone but my niece. If you're willing to try to make a go of it, stand up."

She saw a lot of eyes on her. No one moved. The big man in the front row stood. "I am Ido. My brother, his mate, and I are looking for a home together. Will you take all of us?"

The symbols on his arms bulged as he clenched his fists. He stood taller than any man in the room. His copper eyes bore into hers. His skin was dark, nearly black, while his brother's was brown. The two of them stared as they waited on her answer. His brother's mate clung to his hand, but she stood next to them.

Molly squeezed her hand. Jack looked down at her. "Welcome," Jack said, looking back at the three. Molly stepped towards them. When they stood close enough, Jack reached out to take Ido's hand. "I'm Jack. This is Molly."

"My brother, Gwan, and his mate, Zira," Ido said. He squatted down to look at Molly. "It's very nice to meet you."

"Thank you," she said. She touched the markings on his arm. "These are a tattoo?"

"No, we are born with them. Each has a meaning."

"Will you teach me them?"

"Yes." Ido turned to Jack. "We will join you, if you will have us."

"The homestead has room for all of you," Jack said.

Ido turned to look at Gwan and Zira. When they nodded, he said, "We will join you."

"We got room if you got stuff," Molly said tracing a symbol on Ido's arm.

"Now just a moment," Mr. Ramen said. "We need to be orderly about this."

"We get what you want us to do," Jack said. Ido rose to stand next to her.

"There are procedures," Mr. Ramen said.

"No. We do not have time for your procedures," Jack said. "We followed your procedures with the sick and still we lost half our people."

"More than," called a voice from the room.

"Public safety is one thing," Jack said. "Matters of the heart? Matters of mating? You don't get to dictate how we handle those. I'm not letting the government tell me who to take to my bed or into my heart."

"We aren't..." Mr. Ramen said, stumbling over his words and stuttering to a halt.

"Good then." Jack's face felt hot. She didn't like speaking up. She didn't want to discuss her love life or lack of one. "You aren't going to figure out who you like without mingling."

Laughter met her statement. People rose and stepped across the aisle. Hands touched. People started talking.

"Crude as usual," Olivia said.

"Shouldn't you be picking your mate?" Jack asked.

"My love life is none of your business," Olivia said, but her eyes strayed to Mr. Ramen.

"You should ask him to dinner," Jack said. Tired of the BS, she turned to Ido.

"We have our belongings in the next room," Ido said. "We will gather them."

"I can help," Molly said.

"I'm certain you can," Ido said.

"Can I, Aunt Jack?" Molly asked.

"Yes," Jack said. "When they've got their stuff, take them to our hauler."

"'Kay." Molly took Ido's hand.

Jack watched her walk away. It was the first time Molly had stepped away from her. She wasn't sure who she worried about more—Molly or herself. Closing her eyes, she took a deep breath and realized this was part of the healing process. Molly would grow up. Hopefully, the fear of losing and the pain of grief would become a distant memory. Jack planned to make sure it would, but shit happened.

She walked back down the aisle. People stopped her to talk and ask questions. It started to feel like the community they used to have before. She saw a mirror of grief and pain, but she also saw the light of hope.

By the time she'd made it out the door, she thought she'd shaken hands with one member from every family. Squinting, she stepped out into the harsh light of the midday suns. Her eyes automatically moved to their hauler. Ido stood holding Molly's hand. Gwan and Zira stood next to them. Molly's hand shot up and pointed to Jack. Jack grinned and moved down the steps.

"Our things are in the back," Ido said. "We strapped them in."

"I showed 'em how," Molly said, bouncing. "They don't got much."

"Well now." Jack squatted down. "Do you remember Grandpa talking about how little we came here with?"

"You traveled for four months through space," Molly said. "When you landed you were allowed one crate for household stuff which had to fit in the hauler and a bag each."

"Yes," Jack said. "Clothing and such, we can figure out."

"Mom made…" Molly trailed off. Her chin dropped to her chest and she bit her lip.

"Your mom made beautiful clothes," Jack said. "The memories only honor them, little mite."

"'Kay. Can we go home now?"

"Sure can."

"Do you want us to ride in the back?" Gwan asked.

"It would be very hot and uncomfortable in the back," Jack said. "We use it for animals and stuff, not people. There's two bench seats in the cab."

"We've been to many settlements," Ido said, giving his brother a stern look. "Many treated us as—"

"Less than equal?" Jack finished for him.

"Yes."

"You gonna work a full day?" Jack asked.

"We have no experience with working the land," Zira said.

"You willing to learn?"

"We are," Ido said. "This planet has more open space than we've ever seen before. This is all new to us."

"We'll teach 'em, won't we?" Molly said.

"Yeah. Yeah, we will," Jack said.

Gwan helped Zira step up into the back seat of the cab. He followed her. Ido squatted down to Molly. "May I assist you?" he asked.

"Jack usually just tosses me up." Molly's green eyes sparkling with mischief.

"Imp," Jack said.

Ido glanced at her and smiled as he looked up and down her body. Heat flared in his eyes.

"You can help me this time," Molly said, drawing his attention back to her.

"Front or back?" Ido said. lifting her with ease.

"Front. I sit in the middle cause I fit."

He swung her up to the cab. When she crawled through to the center seat, she turned to show Gwan and Zira how to strap in.

"Do you require assistance?" Ido asked.

"Not hardly," Jack said. She saw disappointment flash in his eyes. "But thank you."

Ido nodded and stepped around her to climb in the other door. Jack reached up to pull herself up. She felt weary and worried. Was she ready for a new man in her life? As she settled into the seat, she realized she'd better get ready because he was here.

They rode in silence through the town.

When they'd left the town behind, the three stared out the windows.

"It's so… green," Gwan said.

"Big," Zira said. "Where does your property start?"

"Not for a while," Jack said. "The roads here are good. We make good time, but the closer we get to the ranch, the rougher the track gets. This land is unclaimed at the moment."

"Will the government bring in more humans?" Ido asked.

"Don't know," Jack said. "From the news I read, the sickness hit the human worlds hard."

"Did you not lock down?" Zira asked.

"Lock down? No. We heard about it one day, and it seemed like the deaths started right away," Jack said.

"You lost many," Ido said, reaching his arm along the back of the seat to squeeze her shoulder.

The warmth took her by surprise. Comfort. Something she hadn't felt in a long time.

"Grandma, Grandpa, Uncle Patrick, Mommy, Daddy, and my two sisters," Molly said softly.

"Were you able to perform your death rites?" Zira asked.

"Government bastards took all the bodies," Molly said.

"Molly." Jack scolded.

"Sorry." Molly leaned on Jack and curled her legs under her. Jack took her hand off the wheel momentarily to rub her arm.

"Death rites do not require bodies," Zira said. "On our world, we honor those who have gone to the afterlife."

"What's an afterlife?" Molly asked.

"It's what we believe happens to people when they die," Ido said. "They go to the ancestors."

"So Mommy and Daddy are with Grandma and Grandpa, who are with their parents and such?"

"This is what we believe," Zira said, watching Jack. "Perhaps you believe differently."

"Depends on the religion," Jack said, clearing her throat. "I like your version."

"Can I join them some day?" Molly asked.

"When you are very old," Ido said, watching Jack.

The hauler bumped over some tracks. Molly jerked in her straps. "Ow," she grumbled.

"Best sit up," Jack said.

With a sigh, Molly sat up.

"What are those?" Gwan asked, pointing out the window.

"Those are our bread and butter," Jack said.

"Bread and butter," Gwan said, not taking his eyes off the large animals.

"They're jumbos," Jack continued. "We domesticated them. We raise them. They provide milk, meat, fertilizer, fibers for spinning, and more."

"How many do you have?"

"Fifteen hundred. We've got four sectors of land. In each sector we keep a third of the jumbos. We rotate the males. When the females go into heat, the males can get territorial."

"What do you have to do with them?" Zira asked.

"The females in the north sector are birthing," Jack said. "First thing tomorrow, I'll head out to see if we have new little ones."

"They're so cute," Molly said. "The moms are super protective, so you gotta be careful."

"It takes two years for them to gestate," Jack said.

"That means to have a baby," Molly said.

Ido laughed and ruffled her hair. "You have five hundred head you need to check on for birthing. This must be difficult."

"They do pretty good." Jack slowed the hauler to cross some deep ruts. A track went off to the left and one to the right. She took the one to the right. The hauler tipped and bumped over the ruts. "We've never had to assist one of the jumbos."

"If it takes so long for them to replenish, how can you harvest them?" Gwan asked.

"Butcher," Molly said. "Gramps always did one a year for our family. All the boys get sold."

"They are large," Zira said.

"When there were all of us, we got through the meat from one in about a rotation," Jack said. "Here, a rotation is about eighteen months."

"Are your seasons equally distributed?" Ido asked.

"No. Winter lasts about two months. Summer, which we're at the start of, lasts about eight months. Towards the end of summer, everything dies. It gets so hot you have to harvest all your garden. You can plant short crops once it starts cooling off, but the last six weeks of summer it's too hot. Everything gets scorched."

"Gotta keep an eye on the sicins and their eggs," Molly said.

"Yes, that's your job," Jack said.

"Why?" Gwan asked. "What's a sicin?"

"It's a bird which lays eggs as big as your fist. If you leave the eggs with the birds, they crack them open for the fluid during the height of summer. We gather them and use them for baking and cooking," Jack said.

"Useful," Ido said. "You make use of everything then."

"Gotta," Jack said. "We're on our own out here. A trip to the store involves a long drive and getting food back from the store is not an easy task. Flour, sugar, tea, coffee, these are things we stock up on."

"We stopped at the store daily," Gwan said. "Our place was so small there was no room for a big cooler."

"We use solar and others," Jack said. "We have a cooler and a deep freeze."

"They're huge," Molly said, yawning. She leaned over on Ido and closed her eyes.

Ido put his arm around her and moved closer to ensure her comfort. His eyes darted to Jack full of concern.

"It's gonna get hot," Jack said. "Sleeping is the best way to get through the heat of the day."

"Naps in the afternoon," Ido said, watching the little girl sleep.

"Yes, for a couple hours, even when we're out in the fields. We find a shady spot and kick back for a bit."

"What should we know about the home?" Gwan asked.

Jack glanced down at Molly. She ran her hand down her arm. "When we first came ten years ago, it was Mom, Dad, my sister and me." Jack took a deep breath. These memories hurt. She didn't want to say this, talk about this. But she had to.

"The main house was built for a family of four," she said as Ido reached to rub a finger down her arm. She glanced at him, grateful for the silent support. "As we got older, other parts were added to the house. My sister wed first, so we built the wing with Molly's bedroom and... We didn't clear anything out."

"You want her to keep the memories," Zira said.

"Nothing's been normal for a while. It's just been her and me. Her mom was the household person. She liked to cook, bake, weave, sew, and do all those things. My cooking is basic. My sewing skills are nearly non-existent. She's missing out. She followed her mom everywhere."

"The females tend the homes," Gwan said, frowning.

"Some of them," Jack said. "Dad and I with—well, with my sister's husband and my intended—tended to the land and animals. I mean, my sister could do all the work in both places, but she preferred to tend the house. Their middle daughter was adept at... fuck." Jack wiped at the tears falling on her face.

"You lost much," Ido said. "Miss them all."

Jack swallowed. "Yeah. Anyways. I moved from the wing built for me and Patrick so Molly could have normal in her wing."

"How kind of you," Ido said. "To keep her as normal as possible."

"So, Gwan and Zira, you can use that wing of the house. I still have some things to pack away, but you can take it over. Part of the problem is that I don't know what to do with... Patrick's family is back in settled space. He's only got a sibling or two. They haven't expressed an interest in his things... it's mostly clothes."

"And your parents' things," Gwan said. He and Zira both reached out to her, touched her shoulder, and held it.

Jack took a deep breath and cleared her throat. "Out here, we keep everything. Shipping things in is expensive. Making is time-consuming. Clothes are clothes. I've been busy keeping up with the ranch."

"And taking care of you and Molly," Ido said. "We will only shift what you're ready to."

Nodding, Jack sniffled, and brushed away the unexpected tears. "Thanks," she said. "Tell me about you. What are you good at? What do you like to do?"

"I studied cooking," Gwan said. "Part of my education involved growing my own food. I've had no practice except small containers in a window."

"Well I can teach you how to grow stuff," Jack said. "Or you can read Mom's logs. From the time she arrived here, she documented what she grew and where. At first, the government required it. They had to show they were making a concerted effort, or the government wouldn't ship supplemental food."

"I've trained as an engineer," Zira said.

"Like mechanical things?" Jack asked.

"Some," Zira said. "What is your power source?"

"We've got wind and solar. Dad looked at water as we're near a stream. I think he had everything he needed but got sick before he finished setting it up."

"Has he been as thorough in his documentation?" Zira asked.

"Had to be." Jack slowed the hauler as she approached the river. "Here's your first lesson. This river winds by our house. In spring, there's no way across it." She stopped in the middle of the stream.

Ido, Gwan and Zira looked one way and then the other. "This rises so much," Gwan said. "What causes such an increase?"

"Way south of here, it's cold for more of the rotation, almost half," Jack said, pointing in the direction. "There's lots of mountains. It's a rough land, really rough from what I remember. Their spring is a little later than ours, but when the snow melts, it runs into all the rivers."

"Making them swell dangerously," Ido said. "But also freshening the water."

"From now until mid-fall we can play in the river, gather water from it if need be. It provides water for the jumbos and other animals. We can fish in it, but we have to be careful about which fish we take," Jack said.

"I'd very much like to learn how to fish," Gwan said, watching the river.

"You said other animals," Ido said. "Are they dangerous?"

"Some are. Some aren't. It's better to assume they are all dangerous until you know." Jack shifted the hauler back into gear. Slowly she drove out of the river and back onto the track.

"How soon will we see the house?" Gwan asked, leaning forward.

"Soon," Jack said. "Watch that way." She pointed out her window. She knew they'd see it in the distance from here. Dad used to have her watch for it as they rode to and from the town. She did the same with Molly, when she was awake.

"Oh!" Gwan and Zira both gasped.

"It's beautiful," Ido said, watching along with his brother and his mate. "Like the woman who owns it."

Jack snorted but stopped so they could get a good look. "I remember arriving here for the first time," she said. "In this hauler, with my dad driving, Mom next to him, and my sister and me in the back. We stopped about here. Mom said, 'There's where we'll put our home.' Dad grabbed her hand and kissed it. When we got to the location, it was perfect. Supplies were flown in by transports, but our belongings were in this hauler. We lived in tents and explored the valley."

"You grew up here," Ido said. "You've been very lucky."

"Yeah." Jack cleared her throat. "Yeah. Let's hope there are more to come. More people and better times."

## Chapter Two

### Learning to Love... Again

For three months, Ido watched Jack teach them about living on this land. Jack... her name was different from any of his people's names. Now he sat in the hauler watching her move through the jumbos. She touched and talked to them and they accepted her. Some of the little ones—could they be called little if they stood as tall as she did?—rushed to her. Her smile lit up each time one came near her. She rubbed and murmured and checked them. These animals rarely got injured. They grazed the land and they gave birth.

This group had been sheared two weeks ago. The fleece felt like clouds in his hands. He'd learned how to clean it, bundle it, and prepare it for shipping. He already knew how to weave, knit, and crochet. He'd been an artisan on his world.

She turned to look for him. He smiled and raised a hand so she could see he was paying attention. She smiled slowly, and at first forced. But her eyes lit up. She'd suffered such grief and loss, but she hid it from everyone. He saw it. He felt it when they walked at night or sat on the porch. He wanted to lift some of her burden, but he didn't know how.

She made her way back to him. Opening the door, he shifted to the passenger's seat. "They look really good," she said. "The new calves are growing. We have more females than males. The males are big though."

"The price for their fleece is up," Ido said. "I do not want to think of the males being butchered."

"How many live in one of the apartments on your home world?" asked Jack.

"They have three bedrooms. As many as a dozen," Ido said.

"Do they have meat daily?"

"It's too costly."

"One of the adult male jumbos will feed our household for two rotations, maybe three if it's big enough. We're five people. You do the math."

"It would feed a lot. Don't you feel attached? They rush to you. They want your attention."

"The males get more aggressive the older they get. You see the playfulness of toddlers. By the end of their first rotation, they're as big as the females. By the end of the second rotation, they are almost double the size of the females."

"Raised to feed people." Ido leaned towards her. "How do you court?"

"Court?" Jack's eyebrows bunched as she considered. "Generally, the man expresses an interest. The woman can accept his interest or not."

"Jack." Ido murmured her name. "I have an interest in kissing you."

Jack touched his cheek. Her eyes dropped to his full lips. She felt her stomach tumble into a mass of knots. She swallowed. "I accept your interest," she said, as she smiled and leaned towards him.

His lips pressed against hers, gently. He inhaled her clean, fresh scent and the musky scent of the jumbos. His hands slipped from her face to her shoulders, drawing her nearer to him, and into the strong circle of his arms. He needed her, wanted her closer to him.

Her breasts pressed against his chest. He felt her heart beating as though she ran. His tongue slipped between her lips. She opened her mouth to him, accepted him. His cock throbbed with need, but he took it slow, as he had for the last three months. His hands brushed down her back, cupped her bottom as he shifted her onto his lap.

Their lips pressed to each other's, their tongues danced, as she wrapped her arms around his neck. His hands caressed her sides, cupped her breasts.

Jack moaned, "Ido." She leaned in again for another kiss.

WHOMP!

Their faces bumped, with their noses connecting sharply.

"Ouch," she said, rubbing her nose.

"Are you all right?" Ido tipped her chin up to check for damage.

"I'm fine. What caused that?" Jack started to shift, then stopped and pressed her lips against his.

Ido held her for several more moments, before letting her withdraw. "It's probably one of the jumbos getting pushed into us," he said.

"Shit," Jack said as she looked out the window. "No, it's Rad Red."

"He's the bull?" Ido leaned towards her. He put his arm around her shoulders. She glanced at him and pointed. "He's big."

"Watch," Jack said. "There are a couple of females in heat. It's why he banged into us. He perceives us as a threat."

"Letting us know not to poach his females. Well, he's... domineering."

"Embarrassed," Jack grinned. Rad Red mounted a smaller female jumbo and proceeded to impregnate her. "He's doing his job. Without him here, the females wouldn't produce calves or milk."

"It feels like we're intruding." Ido laughed at himself.

"We're not watching Gwan and Zira," Jack said. "These are animals following their natural urges."

"Natural urges. Will you follow your natural urges?"

Heat flared in Jack's cheeks. "This is... new for me. I met Patrick when I was fourteen. He is... was my first."

"I understand." Ido watched her stumble through her explanation.

"I... He's gone. I know he's gone and I'm not," Jack said. "I've never spoken openly about these things."

"With him?" Ido hoped he didn't sound jealous. It was difficult to compete with a ghost. "With Patrick?"

"No." Jack leaned into Ido. "We dated and waited. He had experience. I didn't. He said it was up to me."

"It still is," Ido said.

"When we became intimate" —Jack leaned into him, embarrassed but needing him to understand—"he was in charge. He knew what he was doing and led." She covered her flaming cheeks.

"You've never initiated intimacy? Were you not to be mates?"

"Yes, but he called the shots in our bedroom."

"Were there things you wanted to do, to try, but he didn't allow it?"

"When I asked my sister, she said it was normal."

"Is this how you want to continue?" Ido asked, uncertain how he felt about dominating their intimacy.

Jack stared out the window. In her time with Patrick, it was the one thing they'd fought over. Sex. She wanted more. He wanted complete control in the bedroom.

Ido watched an array of emotions wash over her face. He worried he'd pushed too hard. "Jack," he said, turning her towards him.

She smiled, leaned in, and kissed him. "I'm not ready for sex with you yet, but I-I want us to be more open. I don't really know what I like."

"Perhaps we could discover it together," Ido suggested.

"We should start with more kissing." Jack grinned and pressed her lips to his.

*\*\*\**

Ido hurried around the hauler to reach up and help Jack down. His hands on her bottom, he caressed her.

"You could get in trouble for that," she said. "You know I don't need help getting out of the hauler."

"I like helping you," Ido said. "I like putting my hands on you."

Jack smiled and leaned towards him. She wrapped her arms around his neck. "I like your hands on me," she said.

He rewarded her with a kiss. He occupied her mouth while he let her slide down the length of his body. The rub of her against him nearly undid him.

"I like your body next to mine," she admitted softly against his lips.

He pressed her hips to his. "I share your feelings."

Gwan called from the house, "Supper is nearly ready!"

With a sigh, Jack stepped back, putting distance between them, but she gripped his hand with hers. "What do you plan to do tomorrow?"

"Are you going out in the fields?"

"I am, but I thought I'd take Molly. If she wants to go."

"Are you worried about her?" Ido asked, pulling her to a stop.

"She's spent a lot of time with Gwan and Zira. I don't want her to feel like I've abandoned her now you're here."

"I'd like to make it the three of us," Ido said.

"Do you mind if I leave it up to her?" Jack asked.

"Excellent idea." They stepped up on the porch. Walking into the house, the temperature dropped, and it felt soothing. "Ahh."

"It's nice, isn't it?," Jack said. "I'll meet you in the kitchen."

"Of course." Ido watched her walk to the wing of the house she shared with Molly. With five bedrooms in that wing alone, Ido found the space in the house unusual.

"Enjoy your afternoon, brother?" Gwan asked.

"Definitely," Ido said.

"Have you told her about the offer?"

"Not yet. I will soon."

"Better do it before she finds out some other way. You smell like jumbo."

"I'll go shower."

\*\*\*

Jack left her hair down. The long strands reached almost to her waist. She'd meant to lop it off, but her father had liked her hair longer. Deep male laughter echoed down the hall from the kitchen. It sounded like when Dad teased the three girls. Molly's giggles rippled down like a melody to Ido's deep harmony. Jack stopped short and caught her breath. She swallowed past the tears which threatened. She wanted to see how Molly and Ido looked when they laughed. Patrick had made it clear he only wanted the minimum number of children the government required and no more. It was another area where they hadn't agreed. The government had required three. She'd wanted more. She'd wanted the house to sing with laughter.

Had Patrick not been a good fit for her? She'd thought him her soul mate, but now with Ido... she felt so different. Different. There was the word. Having the three of them in the house reminded her of family. Someone always cooking and tending the garden. Someone working on the mechanics. Someone checking on the animals. It was a ranch, for fuck's sake. There was always work.

But before the plague, they'd just done what was needed. She'd taken for granted the laughter and spits of anger. It dawned on her that one of the hardest things since they'd died was the quiet. She and Molly didn't make a lot of noise. With three more in the house, chores got done and noise, family noise, echoed again.

She stepped into the kitchen. Molly leaned over to tease Ido with a piece of Gwan's homemade bread. Before Ido took a bite, Molly snatched it away from him. He laughed and reached for her. She giggled and pulled away. It reminded Jack of how her dad would hold Leah on his lap while he teased Molly and Bridget. She swallowed and forced a smile. "That bread looks delicious," she said.

Molly stopped laughing, bit her lip, and looked down. "Sorry," she said.

"For what?" Jack asked squatting next to her.

"I was…" Molly closed her eyes.

"Doing exactly what you used to do to Grandpa," Jack said. "It's good to remember the laughter. It's even better to have laughter in the house again, don't you think?"

Molly flung her arms around Jack's neck. "Yes," she whispered. "Grandma always scolded but she laughed as much as Grandpa did."

"They sound like lovely grandparents," Zira said. "We should have a place of honor for them."

"What's a place of honor?" Molly asked.

"Most of our homes have one," Gwan said as he placed a platter of roasted vegetables on the table. "It's a small space where we place items we want to keep to remind us of those who have passed."

"What kinds of items?" Molly asked.

"Anything which reminds you of them," Zira said.

"Like Bridget's favorite slingshot?"

"Yes," Ido reassured her. He ran a soothing hand through Jack's hair.

"Scooch over, munchkin," Jack said. "I've got to keep you and Ido apart with how much trouble you cause."

"You know who the troublemaker is," Zira said.

"Who?" Molly gnawed on her lip.

"Ido," Jack said, reaching out to hold his hand.

"Definitely," Gwan said. He placed the last of the food on the table. "Whose culture are we discussing tonight?"

"Gotta do the updates," Molly said, taking a bowl of pickles and putting a spoonful on her plate. "Then we talk about other stuff."

"Yes, ma'am," Ido laughed. From their first night here, they'd come together for supper and discussed what had got done and what still needed doing. Then they'd talk about how things were in each other's cultures.

***

"It's really coming down," Molly said as they rode in the hauler. For the last three days, rain had drenched the area. An unusual mid-summer storm battered the homestead. The creek next to the house overflowed its banks. Working over the last three months, Zira had set up the hydropower stations. It worked well.

"It sure is," Gwan said from the back seat. "Where are we headed?"

"In this southern sector, the creek twists a lot and the land can become a little marsh-like, Jack said. "Jumbos are big and can get stuck. There are some new calves in the area, so I want to check on them." She glanced at Ido. She'd meant to come on her own, but Molly had got terribly upset when she found out what Jack planned to do.

"Calves get stuck," Molly said. "Mama Jumbos are not happy to have their calves touched."

"I told you it would be fine," Jack said.

"But more people will make it safer," Ido said, reaching across to grip her shoulder.

"Might," Jack said. "Might be I'm worrying over nothing."

"What's the plan?" Gwan gripped Zira's hand.

"No plan until I see if there's a problem," Jack said. "This is probably a waste of time."

"Grandpa always said to trust your gut," Molly said. "He said your gut was never wrong."

Jack stared through the windshield of the hauler. She knew in her gut there would be a problem. It was something she couldn't let go of. The more it rained, the more she worried about this location.

"Okay, so if a calf is stuck, we have to get the calf out without upsetting the mama. Molly will stay in the hauler and watch for other jumbos."

"Especially the bulls," Molly said. "They get mean."

"But other mothers as well," Ido said. "They come to each other in times of stress."

"Someone's been reading the material on our jumbos," Jack grinned. "Zira, you've driven the hauler the most. You okay with staying in with Molly?"

"Yes." Zira nodded and leaned against Gwan.

"I know you don't like the jumbos," Jack said. "That's okay. My sister didn't either. They made her nervous."

"They are so big." Zira was relieved Jack understood.

"That leaves Gwan, Ido and me to either pick up and carry the calf out of the muck or put it in the hauler."

"Can you pick up a calf?" Ido asked.

"Depends on the size and how much mud we're talking about."

"Not the yearlings," Molly said. "They're too big."

"Got that right," Jack said. "You gonna be a rancher or something?"

"Not gonna. Am."

"If we're lucky, the crossing won't be too wide and we'll be able to cross shortly," Jack said.

"If it's too wide?" Zira asked, looking out the window at the rapidly moving water.

"We go around. Dad got swept away once. Not ever again."

"What happened?" Ido asked.

"He was on the smaller one," Molly said.

"Yes," said Jack. "Tried to cross thinking the small hauler was heavy enough to keep traction but it wasn't. Hauler got swept downstream and tipped over. Fortunately, Dad crawled out before the cab filled with water but… It was three months before he got sick."

"Lesson learned," Ido said, rubbing his hand on her neck. His warm skin against her smooth neck eased some of her grief.

"There's the crossing," Molly pointed.

"There's still dirt showing on the crossing," Ido said.

"Not much," Gwan said.

Jack lined up the hauler. All five of them were in the cab. There would be no one to get help. She watched the water. It burbled white across the dark ground looking almost like moving snow. Less than a third of the track was covered.

"What do you think?" Gwan asked, leaning forward.

"Slow and easy," Jack said. "If anyone doesn't want to ride, I can let you out, but I think walking would be more dangerous."

Ido glanced down at Molly and frowned. "Molly is too small to walk across it. Zira is probably too short as well."

"Agreed," Gwan and Zira said together.

"Just drive," Zira said. "The sooner you start, the sooner we're across."

"Onward," Jack muttered.

The earthen bridge was wide enough for the hauler as the creek got deeper here. It went under this section of ground, but with the water rising from all the rain, the creek was roaring over the top. Jack lined up the hauler, paused and looked out her window. Ido looked out his.

"You're on track over here," he said.

"Okay," she said, appreciating him checking. The tracks of the hauler moved forward as she eased along the earthen bridge.

"This would be easy enough to shore up," Zira said, watching her side of the crossing.

Gwan watched his side and squeezed her hand. "Perhaps not today."

"There's debris coming down the creek," Zira said. "Looks like a limb off a tree."

Jack glanced out the window to see the tree branch stuck in a curve. Water was gurgling over the top of it and building up behind it. "Shit," she muttered.

"Slow and steady," Ido reminded her. "Good on this side."

The sound of rushing water drowned out quiet conversation. They all spoke up to be heard.

Molly gripped Jack's leg as the water splashed up against the window. Ido took her hand in his big one. "It's all right," he reassured, warming her cold hands. "Only a bit more."

"Tree branch broke loose," Zira said.

"Almost there," Jack said. The water splashed against the side of the hauler.

Molly watched the tree branch tumble towards them. She gasped and bit her lip. Ido looked out Jack's window.

The hauler dipped a little, lurching forward as it left the earthen bridge. A loud scraping echoed through the cab as the water pushed the tree branch along the side of the hauler.

"Take it easy," Zira said softly.

"Definitely." Jack guided the hauler up the slight incline of the bank. At the top of the incline, she looked behind her to see the tree branch tumble away down the creek.

"We will probably need to take the longer route on the way back," Ido said.

Jack wiped her sweaty hands on her jean. "Yeah. You're right."

"How far away is this area?" Gwan asked.

"Do you see that stand of trees?" Jack pointed in front of them.

"It doesn't look far," Gwan snorted. "But how far is it?"

"If we don't hit any additional issues, an hour," Jack said.

"Anything can happen," Zira reminded them. "Is it the main creek which twists around?"

Putting her hands on the wheel, Jack started towards the trees. "No, it's a smaller branch of it. It twists around itself and the low banks. When it's calmer, it's a beautiful area to come and picnic."

"Jumbos," Zira said. "Off to the left."

"That's the herd," Jack said. "Maybe I worried for nothing."

"What's that?" Gwan asked.

"Crap," Molly said.

"Are there four calves there?" Gwan asked.

Jack slowed the hauler. "Bella is one of the bigger mothers. She almost always has twins. She adopts any from mothers who don't have enough milk for their own calves."

"The herd's moving towards her," Zira said. "How many babies are in this herd?"

"A lot. I'll put the hauler between Bella and the herd."

"I'll have to keep moving it to shoo them away," Zira said.

"All while avoiding us," Jack said. "Doesn't this sound fun?"

"No," all four of them said together.

Jack snorted. "Agreed." She drove the hauler until the tracks started to slip. She backed away from the marshy area.

"You've left ruts," Ido said.

"Gives a visual of what to avoid," Jack said.

"They're fillin' up with water," Molly pointed.

"We better get to work," Jack said. Gwan handed her the bright yellow rain jacket. "Zira?"

"I'm good," Zira said, crawling over the seat to get in the front. Ido, Gwan, and Jack opened the doors and stepped out into the pouring rain. Her rubber boots squished in the mud.

*OOOORRRROOOOO!!*

Jack saw Bella call to her herd. "You stay back here until I see who's stuck."

Ido nodded, allowing her to lead them.

"Why do you not object?" Gwan asked. "Do you not want to protect her?"

"I've watched her with these animals," said Ido. "She walks among them like she's one of them. The birth I watched last month, she helped the mother. I trust her and her judgment."

"Perhaps she doesn't trust you. You should have bedded her by now."

"I want more from her than that." Ido's eyes never left Jack. "Would you speak so crudely about Zira?"

Gwan turned to watch as Zira herded the other jumbos away from the marshy area. "You know I wouldn't," he said. "She's everything."

"Then let me find my way with my mate."

Jack waved them over. She pushed one of the baby jumbos away. "We need to lead the babies away," she said as Ido and Gwan approached. "Bella's caught."

"The suction from the mud's holding her?" Ido asked as he gently pushed one of the smaller jumbos towards the herd.

For several long moments, Ido and Gwan pushed the baby jumbos away from their mother, but just as they got the fourth one away, the others circled back and came back to her.

"This isn't working," Gwan complained as the babies returned to Bella for the fifth time.

"It's all right," Jack murmured to Bella, running soothing hands along her face and behind her small ears. "We'll get you out."

"What if we dig out around her feet?" Ido asked.

"Maybe," Jack said, bending down to show how as soon as the mud was moved more slid in place to take its place.

"What about tipping her over?" Gwan suggested.

"Jumbos don't do well on their sides," Jack said. "It's the position they die in."

"What if we put the little ones in the hauler?" Ido suggested. "It gets them out of the way but encourages her to try harder."

"We can start there," Jack said.

"What do you mean start there?" Gwan asked.

"If any of her legs are broken, she'll have to be put down. On her side, we can have the hauler pull her out."

"But she'll be dead," Ido said, seeing the grief on Jack's face.

"Animals die. Sometimes on the ranch, we have to put them down." Jack squelched as she walked closer to them.

Ido gripped her shoulders. She shook her head. "If I've got to put Bella down, I don't want Molly to see." Blinking rapidly, tears joined the rain on her face.

He cupped her cheek. "I'll make sure Zira takes the hauler away so she doesn't. Let's try getting the babies in the hauler first. She's a mother first."

"She's exhausted. She may not have anything left in her."

"We can try this and other things first. Gwan, go tell Zira we need the hauler backed in as close as is safe."

Jack tried to form an argument against his plan, but the thought of putting Bella down hurt too much to not try.

With her nod, Ido said, "Go, Gwan."

Gwan splashed across the field. Stopping so Zira saw him, he hopped on the step and spoke to Zira.

"How do we get them in the hauler?" Ido asked.

"They're hungry. In the box," she started to tell him.

"Grain," he said. "Gwan and I will single one out. You work on getting some of the mud off her."

He started to turn away, but Jack pulled him back. Without looking to see if anyone watched, she pulled him down. Her lips met his, brushed against his, and held for long moments.

Ido pulled her closer. "We'll save Bella if we can."

"She's the first calf Dad helped deliver," Jack said. She shivered as rain dripped under her jacket.

He leaned down for another kiss and hugged her tight to him. Gwan crossed his arms and waited. He waited for several minutes. "Perhaps you can kiss her later so we can get out of this downpour," he teased.

"No time like the present," Jack grinned. "Take the big one. She's mostly weaned."

"Gwan," Ido called as he moved to push the largest calf away from Bella. "Grab a small bucket of grain."

Gwan ran back to the hauler, splashing mud and water as he went.

Ido rubbed the big calf behind her ears. "Come on, little one." He spoke softly as he'd learned from Jack. He leaned into the calf, pushing her away from the others. Little by little he coaxed her towards the hauler. Gwan lowered the gate on the back of the hauler. He shook the bucket with grain.

Hearing food, the calf sped up, more willing to leave Bella. As soon as the first calf was in the hauler, Gwan used a rope to secure her to the side. He left the bucket of grain and grabbed another for the next calf.

Jack rubbed a hand down Bella's side. "I'm just gonna touch your leg, pretty girl," she murmured. "Take it easy."

The deep thrumming sound the jumbos made vibrated through Jack. "We're here to help, Mama," Jack said.

Out of the corner of her eye, she saw Ido get a second calf headed to Gwan. She admired how he handled the jumbos. She slid her hand down Bella's front leg, through the soft fleece, and felt the knee. It seemed undamaged. No swelling. Not dislocated. She assessed as she worked. Using her hands, she dug into the mud and shoved as hard as she could. She felt the top of the hoof and the joint. It didn't seem to be damaged. She pushed mud, getting dirty up to her upper arms. Rain washed away the mud, but this clay clung to her.

Ido pushed the third calf towards the hauler. This one doubled back three times. Gwan stepped away from the hauler to help with the stubborn calf.

Jack worked on the second front foot. Checking the knee as she worked down to the hoof. Bella swayed side to side as the third calf was pushed into the hauler.

*OOOORRRRROOOOO!!*

Jack petted her face. "You're going with them," she assured. "We just gotta get you free."

Bella lifted one of her front feet free of the mud. She pawed at the ground. Jack saw the signs of distress. "Bella, calm down. They're safe. Right there, you can see them," she crooned to the jumbo.

Bella tried to step forward, but the mud and water clung to her and sucked her feet back into the muck. Jack caressed Bella's side as she worked her way to her back leg. She felt the hock, the upper part of the leg. It wasn't swollen or damaged, but the bottom half of her legs were buried in the mud.

With deliberately slow movements, she pushed the mud down and away. Reaching into the creek she diluted the dirt and mud. Bella shivered as the water touched her. She tried to lift her leg, but it squelched and held the hoof. More water. More shoving of dirt. Jack's arms ached from pushing the soaked earth away from the jumbo.

*OOOORRRRROOOOO!!*

Jack glanced up from Bella's leg to see Ido and Gwan loading the fourth calf, tying it to the side of the hauler and giving it a small bucket of grain. Bella did not like being separated from her calves.

She moved to the other side and worked to get down to the hoof. She wanted to remove the mud as evenly as possible. She worked the mud down towards the hoof, but the clinging dirt covered a quarter of the cannon. Bella lurched forward. She wanted to be closer to her calves.

"We brought a halter," Ido said.

"Good," Jack said, digging deeper into the mud. "Put it on her and start pulling."

Ido nodded to Gwan, who moved nearer to Bella's head.

"Do you want me to work on her other leg?" Ido asked.

"No, I've got this end," Jack said. "Go tug. She wants to go. You can hear her grumbling."

"Yes," Ido said. "Be careful."

"Infinitely," Jack said. The back legs were dangerous because jumbos didn't like them being touched and they kicked out if agitated. A kick from a jumbo could kill. Keeping a hand on Bella, Jack worked her way back and forth.

Ido and Gwan got the halter on Bella's head. "We're ready to start pulling," said Gwan, as he wiped rain off his face.

Bella tried to step. Her back leg struggled to get free from the clay. She bellowed her displeasure. They tried three times as Jack cleared more and more dirt from around her.

"Try again," she called, feeling the top of her hoof.

She stepped back from the back hoof and leaned against the back of Bella. She pushed while Gwan and Ido pulled. Bella moved three of her feet, but the fourth remained stuck. Jack stepped closer and used her feet to make a channel in the clay. Water slicked down her face and into her eyes. The men pulled again. Bella stepped free of the clay, stumbled, and nearly went down. She shook her stuck foot to free it from the dirt.

Ido watched as the jumbo finally moved forward. Joy flooded him as Bella willingly followed them to the hauler. He looked over his shoulder to make sure Jack was following, but he couldn't see her.

"Take her," he said, turning back.

Zira opened the door. "LOOK." she pointed to the right of where the jumbo had been stuck.

Something yellow bobbed in the water.

Ido ran, stretching his long legs. As they'd been working with the jumbos, the water had risen over the banks further and swirled in the field. This had caught Jack and pulled her towards the fast-moving and deadly creek.

Ido jumped into thigh-high water and grabbed for the yellow rain jacket. His fingers slid over the wet material. He stepped forward, pushing the water out of his way. Plunging deeper into the swollen creek, he saw an arm move, reach up. He grabbed Jack's hand and pulled.

Her head came out of the water. She gasped for air, choking, gagging, and spluttering water out. He dragged her next to him and wrapped both arms around her. Her chest heaved as she tried to get air in and out. Her arms went around him. On her cheek there was a dark bruise, and blood mixed with the dirt and rain. He gripped her hard to his chest. He felt the pull of the current and carefully stepped back and back.

A hand gripped the back of his coat. "Hand her here," Gwan said. They lifted her over the slide of mud on the bank. Carrying her further from the edge, Gwan laid her down to return to his brother.

"I've got you," Gwan said, tugging Ido. "She's breathing."

"Good." He knelt in the dirt next to her. Rain poured down on them. The dirt and mud washed away, but her face shone white except for the black bruise on her left cheek.

"I've got a heartbeat," Gwan said, checking her neck. "She's breathing."

"Jack," Ido murmured, as he cupped her uninjured cheek.

Her hand lifted. Her eyes fluttered open and then closed. "I'm..." she choked out.

"We need to get her in the hauler," Gwan said.

Gently, careful not to jar her, Ido picked her up and carried her to the hauler. "I'm all right," she murmured as she lay against his shoulder.

Ido frowned deeply. They were so far from help. This field was even further from town than the homestead. What if him carrying her hurt her more?

"Ido," Jack said. She put her hand on his cheek so he looked at her. "I'm okay."

"Not," he growled. "You nearly drowned."

"You saved me," Jack said. She started to shiver.

"I'll keep you safe." Ido brushed his lips across her forehead.

"Give her to me," Gwan said. "You get in the cab and I'll hand her up."

Reluctantly, Ido handed Jack to Gwan. Her eyes stayed on his as he stepped into the cab. He reached down to take her from Gwan.

Molly knelt on the seat. "Aunt Jack," she said, blinking back tears.

"I'm okay," Jack said weakly.

"You gotta get out of the wet clothes," Molly said. "There's blankets in the overhead."

Zira pushed the sliding door open in the roof of the hauler. A small compartment in the top held blankets, a first aid kit, a gun, and other supplies. "Here's the blankets," she said.

"Gate," Jack said. Her teeth chattered and she felt like her whole body was in a deep freeze.

"It's up," Gwan said, stepping up into the cab. "Bella and her four calves are secure. I untied the calves so they could nurse. I gave Bella some grain as well."

"Get your raincoats off," Zira ordered as she turned in the seat. "Gwan, look away."

"G-Gotta g-get ou-out of w-wet cl-clothes," Jack said. Blue tinged her lips and fingertips.

Ido stripped off his raincoat. Mostly he was dry underneath it. He undid her jacket because her fingers were too cold to work the closure.

"Turn on the heat, Aunt Zira," Molly said. "Her boots. Get her boots off. Her feet are gonna be too cold and too wet."

Ido stripped the shirt she wore and the bra. He wrapped a blanket immediately around her top half and started on the bottom half. Jack clung to the blanket hoping for some warmth. Molly rubbed her shoulders like she'd seen her mother do to her father.

"We have to get you warm," Molly said. "We need to head for home."

"C-can't g-go," Jack stuttered.

"Water will be over the earthen bridge," Molly said, finishing for her.

"How do we get across the creek then?" Gwan asked.

Water poured out of Jack's boots as Ido tugged them off. He used one blanket to dry her as much as he could.

"Mol, app-ples," Jack stumbled over the words.

"Through the orchard," Molly said. "I know how to get there."

Wrapping a blanket around her waist, Ido reached under it to pull down her pants and underwear. The wet gear sat in a pile on one side of the back floor.

"Body heat," Molly said. "Uncle Ido, you need to hold her close."

"There's a couple more blankets," Gwan said as he knelt on the seat.

"One more," Ido said. He wanted to wrap her in a cocoon of warmth. His strong Jack. His strong mate. He stripped his shirt off and wrapped it around her. It fell to her knees which she pulled into her. Keeping the blankets around her, he pulled her onto his lap. "I've got you."

"How do we get back?" Gwan asked, taking off his own rain jacket and adding it to the pile of clothes in the back.

"I've got the heat up," Zira said.

"You have to head that way." Molly pointed away from the swampy area.

"Nice and slow," Zira said, more to herself than the others.

"I don't remember an apple orchard," Gwan said.

"They died," Molly said. "Grandma wanted apples, but they didn't work in the soil and the summer's too hot."

"How does this help us get over the creek?" Gwan hung on as the hauler swayed back and forth as they went over ruts. He reached out instinctively to hold Molly in place who still hadn't sat back down. She was watching Jack.

Jack curled into Ido, her arms reaching around him and including him in her cocoon. She felt cold to him.

"The creek is wider there," Molly said, biting her lip but turning around to get strapped in.

"Wider is not good," Gwan said.

"Yes, it is," Molly said. "Even with all this rain, it will be shallow there. It's higher up than the house."

"If you're sure," Gwan said, exchanging a worried look over Molly's head with Zira.

"There's a series of waterfalls." Molly closed her eyes as she tried to remember what her grandpa had told her. "At the highest one, the water gets really shallow. It's safe to cross there most times."

"Well, lead us there," Zira said.

***

Jack stretched as she lay in bed. She didn't remember the trip back from saving Bella and her calves. She remembered clearing off Bella's hoof and feeling a sharp pain when Bella shook her foot. Probably Bella's back hoof had caught her and thrown her towards the water and the rest.

She stared out her window. They'd got her home and in a bath. The only thing she remembered was being in Ido's arms and feeling safe for the first time in an awfully long time. Molly had guided them to exactly the right spot. It had taken most of the afternoon and it was dark by the time they got to the homestead.

A hot bath and a good night's sleep had done wonders for her. The others insisted she rest today. It was the first day in months she hadn't done chores. Ido checked on her frequently throughout the day. Molly brought her breakfast. She'd joined them for lunch and dinner. Now the house was quiet, but her mind wasn't.

Ido was not her first choice, but she hoped he'd be her best choice. She'd made an actual choice, rather than doing what everyone expected. She snorted. In a way, the community did expect them to be together, but whether they did or not, for the first time, she didn't care. She wanted to be with him.

She considered donning something different than her tank and sleep pants, but this was her. She wanted him to take her for who she was. She stepped into Molly's room to check on her. Molly lay sprawled across her bed, stuffed animals hugged close to her and books on the bedside table.

They'd lost their whole family except each other. But Molly loved these new people in their lives. She enjoyed spending time with all of them. She was ready for a new family. Not the traditional one, but maybe a better one.

Walking through the house, Jack saw how things had shifted. The house was changing. She stopped outside of Ido's door. She heard him pacing. With a light tap, she bit her lip. Did he want her? Did he love her?

His door wrenched open. "Jack." He breathed her name as though it was his lifeline.

"Ido," she said, suddenly nervous. She stepped into his arms. She wasn't sure what to say but she knew she wanted to be in his arms. He lowered his lips to hers and closed the door quietly behind her.

"I want to make love to you," he said. "I've been pacing for an hour debating whether to come to you."

She grinned. "I want to make love with you."

"Tell me what you want."

"You. I… I want us to discover each other together. Can we do that?"

"Yes. We can do whatever you want."

"I'm willing to do any position," she said, rolling her eyes. "Most positions, but I have to be honest, I like the comfort of a bed."

"You deserve every comfort," Ido said. "There can be comfort in other places. We can try those another time."

"I don't want to be ordered to do anything."

Ido backed towards his bed, his hands resting on her shoulders. "Partners don't order each other around." He gripped the bottom of her tank top. "These shirts. You need more of them. I love how you look in them."

She grinned. "Good. Ido?"

"Yes," he said, sitting on the bed and guiding her between his legs.

"Less talking, more action." She covered his mouth with hers. Their lips met and she felt all the tension leave her body.

His large hands lifted her tank, skidded across her nipples. She sighed as her gut tightened. Lifting her arms, she helped him get rid of the shirt. Wiggling her hips, she pushed off the sleep pants. He watched her move. His copper eyes darkened as he reached for her.

"Tell me when you want more of something," he said.

"I want more of your body, and less of your clothes," she said, her blue eyes sparkling.

"Easily remedied," he chuckled and moaned as her hands met his and swept up his body, taking his shirt off.

His moan seemed to reach inside her and touch a place so deep and secret. She stepped back. Swallowing, she said, "Take off your pants, please."

He pushed them off, exposing his hard arousal. He let her look, enjoyed the desire he saw on her face. Her eyes drank in his dark skin, the symbols on his skin, all of him. "You're incredible," she said, stepping into his arms. "I… I like the top."

He grinned. His eyes slipped down her body to her breasts. "We can start there," he said. "It's definitely a good place to start."

"Start?"

He leaned back on the bed, pulling her with him. She moved to connect them, but he stalled her. "I like to linger. I want to explore," he said. His mouth covered hers and lingered, with his tongue diving in and teasing hers.

Her hands cupped his face. She pressed her body to his, her breasts tight against his chest.

"You have a beautiful body," he murmured, as his lips slipped along her jaw and down her neck. "I want to draw you like this." He raised his head, looked down at her lips and her breasts. He cupped them, tugged on her nipples.

She closed her eyes and hummed her pleasure as she covered his hands. "I have really sensitive nipples," she said as he tugged again and again.

When his lips wrapped around one, she pumped her hips against his hard maleness. "I like how sensitive they are," he confessed as he moved to her other breast. He cupped them gently, almost reverently. "Shall I linger here?" He tweaked her pebbled peaks.

Her hands gripped his shoulders as her hips thrust against his bulging erection. "Yes, oh, definitely, yes." She watched as he tormented the hard tip. He alternated between soft and rough. The sight of his lips against her made her breathe faster and her stomach tighten with need.

His thumbs massaged her inner thighs. Moving from her knees up, his fingers kneaded while his lips demanded.

Holding him to her, she watched every caress and movement, each adding to her pleasure and desire. Need rose in her as his thumbs slipped higher up her legs. Her breath shuddered through her entire body as his hands moved between them. He slipped fingers into her channel. His thumb slipped over her core, pressed, and teased.

"Oh," she said, surprised. "OH!"

He bit her nipple. She moaned. Twisting her core between thumb and forefinger, he toyed with it as she thrust against him. Her fluid coated his throbbing bulge.

"I… oh…" Her words choked off as he licked his way down her belly.

He slid between her legs and tasted her. Sucking on her thigh, he kissed his way from knees upward. Her hands gripped her breasts. He watched her tug on her own nipples. His tongue slipped around her pleasure center, sucking it in, before nipping it. She arched her back and curled her toes.

"Ido!" Need filled her tone and her belly. She wanted him inside her. She wanted to ride him until… "Ooooohhhh."

He sucked her pleasure center, milking it until her body tightened around his fingers and her hands gripped her breasts. She arched and moaned as he took her over the top.

Panting, she balanced herself, hands on her thighs. "Ido. I like when you linger," she gasped out.

"I plan to linger here for a bit," he said. "Still want the top?"

"How do you want me?"

"Writhing and begging beneath me," he said with a grin. "I'll take you any way I can get you."

"Do you want me to?" she blushed.

"I want to take you over the top of a few more orgasms, and then we can talk about other things," Ido said as he nibbled on her thigh.

"A few more," Jack said. "I definitely like your plan."

He turned her over. Her head hit his pillow. Her black hair spread out beneath her. "Beautiful," he said. "Tug on these while I attend to other parts of you."

"Do you like watching me touch myself?" she asked.

"Yes, and later, I want to watch you do more than touch your breasts."

She raised her eyebrows. She liked pleasuring herself, and the thought of him watching her do it excited her. "I'd be open to that."

He grinned, his teeth flashing white. It was the last coherent thing she said for quite some time. He returned to worshiping her, driving her from satisfied to needy to begging.

Her body accepted each stroke and touch. She welcomed his skill and his patience as he explored her needs. He kept her mindlessly climaxing until she pushed him onto his back and slipped down his body.

"Jack," he growled, holding her tight against his body. "Jack, my love. Take me."

"All of you," she said, as her body rocked against his. Her channel welcomed his hard shaft as she took what she needed from him. She pushed his rigid cock deep into her core. She pushed him back on the bed, held his hands and looked deep into his copper eyes. Her mouth took his, thrust her tongue in as she demanded everything from him.

Ido called her name. "Jack. My Jack."

"Yours," she murmured as he sat up, licked around her areolas, and sucked in her nipple.

"Yes," he bellowed as she held tight. He gripped her hips, held her still as he jerked into her. Her body tightened around his, welcoming his offering of love.

***

Jack traced the design on Ido's arm. He held her tight to him, his body connected to hers, holding her against him. "It's nearly morning," he said. "Will you go back to your room?"

"Do you want me to?"

"I want to spend the next month right where I am." He nibbled on her ear.

"Month? Oh… I …" Jack started to pull away.

"What's wrong?" He held her close.

"I'm not on anything. I stopped… I mean, after all of them died."

"I am. You're safe from pregnancy."

Sagging in relief, she settled back against him. "It's not that I don't want a child."

"I'm not ready for a child," he said. "I want you. I want you in my bed and in my heart. For now, is that enough?"

"It is."

"In our society, the male takes care of this aspect. When I'm ready for a child, I let you know and then you tell me if you are or aren't."

"I like that."

"Good." He tucked her under his chin. "I have something I want to tell you. Please do not—"

"Just tell me," she said, turning into his arms. "I want us to be open."

"I've been contacted by our government. They want me to come back and be the head of the arts council."

"Oh. Do you want to go back there? Is that what you did before you came out here?"

"I was an artist." He brushed the hair back from her face. Wrapping a strand around his finger, he frowned.

"You came because of Zira and Gwan?"

"Yes. For them to be together. They were not allowed to remain on our world, but they couldn't get into the program."

"Because they were already mates," Jack said. "Do you regret making the sacrifice for them?"

"I stopped having regrets the moment you stood up and spoke," he said. "Your bravery and forthrightness appealed to me. How you cared for Molly, the animals, the land—all of it impressed me."

"I won't hold you here if you want to return. Don't worry, Gwan and Zira can stay."

"I can't go. It would rip out my heart to leave you. It would destroy my soul to leave you and Molly."

"Why?" Jack asked, frowning.

"You're my mate. I love you."

"I don't want to hold you here."

"You aren't. I can do my art here. I need some tools and supplies, but when we have time, we'll discuss it."

She hugged him to her. She held tight as emotions overwhelmed her. "I love you," she said softly. "I realized some time ago I loved you, but I was afraid of losing all of you."

"I know," he said.

"Then I got swept away. I could have died, and you never would have known how I really felt about you. I didn't want that."

"Will we share a room?"

"Yes, as soon as Molly is comfortable with the idea."

***

"Why are we cleaning out this space?" Molly asked as she stood inside the door.

"Not cleaning out," Jack said. "Do you remember how Grandpa spent his spare time here?"

"Yeah. He liked to carve and build stuff."

"Yes, he did." Jack lifted her and set her on the workbench. "We had a family."

"You know I'm good with you and Uncle Ido," Molly said. "We don't gotta talk about it."

"This is different," Jack said, closing her eyes. "We've got a lot of memories around us from our first family."

"Grandpa made my bed. He made most of the furniture in the house."

"I want to start making memories with our new family."

"Do you want to clear this out?" Molly picked up one of the tools hanging on the wall.

"No, I want to let Ido use it. What do you think?"

"Does he carve and stuff?"

Jack laughed. "I'm not sure, but back on his planet he was a big deal artist."

"I think Grandpa would like that," Molly said. "Even if he didn't like his baby girl being with anybody."

Jack hugged Molly. "Do you want to go get Ido?"

"Yup," Molly pushed Jack back so she could jump down.

"Daddy, I think you'd like him," she whispered.

"What's the problem?" Ido asked as Molly dragged him to the back of one of the barns. "Where are you taking me, little one?"

"Aunt Jack's got a surprise for you," Molly said.

They stepped through the door. Jack felt a flutter of need rip through her gut. It had been a week since they'd become lovers. They'd moved him into her room four days ago. This was one more step in integrating him into their lives.

"Hi." She smiled at his frown of confusion.

"We wanna give you this," Molly said.

"Give me what?" Ido said.

"Grandpa's workroom. Right, Aunt Jack?"

"Yes." Jack reached for him. "Dad used this space for his projects. He built furniture, made carvings, and putzed around in here. I don't know what type of art you do, but if this will help you do art here, this space and his tools are yours."

Ido pulled her close as his copper eyes brightened. "You two," he said. "This is a wonderful surprise."

"You might hafta make a crib though," Molly said.

"Crib?" Jack frowned.

"Gwan and Zira will need it. She's been sick in the mornings like Mama was. Her belly's getting bigger too."

"It's why they wanted in the program," Jack said.

"It is," Ido said. "Thank the stars in the heavens."

## Chapter Three

### A New Family

Jack watched the suns dip lower in the sky. She heard Ido and Molly clearing the table. Across the homestead, she saw the light in the new buildings. The last six months had been eventful.

Leaning against the porch post, she considered where she'd been a year ago. Alone, raising Molly on her own. Now she looked around and people were there. Family. Ido's family. So many siblings had arrived over the last month, she still didn't know all their names. Zira's family. Friends and others had arrived, easing the crowding even slightly on their home world.

Strong dark arms snaked around her, pulling her back against a hard-muscled body.

"Ido." She murmured his name and tipped her head up for his kiss.

His lips lingered, teased, and promised in a gentle caress. "Jack," he whispered. The timber of his voice vibrated through her, creating need and desire she knew he'd satisfy as soon as they were alone.

By day, she worked. Now she had people around her all the time. Hands to help with the chores. She spent more time teaching than ranching. The garden had expanded to feed the more than fifty people now living on the ranch.

She'd badgered the government until they brought supplies for them to build three more houses and a complex of smaller apartments.

"What do you think of your empire?" Ido teased.

"Our empire," she said. "Most of these people are related to you."

"Some. More will come to learn."

"Yes, we still have room. It feels good."

"Do you think Molly's all right with the plaque?"

"Do you mean the beautiful sculpture you built to remember everyone we lost?" Jack said turning into his arms. At the end of the apartment building, Ido had carved out of wood each of the people they had lost. It was a tableau of life on the ranch.

"She cried so hard," Ido said, smoothing the hair back from her face.

"It's beautiful," Jack said. "You captured so much more than the pictures of them."

A baby cried inside the house. Jack sighed hearing it, and hearing Molly coo to the baby as Zira let her burp her. Two weeks ago, new life had come into their household.

"Are you ready for a child?" Ido asked.

"No, I want more of you," Jack said. "It's good to hear new life. Colleen loved her children. She always wanted a large family and was working her way towards having one. I miss the sounds of them."

"But not the smell," Ido teased.

"No one wants to know what comes out of an infant."

Ido held her close. They watched the suns slip lower. Peace settled around them.

Molly stepped out the door and smiled to see them holding each other. "I finished my chores," she said. "Are you two gonna hang out here or come in to play some board games?"

"Isn't it your bedtime?" Jack teased. "I swear it's past your bedtime."

"I'm nine," Molly declared, standing with her hands on her hips.

Ido pulled her close to include her in their hug. "We can do board games. After we watch the sunset."

The sky lit up with streaks of red, orange, pink and yellow as the first sun slipped beneath the horizon and the second followed.

"You know, if this were one of Grandpa's cowboy movies, somebody would be riding off into that sunset," Molly said. She tugged Ido down to kiss his cheek. "I hope you never ride off."

"I won't," Ido said.

"Good," Molly said. "I'm picking the first game."

"There's too much here which needs tendin' ma'am," Ido said, before his lips covered Jack's in a gentle caress. Her pleased sigh whispered as the last of the suns' rays flared across the deep purple sky.

The End

# The Wyoming Way
## Nancy Golinski

## Late Summer 2017

It was hotter than normal for August, and they'd been at it all day long. Every cowboy was dripping with sweat, and there was a thin layer of dirt and dust on their faces. It was the last cattle run of the year and by far the biggest load being shipped. It required the entire team to get it done.

Spencer Campbell shut the gate and watched the steer pass through the chute, up the ramp, and into the truck. Then he leaned against the post and wiped his face with a rag. They were finally done, and he waved at the ranch hands who were getting ready to leave.

His brother, Paul, walked over and grinned at him. "We should clean up and go celebrate in town."

Spence sighed. "I can't. Charlotte has a dinner planned tonight with the mayor and his wife."

Paul made a face. "Jesus, isn't that the fourth social event you've done this week?"

Spence grabbed the reins of his horse and started leading the mare toward the trailer. "What can I say? My wife likes to entertain."

"There's an understatement," Paul replied drily. Then he changed the subject, "Did you hear Jess Thomas is moving back home?"

Spence paused. "I've heard that rumor a hundred times before. I'll believe it when I see it."

"It's true. I got it from Doc Adams himself. She's moving home to help him with his clinic. She's also going to try to get the Thomas ranch cleaned up and running again."

Jessica Thomas had moved away years ago to attend a veterinary school in Missouri. She never came back, and her brother had let their beautiful ranch fall apart in her absence.

The Thomas ranch was adjacent to the Campbell ranch, and the four of them had grown up together. Jess was six years his junior, and Spence remembered her being a scrawny kid but mouthy as hell. She was also an excellent rider and often challenged him to races. The thought made Spence smile.

"I hope it's true," he said. "Poor Joey has never been the same since his stint with the Marines. He's really starting to lose it. Maybe Jess can help him." With that, he loaded his horse and headed home.

***

Jess led Titus up the ramp and into the horse trailer. He was an Egyptian Arabian chestnut, and he had the high-strung personality to match. She had rescued him two years ago from a farm in southern Missouri. Back then he'd looked nothing like the beautiful and noble beast he would become. She had nurtured his emaciated body back to health, and now she loved that horse with all her heart.

Once the trailer was shut and locked, she opened the door to her pickup and let her mutt jump in. Scout immediately tried to commandeer the front seat, but one look from Jess, and he hopped to the back. He had been found on the same property as Titus, and she had rescued him at the same time. Theirs was more of a love/hate relationship. That meant Scout liked to push his boundaries, and he hated when she reprimanded him.

Jess gave the house one last look before pulling out onto the street. It was a fifteen-hour drive to Wyoming, and she was getting an early start. She had planned her route ahead of time with one overnight stop along the way. That way she could safely exercise Titus and give herself a break in the process.

While she drove, she thought about her life. After high school, she'd left Wyoming to pursue her dream of becoming a veterinarian. She'd worked hard to become a large animal specialist, and she'd spent the last fourteen years honing her skills and saving up money. Her goal was to return home and open a horse rescue on the family ranch. Jess shared ownership of the property with her brother, Joey. He had also left home at a young age and joined the Marines. Their father was still alive at the time, and the drunkard had had little to do with either child. The best he had done was put a roof over their heads, and the two had fled home as soon as possible. But then the old man had died and left the property to them. Joey had returned and tried to make a go of it, but Jess knew he was barely hanging on. The military had somehow damaged Joey, and he wasn't the carefree and sweet big brother she remembered.

For one thing, he didn't want any outside help. Jess often paid cowboys to sneak on their ranch and take care of pressing needs. Sometimes Joey would catch them in the act, and he would throw a fit. The only help he allowed was from her, and she had been paying all of the bills and taxes for years. That had strapped her financially, but she'd still managed to put away a tiny nest egg. It, along with the Bureau of Land Management grant she was hoping to receive, would get her rescue farm up and running.

*** 

As Jess drove into Wyoming the next day, she immediately noticed the deep blue sky and vastness of the land around her. It was such a difference from the traffic and suburbs of Missouri. She rolled down her window and breathed in the fresh air. God, how she had missed this part of the world.

She turned down the long, rambling entrance to the Thomas ranch four hours later. She noticed the overhead sign was broken, and they needed to do a burning to clear some of the brush. When she finally pulled up in front of the house, she sighed. It was more run down than she'd expected. But Jess wasn't one to shy away from a difficult task. She got out of her truck and went to unload Titus.

Joey came out from the back porch door. "So glad you're home, sis," was all he said. They hugged, and then she immediately got to work.

### Early Fall 2017

The Campbells were having Sunday family dinner at their dad's house. His legal name was Paul Sr., but everyone called him Soup. He was a likeable guy who'd inherited the land from his own father years ago. Soup had married the love of his life, Mary, and they'd had two boys together. Both sons had got married, built homes on the vast property, and now worked the land. Paul and his wife, Kate, were never able to have children, but Spence and Charlotte had two daughters. The girls were now away at college.

The family had just finished eating and were discussing the local news. Lately the topic of interest was Jess Thomas. She had only been home a month, but her house and barn were already spruced up.

"She was always a hardworking girl," said Soup. "Sweet too. She would come sit with me and discuss horses for hours. That girl loved all animals and especially horses from the time she was old enough to ride them."

Charlotte made a face. "She sounds like your typical Wyoming girl."

Mary teased. "She was. Your husband took quite a shine to her when they were younger."

Spence looked surprised. "Now why would you say that? I seem to remember us arguing all the time."

"That's why," replied his smug mother.

"Well, she's certainly doing wonders to the Thomas ranch. I hear she's even motivated Joey to get off his butt and help," said Paul.

"Good," commented Soup. "There's some ranch work that women aren't strong enough to do on their own."

Kate laughed. "Sexist, much?" Then she added, "I saw Doc Adams at the grocery store, and he said she is phenomenal with the animals. He is thrilled to have her."

"We'll have to have her over then, so I can meet her," said Charlotte. "I'll invite her to our barbecue next weekend." She had a fake smile on her face and didn't notice the rest of the family rolling their eyes.

*** 

There was a BLM meeting the following afternoon. Most of the ranchers in the area were part of the BLM's Wild Horse Program. They allowed wild horses to roam freely on their land and did not put up fences in certain areas. In this way, the horses could seek out water, food, and shelter as needed. The volunteer group also worked to keep the animals healthy and not over-populated. They were meeting now to discuss the census that would begin that very afternoon.

Jess had joined the group as soon as she got back. She loved horses, and her skills as a vet would come in handy. Plus, it looked really good on paper, particularly now, when she was waiting on the BLM grant.

The room was already packed with testosterone-laden cowboys when she arrived. Jess walked in with her head held high and the confidence of someone who had grown up with all these boys. She secretly laughed as conversation stopped in the room. They were staring at her like they had never seen a woman before.

Spence was sitting in the corner and was surprised to feel himself getting angry. The men were acting like a bunch of lovesick calves, and the need to protect her surged inside of him. He and Paul waved, and she worked her way over to their side of the room. While she walked, Spence had time to take in her figure.

Jessica Thomas had grown up. The scrawny stick of a child he remembered had been replaced by a pretty woman with curves in all the right places. She was of average height, and her wavy brown hair was pulled back in a ponytail tucked under a baseball cap. Her eyes were large, blue, and expressive.

As she walked, one of the younger cowboys called out to her. "Darling, are you sure you're in the right place? The secretaries are meeting down the hall."

Jess stopped and eyed up the man with amusement. Then she replied loud enough for everyone to hear, "Yah, I'm sure. I just castrated three bulls this morning. Want to be the fourth?"

That brought a chuckle from the room, and the red-faced man shook his head before walking away. She continued on and gave both Spence and Paul a hug when she reached them.

"Hi. I've been meaning to come visit, but I've been so busy." She grinned, "It's good to see you both. Neither of you has changed a bit."

Paul laughed and patted his belly. "You're too kind, Jess."

Spence laughed as well. "You haven't changed either. Still as mouthy as ever, eh Sassy?"

She grinned. It was the nickname he'd given her when they were kids.

The meeting started and they took their seats. The discussion was short and to the point. Before they knew it, they were saddled up and riding out to find the wild horses. Jess rode with the Campbells and filled them in on the last fourteen years of her life.

"I always wanted to come back. I just needed to get some money saved and pay off my student loans."

As she continued to chat, she noticed Paul was contributing to the conversation while Spence remained quiet. Some things never changed.

Eventually the group thinned out even more, and Jess found herself riding alone with Spence. Normally she would be content to ride in silence, but she was curious about his life and so commented, "I heard you got married and had two girls. I bet you make a great father."

Spence's face lit up. He told her about his daughters, and she could hear the love in his voice. He was clearly a proud papa, but then a shadow crossed his face as he told her they had moved away to college.

She tried to ease his pain. "Well, at least you can FaceTime with them and call whenever you want. I'm sure they'll be home for the holidays too."

He simply grunted, and they rode on in silence.

Jess idly wondered why he hadn't mentioned his wife. She didn't have time to think about it, though, as they encountered a herd of wild horses around the next bend. They immediately got to work.

Their goal was to obtain census data, but Jess noted one stallion looking to be in pain. She had Banamine on hand and silently motioned to Spence as she pulled the needle out and got it ready. He knew exactly what she planned to do and got in position to steer the horse her way. It took several tries, but they worked well as a team. On the third attempt, Jess landed the shot, and the two grinned at each other.

Two hours later the census data was complete and they were heading back. This time Spence rode slightly ahead, which gave Jess a chance to check out his body. He looked good in his faded jeans. He had always been handsome, but age had sharpened the distinctive Campbell dimples and brown eyes. The scruff on his face made him sexy as hell. His cowboy hat was tipped low to keep out the sun, and all Jess could think of was the Marlboro Man. She chuckled to herself.

They got back to where the trailers were parked, and Spence helped her load Titus.

"He's a fiery one, isn't he?"

She grinned. "I wouldn't have it any other way." Then she added, "It was so good catching up with you and Paul. I'll see you again on Saturday. Your wife invited me to the barbecue."

At the mention of Charlotte's name, Spence made a face, but Jess didn't notice. She got in her truck and drove away.

***

Saturday afternoon found Jess getting ready for the barbecue. She was putting the finishing touches on her makeup when Joey walked in.

"You sure you don't want to come with me? She invited us both."

Joey shook his head. "No way. That woman is crazy. I swear she tried to kill me with an appetizer once. She said it didn't have flour in it, but I still ended up in the hospital."

Both of them had inherited celiac disease.

"Oh, Joey. I'm sure she didn't realize. You know most people have no clue about gluten."

He shook his head. "I'm telling you. There's something wrong with her."

Jess sighed as she grabbed the fruit kabobs and dip out of the fridge. When her brother got one of his crazy ideas in his head, there was no changing his mind.

She headed out and arrived at Spence and Charlotte's house twenty minutes later. She frowned as she parked the car. Nobody was outside, and it was a beautiful day. If it weren't for all the cars, she would have no idea there was a party going on.

She headed to the front door and rang the bell. It was opened by a haughty-looking woman dressed in a sheath dress, pearls, and formal-looking heels. Jess introduced herself to the woman, who turned out to be Charlotte, and was quickly ushered into the house.

Jess looked around and saw the place was packed with fancy-looking guests. She looked down at her own sundress and short boots and felt woefully underdressed. It would appear the Campbells had gone high-class on her. She wondered what the heck had happened to the backyard Wyoming barbecues she remembered from her childhood.

She was never one to worry about her looks, though, and quickly shrugged it off. She smiled at Charlotte and handed her the kabobs. The woman looked stunned and almost miffed at the offering. The whole thing was getting downright funny, but then Jess was distracted when she heard her name called.

"Little Jessie Thomas. How are you, girl?"

It was Soup, and he was dressed in jeans and a plaid button-down shirt. She immediately felt at ease as he engulfed her in a bear hug. She noticed Paul and Spence in a corner of the room talking to a group of men. Paul smiled and waved at her, and Spence gave her a nod before resuming his conversation.

The evening was going well, and Jess was catching up with many of the locals she hadn't seen in years. She had already reconnected with Paul's wife, Kate, and the two had agreed to meet for lunch the following week.

Jess was drawing the eye of many a man in the room, but she didn't notice. What she did notice was how Spence and Charlotte barely said two words to each other. They appeared to have some tension between them, and her heart went out to her old friend.

She eyed the food on the buffet table but chose not to eat anything. Joey's words were still ringing in her head. Better to be safe than sorry when it came to gluten. She noticed her fruit kabobs did not make an appearance. The whole party was starting to feel a bit too over-the-top, but then she got an emergency call. A mare was having difficulty delivering her foal. Jess gratefully hung up and apologized to Charlotte before making her exit.

As she drove away, she shook her head. That was clearly not her scene, and she was happy to be out. Joey was right. There was something wrong with that Charlotte chick. She said a silent prayer for Spence and drove on.

***

When the party ended, Spence helped Charlotte clean up. She was ranting about the various guests, and he was barely listening, until she started in on Jess.

"That girl had some nerve bringing a dish."

Spence sighed. "That's how it's done around here, and you know it. You're the one that has to have these fancy parties."

"Well, I need more than cornhole and steaks on the grill."

"I know. You have made that very clear over the years."

They finished cleaning, and he headed out to the barn to check on the horses. It was something he did more often now, just to get away from his wife.

Spence sighed and thought back to the day he met Charlotte in college. She had been lively, fun, and outspoken, and he had admired her confidence. They dated, ended up pregnant, and tied the knot in under a year. She was from Boston and hated Wyoming on sight. Over the years she'd slowly changed their house, daughters, and social events to suit her needs. Spence went along with it to keep her happy. He took his marriage vows seriously, but it was getting harder and harder to please his wife. Now with the girls out of the house, he was starting to push back a little, which resulted in even more fights.

Spence's mind wandered to Jess as he brushed his horse. She'd looked so darn pretty in that little dress and boots. His mom was right, he'd had one serious crush on her back in the day. But she was so young then, and his best friend's sister to boot, so he had only admired her from afar.

Now she was all grown up, and he couldn't be prouder of the woman she'd become.

## Late Fall 2017

Over the next two months, Jess settled back in her old home nicely. She recruited the help of all the ranchers she knew to get the Thomas property into shape. It was what Wyoming neighbors did for each other, and most weekends there was a crew of volunteers at her disposal. Jess in turn paid it forward by assisting them whenever she could. That usually involved pro bono veterinary work on their livestock. She didn't mind. It was a wonderful system, and it was even helping to pull Joey out of his funk. By Christmastime, he was joking around and acting like his old self.

Jess noticed Spence was often by her side when work needed to be done. They talked about ranch stuff, horses, cattle, and basically anything related to the cowboy way of life. She assumed he was trying to protect her, and one day she couldn't resist commenting, "I can take care of myself, you know. I'm not afraid of these rough and tumble cowboys, and you don't always have to ride with me."

Spence laughed. "Of course I know that." He waved his hand at the ranchers helping that day. "You could floor any one of these yahoos in a heartbeat. I just like riding with you. You're easy to talk to, Sass."

Now Jess was grinning. "When we were younger, you wouldn't have said that. Back then we argued more than we talked."

He nodded. "That's because you were a little know-it-all. Plus, you thought you were a better rider than me, and we both know that's not true."

He was teasing, but she couldn't help kicking up Titus and galloping away. She called over her shoulder, "That's because I *was* a better rider. Still am."

Spence chuckled before spurring his own horse on. "We'll see about that," he yelled. They tore across the countryside and finally stopped when they reached a herd of cattle drinking water at a creek.

Jess sighed happily. "I forgot how much I missed this country. So vast. So open. It makes you realize how precious life is, you know?"

Spence nodded. He felt the same way.

\*\*\*

Later on, Jess was back in the barn brushing Titus. She thought about Spence and how easy he was to talk to. She wished he was still single, as she could easily fall for a man like him. She just didn't get the whole Charlotte thing.

Jess had gotten the whole story from Kate a month ago over lunch. Apparently Spence and Charlotte had had a whirlwind college romance that ended with a baby girl on the way, and two shell-shocked kids trying to do the right thing. They'd somehow made it work, but now they fought all the time and had nothing in common except the two daughters.

Kate had further confided that the Campbells were worried a divorce was on the horizon, as it could mean the loss of valuable land. Nobody liked Charlotte, and they were afraid she would take Spence to the cleaners in a divorce settlement.

Once again, Jess felt badly for Spence. She was also worried, as she knew there was a growing attraction between the two of them. She sometimes caught him checking out her figure, and their conversations while riding were becoming more and more personal.

Jess finished grooming Titus and got ready to call it a night. She vowed in that moment to keep her distance from Spence. She was deeply attracted to him, but she was no homewrecker. With that thought, she headed into the house.

Meanwhile, the man in question was driving back to his own ranch. He reflected on the conversation he'd had with Jess earlier and realized he was becoming more and more attracted to her. She was sexy as hell, and they had so much in common. She filled a void inside him that had been empty for way too long.

Spence rubbed his face as he realized he was in over his head. He was in danger of overstepping his marriage vows, and he didn't want to do that. He knew he needed to keep his distance from Jess. Marriage was sacred, and he was no damn cheater. He pulled into the lane that led to his house and clenched his jaw. In that moment he vowed to stay away.

## Early Winter 2017

It worked for a while. The months rolled by, and the cold kept most ranchers inside or working on their own land. Jess didn't see Spence at all during this time, but she thought about him often.

She was starting to have issues at home with Joey. He had PTSD, and sometimes his perceptions were completely irrational. When that happened, he would fly off the handle about stupid things and then disappear for a few days. Normally Jess could handle it, but then she got a letter from the BLM saying her grant application had been denied. It was a major blow, and she found herself resenting her brother more and more. She was the one doing all the work and paying all the bills. She was also missing her friends from Missouri, which in turn made her miss Spence even more, as he was her only true friend in Wyoming.

Then one Friday morning, everything changed. The weather bureau started issuing warnings about an epic storm. It was expected to sweep down from the north and dump a lot of snow on Wyoming.

The cowboys immediately sprang into action. They had to move the cattle out of danger zones and into areas that would provide some form of shelter. They also needed to put down plenty of hay and make sure their tank heaters were working, so the water supply wouldn't freeze. It was a hectic time, and as soon as a rancher had his own cattle safely in place, they moved on to help their neighbors.

The Thomas ranch didn't have any livestock, so Jess was able to help the Campbells right away. She drove her trailer over and parked it in Soup's driveway before joining the ranch hands out on the land. The Campbells owned a lot of livestock, and it took a long time to move them all to safe areas. By the time they were done, the wind was really howling, and the snow was coming down at a steady pace.

Jess wanted to go after the wild horses next, but the men refused to help. Visibility was getting difficult, and it would be easy to get lost out on the range. They also needed to drive their trailers safely home before the roads became impassable. Drifting snow was a very real problem in Wyoming, and drifts could easily get as high as eight feet.

Jess refused to give up. She went and grabbed a GPS out of her truck and a high-powered flashlight. She knew where there was a good copse of trees on the Campbell property. It would provide the horses with a natural windbreak, and they would instinctively go there to weather out the storm.

Spence watched her with growing alarm as she walked back to Titus and put her left foot in the stirrup. As she went to swing up, he grabbed her arm and stopped her.

"Just where in the hell do you think you're going?"

She glared at him. "I'm going after the wild horses. They'll never survive this storm with just a tree windbreak."

"No way. I know you love animals, Sassy, but it's too dangerous."

She shirked away from his hand and mounted her horse. "There's still time. I can drive them down in under an hour and before it gets dark."

He sighed. "You're better off herding them to the old Jamison homestead. The barn there is still in decent shape, and it's a lot closer."

She nodded. "Good idea. How close is that to the tree copse?"

He scowled at her. There was no way he was letting her go alone. "You'll never find it on your own, especially in this weather. I'm coming." Spence ran over to tell Paul where they were going and then mounted his own horse, Cinders. "Watch your footing," was all he said, and then they were heading out.

It took twenty minutes to find the tree copse. Fortunately, the wild horses were already huddled there. The wind had shifted, and the snow was now coming down hard.

Jess and Spence assessed the situation. With just the two of them, they would need to get the dominant mare moving in the right direction. If they succeeded with that, the rest of the herd would follow. Spence would take the lead, as he knew the way to the old homestead. Jess would bring up the rear and make sure there were no stragglers. Spence didn't like it, as she would be out of his sight, but he had no choice. He kept telling himself what a good rider she was, and that was all he could do.

Their plan worked. The horses didn't want to leave the natural shelter, but with some loud noises and quick checks, they were able to get them moving. Spence led the way with the dominant mare by his side. He would occasionally hear Jess making noises behind him, presumable to bring a stray runner back into the fold. It seemed like forever, but they finally made it to the old homestead.

Spence was relieved to see the barn was still standing. The leeward side had a gaping hole in the wall, but the horses would still be protected. They got them in and placed their own horses in a separate area of the barn. Then they headed to the house to see what supplies they could find.

There wasn't much. They found some old moth-bitten blankets on a shelf, and a rusty bucket under the sink, but there was no running water. Jess immediately grabbed the blankets and explained she was heading back out to dry their horses.

Spence shook his head. Of course she would think of the animals first. He came with her, and they worked quietly to bed Titus and

Cinders down. The wild horses were nervously snorting and stomping the ground, but they would eventually settle in. Jess checked her pockets to see if she had any food. All she came up with was a handful of peppermints. She used those as treats for the two domesticated horses. Then she handed one to Spence and smiled.

He took it and grinned back at her. "Not much of a dinner, but under the circumstances, it will have to do."

They headed back to the house in a blinding snow and knew they weren't getting out of there that night. They looked at the fireplace in the corner of the room. Even if the chimney was clear, which they doubted, there was nothing there to start a fire. Daylight was fading fast, and they realized they were both soaking wet. Jess was also shivering.

"We're going to have to get out of these wet clothes," she said. They headed to the bedrooms and found one bed with dusty sheets still on it along with a blanket. They pulled them off. Spence walked into another room, and then they both quickly stripped down and wrapped themselves in the sheets. They hung their clothes in the bathroom before crawling into the bed and pulling the blanket over them. It was the only way they were going to stay warm that night, and both instinctively knew that.

Spence pulled Jess up against his body and tucked the blanket around her.

"I ought to throttle you for dragging us out in the storm, but I'm glad we did. Those horses would never have survived otherwise."

Jess smiled in the dark. "I know. I'm sorry. I just couldn't bear the thought of them lost in the snow. I know we didn't get them all, but at least we saved some."

They could hear the wind howling around them.

"I just hope the roof holds up on this old house," said Spence. Otherwise, we'll be sleeping out in the barn with the animals."

"We used to do that a lot when we were kids, remember?" sighed Jess.

He grinned. "I do remember."

She rolled over so she was facing him, and she could hear his heart beating in his chest. Then she felt his hand gently stroking her hair and face. He tilted her head up and slowly moved his lips down over hers in a whisper of a kiss.

It was a surreal moment, and they both knew it was wrong. Somehow the howling wind, the precarious rescue mission, and their history all clashed together into a sexually charged intensity. The kiss deepened, and now they were devouring each other. Jess could faintly hear a voice in the back of her head telling her to stop, but a deep yearning for Spence drove her on. He in turn was hearing his own conscience speak, but his loneliness and need for her were far greater. They clung to each other like two lost souls.

Then Spence's hands were down between her legs. He could feel her wetness there, and his own growing arousal was pushed hard against her thigh. He didn't say a word, but he did hesitate, and she could tell he was seeking permission to enter. She answered by wrapping her legs tightly around his back.

That's all Spence needed. He plunged into her body with an unchecked passion. Jess held on to his shoulders, and she raised her pelvis to meet his on each thrust. It was by far the wildest sex she'd ever had, and when she felt her climax building, she couldn't hold back. She howled as she came, and she heard Spence making his own primal noises as he did the same.

When they were done, they lay quietly in each other's arms and tried to steady their breathing. Neither one could find the words to say anything, and they were both exhausted. They fell asleep like that with the wind howling and ice pellets hitting the window.

The next morning Jess woke to an empty room. It was quiet, which told her the storm was over. She got up and went to get her clothes. It took forever to put them on, as they were still soaked and stiff from the cold. As she dressed, she thought about the previous night with chagrin.

She knew Spence's character enough to know this wasn't who he was. It wasn't in her nature either. Now that reality had sunk in, she wondered how Spence was feeling. She guessed guilty as hell, which summed up her own emotions.

She found him in the barn. The storm had ended, and the wild horses had already been set free. Spence had tacked up his horse and was just putting the saddle on Titus. He glanced at her when she walked in but then turned his attention back to the saddle.

"How are you?" she quietly asked.

He just grunted. When he was finished with the saddle, he handed her the reins. "We should get back."

Jess took the reins and sighed. "That's it? You don't want to talk about last night?"

He looked at her, and there was anger in his eyes. "Last night was a huge mistake."

She nodded. "Of course it was. I think we just got caught up in the moment. I'm really sorry, Spence."

He mounted Titus. "Sorry doesn't even begin to cut it. I have a wife and kids, and I take my marriage very seriously. I should never have followed you after those damn horses. You may live the free and easy life, but I do not." With that, he turned his horse and rode away.

Jess stared after him in shock. There were tears in her eyes as she mounted her own horse and followed. She kept a good distance behind and didn't say a word the whole way back. When they finally reached the trailers, she quickly loaded Titus and drove off.

Back at her own barn, Jess got Titus fed and situated. Her tears were flowing freely now as she brushed the chestnut and put a blanket over him. She had never been a one-night stand girl in her life, but that's how Spence was making her feel. She sobbed even harder when she realized she was actually in love with the bastard. Not that it mattered. When she finally regained composure, she went into the house, called the BLM, and quit. She needed to be certain she never ran into that damn cowboy again.

***

Spence agonized over what had happened for a week. He knew he needed to talk to Charlotte and confess, but she was in Boston visiting relatives. That was actually a relief, as it gave him time to think. He realized he was angry with himself and had taken it out on Jess. That wasn't fair, and he planned to apologize to her at the next BLM meeting. When she didn't show up, he decided to drive over to the Thomas ranch. But then an emergency happened with the livestock. When that was resolved, he found out that his mom had gone into the hospital for heart tests. Then his girls came home for the holidays. Before he knew it, a whole month had gone by, and he hadn't talked to either woman.

***

Jess stared at the little white stick in disbelief. It had a plus sign on it, and a hysterical laugh slowly escaped her lips. Single and pregnant at thirty-two—that wasn't how she pictured her life going.

How could it be happening? She wasn't one to sleep around. There had been one boyfriend in college and another in her late twenties. Both times she had been safely on the pill, but she wasn't now. Why take contraceptives when you're not even dating? Oh, that's right. Because you might end up banging the love of your life in an epic snowstorm in the middle of nowhere.

Jess bit down on her lip and thought about what to do. She needed to tell Spence, but he hadn't tried to contact her in over a month. She was certain the news would devastate him. The poor man was trying to make his marriage work, and this would only add fuel to the fire.

In her heart Jess knew their marriage was over, and had been for quite some time. But the two of them would have to figure that out on their own. She couldn't worry about them now. What she needed to worry about was the little baby growing inside of her.

Jess thought about her finances and how best to proceed. Her brother was of little help, but she had great friends back in Missouri. There was also a good hospital there, and she knew she might run into problems with her celiac disease. If she did, her insurance probably wouldn't cover everything. But if she gave up on her horse farm dream, the little nest egg she had saved might fill in the gap.

Jess made a quick call to her best friend in Missouri and had a plan in place an hour later. She would move back to Missouri and stay in the cottage on her friend's property. She would tell Doc Adams she had to leave due to an emergency. She would tell no one in Wyoming about the pregnancy. Someday, when the time was right, she would come back and give Spence the news.

## Spring 2018

A few months went by, and Jess was settled in Missouri. She was having a difficult pregnancy. Part of that was due to the celiac disease, and part of it was due to carrying twins. When the doctor broke that shocking news, all she could do was shake her head. The pregnancy had really toughened her. Instead of being upset, she joked about how it was the stud cowboy's fault. Her friends had long since learned not to ask who the father was. All she would tell them was he loved horses and knew how to ride.

Meanwhile, back in Wyoming things weren't going well. Spence and Charlotte were really starting to unravel. The holidays with the girls home had been great, but once they left, things got ugly in a hurry. The two fought over everything. Spence kept trying to find the right moment to tell Charlotte about his tryst with Jess, but she kept hurling insults his way. He was afraid the news would send her completely over the edge.

Spence's thoughts turned to Jess more and more, and he spent a good amount of time in the barn thinking about her. When he'd first learned she had left, he'd been initially relieved. It assuaged his guilt for a little while. But then he realized how much he missed her. What's more, he slowly came to realize he loved her. At that point, the guilt came back with a vengeance. Spence had never apologized to Jess, and now it looked like he would never get the chance.

Things were equally difficult for Joey over at the Thomas ranch. Without his sister there to calm him down, he was having some truly frightening moments. She had also quit paying his bills, and now he was left with disconnection notices and the realization that his life was not where he wanted it to be.

Unlike Spence, Joey knew where his sister was and decided to go visit. She was sitting out on the porch when he pulled up in the rental car. She had a blanket around her lap, and Scout was curled up against her side. She hadn't known he was coming.

Joey walked up, reached down, and gave her a hug. Then he sat in the seat next to her and started talking.

"I'm sorry, Jess. I know I'm difficult to live with. I'm just trying to work through stuff, you know. Wish you would come back. You keep me on track."

Jess let him ramble and debated what to do. He hadn't noticed her belly yet, but it was only a matter of time. Sure enough, he suddenly stopped talking and honed in on her midsection.

"Did you put on weight?"

She nodded, but he had already moved on to the obvious.

"Oh my god, you're pregnant!" He stood up. "That's why you left. I thought you'd had enough of me, but you left because you were knocked up. Who's the father?"

She sighed. "That's none of your business, Joey, and it really doesn't matter."

He stared at her in disbelief. "Of course it matters. This guy needs to do right by you."

"Oh my god. What is this? The 1950s? No, he doesn't. I can take care of myself. Now drop the subject."

But it was too late. She could almost see the wheels turning inside his head.

"It's Spencer Campbell's baby, isn't it? You two spent a lot of time together. That's why you left town so fast."

She covered her mouth with her hands and muttered, "It's not a baby; it's babies. I'm having twins."

That took Joey by surprise. "No kidding. Mom was a twin."

"I know."

They continued to stare at each other.

"You can't say anything back in Wyoming, Joey," she said. "I don't want people to know. When the time is right, I'll let the daddy know."

Now Joey was laughing. "I would love to see that uptight Charlotte's face when she gets the news. But don't worry, your secret is safe with me."

Jess glared at him. "I never said they were Spence's."

"You didn't have to, sis. It's obvious."

He dropped the subject after that. It was the one thing she could count on with her brother. He didn't push things, and he always respected her privacy. If he said he would keep her secret, he would.

Joey ended up spending the entire weekend. At one point he asked for money to pay his bills, and she had to tell him no. "I would help if I could, but I have a ton of medical expenses now. Once I push these babies out and get back to work, I'll be able to help you. Until then, you're going to have to get a job. How did you pay to get out here?"

He gave her a sheepish look. "I sold my saddle."

"Oh, Joey," was all she could think to say.

## Summer 2018

By summertime, Spence was barely hanging in there. Fortunately, it was their busy season, and he spent most days working outside and away from Charlotte. She in turn was traveling more, and one day she quit coming home altogether. The legal papers arrived a week later. She was filing for divorce and was only asking him to take care of the girls' college and insurance expenses. She did not ask for alimony.

Spence looked over the papers and sighed. He had known it was coming, and he was glad she'd made the move so he didn't have to. He was surprised she wasn't asking for money, though, and wondered if it was a ploy. He immediately called his lawyer, Gary, and then his family to discuss the matter. They met at Soup's house that night.

"If she wanted to, could she take a share of the land?" asked Soup.

"Oh, yes. Wyoming is a no-fault state," explained Gary. "She's entitled to half of everything. The only way around that would be if she were mentally ill or had done something egregious."

"Well she's a bitch," murmured Paul. "Does that count?"

The lawyer ignored him and turned to Spence. "She may change the terms of the settlement once we get into court. I need any dirt you can think of to help protect your assets. What about fidelity? Could she have cheated on you?"

Spence shrugged. "I don't know. Maybe?"

The lawyer nodded. "Let me have my PI look into it. If we can dig up some dirt, that will provide you with a fair amount of protection."

Spence nodded. He thought it ironic the lawyer hadn't asked about his own fidelity. It would never occur to anyone he would cheat. The realization left him unsettled inside.

"That's fine," he said. "Just make sure my daughters are taken care of. I don't want them dragged into any of this."

Gary reassured him and left.

Spence looked at his family and apologized.

"It's not your fault, son," said Soup. "Lord knows you tried."

His mom patted his arm. "She was never cut out for our way of life. You both did right by your girls, and that's all anyone can ask."

***

A few days later Gary gave Spence a call. He didn't beat around the bush.

"She's been cheating on you for over two years. A guy named Kyle Burton who lives in Boston. He's quite wealthy. This could be why she's not asking for money. I'll be in touch."

After the lawyer hung up, Spence sat at the kitchen table and poured himself a beer. It was odd. The news should have angered him or made him sad. Instead, he only felt relief. He completely understood where Charlotte was coming from. They had been so lonely together. Now he wished her well with the Burton fellow, and his thoughts moved on to Jess.

Spence was missing her more and more each day. He often snuck onto the Thomas ranch and did work around their property. It somehow made him feel closer to her. Spence knew he'd blown it with Jess, but he was hoping for a second chance. Maybe when the divorce was final, he would ask Joey for her phone number. He just couldn't believe she wanted to stay in Missouri the rest of her life. What had happened to her dream of rescuing horses?

Spence made a vow right then and there to win her back. He just needed some leverage.

## Early Fall 2018

The leverage he needed was born a few months later. Jakob and Joshua Thomas came into the world on a hot August night. Their mama had a rough go of it during the delivery, but all three were now doing well at home. Best of all, Jess was slowly regaining her strength. The babies had zapped all of her energy during the last trimester. They had also come early, which wasn't a surprise for twins, but had still added an extra layer of risk to the delivery.

A month passed, and Jess was looking ahead to the future. She had already made the decision to move back to Wyoming. Doc Adams still had a spot for her on his team, and she had just reapplied for the BLM grant. There was more money in their budget this year, so it was looking hopeful she would receive some. The only issue remaining was what to do about Spence. The man had a right to know about his sons, but how could she even begin to tell him?

Ideally, she would move back home, settle in, assess the Campbell marriage situation, and broach the topic with Spence when the time felt right. There was only one problem with that solution, and it was staring her right in the face.

The boys looked exactly like their father. It was uncanny. They were identical twins, and they had the same Campbell dimples and brown eyes that were legendary throughout the county. She might be able to convince people the father was some unknown cowboy, but one look at the babies and her secret would be out.

It wasn't fair, really. She was the one who had gone through eight months of carrying them around like a gigantic, heavy bowling ball. She was the one who'd had to pee six times a night, who'd eaten ravenously one minute, and chucked it up the next. Then there was the painful labor itself, which she had gone through all on her own. Well, she'd had three close girlfriends in there with her and the best obstetrician a woman could ask for, but still. The boys could at least have inherited her eyes or something.

But then Jake smiled at her and Josh gave a little burp, and her heart instantly melted. They were the sweetest, most perfect babies on the planet. It wasn't their fault they were the spitting image of their daddy. As long as they rode horses like their mama, all would be forgiven.

Now, back to the problem at hand. How was she going to break the news to Spence? How would Charlotte take it? Could she live with the repercussions? Jess just didn't know.

***

Spence was on the Thomas property patching fences alongside the road. It was far enough away from the house that Joey couldn't hear him, and it would make the front end of their property look a whole lot better. He took a break and was leaning against a tree in the shade, when Joey pulled up in a truck.

"What the hell are you doing, Campbell?"

Spence sighed. He had heard tales of how angry Joey got with trespassers.

"I was driving by and noticed your fences needed some work. I had the tools in my truck, so I decided to stop."

"I don't need any help from you. Get the hell off my property."

Now Spence was angry too. "Come on, Joey. We're neighbors, and we used to be friends. Let me help you. I mean, look at this place. You need all the help you can get."

It was the wrong thing to say, as Joey's face turned a deep shade of purple.

Spence was too far gone to care. "If not for yourself, then do it for Jess. She deserves better than this."

That brought Joey up short. "You're going to talk to me about my sister? How dare you?"

"Yes, I am. Maybe if you had helped her out more, she wouldn't have left."

Spence knew this wasn't true. He knew damn well she'd left because of him, but he was so angry, the words came flying out.

"You're one to talk," sputtered Joey. "You knocked her up and then left her high and dry with all those medical bills and two kids to take care of. Fuck you!"

Then his fist landed on the left side of Spencer's face, and the Campbell man went down to the ground with a thud.

Spence looked up at Joey in shock. "What did you say?"

Joey immediately tried to backpedal.

"Um, nothing, man. I was just ranting. Just get off my property, okay? And, er, sorry for hitting you." He edged toward his truck.

"Joey, wait!" Spencer sprang up and ran to his side. "Are you saying Jess is pregnant?"

Joey swore softly and spit on the ground.

"I promised her I wouldn't say anything. She was pregnant, but she had the babies already. Two boys. They look just like you."

Spencer leaned against the fence in shock. "I had no idea. Why the hell didn't she tell me?"

Joey shook his head. "Um, my guess would be that crazy wife of yours, dude."

Spencer rubbed his forehead. "We're getting a divorce. Joey, you have to tell me where Jess is at." He grabbed the other man by his shirt collars. "I need to see her. I swear I will get it out of you one way or another."

Joey grinned. "Nice to know you care, dickwad. Sure. I'll tell you. Come up to the house, and I'll give you her address."

***

Jess was loading Titus into the trailer. It was a déjà vu moment for her, and she thought back to the last time she'd got ready to leave for Wyoming. This time was different, though.

For one thing, she had to pack a ton of baby gear. Then there were the two drooling infant boys situated in the back. They took up the entire space with their car seats, diaper bags, blankies, and cooler full of breast milk. That meant Scout got to ride in the front, which had the dog grinning from ear to ear.

The other difference was her friends. They had shown up, despite her protests of hating goodbyes, and were sending her off with hugs and well wishes. Jess couldn't have asked for a better lot.

Everyone was still standing, laughing, and chatting when a taxi cab pulled up. The girls watched with interest as a handsome man got out. He was wearing a cowboy hat and jeans, and he had an unmistakable set of dimples and deep-set brown eyes on his face.

Jess gasped.

Spence paid the driver and walked over to where she was standing. He smiled down at her.

"Going somewhere?"

She introduced her friends to buy some time. He hadn't noticed the babies asleep in the back seat.

"I can't believe Joey told you where I was," she muttered.

He smiled. "Yah, well, let's just say I had to beat it out of him."

In truth, the two men had sat at the kitchen table, drank beer, and reminisced for hours. It had rekindled their friendship, but he didn't tell her that. Instead he said, "I had to see you. I've missed you, Jess."

Jess sighed. She didn't know if Joey had told him about the pregnancy, but if he hadn't, it would appear the time had come to fess up. "I was just getting ready to head back to Wyoming." She looked at him and sighed again. "There's something I need to tell you. Since you're here, you're welcome to drive back with me if you like. It would give us a chance to talk."

He grinned. "I would like that."

They said goodbye to her friends, and he threw his kit bag in the cargo bed. Then he looked at her expectantly.

"You said you had something to tell me?"

They were interrupted by a tiny cry from the back seat of the truck. Jake's pacifier had come out, and he was letting his mama know.

Spence opened the back door, bent down, and looked in at the babies. One was sound asleep, and the other was trying hard to work up a cry but was too tired. Spence looked at them in awe and then at Jess. Then he broke down and started crying.

"Why the hell didn't you tell me?" he sputtered out.

Jess moved over and put her arms around him. She saw her friends leaving out of the corner of her eye.

"I'm sorry, Spence. I didn't want to make things worse for you and Charlotte. I was going to tell you when I got back, though. I assume Joey beat me to it?"

He wiped his eyes and then pulled her in even tighter. "He did. God, it's good to see you. I've been thinking about you constantly since you left." Then he pulled away, "Charlotte asked me for a divorce."

Jess immediately felt the shame in her belly. "Oh, no. I'm so sorry. This is all my fault."

He laughed. "I never told her about us." He glanced at the sleeping babies. "Although, I'm going to have to now. No, she asked me for a divorce because she's been cheating on me for a long time. We were never suited for each other."

Jess blinked at the news. "No kidding. All this time I was feeling like a lowlife, adulterating homewrecker for nothing?"

He grinned. "I felt the same way, which is why I was so mean to you that morning. I'm really sorry about that. I was so angry at myself, but I took it out on you. Then the next thing I know, you up and moved away. It devastated me."

She digested his words with a faint smile.

"Well I'm coming home now. We should get on the road if we want to miss rush hour."

He nodded, and after one last check on the trailer hitch, they pulled out.

*** 

They took their time driving and made two overnight stops along the way. They talked the entire time and didn't even hesitate piling into bed together at night. They didn't have sex, though. Jess was just too tired.

Spence didn't care, he was more concerned about connecting with her on a deeper level. It felt like they had known each other their whole lives, and in a sense they had, but there was still a fourteen-year gap that needed to be filled. Jess told him about her life in Missouri, her schooling, her friends, and the job she'd held there. Spence in turn told her about his life with Charlotte and the girls. They had covered a lot of this before while riding together for the BLM, but now they dove deeper. Their conversations were much more personal, and it connected them in a way sex could never have done.

On the third day, they finally crossed the state line into Wyoming. They stopped at a rest stop to eat and change diapers.

Out of the blue, Spence blurted out, "We should get married."

She looked at him over the baby she was burping.

"You call that a proposal?"

Spence grinned as he snapped the bottoms back into place on the other baby. "Well, I'll do it right at a later date, but we should probably discuss it now."

She shook her head. "No way am I marrying you because of the boys. I mean, look how your last shotgun marriage turned out."

He gave her a mischievous look. "Well the way I see it, this is a whole lot different."

"How do you figure?"

"For one thing, we love each other. Always have, really. "

She rolled her eyes but nodded.

He went on. "For another, Charlotte's from Boston and never got it like you do."

"Got what?"

He searched for words. "I don't know. I guess I would call it the Wyoming Way."

She smirked. "Uh-huh. And what, exactly, is the Wyoming Way?"

He gave her a sexy grin as he sauntered over. "This!" Then he pulled her into a tight embrace and gave her a thorough kiss. Josh was tucked under his other arm, and Jess had baby Jake balanced on her hip. The kiss left her breathless and feeling weak-kneed.

Spence finally pulled away and grinned. "So it's settled, then. We're getting married."

She lowered Jake into the double-wide stroller and reached for Josh to set him next to his brother. "Like hell we are," she said.

"Damn stubborn woman. I'll wear you down eventually."

She finished buckling the boys and stood up. "Good luck with that."

***

They broke the news to Spence's family as soon as they got home. Jess had been nervous about it, but the Campbells were ecstatic. They took turns holding the boys, and Soup kept repeating how the family name would be carried on. They all gave Jess a warm embrace and immediately put her at ease. Heck, she'd grown up with these people and had known them most of her life. They were like family.

While everyone was playing with the babies, Spence stepped outside to give Charlotte a call. He succinctly told her about the stormy night and how he had just learned he was the father of twin baby boys.

Charlotte's response was to laugh hysterically. She had to put the phone down to catch her breath. Once she calmed down, she spoke.

"Honestly, Spence, it makes me feel so much better. I don't have to feel so guilty about my own affair. Jess seems well-suited for you with all her horse talk and country charm." She couldn't quite disguise the condescension in her voice. "But are you sure you're ready for babies again?" She started laughing some more.

He grunted. "I don't really have much choice. At least they're boys this time. I never quite understood all that girlie stuff."

Charlotte's laugh was genuine and kind this time. "No, you sure didn't. Are you going to tell our daughters, or should I?"

"I'll do it. Do you think they'll ever forgive either one of us?"

"Here's hoping," said Charlotte. "The way I see it, we did the best we could. Those girls had good lives. Your boys will too." Then she hung up.

Two weeks later, and the divorce was finalized. In the interim, Spence had called both daughters and broken the news. They had been stunned at first, but they both took it in stride. He suspected it would take them a long time to warm up to the babies, but he was sure it would happen. His girls had good hearts.

Epilogue – Two Years Later

A lot changed in two years. Jess settled back in her childhood home, and Spence moved in a month later. It took a lot of convincing on his part to get her to agree.

Joey still lived on the property as well. He built himself a cottage behind the barn and started a small wool farming business. It was a gentler way to work with animals, and it suited him. Having two rambunctious nephews also helped, and they were doing wonders for his PTSD.

Jess still worked part-time for Doc Adams, but recently she had also opened the Wyoming Animal Rescue Center. The BLM grant had finally come through. Now she had a steady stream of volunteers helping with the animals, and they were able to rescue more than just horses. It was a dream come true.

*\*\**

Jess and Spence were at the Wyoming State Fair. They were walking along as the boys rode on ponies, each holding a toddler in place. It was an exciting moment for all of them. The boys were squealing with excitement and chattering to each other.

Spence commented, "They're naturals. They ride as well as their daddy."

Jess shook her head and countered, "Nope. They're even better than that. They ride like their mama."

Spence just grinned and patted his coat pocket.

Jess watched him. She knew there was a ring in that pocket. The man had proposed to her about a thousand times already. She suspected he was going to again tonight. He probably hoped the magical setting of the fair would help his cause.

In truth, he was probably right. Jess knew he loved her and the boys with all his heart. The feeling was mutual. They just fit, and living together had proven that. It was time she took the poor man out of his misery and said yes.

With the ride over, their little family headed toward the games. Spence stopped them on the way and pointed to the sun just beginning to set on the horizon. It was beautiful.

Jess never got tired of that view, or the vastness of Wyoming. She was home, with her family, and living her dream. Spence was right. It was the Wyoming Way.

## The End

# The Cowboy's Heritage
## Patricia Elliott

## Chapter One

"Joey?" Reid McCloud called as he pushed a branch out of the way and continued moving down the trail. "Where are you?"

The prize-winning lamb had gone missing during the storm that had hit their island last night. If he couldn't find the animal, his cruise-faring parents were going to kill him. They'd never entrust the farm to him again, especially his father who was often a recluse and rarely, if ever, went on vacation.

As he was riding, a hawk screeched in the air above him, making him look up at the massive trees towering over him, with branches and leaves so thick they blocked out the light from the forest floor. He placed a hand on his brown Stetson to prevent it from falling off. He didn't know what the hawk was squawking at, but it must have found something good to eat. Grabbing the feed bucket, he rattled it, hoping the lamb would hear it. Joey had started responding to the sound recently.

The bushes rustled beside him, causing him to look down as two rabbits scampered out—young ones, by the size of them. There was an overabundance of rabbits this year, always eating his mom's carrots. It would seem they, too, had gotten used to the sound of the feed bucket.

"Not for you guys, sorry," he said, pressing his heels gently into the side of the horse to get him moving again. Where could the little guy be? Hopefully, he hadn't made it to the cliffs.

Reid stopped his horse, Midnight, at a fork in the path, debating which way to go. The path to the left would take him towards the northern portion of the island, while the right would take him to the sandy beach. He might as well start with the beach, as it was the closest area to the farm.

After a few minutes, he ducked under a low-lying branch and emerged onto the beach. Branches and leaves were strewn about the land. His bright green eyes scanned the honey-colored sand, hoping to see a hoofprint, anything that indicated the animal had been there, but there was nothing new to be seen, except some greenish sea glass.

Slowly trotting down the sandy shore, he checked the shrubs lining the edge to make sure Joey wasn't cowering underneath them. After making two passes, he tugged left on the reins to steer the horse back into the thick forest.

Maybe he should have brought his dog, Frisky, but he was getting old and was in the house napping. His dad hadn't bothered to train another sheep dog yet, and it was beginning to look like he'd have to do it himself. Carefully he made his way through the bush, looking this way and that.

"Where are you?"

He was about halfway back to the fork in the path when a resounding crack echoed around him. Reid glanced up in time to see a branch falling. "Hee-yah," he cried, flicking the reins as he ducked his head forward, squeezing his calves and his heels against the horse.

Midnight bolted forward just as the branch crashed to the ground behind them. Reid let out a breath of relief, and then he continued down the trail until he reached the fork. A few skinny trees were leaning against the more robust ones, having been cracked from the high winds and heavy rain. He really needed to talk to his dad about finding another island or buying a place inland away from the hurricane-force winds.

Taking the opposite trail this time, he scoped out the cliffs, but nothing led him to believe that Joey had ventured out this way. There were no hoofprints in the wet dirt and no wool caught in the thickets. Glancing up at the sky, he noted that the sun was beginning its drop on the horizon, making him realize he'd been out longer than he'd thought. Time was slipping through his fingers. Thankfully, he should still have a few hours of sunlight left. It was the first part of August, so it didn't get dark too early yet.

When he reached the rocky terrain on the west side of the island, he hopped off Midnight and tied his reins loosely around a tree. He'd have to go on foot to check the area. A horse would never make it down the wet incline safely.

Taking one careful step after another, he moved from boulder to boulder down to the beach. There was a path between the large rocks, but you couldn't get to it without sliding down, and he wasn't about to get his pants wet. As he continued making his way towards the water, his radio squealed. "Joey's back. Seems he was hiding behind a hay bale, shaking like a leaf," Chris said, his voice barely heard over the crash of the waves.

"Thanks, Chris," Reid groaned, pinching the bridge of his nose. Coming out here had been a big waste of time. He could have been doing other things. How had they missed Joey when doing their headcount?

Just as he turned to go back towards his horse, something shiny and fishlike bobbing in the water caught his attention. It was half-hidden behind a large rock. Reid hopped from one boulder to the next to get closer to it. On the last rock, his foot slipped, and down he went, sliding to the ground on the other side. As he was falling, he caught his first glimpse of what had washed up on the beach and his jaw dropped with the rest of him.

"It's a— it's a—"

He couldn't even say the word as he sat there dumbfounded, staring at the shiny, whitish-blue tail, with his ass aching from hitting the edge of a rock. Reid reached out and poked it, then looked out over the ocean, and then back to the latest visitor to his island. It was a… a fish and a woman. Well, half of each anyway.

Hell! He must have hit his head on the way down. There was no way she could be real. Mermaids don't exist. They just don't. Rubbing his eyes, he opened them again, only to find the mermaid still there. Her eyes were closed, half hidden by long, pure white hair, currently red with blood.

"It's not real. It's not real," Reid muttered, his head reeling at the discovery. His gaze ran the length of her body, past her seashell bra to where her tail began at her waist. He couldn't help but run his hand along it, trying to find a seam or an opening that would show him it was fake, but it blended perfectly with her skin. Her white, almost rubber-like scales were shaped like diamonds with a bluish outline. Her fluke, much like a dolphin's, was floating in the water.

Reaching out, he gently checked her neck for a pulse. It was faint, but she was alive. He sighed in relief, then closed his eyes and shook his head. This was too crazy. He had to be unconscious and dreaming. Yes. It had to be a dream. Or maybe he was going nuts from being on the island for too long.He needed Chris. It was the only way he'd know if what he was seeing was a figment of his imagination or if she was actually lying there. Grabbing his radio, he called him.

"Get to the rocky beach as fast as you can. I... uh... need your help with something." He didn't want to tell him what it was about because he had a sneaky suspicion Chris would call for help, thinking he'd injured his head.

"On my way," came his friend's reply.

Dropping the radio to the ground beside him, Reid took a deep breath, inhaling not only the salty smell of the ocean, but a coppery one too. He glanced down at the mermaid and brushed the hair back from her face. Hopefully, Chris wouldn't be long because she needed someone to look after her wounds, and he couldn't do it here. He didn't have any of his first aid equipment.

He ran his finger along her smooth, pure-as-ivory skin. It was like it had never seen the light of day, nor been damaged by the sun. "Where'd you come from?" he asked in a quiet, inquisitive voice.

Around her neck, she had a necklace made from sea glass and pearls, tied together with a seaweed braided chain. There was something authentic about her. Something more than just a woman being a professional mermaid, which he found out was a thing some women actually did. Standing up, he slid his hands under her armpits and tried to pull her across the rocky shore, but it was harder than he'd expected. Her slender upper body was easy enough to lift, but her tail weighed a ton like it was one big muscle.

Reid maneuvered the mermaid through the small pathway between the big boulders to the back of the beach. There was no way he'd be able to get her up the incline and over the big rocks without Chris's help. Setting her down gently, he waited for his friend. They had to get her inside before the next storm hit.

While he sat there, the woman began to shimmer brightly and silvery ribbons of water swirled around her, making him shield his eyes. When the glare dissipated and he could finally look at her, there she lay with legs instead of a tail. *Oh, God.* He was becoming a chucklehead—a fool. Maybe he'd been alone for too long, and his mind was spinning some bizarre fantasy about being with a mermaid.

He was sitting there, scratching his head, when his friend's face popped over the boulder above him. "Well, I'll be darned. Look at what the storm rolled in."

Reid was too flabbergasted to answer him. "She had…she had a—" he stuttered, as he continued to stare at two very sexy legs and her naked womanhood, her tail long gone.

"Is she okay?"

"She's alive," he replied finally. That was much easier to say than what he'd been attempting to. "We have to get her back to the house."

"Where do you think she came from?"

Reid shrugged, looking down at her. "Not a clue."

"When we get back, are we going to take her to the mainland or call for help and get them to bring a medivac in?"

That was a good question. If she was a mermaid, then she'd become part of a freak show in a circus, and he couldn't do that to someone, even if she was the discovery of a lifetime. His grandmother had taught him to do unto others as you'd have them do to you, and he most certainly wouldn't want to be studied inside and out, as she was sure to be. Mind you, he still wasn't sure whether he'd seen what he thought he'd seen, or whether he'd imagined it, because she had legs now and not a tail.

As he was staring at her, he heard a click and looked up at Chris, who still had his phone in his hand. "Really, dude?" Reid commented, quirking an eyebrow.

His friend grinned and shrugged as he put his phone in his pocket, then held out his arms. "You can't tell me you didn't think about doing the same thing."

Reid just shook his head and lifted the young woman in his arms. Seeing as she was much lighter now, he had no trouble lifting her high enough for Chris to grab her.

"Careful," Reid said, as he tried to prevent her hip from scraping against the edge of the rock. He didn't want to scratch her beautiful, alluring body. Chris took her from his arms and carried her over to the horse as Reid worked his way up the incline carefully, his mind reeling. Was he dreaming? How could she be real? It was like he'd stepped into a movie.

They laid her over the back of Reid's horse and slowly made their way back to the house, her breasts bouncing with each step, making his member wake up and take notice. He averted his eyes, hoping it would ease the ache building inside him. When had he turned into such a pervert?

"She's really quite something, isn't she?" Chris said, breaking the ten-minute long silence.

"I hadn't noticed," Reid murmured.

Chris laughed. "Is that why you've been staring at her rack since we left the beach?"

"Shut up." He released the branch he'd just pushed out of the way, hitting Chris in the knee with it.

"Ow," his friend said, rubbing his knee.

Reid turned back to face the trail, a smirk playing on his face, until he ran into a branch, knocking himself to the ground with an oomph.

Chris doubled over with laughter on his horse. "Serves you right, asshat."

Reaching up, Reid gingerly touched his forehead where a large goose egg was forming. Now he matched the woman castaway with the bump on her head. This was definitely not another normal day on the farm.

After a short while, they reached the house. Chris turned to tend to the horses, while Reid took the unconscious mermaid inside.

If his mom were here, she'd admonish him for not having already given the young woman the jacket off his back. Stepping into his living room, he came to a stop. He wasn't sure whether to lay her on the couch or put her upstairs in the spare bedroom. But he knew that the bed in the guest room wasn't made up yet, and it didn't seem right to put an almost naked woman on the couch… not with Chris' peeping eyes.

So he took her to the one bed that was ready to sleep in.

*His.*

## Chapter Two

She opened her eyes, staring at an unfamiliar ceiling that appeared to be moving as her vision swirled like a cloudy mist. Her head was pounding like an oil drill on the ocean floor. She shook her head, trying to clear away the school of minnows that clouded her mind. What had happened? Where was she?

There was a storm. That she could remember, but beyond that, it was like a wall of seaweed blocking her way. Her heart hammered in her chest, keeping her frozen in place on the bed. She gripped the soft white material covering her and held it tight. Thoughts raced through her mind. Visions of tumbling in the surf assailed her, ending with a giant rock that had made her world go black.

What had she been doing in the water? Was that a dream? Why was she now in a room? Nothing made sense. Nothing felt real. Not the walls around her. Not the bed she was in, nor the stars glowing on the ceiling in the dark. Stars were outside, not inside. She gave her head another shake as panic welled inside her. Pushing the sheets away, she sat up and threw her legs over the side of the bed. She stared at the pale limbs, blinking rapidly. Something felt wrong. Totally wrong.

As she sat there wiggling her toes, a smell wafted into the room that she couldn't quite place, but it smelled delicious. Wanting to know what it was, she stood up and nearly tumbled forward on her shaky limbs. She held her arms straight out beside her and tried to regain her balance, noticing she was strangely naked, except for an odd shell bra covering her breasts.

Glancing around the room, as her vision slowly cleared, she noticed a set of clothes on a chair in the corner. The top was easy enough to put on, but she flipped the other article around in a few circles, trying to determine how it worked. It seemed foreign to her.

"Pa..." She pressed her lips together as she tried to remember the word. "Pants!" she said, her tongue sticking to the top of her parched mouth. The sooner she got dressed in the strange contraptions, the sooner she could figure out where she was and get a drink.

Sitting down on the side of the bed again, she slipped one leg into the pants and was about to put the other in when someone stepped into the room. She let out a high-pitched cry, putting a crack in the bedroom window. The man covered his ears and squinted his eyes.

"Oh, hell! I'm sorry," the man said, lowering his hands and turning around to give her privacy. "I... uh... just wanted to see if you were up to eating anything."

"Where a-am I?" she asked, stumbling over the words.

"You're in my home," he said. "Are you decent?"

"What do you mean?"

"Are you dressed?"

"Oh, sorry. One second." She slipped her other leg into the pants and pulled them up to her waist, but they were super loose, so she bunched the material together in her hand and held it. "Okay."

When the man turned around, a grin spread across his face. "They don't fit, do they? Be right back." He disappeared out the door, but then reappeared a minute later with a long snake-like object. "Here, try this."

She grabbed it and held it up in the air. "What's this?"

"A belt," he said, holding his hand out. "May I?"

"Thank you."

He moved towards her, and she sucked in a breath, dropping her gaze to the floor. His musky cinnamon scent wrapped itself around her senses in the most delicious way.

"I won't hurt you. Don't worry," he said, his voice dropping an octave. Once he threaded the belt through the loops on her pants, he stepped back, giving her space again.

They stood there a moment in silence, neither sure what to say or do. He was the first to speak because she couldn't find her voice yet. "What's your name?"

"I'm... I'm, uh." *Oh flippers.* How could she not remember her own name? Tears welled in her eyes as she brought her hands to her mouth. Her mind had been wiped clean.

"Oh dear," the man said softly, a genuine look of concern passing through his blue eyes. "You must have amnesia."

"Am what?"

"Am-ne-sia. It's where you forget your past, or at least part of it. Can you remember anything?"

She shook her head from side to side, her hair once again partially covering her face. "No. Nothing, except the water," she said, her chin trembling as an extreme wave of exhaustion rifled through her, followed by nausea. "I don't feel too good."

Reid rushed to her side and helped her back into bed, then sat down beside her. "You hit your head pretty hard, so you probably have a concussion. Do you need an aspirin or Tylenol?"

She glanced at him blankly. "Huh?" The words were not familiar to her.

"Of course. You probably don't have them where you're from."

Upon hearing his words, she shot upright, almost knocking him off the edge of the bed. "You know where I'm from?" That was good because she had no idea. But he only shook his head, and her hope deflated again, her mind flooding with questions. Where was she from? What was she doing before she lost her memory? Why was she here? Why did everything feel wrong? She raised her hands and waved them like a fan in front of her face. This couldn't be happening.

He reached out to pat her leg, but she scooted away from him. "It's okay. I'm going to help you figure things out."

"I don't know you." Who was he? Could he be trusted?

"The name's Reid. This is my place. Well, my parents' place, but they are away right now."

She glanced around the room frantically, looking for something, anything familiar. "I need to go. I have to go." Being alone with him didn't feel right. Nothing felt right. She didn't look or feel like herself, especially her voice. Her tongue kept tripping over itself as she tried to sound out the words in his language. Even her body had this strange tingling thing going on between her legs.

"I promise you're safe here."

"Can you, like, go over there?" She pointed towards the door. He made her uneasy. Every time their eyes crossed paths, her insides warmed. And she didn't like it. All right. She did, but didn't at the same time.

He took a moment to study her before standing up and moving across the room. "What should I call you?" he asked, as he leaned against the door frame with his arms folded across his chest. His sleeves were rolled up to his elbows, giving her a glimpse of strong solid arms "Do you have a preference?"

She lost her voice for a moment as her gaze travelled up his arms, and suddenly she could envision them wrapped around her. Her face heated at the thought. Oh goodness, she was going crazy.

"Hey, you okay?"

"Huh?" Her head snapped up.

He smirked and his eyes twinkled, making her cheeks burn with fire. "I was wondering what I should call you. I was thinking maybe Jill," he said.

She scrunched up her nose and shook her head. That one didn't suit her at all.

"How about Nancy?"

Holding a finger against her lips, she thought about that one, but then shook her head again. That one wasn't her either, but it spurred another name in her mind. "Can you call me Nerina?" She wasn't sure why she was drawn to that name, but she liked it.

"Do you think that's your name?"

"I... I don't know," she stammered, but it felt familiar and she needed familiarity.

"Okay, Nerina, it is. Well, I'm going to go finish cooking breakfast.

Come down when you're ready. There is a towel in the bathroom if you want to shower first."

And with that, he turned and left the room.

## Chapter Three

Reid faced the kitchen counter and dished out their food, heaping a pile of eggs and bacon onto his plate. It was one of his favorite ways to start the day. On her plate, he'd put three slices of bacon and a smaller portion of scrambled eggs, unsure of how hungry she'd be.

He hadn't counted on her having amnesia, so there was a vicious debate inside him as to whether he should call a doctor or a vet, considering she was part fish—if he hadn't imagined that particular part, which could very well have been possible. He had hit his own head too.

There was the possibility, somewhere in his weird brain, that he wanted to make love to a mermaid, and that's why he'd thought he saw a tail instead of two very delicious-looking legs. In a way, he wanted to see what would happen if she went into the water.

"Oh crap, the shower." Could any type of water make them change? He stopped for a moment and listened. There were no great cries of anguish or any thumps of her falling over, so he decided maybe normal water didn't do anything. He would just have to be patient and find out when she was ready. There were times he'd had to wait up all night for a foal to be born, so patience had become his middle name.

The only thing he worried about was her being out of the water for too long. Would that affect her? Fish couldn't breathe without it. But what about mermaids? Were they air breathers, or did mermaids have the ability to extricate oxygen from the water? He had so many questions, but there didn't seem to be any way to get the answers he was looking for. And that alone was driving him nuts.

As he scooped the remaining eggs from the frying pan to his plate, he heard a shuffling sound. Turning around, he saw Nerina standing in the doorway, playing with her hair, her bright turquoise eyes cautious. He's never seen anyone with eyes that matched the ocean in the Bahamas. They were as mesmerizing as they were beautiful. Otherworldly. Her curly white hair flowed over her breasts, which were now hidden by his mother's pink t-shirt.

"What's that delicious smell?" she asked.

"Bacon."

"Bacon?"

"You've never had it before?"

She wandered over to him and peeked around his shoulder at the food on the plates. "Not that I'm aware of."

"It's from a pig."

"An animal?" Nerina asked.

He nodded, then gestured towards the table in the corner. She stepped past him and moved towards the table, and as she did so, her salty ocean scent filled his senses. There was a sweetness to it that he couldn't quite put his finger on. Something alluring that drew him in.

"Can you show me a pig?"

"We don't have any on the farm, but, here, give me a second." He placed their plates on the table and then disappeared out of the room. Quickly, he made his way to his dad's office where he knew a set of encyclopedias were, and then grabbed the necessary one and went back to the kitchen. It was at times like this he wished his phone had internet.

Opening it to the section about pigs, he turned to show it to her.

"Oh, I don't think I've seen one like that before."

"Probably not," he said, then quickly berated himself. The last thing he wanted was to say anything that would make her think he was crazy. Grabbing his fork, he dug into his lukewarm eggs, stuffing some into his mouth.

She picked up a fork and examined it, touching the end of the tongs. "Ouch," she said, sucking on her finger.

The seemingly innocent action sent a spark of excitement to his groin, making his cock twitch. There was a sweet purity that bounced off her in waves, and it made her more tantalizing somehow. It made him want to take her into the hayloft and make sweet, passionate love to her, but he knew they couldn't go there, given the circumstances.

He was having a hard time judging her age. She looked young. Her skin was smooth and without wrinkles. She didn't even have crow's feet when she smiled. But her white hair was throwing him for a loop. Did mermaids age differently? Did they live longer or shorter than humans?

He watched as her slender fingers ran over the fork, her forehead wrinkling with confusion. "Never used one before?"

"Don't think so."

"Watch," he said, giving her a demonstration.

She fumbled with the utensil as she tried to position it in her hand like he did, but, in the end, she just wrapped her fingers around it in a fist and dug into the eggs like nobody's business. "These are delicious," she said.

He smiled. "They are the house specialty."

Nerina used the back of her hand to swipe at the juices on her lips, locking eyes with him. Pure sensuality swirled in her gaze like a whirlpool, pulling him under with the strength of a goddess. Suddenly dizzy, he swayed in his chair until she looked away. She appeared to be unaware of her effects on him. Reid gave his head a shake and let out a noisy breath, trying to clear away the cobwebs.

"I have to head out and tend to the farm. Will you be okay?" he asked. She gave him a non-committal grunt, and then continued eating. Nerina definitely didn't have a lot to say compared to the last girl he'd dated. "Don't go anywhere, okay?"

Nerina gave him a thumbs up because her mouth was full, but she kept her eyes down. Disappointment filled him because her eyes were absolutely electrifying. Did she know the power she had in them? Reid contemplated saying something, but he didn't want to sound like he was coming onto her.

Reid left the room and headed outside toward the barn. Chris was sure to be out there mucking out the stalls as he usually did this time of day. He could bet that the first thing out of Chris's mouth was going to be a wisecrack, per his usual self. Usually Reid didn't mind them, but today he was unsettled enough as it was already.

As soon as he stepped inside, Chris poked his head out of a stall, his hair stuck to his sweaty forehead. "So, ya get any last night?"

"Jeez, man! It's too early for your mind to be in the gutter."

"It's never too early."

Reid walked over to the tack and grabbed the halter. "I guess that's why you're the one cleaning out the muck, eh?"

"You could always do it, and I'll go entertain your new friend."

His chest tightened, and he cast a glare Chris's way. "Like hell you will."

Chris held up his hands in surrender. "Easy, dude. I won't tread on your property."

That was the difference between him and Chris. The man was a womanizer and treated them much like property to be obtained and then discarded after you'd had your fill. Reid had been taught to treat them as he wanted to be treated.

Reid opened the stall and stepped inside to prepare his horse. "I'm gonna go check the fence line and see if the storm overnight did any damage."

"I've already run the line. Everything appeared okay this time around."

"Thanks, but I'm gonna go out anyway. I need the fresh air," Reid said, pointing to the manure in the wheelbarrow.

"Ya, okay," Chris said. "I'll clean the stalls and feed the animals while you go for a joyride."

"That is what I pay you for, isn't it?" Reid commented, winking at him. "I won't be long."

He did his fair share of shoveling the muck, but today he needed to get out there and clear his head. Maybe even try to find a clue as to where his new lady friend was from.

After he'd finished prepping the horse, Reid led him outside and hopped onto his back. This was one of his favorite places in the world. You tended to see things from a different perspective as you sit up on their back. The world's problems seemed to fall away.

He cantered across his field, breathing in the clean crisp air. The air never smelled fresher than it did after a good storm. They were far enough away from the city to not really get the pollution from their factories, but you could still smell a major difference permeating the air.

Once he arrived at where he found her, he hopped off his horse and made his way down the rocky beach. The sun sparkled like diamonds on the water today, making him shield his eyes. It looked like the storm had finally passed overhead completely, giving them a little reprieve. He hoped that the recent storms weren't an indicator of how bad fall was going to be this year. Reid breathed in deep as he crossed over the boulders, relishing in the salty ocean smell.

"Man! I love being out here." There was no place in the world like it. He couldn't even imagine living in the city. There were always too many people walking the streets, so many that you'd just about trip over them. This place, surrounded by water in all its serene beauty, was his home.

And it made him wonder where Nerina's home was. Was it nearby? Was that how she'd ended up here? Could they be under his island? He knew there were underwater tunnels that spread the expanse of the island, but he had never bothered to explore them. Now he was tempted to go buy scuba gear and find out what was down there.

As he stood there thinking, there was a rather large splash in the water on the other side of a boulder near where the island curved. He couldn't quite see what it was. When it happened again, he slowly made his way over and saw a black fluke dip under the water. Reid's jaw dropped. Another one? Were they looking for Nerina?

He cupped his hands around his mouth and called, "Hey you!"

Reid shielded his eyes from the sun and looked out over the sparkling diamond ocean, but the creature never surfaced again. "Damn," he muttered.

Knowing there was nothing else he could do, he turned around and headed back home.

## Chapter Four

Nerina stepped outside and found herself surrounded by rather large birds. She'd heard them from the kitchen clucking loudly and went to see what was causing the racket. These things were bigger than most birds she'd ever seen. There were other animals around, too, and she didn't know what they were either. Some were white, about the size of the dog in the house.

There were two other larger animals, like the one Reid had hopped on earlier. He'd looked like a god on a water horse as he'd ridden off. And that had done strange things to her senses, sparking an awkward feeling down below. In fact, she'd needed to go to the bathroom and dry herself.

She couldn't recall ever feeling this way with anyone, but then again, she had no memory of her past. Was there someone waiting for her? For some reason, she didn't think so. There was no way she'd ever forget a person who made her feel like this. It was too unfamiliar to her, and it felt like she'd woken up on another planet, in another dimension. But that was crazy, wasn't it?

"Would you like to feed them?" a voice asked from behind her.

Letting out a high-pitched squeal, she spun around, and her feet got tangled together. In one horrifying minute, she was falling face-first into the wet mud and couldn't do anything to stop it. The birds let out an unpleasant squawk as they scrambled to get out of the way.

Instead of coming to help her, the man with dark brown hair doubled over laughing. "Oh God, you should see your face."

Nerina glared at him with a mud-covered face, the smell of bird poop stinging her eyes. *Oh, great gods of Marianas*. This was embarrassing. Digging her fingers into the mud, she wrapped her hand around some and sat back on her haunches.

"Amusing, is it?" Nerina raised her hand and threw the mud at him. He was too busy laughing to see it coming, and it hit him right between the eyes. That shut him up. And just when she was about to speak again, a sexy laugh broke the air behind her.

"Stop terrorizing our guest, Chris."

"Me? She's the one who—" He stopped talking when he saw another fistful of mud clenched in her hand. "I swear if you hit me with that—"

"Can you take Midnight back and give him a bath, please?" Reid interrupted.

Nerina sighed with relief when Chris agreed and soon disappeared into the barn, leaving her standing with Reid. He let his gaze travel the length of her body and then back up again. "Looks like you could use one too."

Her cheeks burned beneath the mud, and her insides were doing the crazy dance again. Her gaze dropped to his lips. What would it be like to be kissed by him, to be touched by his hardworking hands? The thought made the fire in her cheeks flare hotter than the lava vents on the ocean floor.

"Come on," Reid said, taking her by the hand.

She didn't want to speak, afraid that she'd invite him into the bath with her. There was an undeniable pull in his direction, a strong current that flowed between their hands. Attempting to break his hold on her, she pulled her hand free and stepped ahead of him, wiping the mud from her face.

"Could I have another shower? I liked that." It reminded her of the time that she had showered under the waterfall. It was a no-no. She wasn't supposed to go to that place, but she loved it. The way the water felt as it dripped down her body.

The thought made her freeze, and Reid bumped into her back, almost knocking her to the ground. He reached out and grabbed her shoulders to steady her. "I'm sorry. You okay?"

"I just remembered something I did before," she said, not even paying attention to the fact that his hands were still on her shoulders, as the memory grew more vivid by the minute. The trees were green with the color of summer, berries rampant on the bushes that surrounded the alcove. She'd been swimming in a crystal-clear pool. "At least, I think it's a memory."

"What did you see?"

She turned in his arms and looked up at him, feeling that unfamiliar pull in his direction. It was like her spirit was reaching out to him, and she knew he felt it, too, by the darkening of his irises as he searched her face for answers to other unspoken questions. Nerina swallowed hard. She couldn't understand what was happening as heat spread from his palms to her body like a warm solstice breeze.

"I…" She scrambled through her thoughts, trying to remember what she'd been thinking about before, but it had fled from her mind. All she could see and feel was him. She placed her hand against his chest and felt his heart racing.

His hands dropped to her waist, pulling her close. "Nerina," he said huskily, staring at her lips. It made her want to sing to him, and she couldn't say why. Did she know how to sing? Should she try? But before she could contemplate the thought any further, his mouth was against hers, tasting and claiming them as his own, like they belonged to him.

Rising on her tiptoes to match his height, she slid her hands up his chest, linking them behind his head to deepen the kiss. She wanted to drink in all of him, his salty scent from having been out near the ocean. She craved more of him, wanted more of him. Her breasts ached as they brushed up against his hard chest.

Reid picked her up, and she wrapped her legs around his waist, feeling his manhood pressing against her. She shivered with delight, and it made his cock jump with pleasure. He used a nearby tree as leverage, so he could daringly slip one hand under her shirt and caress her bare breast, pleased that she'd removed the rough shell bra. Her nipples hardened under his touch, and he groaned. He was quickly losing his grip on his sanity. Everything told him not to touch her, not to go there, but he had to.

"I want to make love to you," he murmured against her lips.

"I think I'd like that."

He released her and then took her by the hand. "Come on. I know a place."

"Your house?"

Reid shook his head. "No. I want to do it in a place as breathtaking as you."

In fact, it was a spot he had never taken a girl before, as they never usually came to the island. But it was a place that meant something to him. He couldn't say what it was, but it felt like home, like he belonged there.

Her face lit up and a smile, more beautiful than he'd ever seen, spread across her face. His heart broke open just a little. It made him feel as though he'd crossed over into another dimension, another world where only purity and beauty existed. Not that his thoughts were pure and holy, but she was like this goddess sent to him from the next world over. Were mermaids goddesses? They were the things of mythology and legend, but he had a live one here, in his arms.

He guided her through the forest towards his special place, but she suddenly stopped, and it made him look back at her. She was biting her bottom lip, worry etched into her brow.

His gut clenched, and he wondered if she'd changed her mind. "What's wrong?"

"It's just—"

Just as she started to speak, a thought popped into his head, and he slapped his forehead. "Oh, right. You might be married." Why hadn't he thought about that before?

"No. That's not it. At least, I don't think I am."

He let out a whoosh of air that had been trapped in his lungs. "Phew, you had me scared there for a second. But, if that's not it, what is it?"

"I-I don't think I've mated before," she stammered, looking to the ground as she fiddled with her thumb.

Reid choked on the saliva that had gathered in his mouth and pounded his fist against his chest as he tried to catch his breath. "Mated?"

Now that was a word people didn't normally use with sex unless they were looking to have kids, and that broke the spell he'd been under. That wasn't even an option for him or for her. She wasn't exactly human. He didn't have a right to go there with her, even if having sex with a mermaid consumed his waking thoughts.

"Did I say something wrong?" she asked, her eyes big and round.

"I just realized that if we have sex, I would be taking advantage of you. Come on, let's go back to the house."

"What if I said I don't care?" she argued, slowly unbuttoning the shirt he'd given her to wear. Her eyes began to sparkle the same way they had earlier. Reid dropped his gaze to the ground, not willing to get pulled in again. There was something in her eyes akin to magic and it made his head all fuzzy, like he'd had a few drinks, causing all his common sense to flee away.

"My parents raised me to be a gentleman, and you are a guest in their house. They'd kill me if I was anything but well-behaved," he said. If he could focus on them, he'd be able to hold himself together.

She moved closer to him, not willing to be dissuaded. Their eyes met again as her lips formed a perfect goddess pout. It was like she'd spent a lifetime perfecting it. His cock hardened, viciously so, and pressed against his briefs. It wanted out, and, God, he wanted to let it out. He groaned again and took a step back, hoping some distance would clear his head. Now he knew what a rope felt like in the game of tug-of-war.

*Doggone it!*

He wanted her. But she was hurt, and this behavior could be out of character for her, making her act irrationally forthcoming. It was up to him to do what was right. "Why don't we revisit this topic after your memory comes back?"

"My memory may be gone, but my body isn't."

*Why here? Why now?*

Suddenly he wished that sex wasn't such a rarity in his life because he was now craving it beyond belief. And not just with anyone, but with her in particular. She had a rare unearthly beauty, almost like she didn't belong here. He knew that if he tasted her body once, it would be like a lifelong spell had been cast on him, and he'd never get enough. How was it possible to feel that way so quickly? They didn't even really know each other, and, hell, she didn't even know what she was.

"Hun, we need to talk."

"I don't wanna talk," she murmured, walking her fingers up his chest, pausing momentarily over his nipples, circling them lightly.

She was doing a heck of a job killing every ounce of resilience he had. If he didn't say it now, he never would. "You're a mermaid," he blurted.

There. He'd said it. It might have made him look and sound crazy, but he didn't care. Reid needed Nerina to pause a moment so he could gather his wits. But she didn't miss a beat. Laughter reigned in her eyes as she stood on her tiptoes again and pressed her supple lips against his neck, sucking lightly. It was like she didn't hear him, and his battle of wills was slowly being lost. What would it be like to have those lips close over his erection?

"Are you a siren?"

Nerina giggled, and, and the sound swirled around his heart, threatening to break the last strand of his will.

She paused a moment and looked up at him, fluttering her eyelashes. "We can play it that way if you want."

"You're killing me, woman! I'm trying to do the right thing here."

A sexy smirk spread across her face, and she ran her hand over his erection. "You aren't trying that hard."

That was his problem. He didn't want to try. He wanted to give in, but there would be hell to pay if he did. When she brushed his cock a second time in the opposite direction, he sucked in a breath and was unable to stop himself from reaching out to her. Her nipples were hard against his touch, and he knew her pussy would be just as ready for him.

Nerina took his hand and guided it down to the waistband of her sweats. "It's all right," she encouraged. "I won't tell anyone."

Yep, that cinched it in his mind. She was definitely a siren from another world. Unable to help himself any longer, he loosened her pants, and they dropped to the ground, giving him a full view of her womanhood. Wet and glistening. His cock ached at the sight.

"We shouldn't," he groaned.

"We shouldn't have fun?" she asked, all innocent-like while at the same time undoing the belt on his blue jeans. He had on his blue briefs with the usual slit down the front. Nerina slipped her hand inside and pulled him out, his cock springing upward.

When her hand wrapped around him, he dropped his head back and closed his eyes. The electrifying power of her touch doused any reluctance he had left. He wanted this. Her. All he could think of now was burying himself deep inside her and making her his. And by the look on her face, she didn't have a problem with that at all. So why should he?

Having made the decision, he pulled her hand away, then tucked himself back inside and pulled his pants, as well as hers, up. In a split second, he had her up over his shoulder and was on his way to the spot he had planned to go before—the waterfall.

## Chapter Five

Excitement built inside her as she bounced over his shoulder. She'd never been in this position before, but she liked it, liked how it gave her an unadulterated view of his butt. She reached down and slapped it. He did the same to hers, making the ache inside her double.

"We'll be there soon," he said, his voice raw and deep.

It wasn't soon enough for her liking. She wanted to be there now. Reaching down, she tried to pull his pants back so she could slip her hand inside, but the belt held them snug and firm against him. Nerina let out a puff of air, her hair dancing from the breeze.

She couldn't say why she wanted this so badly—why she wanted him the way she did. He had this aura about him that drew her in like a minnow to an anglerfish, a very deadly combination, but her feelings were too strong to ignore.

By the time he came to a stop in a small clearing, the sun had passed the halfway point in the sky and was beginning its descent. He put her down, and she turned around to see where he had brought her. Across the way was a roaring waterfall that emptied into a crystal-clear pool. The rays of the sun sparkled against the surface.

As Nerina walked towards it, a mist blanketed the surface and all the hairs on her arms stood on end as fear punched her in the gut. She backed away, backing right into Reid. He placed his hands on her shoulders to steady her.

"Wow, are you okay?" Reid asked.

"The house, take me back to the house," she begged. "Please."

He scratched his head, his curiosity piqued. "What… what's wrong?"

Nerina wrapped her arms around herself, looking from her left to her right. "I don't know. I just don't like this place."

Nothing about this made sense. How could a mermaid be afraid of the water? Had something happened prior to her landing on his island? Could she have been in trouble? He'd assumed that the storm had marooned her here, but now he was feeling like there was something more to it.

"Come on," he said, holding out his hand. "I'll take you back."

She grabbed his hand in a death grip. Reid gently squeezed back and then led her out of the clearing. He'd been hoping that they could go swimming and have some fun in the water, but now he was more concerned about her well-being than getting some action.

As they made their way back towards the house, the tension slowly drained from her body and her grip loosened. He glanced at her. Her lips were pulled to one side, and her forehead was creased in confusion. She looked as confused as he felt.

"Do you want to talk about it?" he asked when they finally entered the field back at the farm.

She shook her head. "I still don't remember much. I just had a weird feeling back there, like something was pulling at me."

"You must be able to feel something in the water I can't."

"And you think it's because I might be a mermaid?"

He shrugged. "I did see you with a tail. A mighty fine one, I might add."

Nerina chuckled. "You're crazy."

"That wouldn't surprise me," he said, joining in the laughter.

They stepped inside the house, and he shut the door behind him. Before he had a chance to say another word, she pressed him up against the door and kissed him with even more ardor than before.

Reid should have stopped her, but he couldn't. Her lips were as intoxicating as the rest of her. Picking her up, he carried her upstairs to his bedroom, relishing in the feel of her light kisses against his neck. Her lips held a power unlike any other. It was like she was made for him.

Once inside his room, he put her down, unable to believe that he was standing in front of the most beautiful woman in the world. Very few women had the ability to draw him in with just a look, but her eyes were like a treasure trove that went on forever.

She reached out and made short work of his pants and underwear, releasing his erection. Her eyes were glued to it in awestruck wonder, which made him want her even more. She reached out and touched him. He sucked in a breath as the sensation raced to his core.

When her fingers wrapped around him and moved up his length, he stilled her hand. "If you keep doing that, I'm going to come, and I want to be inside you before I do."

A sensual smile played on her lips. "This is what you want, right?" she asked, squeezing him gently.

"God, yes!" he groaned.

Nerina ran her thumb across the head of his cock. "Does it get any harder?"

Grabbing her hand, he pulled it away, backing her towards the bed. "If it did, I'd explode," he said, as he helped remove her shirt. Reid's eyes feasted on her newly revealed flesh. "You make me think of an angel." She had no flaws. Everything about her was perfect.

"Really, an angel?" She looked up at him, her eyes wide. "When my mom went to school, kids made fun of her. They said she looked like a zombie."

As soon as she finished speaking, Nerina froze.

Reid took her hands in his. "You remember?"

She shook her head. "No. Occasionally, I get an image or remember a phrase, but that's it."

"Have you remembered anything that might tell you where you're from?"

Pain flashed in her eyes as she shook her head again. "I have a feeling it was more like a prison than anything else."

"Well then, I'm going to make it my mission to make you feel free," he said. "First step is getting you out of these clothes."

"I'm up for that."

"I think you have our roles reversed," he said, pointing to his cock. "I'm the one who's up."

Nerina's sweet laughter filled the room. "Yes, I suppose you are."

Reid loosened the belt on her pants, and they fell to the floor. He whistled as his gaze took in her tiny frame, his fingers exploring her pale, flawless skin. He felt like he was dreaming. His mother once said that someday a woman was going to fall into his lap that he couldn't refuse, but he didn't think she meant literally.

He wasn't going to question it though, not when he had a beautiful, willing woman in his arms. Mermaid or not, opportunities like this didn't come around every day. Not for him, anyway. Letting his fingers trail up her abdomen, he brushed them over her hardened nipples. God! Even her breasts were perky, sexy.

They crawled onto the bed and he took a position beside her, slipping his arm under her head. His lips met hers, and they slow-danced across the great abyss until nothing else existed. Not the bed. Not the house, Not the world. Just them. His hand closed over her breast, needling her nipples with his thumb and index finger while his mouth closed over the other, sucking as a baby would.

Her back arched and she gripped the sheets, giving him even better access to her breasts. He rolled his tongue around her nipple. She whimpered with delight and turned towards him, tossing her leg over his hip, his erection pressing against her belly.

"Please, take me," she begged.

"All in good time," he whispered as his wandering hand slipped between her folds, loving the feel of her wet silk against his fingers. She moaned and bucked against his hand. Most women he'd been with took ages to get aroused, but she was already ready for him. Sexual energy buzzed in the air, filling him with lust, making him realize that if he made her orgasm without being inside her, he'd come just listening to her. And that was the last thing he wanted.

Rolling on top of her, he positioned himself at her entrance, her silk coating the tip of his cock. Desire flooded him and he took a breath, trying to hold himself back from pounding into her. If she was a virgin, it would be painful, and he didn't want to cause her pain.

"Yes, please," she begged, wrapping her legs around his waist, opening herself up to him. Her words rang like a siren's song, making him plunge uncontrollably into her depths. It was only after he was inside that he paused, trying to figure out how that happened.

"Are you okay?" he asked, giving her time to adjust to him.

Nerina didn't respond. Her wide eyes were staring past him, as though she were looking at something on the ceiling. He twisted and looked up, but nothing was there. "Nerina, talk to me?"

It was like she wasn't there and had disappeared on him somewhere. Reid waved a hand in front of her face, trying to get her to come back to him. "Nerina, do you want me to stop?"

Finally, her eyes refocused on him as she gave her head a little shake, her smile returning. She reached up and framed his face with her palms. "I'm probably going to be dragged to the bottom of the Marianas Trench for this, but heck no. I want to do this. I want you."

Reid sighed in relief, resting his forehead against hers. "Oh, thank God!" If she told him to stop, he'd have to rely on the sheer will of his strength to pull back, and he didn't think that was possible. Not when there was something in the air entwining them together. It was like he was watching the action from a distance, through eyes that weren't his own.

Supporting his weight on his forearms, he pulled out of her and then watched as his cock disappeared inside her like magic. Nerina tilted her hips, taking him in deeper. Reaching up, she grabbed the posts of his bed and met him thrust for thrust. When her muscles began to clench down on his cock, her eyes locked with his.

He could see the entire ocean within her irises and felt himself falling under her spell. A place he could see himself indefinitely. When she came, she cried out his name. And he quickly joined her, moaning in ecstasy—his seed becoming one with hers. After a minute, his arms gave out, and he collapsed on top of her, breathing hard.

"Wow," was all Reid could say, his hands tangling with hers.

"My thoughts exactly," she whispered shyly, yet in that moment, he could see a change in her eyes. A knowledge that wasn't there before, but he was too tired to ask about it.

"Good night, Nerina," he said, drifting off to sleep.

*Oh goodness, I gave him the name of my mother*, she thought to herself, smacking her forehead.

## Chapter Six

### Present day Atlantis

"My queen, come quickly," her lady-in-waiting said, poking her head around the door frame. "You're needed in the vault."

Queen Nerina swam after her, trying to keep up with the spry young lady, who was moving better than she was these days. After her close call with a tiger shark, her tail didn't work as well as it used to.

The young woman stopped at the door to the vault and Nerina swam inside, skidding to a halt at the sight before her. The heart, the very living core of their great city, was sparkling brighter than it had in a long time, its synapses firing wildly into the veins that spread throughout the city, providing them with light and life.

Her jaw dropped and her eyes widened. The last time it did that was when her youngest child, Prince Adrian, was born, but it wasn't Nerina who was pregnant this time. Her days for having children were over and that could only mean one thing.

*Oh child, what have you done?*

A guard with a black tail stopped in the doorway, knowing he was forbidden to enter the sacred place. "My queen, may I have an audience?" he asked.

"Speak." Nerina said, turning to face him, her whitish-blue tail sparkling with the same life-force as that of the heart.

"We've found Princess Nixie."

"Where is my daughter?"

"She's on an island to the north, with a human. Shall we retrieve her?"

"That won't be necessary. This one needs a mother's touch," she said, especially if her suspicions were accurate. If her daughter was carrying new life within her, then the man's past had to somehow mingle with theirs.

Could he be a long-lost son of the northern tribe? It was believed that their ship had been lost on the journey to Earth. They had seen it collide with an asteroid prior to entering Earth's atmosphere. Four hundred people had been on that ship when it crashed into a volcano, causing it to explode.

"Prepare my orca," she told the guard, and then she returned to her royal chamber, her mind spinning. They had spent days looking for Nixie. No one had seen her leave, so they had searched every house in the city to no avail.

As Nerina was getting ready to go, King Wade entered the chamber. "Where are you going?"

She swam to her treasure chest and pulled out her bag with human clothes. "To get our daughter."

"I'll gather the guard."

"I don't think we'll be needing them, darling." Nerina pulled her hubby into her embrace. "I believe our daughter has found her suitor."

"What about Kai? We already promised her to him."

"What would you have done had my father chosen someone else for me?"

Wade's lips pulled to one side in a grin. "I'd have fought for you."

"Then our daughter deserves to choose her own, don't you think?"

She didn't think anyone else of the royal lineage existed, so their choices were slim to none. But if her hunches were correct, then maybe their people had ended the search too early all those years ago.

Wade planted a kiss on her cheek. "You're right. I should know better than to argue with the mother of my child."

"See," she said, winking at him. "You're learning."

Wade laughed. "Come on. Let's go see who our daughter has chosen."

***

"Nerina?" Reid asked, as he came up behind her. She'd been standing at the window, staring outside for at least an hour, not saying a word. Something heavy was weighing on her mind.

"My people are coming."

He pushed the curtain further back and stared out into the darkness. "How do you know?"

"I can feel them."

"Like telepathy of some sort?"

"Kind of." Actually, she had no idea what it was called. They were all interconnected with the life-force that powered their city like a symbiote. The royal family had been chosen by the gods to be the very heart of the merpeople, the life-givers of their fair underwater city. It was mostly passed down on the woman's side, which was why it was her duty to bear the next female heir to pass on the legacy, but she had to mate with a man of royal blood or the line would end with her and so would their city.

Sadly, there weren't many men to choose from, so her parents had chosen Kai, but she didn't love him. Never could. He was a cocky, arrogant merman, who acted like he was the king of the castle and she was just a lowly mermaid, not worthy of being treated with respect. He was good at being charming in front of her parents, but in private he was anything but. They refused to listen to her complaints, claiming that she had a destiny to uphold. Nixie had wanted the chance to choose her own destiny, be her own person for once in her life instead of being stuck locked in the castle.

That's why she'd jumped into the forbidden portal, trying to get away from the cosmic law that held her to Atlantis, but after doing so, she'd found herself in the middle of a storm that even she couldn't calm. Her powers hadn't yet reached their full potential, and she couldn't control the storm as her mother could. She'd gotten trapped in a riptide and struck a rock. That was the last thing she could remember before waking up on Reid's bed, right into the path of her new destiny.

"Do you remember everything?"

She nodded.

"Who are you?"

Turning to face him, she looked into his eyes. Worry was etched into every line on her face. "I don't know how to tell you this without scaring you off."

"Honey, if seeing your tail didn't scare me off, nothing will."

"My name isn't Nerina. That's my mother. I'm Princess Nixie Cordelia Albion."

Reid froze. *Holy shit.* He'd slept with a princess. That was certainly going to go over well with her parents and his. Weren't they supposed to be married to someone before being deflowered or risk a scandalous rumor that could hurt the crown?

*Ugh.* So much for being the gentleman his parents had trained him to be. Reid stepped back and frantically picked his clothes up from off the floor. "My underwear. Where's my underwear?" He knelt down to check under the bed.

She smirked. "You'd think I'd be the frantic one, since it's my parents that are coming."

"Your parents? The king and queen?" Reid stood up and buried his hands in his chin-length blond hair, a new sheen of red creeping up his neck. "Shit! Why wouldn't they just send a bodyguard?"

"My mom is quite hands on, much to our guards' displeasure."

"She's not going to kill me, is she?"

"Relax, cowboy. If anyone is going to get into trouble, it's me. I'm, uh, how shall I put this?" she said, biting her bottom lip before continuing. "I'm betrothed."

"But I asked if you were married."

"Amnesia, remember?" she said, shrugging like it meant nothing to her. "I have no plans to marry him, if I have any say in the matter."

Reid's mind was spinning. In fact, the room was spinning. Breathe. He had to remember to breathe. In through his nose, out through his mouth. This was crazy. Nuts. Why did he think having her in his bed would be a good idea? He should have waited to find out who she was first.

Would he have to fight for her honor against the man to whom she was betrothed? Reid rubbed his temples, hoping to ease the headache that was starting behind his eyes. He should have been thinking with his big head, not his little one.

"I'm sorr—"

She raised her hand and silenced him with a look. The water in the cup beside the bed bubbled. Steam twirled like tendrils into the air. "Don't be sorry, because I'm not."

He looked between the water and her. She was in a different league than he was. He had no business touching her or interfering with their ways. What the heck was he thinking? There had to be a reason they'd picked that man or merman for her. Didn't royals only pick those who could further their cause and their throne?

"And here I thought you were just a siren."

Nixie laughed. "I suppose you could call us that. Apparently, it's how our race was able to thrive after we arrived on your planet."

The story just kept becoming more and more bizarre. "So you're telling me that you aren't just a mermaid, you're an alien too?" Okay, now he knew he had fainted at the beach, and he must be in a coma or something. Real life just wasn't this bizarre.

"As are you," a voice said from behind him. Reid spun around and found himself face to face with a woman who looked like the spitting image of Nixie, except older, wearing a green and blue dress with flowing tendrils that reached the ground. It almost had the look of a jellyfish. A crown of green sea glass and light pink shells rested on her head. Behind her stood a man wearing the same colors as the woman's outfit, except his was hardened armor. In one hand he carried a three-pronged spear, a trident.

Was that King Triton's trident? Reid swallowed hard. "Hi," was the only word he could muster the courage to speak. He wasn't sure what they meant by "as are you."

"Are you here alone?" the king asked.

"My parents are on a cruise." His voice came out more croaky than he expected it to. When he'd woken up that morning, this outcome was the last thing he expected. He now had three aliens in his bedroom, and it kind of reminded him of the first time he had been caught having sex when he was sixteen years old. "I'm sorry. I didn't know who she was."

For a moment, they ignored him and examined Nixie. The queen ran her thumb over Nixie's goose egg. "Did he do that?" she asked her daughter.

"Of course not. He's been the perfect gentleman."

Her dad snorted as he eyed the messy bed beside them. "As much of a gentleman as I was at that age, I'm sure."

Reid's face warmed. He knew the king was acutely aware of what they'd been up to. "I'm so—"

Nixie kicked his shin. "Stop apologizing. We did nothing wrong."

"Manners, young lady, and you most certainly did. You weren't supposed to leave the palace. It's too dangerous."

"I didn't, not exactly."

"Then how did you wind up here?"

"The portal."

The king and queen glanced at each other in surprise. That was a first. Wade couldn't recall a single time he'd seen it active. "Could it be him?"

"What?" Nixie studied her parents. "What's going on?"

"In our history books, it speaks of a portal that once connected the north and south realms, but after we landed on earth, we lost contact with the north. We thought they all perished," said Queen Nerina as she circled Reid. "But we were wrong, weren't we, Reid?"

"I have no idea what you're talking about."

"New life has already begun inside Nixie, and not just any life. The child has made our city hum with energy unlike any other."

Reid glanced at Nixie's belly and backed away from them. "New life?" Had he been sucked into some weird type of psychotic game? "This is far too crazy."

"Far from it. You are an ancestor of the royal bloodline."

"I might be king of the saddle, but that's about it," he responded, suddenly feeling lightheaded. "I need to sit down." And he did just that, plopped his butt on the floor in his bedroom.

Was this the reason his parents had decided to live on an island? They'd spent his younger years inland, but his dad had said there was something calming about the sea. But not once did he mention anything about their past being this bizarre. That was a pretty big detail to leave out of their conversations.

He couldn't even contact his parents because their phones were on airplane mode. And if their itinerary was correct, they wouldn't reach the next port until the day after tomorrow. How was he going to tell them he'd knocked up a girl, and not just any girl? A princess from a species he knew nothing about. Was Reid who the queen said he was?

That begged the question. Were his parents his real parents or was he adopted? Nothing made sense anymore. And now these strangers were telling him he was going to be a father, and to what? A mermaid?

Queen Nerina knelt beside him and placed a hand on his knee. "I know how all this must feel."

"How could you? You're the queen, for Pete's sake."

"Do you think I was born a queen? I was raised on land, just like you were. No one told me a thing. Ironically, I found out much the same way you just did. It wasn't until after I got pregnant and things snowballed that the truth came out," Nerina said.

"Is that your way?" he asked. "Sending your kids to live on land?"

Wade came and stood behind his wife. "It used to be, back when we were at war."

"I guess war isn't just a human thing, is it?" Reid commented.

Wade shrugged his shoulders. "I dare say it's universal. There is always someone who wants more power. Thankfully, we are at peace right now. But back then, a royal child was given to special families on land who were hired to protect them. And when the child came of age, they were returned to Atlantis."

Reid couldn't imagine a parent leaving their child behind, to never see them until they were ready to return home. When he had kids, he wanted to be with them twenty-four hours a day, seven days a week. He didn't want anyone else raising them. And that gave him a royal dilemma, excuse the pun. He hadn't planned on knocking anyone up.

"So Nixie is pregnant with my child?" A mixture of horror, fear and amazement crept into his voice. They'd only done it once, and only today for that matter. Wouldn't it take a while for them to find out? Were they conning him?

"I'm sorry. I didn't know that was going to happen," Nixie said, cringing as she wrapped her arms around herself, looking as lost as Reid. He stared at her, not even sure what to say.

If she was pregnant, was his child going to be raised on land or in the water? Was the baby going to be raised by someone else or by them? Standing up, Reid pressed a hand against his forehead, trying to stop the drum pounding in his head. He couldn't sit anymore. His legs were antsy, and he needed to move. In fact, he needed to get away and do some thinking.

"I… uh… need to go do my chores."

"Can we help?" Nixie asked.

"No!" he said, a little more sharply than intended. "Sorry. I need time to think. If you're hungry, help yourself to whatever is in my kitchen." With that, he turned and hurried out of the room.

He didn't stop until he reached the safety of the barn, but he skidded to a halt when Chris came around the corner with a bale of hay. "Crap,"

Reid muttered under his breath. He'd almost forgotten about him.

"What's with the frown?" his friend asked.

"I, um…" Reid turned and looked toward the house, still at a loss for words. "You wouldn't believe me if I told ya." Their existence was obviously a secret from the world; otherwise they wouldn't still be classed as a myth. That alone made him hold his tongue. But Chris was his closest friend and was like the brother he never had. They'd grown up together. Chris's parents were their stable hands when they were alive, and Chris had stayed on the farm after an accident took their lives.

"Try me."

Reid was sorely tempted, but he wanted to talk to his parents first before letting any cat out of the bag. There was more information he needed before he could make any sense of it all. But that meant waiting for them to get to a port. That is, if they were actually on a cruise. What if they were in the ocean, not on it? That made way more sense.

Walking over to the tool closet, he pulled out a shovel. He needed to do something physical and work off all the excess energy that had built up. "I will. Just not right now."

Chris reached around him and grabbed a second shovel. "Let's finish these chores and then go for a drink somewhere."

That sounded so tempting, but he couldn't very well abandon the king and queen of Atlantis, could he? His parents would kill him for being so disrespectful. Sometimes he wished he wasn't so bound by principles.

*Where were your principles when having sex with her?* his conscience argued.

"Shut up," he muttered.

"Geez, sorry." Chris held his hands up.

"No, not you," he said, looking over at his friend apologetically. "I've got a lot on my mind."

"That's exactly why you need a drink."

"I wish I could, but I have company at the house." Reid gestured towards the house.

"You mean those regal dudes that I saw go inside?"

Reid just about dropped his shovel. Had he seen them come out of the water? "You saw them?"

"Ya, they were standing on the dock. But the odd thing was, there wasn't a boat."

"Someone probably dropped them off." Reid couldn't say why he was covering for them. He didn't owe them anything, but what if he was one of them? Then their secret wasn't just theirs to keep; it was also his. Humans weren't always known for being compassionate to those who were different.

"I've never seen them before," Chris said.

"I think they are friends of my parents. I said I'd try to contact them."

"They look like Nerina," Chris stated.

*Drat.* His friend had already honed in on that. The surprise must have registered on his face, because Chris said, "Holy shit! It's them, isn't it? How the hell did they find her?"

That was a question Reid wasn't entirely certain about. "Beats me."

"Did she recover her memory?"

"Yes."

Chris dug into a pile of used hay and chucked it into a nearby wheelbarrow, then leaned with his forearm the upper edge of the shovel with the bottom resting on the ground as he looked at Reid. "That was quick. Do you think she was pulling your leg?"

Honestly, that thought hadn't even crossed his mind. He knew in his heart he could trust her. Just how he knew that, he wasn't sure. There was something about her that screamed innocence. He half chuckled. Well, not so innocent now.

Reid shook his head. "No."

"How can you tell?"

"There's just something about her that strikes me as genuine."

Chris studied him for a moment before a huge grin spread across his face. "You guys did it, didn't you?"

Reid's face heated. "Just finish mucking out the stall."

His friend laughed. "How was she?"

"Just leave it alone," he snapped.

"Wow, chill."

Guilt riffled through him. He rarely got angry or upset so easily. Chris had always been a good friend, and he didn't want to ruin that now, not when he had a feeling he'd need their friendship in the coming days.

"Sorry. Maybe we should go for that drink after all," Reid suggested.

"The last one to finish their stall pays for the drinks."

"You're on."

## Chapter Seven

"How come you never told me about your time on land, Mom?" Nixie asked as she curled up on the couch, waiting for Reid to come back. Her parents had sat down on the love seat across from her.

"Because it's another story for another time."

"Please?" Nixie begged. She really wanted to take the attention off herself.

"What we need to discuss is what we're going to do about your situation," King Wade said.

"I'll marry him if you want," Nixie said quietly. It was a decision she could live with. In the short time she'd known him, she had connected with him in a way that she hadn't felt with anyone before. And she knew that if she had a kid out of wedlock, the merloids would have a field day with the story.

Her dad straightened his back and shook his head, looking every bit the king. "You're too young to get married."

"Well, what then, Dad? I don't see any other choice."

"For now, we're going to go back home. We need time to discuss this and come up with a more reasonable solution."

She mimicked his posture and defiantly said, "I'm staying here then."

Just then, Reid walked into the room. He glanced between the two, and she knew they looked like they were about to go into battle. Nixie walked over to him and threaded her arm through his, but he stepped away.

"Look, I don't want to trample on anyone's toes," he said. "My parents aren't due back for a while, and they won't be in contact range until the day after tomorrow, so go with your parents, Nixie."

Nixie drew in a ragged breath, her heart tearing in two. He didn't want her to stay. Had she read him all wrong? She studied his features, his eyes gaining the most attention. He was trying to avoid looking at her, but when their eyes did cross paths, he wasn't even looking at her the same way he had previously.

Turning away, she covered her mouth to stifle a sob, her eyes filling with tears. How could she have read the situation so badly? Unable to say another word, she raced towards the door and down to the dock. Nixie shed her clothes along the way, except for her shirt, and dove off the dock.

Just before her ears submerged, she heard him yell her name, but she refused to respond. Beneath the surface, her body temporarily glowed a bright blue color and a silver ribbon swirled around her legs as she made the transition.

Unsure of where she was exactly, Nixie swam down to the ocean floor and touched it. It hummed with energy beneath her fingers, revealing which way she had to go. Just when she was about to swim off, a hand grabbed her arm.

She let out an ear-piercing cry that made all the sea life duck for cover and twirled around to face her captor. But the minute her eyes fell on Reid, her fear dissipated, and anger took its place.

"Let me go."

He pointed towards his throat and then the surface and mouthed, "Please."

How could he be a mermaid when he couldn't even breathe underwater? He didn't even have a tail. Could her parents be wrong? Maybe another royal family member had got pregnant that they didn't know about. She should have paid more attention to her history classes, but she'd found them boring. She loved the present day better.

Unable to stay down any longer, he swam towards the surface, beckoning her to follow him. She should swim away, go back to the castle and leave him alone, but something inside her heart refused to deny him the opportunity to talk. She climbed up on the dock to sit beside him.

"You might want to hop in the water so Chris doesn't see you," he said.

"Why did you bother coming down to get me if you just want me to get back in?"

"I don't mean to sound like I'm trying to get rid of you. I just know that you guys like to keep your existence a secret, and Chris is the loud type. I don't know what he'd do if he found out."

She crossed her arms over her chest, her eyes wary. "That doesn't answer my question. Why did you come down and get me?"

Reid looked out over the ocean and ran a hand through his blond hair, ruffling it scrumptiously. The look in his eyes was one of confusion and pain. "I couldn't let you leave knowing that I'd hurt you."

"What did you think I would do? You told me to leave."

"Things are moving too fast. One minute I'm a normal man making love to a mermaid, getting lost in a fantasy; the next, I'm being told I'm one of you, and not just one of you but a royal, and that you're carrying my kid. I'm sorry. It's a lot to process."

Nixie looked down and fiddled with one of her scales, tracing the light blue color. "I'm sorry. I didn't know that was going to happen."

"How did they even know about... you know?" He pointed to her flat belly.

"The royals are connected intimately with Atlantis. It's not just a city. It's a being of its own right. Our life-forces work together to keep the city going. It knows when a new royal child is on the way. One that will take the throne someday."

"Are you in line for the throne?"

Nixie nodded. "When my parents are ready, I and my mate will take their place. I want that to be you."

"Nixie, we—I—" Reid was at a loss for words. Things didn't generally happen in this order. People meet. They date for a while, and then they decide if they're going to get married, and somewhere down the line, kids enter the discussion. But here, the kid discussion was upfront, and then came the proposal.

Nixie was so beautiful and unique—a woman you could search the globe for and never find. He didn't want to lose their new budding relationship, but if what her parents had said was true, he had so much to find out before he made a lifelong decision that affected them all.

"I'm not ready. I can't make a decision like that until I know who I am. It's not fair on you or your family."

Nixie took off her necklace and held it between her hands, her palms glowing. When she was finished with whatever she was doing, she handed it to him. "Use this to contact me before the next full moon."

"What happens then?"

"That's when my parents will announce my betrothal to Kai."

"How can I call you with this?"

"Just put it on the water and I'll know."

"Okay."

With a quick kiss, she dove under the water. Her parents quickly followed. Reid stared out over the ocean, still reeling from the shock of the new revelations. Chris walked up behind him and placed a hand on his shoulder, causing Reid to spin around and nearly knock his friend over.

"Don't do that," Reid growled.

"Geez, you're jumpy." Chris looked around. "Where'd your company go? I could swear they were here a minute ago."

"Gone for now."

"Great! We can go for those drinks now."

"Hell ya." Reid grabbed Chris by the shirt and practically dragged him to their boat. Maybe a few beers would make his head clearer again. He could only hope.

***

Reid's parents, Jodi and Ian, had finally got his message and had abandoned their cruise to return home. Nixie had been gone a few days, and he felt empty. Her presence had somehow filled a part of him that had been void. A void he had never noticed before.

"What's the emergency?" his mom asked.

"I think we should sit down," Reid said. "It's a doozy." He still wasn't sure what part of the story he was going to start with, but he knew they needed to talk about everything.

"What's wrong, son?" his dad asked, giving his wife a squeeze on the shoulder as they sat there. Reid studied them. How could he not have realized that they looked nothing like him? His father had black hair and his mother red. They shared no common features.

"I met someone."

His mother glared at him. "You called us back because you met someone? I had a hard enough time getting your father out of the house. Couldn't this have waited?" As she continued to stare at him, her eyes widened with knowledge only a mother could have figured out. "Oh, son, you didn't."

Reid nodded, his face reddening. "It kind of just happened."

"How far along is she?" his mom asked.

"That's the thing. We only did it a few days ago."

"That could mean it's not yours," his mother replied hopefully. "You don't usually find out for a few weeks."

He would have thought the same if the circumstances weren't so bizarre. "I didn't call you back here to talk about that, though."

"Oh gosh! What else could there be?" his mother asked, biting on her nails.

Reid let out a big breath before blurting the next three words. "Am I adopted?"

"Oh." His mother sucked her bottom lip into her mouth. His dad sat frozen in his spot, his back ramrod straight. Neither chose to speak up first. He could sense that they knew something.

"Please, I need to know."

His mother was the first to react. She stood up, her hip cracking, and went over to the filing cabinet in the corner of the living room. She pulled out a yellow manila folder and sat down on the coffee table in front of Reid.

"We found you on the beach in nothing but a teal blanket. No one else was around. We tried to find out who your parents were, but we came up against a brick wall every time. After a year, the ministry finally let us adopt you," she said.

"Why didn't you ever tell me?"

"I guess, in our eyes, we never considered you anything else but our son. You were ours in every way." She handed him the envelope. His dad remained silent but watched the exchange intently.

"Did I ever exhibit any unusual talents?"

"Aside from swimming as soon as you touched water, nope. Why the sudden interest in your past, son?" his dad asked.

Not answering right away, Reid opened the envelope and pulled out some pictures and the adoption papers. In one picture, his mother was holding a young baby on the beach.

"The woman I met happens to be a mermaid," he answered.

His dad's eyes narrowed as he studied Reid. "Did you fall out of the loft again?"

"Her parents were here too."

"And?" his mother pressed gently.

Should he tell them? They were going to think he was crazy and probably send him to an insane asylum. But he didn't know what else to do. He needed to know what they knew.

"They told us she was pregnant with the next heir to Atlantis, and that I was one of them."

"Seriously, son? I think they just pulled one over on you," his dad said, standing up. "I'm going to my den."

Did they honestly not know anything? Hadn't anyone tried to find him? Why had he been left on the beach? Too many questions and not enough answers. "Mom, Dad, please. If you know anything, I need to know."

"Don't you think if you were one of them, you'd have a tail?"

"I may have the answer to that." Queen Nerina's voice piped up from behind them. They all spun around and there stood Nixie's parents, with her behind them. This time, she was wearing clothes, instead of being naked, and looked every bit a princess, with the crown of shells on her own head. She wore a skin-tight aqua outfit, with a cape that had the Atlantean trident crest.

"Who the hell are you?" his father demanded. "And how the hell did you get into my house."

"Dad, you might want to mind your tongue," Reid whispered in his ear. "This is Queen Nerina and King Wade."

"King-smeen, I don't care. No one comes into my house uninvited."

"Please, excuse the intrusion. We were informed that you had made it back, and we felt the need to come and explain everything ourselves. I'm Queen Nerina," she said, bowing her head slightly towards Reid's father.

His father eyed the visitors with a gaze full of cynicism. "My son tells me that you're merfolk. Prove it."

"Dad!"

"It's alright, Reid," Queen Nerina said, pointing to a cup. "May I?"

His dad gestured towards the cup. "Be my guest. It's probably cold anyway."

They watched as the queen held her hand about an inch over the cup. "One of the things my family can do is this." Within a minute, the coffee in the cup was steaming again.

His dad's eyes narrowed, his arms crossing over his chest. "That's just a magic trick."

"Do you need to see their tails to believe the truth, Dad?"

His dad nodded, and they all filed towards the dock. Reid was happy that it was a private one and no one else could see what was about to happen. Nixie and her parents dove into the water and then surfaced a minute later, pulling themselves onto the dock—tails and all.

"Is that proof enough?" Reid asked his father.

And for once, his dad was without words. The truth of the matter sank into the depths of his gaze. For a few minutes, no one said a word. His father and Wade stared at each other. It was almost like a battle of wills was being fought between the two alpha males.

"What do you want with my son?" his dad asked.

"They have no idea about Atlantis, Queen Nerina," Reid said.

She nodded. "Just give us a second and then we'll go inside and talk."

After the tails disappeared, they returned to the house, and Nixie's family revealed the truth of where they were from, like they'd told Reid not that long ago.

"Okay, but what does that have to do with Reid?" his mother asked.

"We thought that the northern tribe perished in the descent and that my people were the last to survive, but we now know that isn't true. Reid is a descendant from the northern royal family."

"But if you guys arrived centuries ago, how is that possible?" his dad inquired.

"We weren't sure what had happened back then, so when we returned to Atlantis a few days ago, we hunted down the best historian we had. After some research, we discovered that while the ship died, a few families managed to survive. And their king knew that the only way they'd make it on Earth was to transition into being human. They didn't know that our ship had landed safely.

"But to make the transition and allow his people to live as one of you required the combined powers of the king and queen. They had to give up their life-force to do it. But they saved at least thirty people. Their two kids, with their mates, along with a few other families."

Tears shimmered in his mother's eyes. "How sad. But that still doesn't explain how we found him on the beach."

"No, I suppose it doesn't, but it does explain how their blood lives on in Reid," Queen Nerina said, "and how he managed to produce a royal heir. Albeit, I would have preferred them to be married first."

"I know I said that they were too young to get married, but after all things considered, we feel that it's the best way to move forward," King Wade said. "A union between the two tribes would be historic for our people."

"Don't you think that's for the kids to decide?" Reid's mother asked gently.

The four of them turned to look at their two kids. Reid walked over to Nixie and leaned down, whispering, "Come on. Let's talk." She took his hand, and they left their parents in the living room.

Once outside, he said, "It was getting too crowded in there."

"Don't I know it."

They made their way down to the rocky beach where he'd found her, and they sat on a large boulder. "When I found you here, I never expected things to turn out this way."

"Me either, but I guess we have some big decisions to make," she said, looking out over the ocean with her big turquoise eyes. "Would it be such a bad thing to be married to me?"

That wasn't what Reid had a problem with. "What do I know about being a royal? I still don't know who or what I am." She deserved more than anything he could give.

"I know enough. You are caring, loving, gentle. Everything I could ever want in a mate."

He cupped his hand under her chin and encouraged her to look up at him, "Would that be all I am to you?" He still had no idea what was expected of him. Would he just be a baby daddy?

"No. You'd be that and so much more. You'd be my mate, my lover, my friend, my king. And I'd be your queen."

He brought his other hand up and framed her face, allowing himself to get lost in the love he saw in her eyes. How that had happened so quickly he had no idea, but it made him believe in love at first sight. "I like the sound of that."

"Me too."

"So does that mean we're engaged now?"

"Not quite," her father said from behind them. "You need the queen's blessing."

"Come on, Dad," Nixie complained. "You just said we could inside."

Queen Nerina held her hand out to Reid. "There is one last thing that needs to be done."

Reid stared at her hand, unsure of what to expect if he were to touch it. "You're not going to kill me, right?" They had every right to after what he'd done.

The king gave a hearty laugh. "If you don't take her hand, you can't marry our daughter."

The queen wiggled her fingers at him, and he reached out, wrapping his large hand around hers. She then placed her other hand on top, closed her eyes and reached out to the water with her other. A small water vortex appeared and flew up into the air, then enveloped him like a cocoon. After a second or two, the water exploded into a thousand tiny particles before disappearing. He suddenly felt re-energized and full of life.

"What just happened?" he asked.

"I've restored to you that which had been lost." Queen Nerina rose on her tiptoes and kissed each of his cheeks. The king followed suit, but instead of kisses, he gave Reid a manly handshake.

His parents hadn't said a word as they stood at the end of the dock. His mother had her hands against her chest, her chin wobbling. She looked lost. He went over to her and pulled her into his arms, holding her close.

"You're leaving, aren't you?" she whispered.

"I have to go find out who I am."

"Please, promise me that you'll come back," she begged, holding onto his shirt tightly. "I don't want to lose you."

"I will. I promise." He couldn't have asked for better parents. They'd given him a safe haven to grow up in. A wonderful island to live on, and a love that was endless, despite his many shenanigans throughout his youth. He was certain he was responsible for a few of the grey hairs on his mom's head.

She gave him one final squeeze before letting go, tears falling down her cheeks. "Then go. Learn who you are, but I expect to hear all about it."

He wiped the tears from her cheeks. "Please, don't cry, Mom."

She leaned against his palm, holding it against her skin. "I knew one day that you'd move out, but I didn't think that you'd go somewhere that we couldn't visit."

"One day soon you may be able to," Queen Nerina said with a warm smile.

"We have to go," King Wade said. "It's a long journey back."

The queen, king, and Nixie dove into the water and then surfaced a few seconds later, beckoning to him. It all still felt like a dream, but something felt right, like his destiny had finally made itself known.

"Do us proud, son," his dad said, giving him a rare hug of his own, holding onto him tighter than ever before.

"Always."

"Don't forget about us," his mother pleaded.

"Never!" And with that, he turned and dove into the water with a tearful smile of his own. He always thought the island would be his future, but when one door closes, another door opens. And this door was so much more interesting than anything else he had planned.

And, somehow, he had a feeling he wouldn't regret a thing.

## The End

# Bird That Sings
## Dee S. Knight

*What the hell?*

Owen Gilchrist stared up at his horse from the ground. The two were atop a hill surrounded by green pastureland. If he twisted, he could see the house and barn, a mile away. But he wasn't supposed to be on a hill a mile from home. He was supposed to be mending a section of fence line near the road, a quarter-mile from the house. How the hell had he landed here, on his butt, while his horse lazily munched on grass and stared at him as though he had two fucking heads?

Gingerly, he checked his limbs to make sure he hadn't any injuries, though he wasn't in any pain. Nope, nothing wrong that he could tell. So, he hadn't been thrown from Goldie's back. He must have set himself on his ass with the view of the surrounding hills and grass.

His two hundred head of Limousin cattle were in the far distance. In summer, the high pasture area was lush with grass, and the streams that supplied Cottonwood Creek provided plenty of water. Owen could see the ranch Jeep headed down from checking on the cattle. Calving season had ended only a couple of months ago, and this was a critical time for the young critters. Jerry would laugh his ass off if he found out that Owen had had another "episode," so he'd better get himself in gear and get back to that fence.

Owen stood and slapped at the back of his Wranglers before taking Goldie's reins and climbing back in the saddle.

"How'd we end up here, girl? Huh?" Goldie kept her own counsel and chose not to answer. She was Owen's favorite female for that reason. He could say anything to her and she wouldn't get pissed. He could go out with the hands and blow a hundred bucks on beer and poker and she never sulked. She never tried to trap him with that age-old trick question of whether her butt looked big in that dress or those jeans or those slacks. And best of all, she never brought up the subject of marriage or moving their relationship to the "next level." He and Goldie enjoyed their relationship just as it was—he brushed her down and fed her oats, and she didn't throw him.

He urged Goldie into a lope down the hill and across one of the lower pastures toward the section of fence where he'd been working. A few minutes later, Goldie was once again feeding on the rich grass their spring rains and warm early summer days had provided. Fortunately, he'd pretty much finished the repairs before he'd lost contact with reality, so an hour had him gathering his tools. Jerry would come and get them in the Jeep. He jammed his work gloves in his back pocket and hoisted himself into the saddle for the ride home.

Suddenly a sense of unease struck him. The hair stood up on his nape and a frisson of fear skittered down his back. His head snapped around to the hill where he'd been sitting earlier. A figure stood there watching him. The shape was so amorphous he couldn't even tell if it was male or female. Goldie whinnied and took a step back. Did she sense something on the hill too, or just his fear?

"Whoa, girl." He stroked her neck and made calming sounds. As he watched, the figure turned and struck off down the other side of the hill.

"Come on, Goldie!" Owen dug his knees into Goldie's side and she took off at a gallop. In less than a minute they were again atop the hill. Owen jumped off and ran to where he'd seen the figure.

There was no one in sight. No one. In any direction.

These were pasturelands, damn it. There were trees in bunches on some of the far hills, but this was not forested acreage where a body could run and hide. The vista was vast—northeast toward the grazing cattle, south to the house and barn, north to the Yellowstone River, and west, well, to not much until you reached the interstate highway, and that was a long way off.

Crossed between frustration and relief, Owen slapped his hat against his legs and swore. "That wasn't my imagination, Goldie. No sir, it wasn't."

But there was nothing for him to see now, so he huffed out a breath and let Goldie take him home. This was the third incident in a week. What should he do about it? What could he do?

\*\*\*

"Pass the beans, please." Ross, Owen's younger brother, held out the bowl for him to take.

Meals on the Crosshatch G ranch were served at the house. Owen employed four hands and his brother, except during roundup, when they brought the cattle down from the high pastures in the late summer-early fall, and again in the spring when they took them back up. During those times, they were mostly out of doors and ate off the large, wood-fired grill brought along in the "chuckwagon," a four-wheel-drive camper that supplied all the basics. But most of the time it was just the six of them: Owen and Ross; Jerry, his foreman; and Hank, Mike, and Tom, his hands.

"How does everything look up at summer?" he asked Jerry.

"Good. They'll be ready to move to the west pasture in a week or so." He dug into the serving of shepherd's pie on his plate.

Ross drank half of the iced tea in his glass. "Hank and I are spraying tomorrow." This comment was met with a groan from Hank. In addition to the cattle, Owen farmed acres of hay and alfalfa, raised to feed the cattle throughout the winter.

"Tom, you and I are back on fence duty. We need to restring barbed wire in a few patches up north." Owen ran through other chores in his mind. There was always so much to do on a ranch, some of it boring and some of it too exciting or scary to be fun. At least they had calving and branding behind them for the year.

He hesitated before asking the question he'd been dying to ask all evening. "Did any of you all see anything strange this afternoon?"

Ross answered first. "I was out at the windmill all afternoon digging ditches for that new pipe. I didn't see anything but mud all day."

The others all murmured that they hadn't seen anything. Jerry gave him a focused stare. "I saw *you*, up on the hill again. I thought you'd meant to be fixing that fence down by the road."

"I *did* fix the fence. Didn't you notice when you stopped by to pick up the tools?"

"Yup, I saw all right. But I still saw you up on the hill. What were you doing? Having a picnic?"

Owen felt his cheeks heat. What could he say to that question? "Did Mrs. Walther leave us any dessert? I could go for something sweet." Bonita Walther lived in town. Twice a week she came out to clean house and cook enough food to last several days. The men took care of their own breakfast, slapped together sandwiches for lunch, but enjoyed her casseroles, soups, and stews most nights.

"Me, too," chimed Ross. "I think I saw a peach pie on the counter." He stood and picked up his dishes. "I'm on kitchen duty tonight so I'll check."

Hank, Tom, and Mike rose to take their dishes into the kitchen too. Jerry and Owen faced each other across the table.

"Lost time again?" Jerry asked.

"Yeah."

"You need to do something."

"What would you suggest?"

"Call your sister-in-law. Isn't she involved in some New Age woo-woo stuff? Maybe she has some ideas."

"I don't need woo-woo. I need a pill or something to knock this shit off." Owen hadn't meant to speak so harshly, but Jesus, he wasn't crazy or into crazy shit. He wasn't getting enough sleep or something. That was all.

"What can it hurt? Besides," Jerry said, "you haven't talked to Brendan in a while." He stood up, gathering his dishes and Owen's. "Think I'll help myself to some of that pie and a cup of coffee."

Owen stood too and stepped out onto the front porch. Twilight was the point he liked best. The cottonwood down by the creek stood in stark silhouette against the barely lightened sky. The temperature had dropped a good twenty degrees from the afternoon's high and the air felt crisp and cool. An owl hooted from the barn roof and, if he listened carefully, he could hear the horses settling in for the night.

*Maybe Jerry is right.* He plucked his phone from his pocket and punched the numbers that would connect him with his older brother, Brendan.

Brendan was a police detective in a small Idaho town. The brothers had been close growing up on a ranch where their father had trained horses, but by the time Owen had bought his own ranch, Brendan had moved to Idaho and given up ranching and horses. Owen missed seeing him, especially since Brendan had married and now had a couple of kids. Their lives seemed too divergent.

Would his mystery bring them closer? Or would his brother brush him off as a crackpot?

*** 

"Hello?" The voice on the other end was decidedly feminine.

"Amanda, it's Owen. How are you?"

"Owen! How wonderful. I was just thinking of you." Since Amanda was known as being a psychic, her words didn't surprise him. Nor, since she often sensed trouble in the future, did they bring him any comfort.

"Something good, I hope?"

"Depends," she said in a teasing voice. "Brendan and I were wondering if you'd mind if we came out on vacation again this year. We'd try not to come at too busy a time."

"That would be great! Just let me know when. I can't wait to see how much the kids have grown."

"I'm so glad! We can't wait to see you and Ross, either. I'd let you speak to Brendan, but he's not home."

"That's okay. I really called to talk with you. I, uh, I need help with something."

"Sure, anything."

In as succinct a way as possible, Owen explained what he'd been experiencing. "I know how this sounds," Owen said, "but I'm not quite sure what to do. It's getting a little worrying. We do some pretty dangerous things around here. I can't afford to lose control. Or time."

Amanda was quiet. Then she asked, "Have you seen a doctor?"

Owen let out a silent huff. "No. I guess I should. I'm sure it's just a matter of my not sleeping enough or something. I just thought, you know, with your special powers or something, you might have a different insight."

She chuckled. "My special powers? I'm definitely not Wonder Woman, but I know what you're trying to say. I can tell you that I haven't had any 'insights' about you. I would have called if I'd seen anything."

Owen sighed out his relief. "Good. I'll check with Doc—"

"But that doesn't mean you should dismiss a mystical answer. I have a friend who might be able to help. Would you mind if I passed her your number?"

Owen wrinkled his brow. "Uh, no. That'd be fine. Thanks."

"Either she or I will get back to you. Her name is Debra Mason, and she teaches here at the university. Until then, take heart. We'll get an answer for you, one way or the other."

"Thanks, Amanda. Love to you all. Looking forward to your visit."

Owen ended the call and stared out into the darkening night. Then he swung around and went back into the house.

***

When the phone rang two days later, Owen had his hand on the doorknob to return to work. He'd come back for another roll of barbed wire and had taken refuge in the house for a few minutes to have a quick glass of iced tea and to fill the thermos to take back for Tom.

"Hello?" He sounded terse, but it had been hot repairing fences. His sweat-soaked shirt turned cold in the air conditioning.

"Hello. I'd like to speak to Mr. Gilchrist, please. Owen Gilchrist?"

"You have him."

"Mr. Gilchrist, my name is Debra Mason. Amanda Gilchrist asked me to call you."

"Oh, right. I'm sorry Amanda bothered you. As it turns out, I think everything is fine. I haven't had any problem the last couple of days, and I think I was imagining things. But I appreciate your call." He started to end the conversation when she spoke again.

"I'm happy you haven't had any more episodes. But it's too bad, really. I'm from Chicago and was looking forward to being able to see a real ranch and cowboy. But if you don't need me... It was nice to speak with you."

"With you, too. Thanks for calling. Sorry to put you out."

"No worries. Bye."

After he pressed End, he thought about her voice. Soft. Gentle on the ear. Did she look as good as her voice sounded? He wouldn't have the chance to find out now, and that saddened him. He'd felt an immediate connection with Debra Mason. Or maybe he was being as "woo-woo" as his sister-in-law.

Owen grabbed the thermos and strode out the back door and to the driver's side of the pickup. He'd left Goldie in the paddock today since he was working alongside Tom, and they needed more equipment for the day's job. He missed being out with her, though. Any day on horseback was better than a day without. Maybe later he'd take her for a ride.

Suddenly, Owen saw no truck in front of him. The barn was missing, and the paddock. He turned to find the house had disappeared. Around him, prairie grass rose waist-high and swayed in the breeze that hadn't been blowing a few seconds ago. Looking down, he saw moccasins, and a soft leather dress that extended to mid-calf. Both the moccasins and dress were adorned in exquisite and intricate bead embroidery. A long braid of ebony hair fell over one shoulder.

A horse whinnied softly a few feet away. She—the girl he saw when he looked down his own body—made a clicking sound and the horse came immediately. Upon his back she jumped, and they galloped away to her favorite spot atop a hill—his hill. From there she could see north to the Rock River and the camp where her father held the title of chief. But her gaze focused on the east. *Tatanka*, or bison as she'd heard the white man call them, roamed in the valleys between the hills. She had heard her father speak of the increased numbers this year and the hunting would be good. Watching the *tatanka* gave her peace, knowing that her people would be fed well this year.

But it wasn't *tatanka* she searched out today. It was trouble. She didn't know how she knew, but she did. Her sixth sense never forsook her. She turned her pony to the north. Trouble for her people would be coming from along the river. And it wasn't going to be long in coming.

One blink was all it took to bring Owen back to himself. His heart raced when he realized where he was. He sat upon Goldie's bare back, facing east, just as he had twice before over the past ten days or so.

He shook his head and quickly checked his clothing. Wranglers with leather chaps covering from his waist and down his legs, protection against working with barbed wire. A long-sleeved cotton chambray shirt; worn, scuffed boots. In other words, standard work clothes. His hat, pulled low on his head, had withstood the gallop from the barn to the hill.

*What the fuck?*

As far as he, Owen Gilchrist, was concerned, he had no memory of leaving the house, mounting Goldie, or the ride here. As for the girl, the Indian girl he imagined, he remembered every second. The horse had been a Painted Pony. But not any type of Paint. It had been one with medicine hat markings—white with color on the tips of its ears and on the top of the head, like a top hat. While Paints carried high values among the Native Americans, these particular markings carried spiritual meaning. Indians believed medicine hat Paints had the power to protect the rider in battle. Owen didn't know about that, but he knew the horse had moved like the wind, and the girl had ridden as though she and the horse were one.

He somehow knew now that this spot had been a favored place of the girl's, and even now he felt her sense of peace. Except when he looked east, over the valley. What had she been looking for?

To give *himself* a feeling of peace, he turned and looked back at the homestead. The house and barn stood right where they should be. He breathed a sigh of relief.

"C'mon, girl, let's go home." Owen turned Goldie and nudged her into a lope. Energy expended, he felt emotionally and physically drained, but he and Tom still had hours of work ahead of them. He had to take a moment for one more thing, though, before he headed back to the fence line.

***

"Dr. Mason?"

"Yes. Is this Mr. Gilchrist? I just had the most peculiar—"

"I just had another episode. *What?*"

"*What?*" They spoke over each other, but their mutual shock came through loud and clear.

Owen started again. "I just had another episode. Right after ending our last call. Except this time was different. Looks like I need your help after all if the offer is still open?"

"Of course."

Owen heard paper being moved, like pages of a book.

"Look, our summer break started last week. I'll need another day to tie up last semester's work, and I'll be free for the next couple of months. Would it be all right if I drove up for a day or two and talked with you about what's happening?"

Owen thought through all the work he had to do. The chores never ended on a ranch, but this—this *whatever* was happening to him, had to stop. If Debra Mason could help, he had to make time for her.

"I'll make it work. What day do you think you'll be here?"

"Thursday? Will that work for you? Then we'll have the weekend to talk."

He gave a dry laugh. "You said you'd never been on a ranch before. First thing you'll learn is there's no such thing as a weekend. At least not in the sense of time off. We work every day. But Thursday will be fine."

"Which city is closest to you? Is there a hotel you can recommend?"

"Dr. Baker, the closest hotels are in Miles City, and that's too far to drive back and forth. Stay here on the ranch. We have space, and we'll get through our work together much faster."

"Oh! Okay, thank you."

He gave her directions to the ranch from Interstate 94.

"I'll see you Thursday evening, then. Since we'll be working together, you'd better call me Debra, don't you think?"

Her voice had dropped an octave, though Owen didn't think she'd done it with any purpose in mind. It sank below his conscious mind and hit a spot that made his cock stir. "And you should call me Owen."

"Thanks, Owen. And just so you know, her name is Bird That Sings. See you Thursday."

She ended the call, but Owen stood holding his phone. The blood had drained from his face. He gripped the steering wheel of the pickup and took a deep, steadying breath. He'd said he'd had an episode. He hadn't described it to her. Yet the name, Bird That Sings, struck a chord in him, as though the girl he'd seen earlier nodded her head and smiled.

What the hell was happening to him?

\*\*\*

In Milford, Idaho, Debra Mason, professor of psychology, sat back in her office chair and stared at the opposite wall. She'd never met this man, Owen Gilchrist, yet she knew him. And knew him in a deep sense, in an emotional way. She didn't know how yet, but meeting him was something she looked forward to. Maybe the man would affect her as strongly as did his voice? One could only hope. "But first," she muttered, "I have to get through this paperwork." Once that was finished, she could go home to pack and leave the next day. If she could get away early enough, she might get quite a ways across Montana before stopping for the night. She'd never been to Montana, having driven to Milford from her previous position in Nebraska, and she intended to enjoy the trip.

Her heart beat fast in anticipation. For the trip, yes, but more for her destination and the cowboy who'd captured her attention so thoroughly.

\*\*\*

"What beautiful country," Debra murmured to herself. In one state she'd driven through awe-inspiring mountains—the northern section of the American Rocky Mountains—and across the Continental Divide. She traversed wide plains. Signs for Yellowstone National Park showed up, pointing the way less than a hundred miles south of her, and then she found herself in a flatter landscape. Finally, she drove through hills and crazy rock formations.

For a good portion of her trip, the Yellowstone River had been her companion east, and having looked at her map before leaving home she knew she was partially following the Lewis and Clark Trail in reverse.

For someone who had always loved history and nature, this trip had already surpassed dreams she'd had when she took her teaching job in the Northwest.

In Miles City, she found a motel room and then ventured into town to find something to eat. A steakhouse filled the bill. When she returned to her room, she read again the directions Owen had given her and traced the roads on her map. Confident she knew where she was going, she fell into a deep sleep. Somehow, she knew she would soon need all of her energy.

Breakfast the next morning consisted of a bagel, coffee and an apple, all of which she picked up to go.

"Have far to drive today?" the desk clerk asked when she checked out.

"Not too far. I'm heading for the Crosshatch G ranch. It's just before I get to the town of Mildred."

The man snorted. "Can't really call Mildred a town. But you'll only need a couple of hours, however you go. Nice day for it." He glanced out the glass-fronted doors.

"Thanks! I enjoyed my stay. This is my first time in Montana."

"Well then, welcome. And enjoy the rest of your time in our beautiful state."

Smiling, she dragged her suitcase behind her and carried the coffee and her breakfast in the other. Once settled in the car again, she set her GPS for the road where Owen told her to turn off US Highway 12, slid her favorite CD of Neil Diamond in the CD player and took off.

Two hours later, she needed a bathroom badly. The ranch seemed to move with every mile of driving, and she just *knew* she'd never get there. The road twisted, mixed short straight stretches with ninety-degree turns, and in general made her keep her speed down. It was bleak but beautiful out here. Emphasis on the work *bleak*. She'd seen miles of fencing, hundreds of cows, and enough hills and valleys and creeks to last a lifetime. But no people, and no ranch.

Twenty minutes later, despite her dire predictions, she reached the turnoff to the Crosshatch G. In less than a mile she spied the house. "Thank God!"

She pulled in front, shoved the gearshift in Park, and turned off the engine. Trying to appear professional, she nearly ran up the front steps and knocked on the door. No answer. She paced a few times up and down the porch and tried again. This time when no one answered, she tried the door. Finding it unlocked, she called out, "Hello? Anyone home?"

With no reply, she dashed in and down a hallway off a very tidy living room. There she found a bathroom.

"No more coffee for you while you're driving backroads, missy."

Relieved and happy to be at her destination, she washed her hands, fixed her hair and straightened her clothes. Satisfied she didn't look as though she'd been traveling for almost three hours, she swung open the door and took two steps out… and crashed into a solid chest. A solid *male* chest.

A rugged hunk of a man grabbed her shoulders to keep her from bouncing back into the bathroom. His body was solid and tall. She was five eleven, yet he made her feel small and feminine in comparison. She looked up into blue eyes and black hair—so different from Brendan—and sharp facial angles. His dark beard already shadowed, though it was still morning.

*Oh, my God. Please let this man be Owen Gilchrist.*

"I sure hope you're Debra Mason and not some lost tourist who stopped in to use the toilet."

He still had his hands on her shoulders, and for the life of her she didn't want him to remove them. The connection she'd felt between them all the way in Idaho exploded here, next to him. Heat raged through her. She wanted to ravage him with her passion, seduce him with her desire, possess him with her hunger. It was all she could do to tamp down the thunder of her heartbeat and control her feelings with a wan smile. If he detected even half of the emotions running wildly through her, he'd run away, screaming for help.

"I *am* Debra. Sorry to barge in, but I did knock and honestly, I couldn't wait any longer."

Grinning, he answered back, "Twisty, bumpy kind of road, isn't it? I'm Owen, by the way. I didn't expect you until later."

Debra twisted her hands in an effort to keep them from wrapping around him and pulling him into a hot, greedy kiss. "Thanks so much for hosting me. It would have been awful making the trip out here from Miles City every day—even for a weekend."

Owen dropped his hands, mores the pity. "No problem. We have plenty of room. Hope you don't mind being the sole woman, though. Our housekeeper and cook is off for a few days."

"What?"

"Oh, don't worry," he hastened to add, "she left us plenty of heat-and-eat dinners. We wouldn't expect you to do anything." He gave a sheepish half-smile and rubbed the back of his neck. The very part Debra had a sudden urge to nibble and then cover in kisses.

"I have to admit, though, that not everyone knows why you're here. Just my brother and my foreman. The other guys, Hank, Mike, and Tom, think you're here to do research on ranching for some project. Sorry to put you in the middle of a white lie, but I don't want them thinking they're working for a crazy guy."

Debra took a deep breath and stepped back, halfway into the bathroom. "I'm sure you're not crazy, Owen. Not because of what you're seeing, anyway."

He frowned. "What do you think it is, then?"

"I'll want to spend some time talking with you and see where on the ranch you're having these episodes, but I'm pretty sure you're experiencing something natural. Memories of a past life."

It was all Owen could do to tear his eyes from Debra Mason's drop-dead gorgeous face. He didn't think it showed, but from the moment she'd crashed from the bathroom into his chest, he'd been drawn to her like a pony to hay. Auburn hair and hazel eyes held him captive, and he couldn't believe how lucky he was that he'd be spending time with this woman for the next couple of days.

Then she mentioned some shit about a past life.

"What?" he sputtered.

"Past life. Reincarnation."

Yup, he'd heard her right. "Sorry, but that's bullshit."

She straightened her shoulders and crossed her arms across a pair of beautiful tits. But he would not be distracted. "I thought you might be into some New Age stuff because you're a friend of Amanda's, but I never expected you to come up here and spout crap about a past life."

"If you thought I was into New Age 'stuff,' then reincarnation should have come to mind. It's natural. We all have past lives. It's just unusual to remember them. You're one of the lucky ones. And what makes you think it's bullshit, anyway? Have you made a study of it?"

He jerked back. "Hell no. It's a fact. You die and that's the end of it. Everyone knows that."

"Everyone does *not* know that." She emphasized her point by poking him in the chest with her index finger.

"What's going on here?" Ross stood at the end of the hallway while Owen and Debra glared at each other.

Owen breathed out a sigh. Debra was supposed to be here to help him get past these visions. Instead, she'd started his blood boiling, first with an unexplained passion and then with anger. And maybe a tinge of fear?

"Come on. Let's get out of the hallway, at least." He led the way past Ross and into the living room. "This is my brother Ross. And this," Owen said, gesturing toward Debra, "is Amanda's friend from Idaho, Debra Mason."

Ross held out his hand and she shook it. "I understand you teach. What area?"

"Psychology. I'm a licensed psychologist but don't have a practice."

Ross grinned. "Just for special nut jobs like Owen, huh?"

She smiled back at Ross. Damn it. A hot spur of jealousy raced through Owen. He didn't want her smiling at other men. Not even his brother.

"You might say that."

"Well, he needs help, for sure," Ross commented. "So, reincarnation, huh? I've always been interested in that."

Owen snorted. "You sure as hell have *not*." Owen suspected the beautiful doctor was what interested Ross, not her crackpot ideas.

Ross ignored him. "What are you going to do with him? I mean, how can you find out more?"

Owen knew what he'd *like* her to do with him, and he wasn't ashamed to admit it. To himself, anyway.

"We don't need to get into that, because she's not going to do anything. There's no such thing as past lives, and I won't be prodded or poked to try to prove there is." Although he wouldn't mind doing a little poking.

Debra turned a narrowed gaze on him. "Don't worry. I wouldn't dream of poking or prodding, Mr. Gilchrist. Thank you for the use of your bathroom. I'll be heading back to Miles City now."

*What the fuck?*

"Jesus, Owen. You and your narrow-mindedness has just cost us the prettiest houseguest we've ever had. I wanted to learn more about what she had to say." Ross nearly pouted.

For Christ's sake. Acting like a child, at his age. "You're nineteen, not seven, and you have work to do. If you and Jerry have finished in the hayfield, go on out and work on the fencing. Tell Mike I won't be back out today."

Ross frowned but grabbed up his hat and stomped to the door. "Nice to meet you, miss," he said. With a stink-eye look at Owen, he added, "If he can apologize, I hope I see you later at dinner." With the dismissal of thought that only youth could get away with, Ross was whistling by the time he reached the bottom of the steps.

Owen faced Debra, who, he noticed, was not showing a dismissal of thought. Anger darkened her eyes, and her mouth was set in a firm line.

"I apologize," he said. "I just don't believe. But maybe if you explain why you do, I'll find something that makes sense."

She huffed out a breath. "Okay. Before that, might I have a glass of water?"

"Sure. Come out in the kitchen. This is where all the important things get discussed, anyway."

He led her into the kitchen where he filled a glass with bottled water. "Our tap water comes from a well. It can taste a bit minerally to someone who's not used to it," he said, handing it to her.

"Thanks." She took a gulp. No dainty sipper, his Debra.

*His* Debra? Where the hell had that thought sprung from?

"In my line of work, lots of people doubt reincarnation. A lot don't believe in God at all, so to them, dying is just a black void of nothingness. Many of those who believe in God think the soul goes somewhere but never back to earth. Some few believe that the soul inhabits another body at some point and lives again, in order to correct past mistakes or improve on the lives they lived before."

"But they don't remember those lives?"

"No. You see how that would be overwhelming, right? Most of us have enough trouble taking care of ourselves in *this* life, much less trying to find our way through a labyrinth of multiple lifetimes."

"So, how's a guy supposed to correct mistakes he doesn't know he made? That seems pretty damn unfair."

"I know, right? We're supposed to be good people, striving for perfection, while getting through life. But we have help. Some experts in the field believe that we tend to run into the same people lifetime after lifetime—those who were friends and those who were foes previously. We can glom on to new people in life, but if they are important, they're probably someone you knew before."

"So, you think I knew this Indian girl in a previous life, is that what you're saying? I somehow knew Bird That Sings?" He tried not to look skeptical, he really did. But his eyebrows rose in doubt of their own volition.

"No," she said, looking like the cat that snuck up on the canary and gobbled him down. "I think you *were* Bird That Sings."

The look of shock on Owen's face would have made Debra smile, had she not known how close he was to dismissing her altogether.

"Impossible. She's a girl."

Debra shrugged. "The thought is that we experience both genders, and all races, religions, and socio-economic groups. The cosmos wants us to have the full complement of lives. Until we reach perfection, of course. Then we go to another plane of existence. Or that's what's presumed. No one really knows."

Owen snorted. "'No one really knows' is how you can explain this whole pile of—" He gave her a sheepish smile. "Sorry."

"Lots of very intelligent people have believed in reincarnation," she said. "You should do a little research on it before you knock it."

"I'll do that." He looked at the clock. "You arrived early. Are you tired or would you like to see some of the ranch?"

"I'd love to see the ranch."

"Can you ride a horse?"

"Barely. It's been years."

"I have a real gentle mare you'd be safe on. Want to try?" He gave an appraising look at her body. "You're dressed well enough if you'll change shoes. Shall I bring in your suitcase?"

"That would be great, thanks. I brought some running shoes I can wear."

Debra stared out the window over the sink while she waited for Owen to bring in her things. Past the barn and just to the left, the land seemed to extend forever. She exhaled a sigh on a prayer of thanks for affording her this opportunity. The tenseness of their argument washed away, leaving her relaxed. She couldn't wait to see more of the property. Something about it called to her. She felt at ease, though she knew nothing about ranches.

Minutes later, she exited the house and walked toward the barn where Owen was saddling a dark brown horse. "She's beautiful."

"This is Maggie. I rescued her last year when she was discovered mistreated. She's a sweetheart. We don't exercise her as much as we should. There's little time for pleasure riding here, so this will be a treat for her, won't it, girl?" He patted her withers and handed Debra the reins. "Come on. I'll give you a leg up."

Cupping his hands to form a step, Owen bent his knees to allow Debra to insert her left foot. As she jumped, he gave her a boost and she slipped her right leg over the saddle and settled into the seat. Maggie stood like a rock, for which Debra was grateful. It would take her a few minutes to feel secure riding again.

"Okay?" Owen asked.

"I think so."

"This is Goldie," he said, indicating the Appaloosa standing just a few feet away. With the smoothness of a glider sliding through the air, he took the saddle.

"How long have you been here?" she asked. They started at a walk past the barn. At a tall gatepost, Owen leaned down and lifted the latch. When she followed him through he secured the gate again.

"About six years. My brothers and dad and I lived on a ranch the other side of Miles City when we were growing up. Dad trained horses but he never had any interest in owning his own spread. From the time I left school it was what I wanted, so when I came into some money I started looking. Found this place. The moment I set foot on the property I knew I wanted it. It felt like home from the first moment. I hadn't even examined the barn or house or pastures. I would have offered exactly what the owner was asking in order to make sure I got it."

"But you didn't."

He laughed. "Hell no. I took a fine-toothed comb to everything. I'd come into some money, but buying this would have taken two-thirds of it. I couldn't afford to be blasé. We dickered back and forth, and eventually came to a price we were both happy with."

While they talked, Debra's head felt like it was on a swivel. She couldn't take it all in, and everything she saw filled her with delight. She'd never seen anyplace so beautiful. Glancing up, she asked, "Is that an eagle?"

Owen checked where she was looking. "A hawk. But we have eagles, so you might see one eventually."

She wanted to laugh in sheer joy. How had she missed this all her life? She could see why Owen felt this place was home. And here she was, a city girl from Chicago. Something about it drew her.

The pastures were rolling, with trees interspersed here and there. For the cows? Water ran alongside on their right, streaming away and then back, over rocks and through grass, seeming at once to be a trickle and then a rush. Though they weren't riding through trees, she heard birdsong from all directions. The sky was a deep azure and the sun warmed her.

"Are Ross and Brendan your only brothers?"

"Yes, thank God! Mom couldn't have taken any more of us. Brendan's the oldest. Three years before me. Ross was Mom and Dad's surprise. Twelve years later. And then Mom died a few years after that. Our house was pure testosterone." He smiled. "Do you have any siblings?"

"A sister. She's married with two gorgeous girls. They're still in Chicago." Debra guided Maggie closer to Goldie so she could see Owen's face while he talked. "Brendan wasn't interested in being a rancher, but Ross is?"

This time Owen laughed outright. "God only knows what Ross wants to do with his life. When he graduated from high school he told Dad he wasn't ready for college, so I offered him a job. So far, he hasn't shown any interest in doing anything else. I figured sooner or later he'll decide he wants to go to school, or he'll find someone he wants to marry and she'll tell him what he wants to do with his life."

Debra laughed too. "We're good at that," she agreed. "How big is the ranch?"

"Not large by Montana standards. About four hundred acres and about two hundred head of cattle."

"That sounds like a lot to me!"

"We have fifty or so acres in hay and alfalfa production. It's a lot to keep up with, I'll grant you." He shot her a sharp look. "That's why I have to get through this mess. It's interrupting my work. If this were calving season, I'd be going crazy right now."

Debra examined where they were. High on a hill. She could see a river far off on one side. The Yellowstone. Somehow, she knew it. *The Rock River.* The whisper in her head surprised her.

Grazing cattle filled the valley below. Owen helped her off the horse and they stood looking over a large portion of his ranch.

"This is where they used to meet," Debra announced.

"Yes," Owen agreed. Then he took her in his arms and kissed her.

Debra tasted sweeter than honey. His tongue pressed into her mouth and conquered it, sweeping across her teeth and swirling over her tongue. She moaned and wrapped her arms over his shoulders and into his hair. Nothing had ever seemed so right. No one had ever inspired such strong feelings, such a need to protect, to cherish. He didn't know this woman, yet there was a sense of familiarity he couldn't deny. A sense of intimacy.

She ground her hips against him. His cock grew longer and hard as stone. He could pound nails with it, but he wanted to pound her, slam into her body over and over until they both reached sweet relief.

He reached into her slacks and beneath the elastic of her panties, seeking that honey spot where he could penetrate her with at least his fingers. Ah! There. She was wet as the stream that joined with Cottonwood Creek below them.

"Wet," he murmured against her lips. "And hot." In response, she arched her back and raised her leg over his hip.

"I need you," she whispered on a moan.

Owen helped her to the ground. He dragged off her shoes and quickly stripped off her slacks and panties. Unbuttoning his jeans, he pulled them over his hips and freed his cock, thick and engorged. He gave it a long stroke. Debra followed his movements with her eyes that reflected a hunger that he shared. He fell between her outstretched legs. Her eyes glazed in heated desire. That's what Owen thought—and he knew his looked the same.

"What are we doing?" he asked.

"What we have to. If I don't have you inside me, I'm going to die."

"I don't have a condom."

Debra's eyes cleared. "Are you clean?"

"Hell yes. You?"

She half sat up. With one hand she grasped his nape and pulled him in for a fierce kiss. With the other hand, she stroked his cock. "Clean and on birth control."

Without another thought, he thrust into her, knowing in the back of his mind that he didn't know this woman, that he should have used more finesse, that they were here on his hilltop and any number of his men could see what they were doing. He didn't give a fuck. He had to have this woman. She must have felt the same. Locking her ankles behind his back, she bucked against him.

He pulled her blouse up to her chin and pushed her bra up. Taking a nipple between his teeth, he bit lightly and then soothed it with his tongue. She cried out but answered his actions by scratching his back. Pain sped his movements, driving into her. As he took her mouth and her tongue, they came. Her cunt milked his cock like a vice. Spilling his cum into her brought such a feeling of happiness, of peace and joy, that tears filled his eyes.

*Fuck!* What the holy hell was going on with him?

Owen broke the kiss in an effort to pull air into his lungs. Panting, he rested his forehead against Debra's.

"What did we just do?" she asked. "We don't even know each other."

"I know. I can't explain it. All of a sudden, I just had to have you. I'm sorry." He rolled off her and threw his arm over his eyes. His cum and her juices made his cock glisten in the sunlight. The scent of sex overrode the rich smell of grass.

"I'm really sorry," he repeated. "I've never done anything like that before."

"I wasn't a stump, you know. I participated, too. I needed the same thing you did and have no idea why."

"It was—" Owen stopped, not quite sure how to describe what they'd done, how he felt.

"Spiritual?"

"Yeah," he agreed. "An experience on another plane. Something unlike anything I've ever felt."

Owen sat up, then stood. He avoided looking at Debra as he fastened his jeans. "We'd better go. The sense of peace I've felt up here is gone. Even the horses are skittish." Goldie's eyes were wide and she threw her head back and forth. Maggie had started edging toward home, he grabbed her reins just as she looked ready to run.

When he turned, Debra was tucking her blouse back into her slacks. Seemed she was having a hard time facing him, too. Taking Maggie's reins from him, she said, "If you'll give me a boost, I'll be ready."

*\*\*\**

The ride back was nothing like the fun, leisurely trip to the hill. Owen said barely a word, and Debra obliged him by staying quiet, too. What had happened on the hilltop couldn't be explained, but she knew one thing—it had shattered her. She'd never had an orgasm like that. *Never.* Overpowering. Life changing. Supercharged. She still felt small aftershocks in her pussy, and rubbing against the saddle wasn't helping a bit. If she could touch herself, she'd go off again like an explosion. When had anything like that ever happened to her before? In her dreams, maybe. Never in real life.

At the barn, she was halfway to the ground when Owen grasped her waist. Even through her clothes his touch scorched her skin. Her breath caught in her throat and she couldn't speak.

"What the fuck are you doing to me?" His voice in her ear was rough and deep.

With reluctance, she twisted away. "Do you need help with the horses?"

"No. Best if you go inside."

Swallowing the need to do what she wanted, smother him in a deep kiss, she turned and nearly ran for the house.

A stranger in the kitchen introduced himself as Jerry, the ranch foreman. "Nice to meet you. I'm Debra Mason."

"Glad you could come all the way out here." Jerry glanced out the window as though ensuring they were alone. "I sure hope you can help Owen. He's fearing he's losing his mind."

"I don't know. I'm going to try. Can I help with dinner?"

"No, ma'am." Jerry peered into the refrigerator. "Hope you like chicken. It's fried, and we have mashed potatoes and greens to go with it."

"That sounds delicious. I'll go and clean up a bit and maybe come back and keep you company?"

"That would be nice." He smiled and then set about pulling dishes from the refrigerator.

Once in her room, Debra stripped and lay on the bed. Stroking her fingers through her folds, she thumbed her clit and inserted her middle finger in her pussy. Closing her eyes, in no time at all, she came again, biting her bottom lip to keep from crying out. She heard more voices in the kitchen and hallway outside her door.

Before she made herself come, she'd pictured Owen's face above her as he'd been not half an hour ago. Instead, as all of her nerve endings flared like fireworks on the Fourth of July, she saw the face of Bird That Sings and a voice in her head whispered, "My beloved."

\*\*\*

"Look," Debra said, sounding as exasperated as she felt. "Regression hypnosis will clear things up. I feel certain."

"*Look*," Owen said in response, "I am not going to let you into my head. That happened enough this afternoon up on the hill." He was leaning on the porch railing while Debra sat in a wicker chair. Owen had suggested they talk on the porch while the rest of the men cleaned up after dinner.

"You are *not* going to blame me for what happened earlier," she said. Heat filled her voice and she fought to calm it. She was the psychologist. She should be able to control her emotions. But damn! The man could make a nun swear.

"Don't get me wrong. The sex was great. Fabulous, even, but—"

"You know we can hear you in here!" Jerry called out.

"But keep on talkin'," Ross called. "I want to hear more about that fabulous sex!"

"Damn it! Now, look what you've done."

Debra opened her mouth to rebut his statement but decided not to bother. "Okay," she said, standing. "I hope your problem straightens itself out. I'll be out of here tomorrow morning."

Owen scraped his hand across his nape. She waited. He heaved a sigh. She reached for the door.

"What does this hypnosis do again?"

Debra sighed a little herself, but inside. Somehow, out there that morning, she'd been caught up in Owen's past life—for that's what she was sure he was dealing with. She wanted to know how and why.

"I'll help you relax. Then I'll guide you into the past. We'll see what happens. There are no guarantees, but I've seen this done and I've had some success with it myself."

"How many have you done?"

"A dozen. Nine have borne fruit. Three patients were too resistant either to the hypnosis or the idea of regression. If we do this, I want you to promise to be open to it."

Owen turned and stared out into the yard. Debra moved beside him. The sky sparkled with a gazillion stars. A shooting star fell to earth and she silently made a wish.

"This isn't just for you," she said in a low voice. "Something happened to the two of us today. The *two* of us. I want to know what's going on as much as you do."

"I'll do it. When?"

"First thing tomorrow. When the men have gone out and the house is cool and quiet."

"Okay," he said, and she didn't hear the reluctance she'd expected. "We turn in early on the ranch, so I'll see you in the morning. Breakfast is at five-thirty." With that, he left her on the porch.

When the door opened a few minutes later, she thought he might have come back. Instead, Jerry spoke. "Thanks." Then the door closed again.

***

"Tom and I are going up to the pasture to check on things. Won't be back until tonight." Jerry talked as he carried his breakfast dishes to the sink. "Ross, if the fence work is finished, will you and Mike start cutting the hay in the north field? There isn't supposed to be any rain for a few days. It you cut it today and tomorrow, we can get it all bailed by the weekend."

"Hank, I *think* we've got all the fence repairs done, but ride the line, will you, and double check?" Owen gave the order. "And then maybe ride out and help Jerry and Tom. I want to be sure all our calves are thriving. We had a good number this spring, and it might take a while to check them all."

"Will do, boss," Hank said. He followed Mike, Tom and Ross out the back door.

"I'll take care of cleaning up," Debra said. "Breakfast was delicious. Thanks."

"I appreciate the help," Jerry said, "but just take care of that one." Pointing to Owen, Jerry grinned and left the house.

"When do we start?"

"Right now, Debra answered. "You'll need to stretch out and be comfortable. Couch or bed?"

"Bed." He led the way to the room at the end of the hallway. It was masculine without being too over the top. Browns and beige dominated the color scheme. The bed was generous in size, as befitted his over six-foot frame. A tallboy dresser with a few family photos took up one wall. A desk with books, lamp, and his hat sat below a window on another wall. The fourth wall sported a door that led into a closet or bathroom. Since it was closed, she couldn't be sure which.

"Take off your shoes. Loosen your jeans or shirt, or anything that restricts movement or your breathing. And then lie down so that you're comfortable."

While Owen took care of that, she pulled down a window shade, plunging the room into semi-darkness. She moved the desk chair to beside the bed.

"Comfortable?"

"As I can be," Owen said. Tension in his voice told her that she needed to start before he decided she was finished.

"Take a deep breath," she said, keeping her voice calm and even. "And another. Good. Now, close your eyes and listen to my voice. Only my voice. Picture a staircase going down into a darkened space. There are many steps. Take the first step. It's cooler than in the room you just left. Take a breath. The air is sweet. You feel relaxed.

"Take the next step. Your mind is clear. You have no worries, no thoughts except continuing on. You're relaxed and feeling sleepy. You're fifteen years old. What are you doing?"

"Helping my dad with a new mustang they just brought in. He's feisty, but my dad can handle him."

Owen's voice was younger, eager. "You like helping your dad?"

"Oh, yes, ma'am. My dad's the best, and the best horse trainer in Montana, too."

"Take the next step, Owen. You feel your breathing deepen. You're five years old. What are you doing?"

A young boy's giggle emerged from adult Owen's mouth. "I'm holding a puppy. He's funny. Mama said I can hold him if I'm real careful. I can't wait to go outside and play with him."

"That's good, Owen. Take another step now. You're sleeping and calm. Your breathing is steady and deep. Take the last step. Open your eyes. In front of you is a door. Do you see it?"

Owen opened his eyes and stared at the ceiling. Then he nodded. "Yes."

"We're going back to before you were born. Back many years. Back to when buffalo roamed the hills of eastern Montana. Open the door, Owen. What do you see?"

"I'm riding Wind Runner up to the top of the hill. It's my favorite place." Owen's voice wasn't feminine exactly, but lighter.

"Are you Bird That Sings?"

"Yes."

"What do you have on?"

"A dress made from tanned hides. I wish I could wear leggings, like Silent Bear. It would make riding so much easier."

"Who is Silent Bear?"

Owen wrinkled his brow. "He's my intended. We're to marry at the next full moon."

"Are you looking forward to that?"

For several seconds there was no reply. Was it Silent Bear she'd felt on the hill? Was it he who whispered something about a beloved?

"I will make him a good wife. He will be a good provider."

Not exactly a rousing endorsement of love and marriage.

"Are you on the hilltop now?"

"Yes. I love it here. But lately, I've felt something wrong. Something is in the wind. I'm frightened."

"Look down in the valley. What do you see?"

"Buffalo. Many buffalo. On the banks of the Rock River, I see my father's camp. But off in the distance, up the river, I see the dust of horses." Owen gasped, and worry marked his face. "This is the change I've dreaded."

"Take a deep breath. Nothing can hurt you. You see these things, but you are no longer part of them."

The worried look on Owen's face smoothed out. "We're going to go forward a few days," Debra said. "What is happening?"

"Bluecoats are in my father's tent, talking. Many of us are gathered to watch the men, waiting for them outside. I am in front, as befits my position as Chief Shadow's daughter. My brother and father are inside. Silent Bear stands behind me, close, as though I need protecting. I don't."

Owen kind of stretches to his full length, and Debra can picture Bird That Sings doing the same. Then he gasps again, but this time not in dread.

"One of the bluecoats is looking at me. He is handsome. His eyes are the deepest blue like the autumn sky and his hair is red as the sunset. He is smiling. Can I smile back? I can and I do. I feel Silent Bear stiffen behind me, but I don't care. This man's smile makes my heart race faster than the rabbit runs. He is tall and strong—a worthy man. What is he called? I wish we could talk, but I don't know the white man's language."

Owen put his hand over his heart. "Oh! He makes my breath catch. I've never felt this way before. Silent Bear has touched his lips to mine and my heart doesn't jump the way it does with just a smile from this bluecoat."

"You're doing well, Owen. Let's move forward a month or so. Where are you?"

"On the hilltop with my beloved."

*Silent Bear?*

"We have met here every evening for the past week. We speak with hand signals, and with our hearts. He told me several moons ago that he is leaving and today is the day our time is ending. I want to die. I can't stand the thought of never seeing him again. I have given him my heart and he has given me his.

"When the bluecoats first came to our camp, they spoke with Father about hunting *tatanka*. Father laughed and told them that there are so many *tatanka* they will last forever. So now his men have enough meat to continue on their journey and they are leaving, going toward the evening sun. If only I could go with him!"

Owen sighed. "He holds me. He is loving me as though he never wants to let me go. I feel him inside me and I wrap him in my arms. How can I go on without him? Tears flow down my face. I will never marry Silent Bear now—I cannot. My beloved, my Mark, is the only man I will ever love. I pray he will leave me with a baby.

"*Mark!* I cry his name silently, knowing he must go and I cannot. He rides north, towards the river and his own encampment. Soon he is only a speck in the fading light. I fall to my knees and sob. From behind me, I hear a sound. It's Silent Bear. 'You disgrace me,' he says. 'You are betrothed to me, promised to *me*, and you lie with that white man.' I tell him that I will not marry him. I cannot now that I know what true love is. He raises his rifle, and before I know to say or do anything, he shoots."

"Pain," Owen cries out.

"You don't feel the pain. You are an observer, remember."

"It's all right. It's over." And Owen is quiet.

"Owen, do you hear me?"

"Yes."

"You're going to come forward now. Listen to my voice. Go back through the door. Start climbing the steps. With each step you will come towards present time. Are you climbing the steps?"

"Yes."

"As you come forward, you will feel refreshed and well-rested. Each step brings you closer to waking up. You will remember everything and will feel content with the knowledge, not disturbed. Are you at the top?"

He nodded. "Then wake up, Owen."

For a moment Owen simply blinked. Then he turned his head and stared at Debra. "Did it go all right?"

"That depends on you. How do you feel?"

"Great. Like I've been asleep a week." He scrubbed his hands over his face and swung his legs over the side of the bed. "That was weird."

"But productive, don't you think? We have a starting point to discuss why you're seeing and feeling these unusual things."

"So you think I was an Indian girl, in love with one man and engaged to another? That I was shot by that Silent Bear guy?"

"What I think doesn't matter. What do *you* think?"

"I don't know. You're right, though. It's given me lots to think about. It seems the whole major points dealt with change. Maybe that's what I'm being warned about? Changes coming in my life?"

"That seems logical."

"Great. If there's one thing I have a hard time dealing with, it's anything that will take time I don't have. Change means inconvenience, lack of routine." He shook his head.

"Well, Debra, I want to thank you. I know I gave you a hard time, but I honestly feel better. Maybe that cleared all the cobwebs out and I can get on with my work." He reached for his boots. "Speaking of which…"

"Right," she said. "Look, I don't want to be in the way. I'm going to clean up the kitchen and get on my way home."

Owen frowned. "No! I mean, I'd like you to stay." He cupped her cheek and stroked it with his thumb. "We haven't figured out the part you played in this mess. You felt something up on the hill yesterday."

"I think I was caught up in your emotions. I don't think it can be more than that."

"Stay," he whispered. "I have work I have to get done during the day, but I'd like to get to know you better."

"No time. You go to bed early on the ranch, remember? And your days are full. It was great meeting you, though."

He studied her eyes, leaned forward and gave her a kiss. "I've never felt with anyone what I feel with you. I think I could love you."

*I know I could love you.*

## Epilogue

"You aren't going to believe this," Debra said to Amanda three weeks later. "My mom was going through some of my dad's parents' things and found some genealogy material. My dad's great-grandfather was in the army during the Civil War and stayed in for a few years afterward. He was in a troop that came west. Right across Montana and Idaho and into Washington!

"It's so exciting! I didn't know I had any attachment to the west until now. I felt a real affinity for Owen's ranch. Maybe that's why." She turned in her chair and twirled a few strands of hair with her fingers. "Speaking of which, have you heard from Owen?"

"Just that he's feeling so much better. Whatever you did seems to have helped a lot; I can't thank you enough. He's a really special man. He asked about you, by the way."

"He did? Why didn't you tell me?"

Amanda laughed. "I'm telling you now. I swear he's sounding like a man in love. You *were* only there a couple of days, right?"

"An intense couple of days."

"I guess so. He mentioned he might come to visit next month. He's never taken time from the ranch to come here, so I can only think it's you that's forcing him into such drastic measures."

Debra's heart skipped a beat and then took off running. "Maybe it's time I give him a call."

"Let me know what's going on."

Debra promised and disconnected. Should she call? *Yes.*

The phone rang three times before she heard, "Yes?" It was him— Owen—the man she'd thought she might never hear from again.

"Owen?"

"My God, Debra! Where are you?"

"Home. Listen, Owen, are you sitting down?" She explained about the paperwork her mother had found. "My ancestor's name was Mason, Lieutenant Mark Mason. From other papers Mom found, he had red hair like most of the men in Dad's family."

"What?" Owen's voice was firm, but she heard the disbelief he must have felt.

"I think... I think he's Bird That Sings' bluecoat."

She took a deep breath. "There's something else, too. You're not going to be happy about this, and I'm so sorry, but you deserve to know. I'm pregnant."

"How can that be? You said you were on birth control."

"I was. I am, or I was before I saw the doctor this afternoon. I remember how you feel about changes in your life, and I promise I will take care of the child myself. I just thought you should know."

"I'm going to be a father." He said it wonderingly. "Come back, Debra. You belong here, on the ranch. Our kid should grow up with his legacy."

"Or *her* legacy."

"Yeah, maybe, but my family has a proud tradition of boys." He actually sounded proud. And smug. "Or we can get married down there. Or in Chicago, if you want, though I can't take too much time away. Cattle don't care if I'm in love or getting married or what."

"We hardly know each other. It's only been— Hold on. Did you say love?"

"I can't get you out of my mind. I dream about you. I *day*dream about you. I can't go up to my favorite spot without remembering what it was like there with you. I love you. When you know, you know."

"But Owen, we only spent two days together."

"So what?" he said quietly. "Bird That Sings only spent a few weeks with her bluecoat. She wanted his baby, and now we're—"

"I know," Debra whispered. "I love you, too."

## The End

## Craving Her Cowboys
## R.M. Olivia

"So, this is it. Really and truly it. The first day of the rest of my life, the day I make my escape."

I sighed, exhaling a large breath. The bright sunshine and bird song outside my window felt like a definite contradiction—another utterly gorgeous day like any other in the Lone Star State. After I left Edward, the Earth would keep on spinning, and no one would be any wiser. I'd woken up today like I did each morning, but today was different. This feeling of foreboding, a living nightmare that surrounded me each night when I went to bed and greeted me first thing when I woke up to his snores, had come to an end. Finally, I'd paid attention to my gut.

And here I stood, stuffing the contents of my life into an oversized gym bag. Soon to be on the run. With one foot out the door of my old life, the other racing towards the new. Sudden waves of trepidation and excitement passed over me. Now that I was leaving, what next? My emotions tugged at me. I knew I'd be facing my life alone. For the first time in years, decades even, I'd be without a man. Leaving this one was far from a loss, but still…

Could I handle what lay ahead of me? Getting lost in my thoughts? And being all alone? Hearing the sound of my own voice and learning to enjoy the pleasure of my own company? In two months, I'd be thirty-three, and I'd spent half of my life wrapped up around someone else. So, having a partner was the norm. My norm, no matter how much my heart told me otherwise.

When my mother said never to ignore my instincts, I should have listened. But you know what they say about love. I was blind. Blind to his dark side. Blind to what a healthy relationship truly meant.

I played with the ring on my finger before slipping it off one last time and leaving it on the dresser. What did my soon-to-be-ex call it?

My little present. Not an engagement ring, because he couldn't be sure about making such a big commitment. He didn't want to be pinned down. Only I hadn't believed him. Hadn't believed his words. Or his actions. What did that make me? Had I seen the writing on the walls and ignored it? I covered my face with my hands. I'd worn the cheap band proudly with thoughts of marriage and children, never fully realizing that it was just something to show ownership. Something to keep the other men away. Now I planned on keeping him away. Permanently.

"Stop complaining. We've been over this. Can't you see I'm trying?" His weak words played in my head like a broken record. They were engraved in my memory.

Unfortunately, some people just never change. Instead, they grow another year older and uglier. Both inside and out.

I took a pillow and a blanket and stuffed them into my bag, struggling with the zipper. They wouldn't fit completely. I removed the blanket, folded it, and threw it over my shoulder.

Then I opened my closet door and removed my go bag. I'd hidden it in the back behind his clothing. I'd meant to move it into my car, but something always came up. The closet had been a safer proposition. Edward rarely went inside besides grabbing his daily uniform of t-shirts and slacks.

"Shoes. Heels or sneakers?" I said aloud before tossing some of my designer pairs into my bag. They'd nearly cost my entire paycheck. I shook my head. You can take the girl out of the fancy neighborhood, but you can't take the fancy out of the girl. Manolo Blahniks were less than practical, but my cousin would definitely be impressed. I'd be able to feel like we shared something in common. And feel like I had not made the biggest mistake in my life by moving away from my family's luxurious accommodations into a cheap nightmare.

A bug ran across the floor, nearly dive-bombing my feet. I jumped. With all the money Edward had been saving, you think he'd be rich. Instead, the money went straight from his pockets to his bookie.

I knew he'd flip out once he discovered what I had done. But leaving him had been my only option, especially after last night's argument.

My head began to throb. I reached into the dresser drawer and removed a bottle of Tylenol, spilling two into my palm. I downed the oversized blue pills with several swigs of water. I wiped the sweat from my brow and frowned—only mid-morning and already close to eighty degrees. The afternoon would only get hotter. I turned up the air conditioner. Might as well be comfortable before this became nothing more than a bad memory.

I opened my jewelry boxes and emptied my earrings and necklaces. It was bad enough that he'd taken one of my favorite chains and hocked it for gambling money. I would not allow him to take anything else. He had stolen more than enough from me. By leaving him, I was getting it back—my freedom and my peace of mind. No man would lay a finger on me ever again.

I looked down at my Smith & Wesson.

"Thanks, Mom." I'd been taking lessons since the start of the new year with the gift certificate my mother had sent me. A gift I never thought I'd actually use. Now, I was just thankful. I could protect myself. Hold my own.

But actually pulling the trigger, now that was another story. Proof of the pudding being last night.

What was wrong with me? I'd had the gun within reach, and I'd faltered. Once Edward hit me, I should have shown him what I'd been doing with my time. My Tuesday evening book club that never was.

But no… I didn't. Fear held me back. Kept me silent and submissive. Since he had so many friends on the force, I knew I'd never win.

I grabbed the heart-shaped picture frame on the dresser and tossed it to the trash. Once he came home, he'd get the message loud and clear. We were through.

I thanked God we'd never had children. Once I walked out the door, I'd have nothing tying me to Edward Greene. Nor this godforsaken town.

I shivered. It had gotten cold in the apartment. I threw on a hooded jacket. If I left the air conditioner running for hours until he got home, that would drive him crazy. Not to mention the electric bill would be higher this month. I smiled.

I took pen and paper and began scribbling before ripping the paper up, tossing the pieces into the air, and watching them rain down onto the shitty carpet below. I wouldn't leave anything behind for my ex. Not in writing. I wouldn't waste a drop of ink on a goodbye letter. A letter that he didn't deserve.

Instead, I pulled out the torn envelope hidden in his underwear drawer. His secret photos of his mistress and a pile of love letters. It blew my mind just how romantic he could be when the woman wasn't me.

"Asshole." I'd leave the photos and letters on his side of the bed as a parting gift, my fond farewell. But not before adding my special brand of payback.

I took the pictures and flipped them over, writing in capital letters: SURPRISE. YOU THOUGHT I DIDN'T KNOW.

But a woman always did. I wished his girlfriends luck, as they would need it. Hell, they'd need a hell of a lot more than luck to deal with him. Simply a miracle.

"Let him be someone else's nightmare," I said to the mirror, passing a hairbrush through my waves of auburn. I tossed the brush into my bag, eyeballing the rooms. What else could I take without being too much of a struggle? What could I fit inside my old car?

My grandparents' old furniture caught my eye.

"Damn," I whispered, touching the cute red kitchen chairs and the cherry wood table. Both old-fashioned yet comfortable. Both gifts from my grandparents. Things I'd miss. I remembered Sunday dinners at their house. The scent of freshly baked bread on the table and meat or fish cooking on the stove. The five of us all gathered around at the table, a prayer on our lips about to give grace. Their house had felt so big. Everything had seemed bigger when I was a child. Besides the furniture, I had a few photos for memories—nothing else. I felt a tear in my eye.

Giving up furniture was a small price to pay to start afresh.

"I'm sorry, Grandma. I know you would never want him to have your things, but I have no choice." I couldn't sneak off with a U-Haul. This was the only way. Come hell or high water, I was leaving. I adjusted my posture and straightened up.

"Grandpa Phil, I finally grew a backbone. I finally woke up. And I'm leaving." I breathed, squeezing an extra pair of socks into my bag.

The sound of an old car engine growling in the distance snapped me out of my reverie. No time for memory lane; I couldn't linger. Couldn't run the risk of him catching up with me. I shook my head.

My cell phone beeped, nearly making me jump. A text from Edward? My breath caught in my throat.

"Holy shit."

*Is he coming home early? Meeting canceled? He could very well be on his way. I gotta blow out of here. Now and not later, if I want to survive.*

My hands shook as I reached for my phone and read the text.

>Coming home early.

"Fuck," I whispered.

With that, I locked the door and jumped into my car. I had a tank full of gas, all my important papers, and money. My last paycheck had been deposited into my account, along with the money I'd been squirreling away in my own version of an "F you fund."

I looked back towards the apartment. If I move some things around in the trunk, maybe I could fit in the table.

The nefarious ringtone on my cell made up my mind for me. My ex-boyfriend was calling. I could not return. I had to leave. And I had to go now. The opportunity for a clean escape might not come again.

I put my cousin's address in MapQuest on my phone and waited for the direction to appear.

Dallas was a few hours away, but I'd make it. I'd wake up tomorrow morning at Lucinda's in the lap of luxury. With all of this behind me. Saying "Edward who?" And since he had another woman, he wouldn't waste time chasing after me. I prayed. Alone for once, and it actually felt good. My fear vanished with each exit I passed.

Cousin Lucinda in Dallas. Might as well have been a foreign country. What did her husband do anyway? I couldn't put my finger on it. I think I'd read online about their wedding. He came from a family of businessmen and doctors.

I knew I'd have to confide in Lucinda once I arrived. She'd probably feel so bad that she'd let me stay until I got back on my feet. Once I'd settled in, I'd start looking for a job. Then, once that panned out, I'd get a place of my own.

I only hoped Edward didn't look for me. I knew I couldn't run forever. I bit my lip and felt the tears roll down my cheek before I flicked them off my face.

"Enough. You left him. It's over," I said, tightening my grip on the steering wheel.

Although my cousin and I had never been particularly close, I doubted she'd turn me away. Not in a situation like this.

I pressed on the gas, increasing the speed and distance between my past and present. I continued driving until I finally found a safee place to pull over.

>Hey, Lucinda. It's me, Riva. I'll be in the area and want to come by. Love to spend some time with you. TTYL, R.

*Text me back, Lu. Pretty please. Sooner the better,* I thought.

Since Lucinda had married well, she'd gained a grand style home with extra rooms that they never even used. Between the maids, housekeeper, and spacious grounds, she won't even notice I'm there. I sure hoped to God she'd be home. Otherwise, I wasn't really sure what I was going to do.

I looked over my shoulder in the rearview mirror. If I jumped on the next exit, I'd be there in no time. I released my breath, and my rapid heartbeat seemed to slow. Had I been holding my breath this whole time?

The sign said *You are now leaving Fredericksburg.*

"Thank Goodness."

I was out of that town. Dallas, here I come.

\*\*\*

I yawned. I'd been driving for who knows how long. My legs and lower back ached, and I wanted nothing more than to go lie down somewhere. And take a long hot shower.

"Thank God," I exclaimed, pulling into a parking lot directly in front of a rest spot. I watched truckers and tourists wander around. I'd freshen up, have a snack, and be on my way.

I used the bathroom, washed my hands, and splashed some water on my face. I frowned at my reflection.

"When this is all over, you deserve a vacation," I told myself, stretching out my legs before heading back to the car.

"You have one new message," my phone voicemail said.

"It's Lucinda. Thank God. She saw my text and has got back to me. Alleluia!" I pumped my fist into the air.

*Riva? They told me you quit work? Where the hell are you? I know you're there. So, pick up. Pick up the fucking phone now!* Edward continued to rant and rave until he finally got cut off.

I hit erase.

"Holy shit!" That had certainly got out fast. How did he know? Who squealed? Probably my ex-coworker. That bitch had never liked me and was jealous of my relationship. She should be thrilled with me out of town. She could pick up where I left off.

I'd told no one of my plans, not even my girlfriends. They had their own lives to manage. The fewer people who knew, the better.

I started up the car and headed back onto the expressway. Without traffic, I could make it to Lucinda's house in less than three hours. I glanced down at my phone.

"Fingers and toes crossed, I'll be in a queen-sized bed tonight with 700 thread count Egyptian sheets." I checked my voicemail and text once more.

My cousin still hadn't responded to my message.

"Oh, God." She was probably not home. Out shopping or having lunch with friends. She didn't work, and I wasn't sure just what she did all day. I hoped she'd be home by the time I arrived.

I popped in one of my CDs and tried getting my mind off my worries. Maple trees and mountains took the place of strip malls and residential neighborhoods.

I traveled along the stretch of highway. I was counting the exits until civilization returned. The area became less of a city and more like the sheer wilderness.

Suddenly I hit the brakes. A cougar had stopped for a few seconds in front of the car. I felt its eyes on me as it opened its mouth in a scream before disappearing into the woods.

"Like a bad omen." I tried not to believe in these things, but the wild cat's presence sent a chill down my spine.

"Close call."

I'd been having one too many of those lately. I loosened my grip on the steering wheel—no need for white knuckles. The danger has passed, I told myself, singing along with the music.

A sudden and complete silence made my ears perk up. What in the world? I turned the volume up. No music. None at all. I turned the dial, but nothing. Then the lights all lit up on my dashboard like a Christmas tree.

"Oh, God. Please, not now. Not when I'm almost there. Pretty please," I begged. I thought we had come to an agreement, the car and me. I'd keep getting her repaired as long as she'd get me where I needed to go. So far, neither party had reneged, until now....

"Please, oh please. If I can only get to Dallas. I'll park in front of Lucinda's. Then I can call for help. Give me a break."

But a break was not in store. The car refused to compromise. The sound of an engine in slow motion grated my ears.

"Turn right," the directions said on my phone.

"Shit, I can't," I mumbled, struggling to comply. The wheel suddenly became impossible to turn. I prayed there was a parking lot somewhere, someplace I could pull in safely before my car gave out for good.

God answered my prayers a few moments later. I pressed lightly on the brake and rolled into a parking lot—a cheap storefront with the words *Evans Brothers' Auto Repair. Come on in. We've been waiting for your car* caught my eye.

"Thank you, Jesus." I turned the car off and slammed the door shut.

I glanced down at my clothing. My choice of attire spoke volumes. Jeans and a tank top. Harried and in a hurry. The humidity had turned my wavy auburn hair into a puff and my makeup was nearly melted off my face.

"Don't let this be expensive," I whispered, heading up the steps into Evans Brothers.

A front window revealed a medium-sized storefront—an office with a man hunched over a calculator, a pencil behind his ear. A few feet away was a garage with multiple lifts, cars and trucks in various states of repair.

I swayed on my heels and paused, peering inside. I raised a fist to knock. The sound of engines running drowned me out. The man at the desk stood up and walked to an old truck, lifting the hood.

Another man took the first one's place at the desk. I turned my head to stare. A pair of the most startling blue eyes stared back at me. The man stood up from his seat, pushing his chair in. He walked closer towards me. A torn t-shirt revealed a nearly printed-on six-pack. Tattered jeans showcased his perfect ass. A cowboy hat sat on top of his dirty blonde hair.

I felt my jaw drop. Did he work there? The mechanics I knew never looked like that.

The man gestured with his hand.

"Come on in. May I help you, ma'am? You lost?" His southern drawl made my heart race. I closed the door and entered the shop, catching a whiff of aftershave. I felt my throat close up.

"Ma'am?" His sea-blue eyes twinkled.

"Huh? Oh. Uhh…?"

"Is something wrong with your car, darling?" The man repeated.

Darling? I blinked. He called me darling. I bet he calls all women that. This is Texas, after all. I cleared my throat.

"Pardon me. My car is on its last leg. All the dashboard lights went on. Can you help me?"

The man frowned and removed his hat, scratching his head.

"When was the last time you changed the battery?"

I grimaced. "I-I don't know,"

The man bit back a laugh. "How's that?" he taunted.

*Jerk*, I thought, but kept silent.

From the looks of it, I was good and stuck, with help nowhere to be found except for Mr. Cowboy. I looked around the shop and noticed the frames on the wall with newspaper clippings, and plaques from other companies.

"Impressive," I mused. Mr. Cowboy stared at me again, only this time with a grin on his sexy lips.

"Please get me your manager so I can get this car up and running, thank you,"

"You can do what you like. But lady, when your car truly dies and you get stuck, don't blame me. I only tried to help," he replied, wiping his hands on his shirt.

"Dies?" I repeated. "I hope not. There's life in her yet."

I watched another mechanic, the one from earlier, underneath a Camaro. Wrenches and car parts covered every corner. Calendars and posters of women in various states of undress decorated the walls.

I moved closer to inspect the strange man, catching a glimpse of a person. The nails were caked with mud and dirt. From this angle, I saw a very well built man with a six-pack that people paid for in the gym or under a surgeon's knife.

A very well-built man with a six-pack that people paid for in the gym or under a surgeon's knife.

"Wow," I whistled under my breath.

"May I help you?" the man asked, crawling out from the car.

A pair of the bluest eyes stared at me, making me break into a sweat. A face nearly identical to the other mechanic's caught my attention.

"You're twins?" I gasped. Warmth flooded my cheeks.

"What gave it away?" The other mechanic laughed, and his brother joined in. He ran his hand through his wavy dirty blonde hair. A small smile tugged at his lips.

I looked down at his shirt; a name tag caught my eye.

Gage Evans.

I glanced back at the other mechanic. Evans. I frowned. Shit. They were the owners. I'd just put my foot in my mouth—big time. I slapped my forehead.

"Umm, yes, Gage. I… my car is dead." I sighed.

"OK, where is your car, Mrs…?"

"Right outside." I pointed. And I'm not married. So no Mrs."

He shook his head.

"I'm Gage Evans. And you are?" He extended his hand.

"Riva Stewart. Nice to meet you. I hope you can fix my car, so I can be on my way." I frowned."Let's see," Gage replied.

I stood for a second, my feet planted firmly on the ground, and eyeballed him. He was a foot taller than me, at least. He had to be around six foot three, with dimples, full lips, and eyes like two pools of crystal water. The warm tan on his skin complemented his hair and eyes. From his t-shirt, I could guess that he had impressive abs. He wore a pair of jeans and sneakers. Strong legs, muscular thighs, and… big feet. I averted my gaze.

"Ma'am?"

"Huh? Oh yeah. My car is in the parking lot. Please come this way."

I led Gage into the parking lot, which had got busier. Some people he knew passed by, and he nodded his head in greeting, making small talk. I dug my heel into the dirt and frowned.

"Do you think it's electrical? Or the engine?" I gulped. I didn't have several thousand dollars to spend on car repair. This could not have happened at a worse time.

"I'll go check, then I can make a few suggestions."

"All right."

"I won't be long, ma'am," Gage replied, lifting the top of the car and sticking his head inside.

"It's Riva."

"Alright, Riva. Just give me a few minutes."

"You gonna be here long?" his brother asked.

I stared at him, taking in his looks with curiosity. His eyes had an earth green tone compared to his brother's. A tiny scar decorated his chin. He flashed me a slightly crooked grin. He copied Gage's mannerisms, running his dirty hand through his hair, making me cringe.

"Do you still want to speak to my manager?" he teased, nearly burning me with his gaze. I felt his eyes pass over me from head to toe, stripping me of my clothing.

I shook my head. "Sorry," I whispered.

"I'd shake your hand, but I think you'll need some soap and water afterward," he smirked, flashing his dirty palms.

"That's all right. I'll pass." I looked up at him, catching his gaze.

Two brothers. Too much to handle. Imagine being in the middle of that sandwich, I thought, and my cheeks burned hot and red. Too bad a long-term stop wasn't in my plans. I'd get the car fixed up and be on my way—sexy brothers or no.

"I'm Riva, Riva Stewart. My car died suddenly. I was able to steer into the parking lot, and the rest is history."

I felt him study me, from my impractical choice of heels to my form-fitting pair of jeans, before landing at my breasts.

"Clay Evans, and that's Gage. We're brothers, and we own the garage here."

"Yes, I figured that much out," I answered, crossing my arms against my chest.

"How can you even walk in those things?" he snorted.

I raised a brow. "Exceedingly well," I replied. I walked towards his brother, hoping to get a better look at my car. I watched him slide behind the wheel and start the engine. He paused for a second, a thoughtful expression on his face. He listened to the terrible sound the engine made.

"What's wrong?" I asked. My foot turned inward as my heel caught on the curb.

"Ouch, son of a—!" I yelled out. I was about to lose my balance and fall flat on my ass in the middle of the parking lot. *Floor swallow me now.* I grimaced, mentally preparing myself for the humiliation. Then I felt a pair of strong arms around my waist, holding me.

"Careful," Clay replied. I breathed in a smell of sweat mixed with cologne and the slight fragrance of grease and filth.

"Yuck. You got dirt on me," I complained.

"Sorry darlin', those are just not the shoes to wear in a place like this."

"Yeah," I snorted.

I frowned, brushing the dirt off my top. The way my poor shoes looked... like I had worked at the garage all day. Filth covered the heels, and there was a fine film of dust over the tops.

"Damn it." I sighed.

"You're coming to the office with me so I can examine you, and then we'll figure out what's next." He put his hand up to silence me. "No arguments!"

"So, you're a doctor now too?" I rolled my eyes. But it did feel good in his arms.

He placed me down softly onto a chair in the office. Under the glare of fluorescent lights, he removed my shoe and examined my foot.

"Not broken or twisted. Just a few scratches. You turned your foot in when your heel got caught."

I winced. Shit, these shoes pinched. They hurt more with each step. Absolutely gorgeous, but they left an imprint on the tops of my feet like a hand had squeezed them. Besides these and a pair of flats in the car, I'd had to leave all my favorites at home. There was no room.

"Do you have other shoes in your car? Sneakers?"

I shook my head. "I don't wear sneakers. I do have a pair of Mary Janes in the back seat,"

"Mary Who? I won't ask. Hold on."

I stared at his hands. Really? You're going to touch my shoes with those filthy hands.

"Oh, I nearly forgot." He rolled his eyes.

I heard the sound of the faucet, and he returned a few seconds later.

"All washed up." He left the garage and came back a few moments later with my flats in hand, and I slipped them on.

"What a gentleman."

"And I thought you were raised by wolves," Gage replied, slapping him on the shoulder playfully.

"Is it going to be expensive?" My eyes grew big, imagining the new costs boomeranging.

"Don't worry about it. You look like you have enough going on in that head of yours. We'll be more than fair," Gage said.

"You should only know," I said under my breath.

I watched the two exchange a glance.

Gage cleared his throat and drummed his fingers on the countertop.

"I think I figured out the problem. It's electrical."

I rolled my eyes. "When do you think the car will be ready? I really need to be on the road again by evening at the latest."

Clay laughed.

"We need to order parts, with your permission, of course. Then it will take two days at the very least for them to come. And we can't even be sure that is all that's wrong with it until Gage puts it up on the lift."

"Are there any other mechanics nearby who can have the part for me sooner?"

Gage scratched his chin. "I know a friend, but I think he's closed today. Vacation."

"Of course," I snapped.

"I don't know how you girls do it," Gage smiled.

"What?"

"Wear shoes like that. But hey, you can give birth, so I guess shoes are nothing." He shrugged.

"Yep." I frowned.

Only a few more hours to Dallas. Now, that plan had been scrapped. There'd be no Dallas, and no staying at my cousin's stately home. Just a jalopy of a car, bags, and judgmental gazes of the mechanics. I knew those expressions. The comments under their breath. What woman shows up like this? A tumbleweed in stilettos. Very impractical.

The damned convertible had crapped out in the middle of nowhere— some little one-horse town near Fort Worth. Christiansville, TX, to be exact.

*Christiansville Welcomes You. Don't forget your saddle!* the sign read, with a little picture of the Stetson man on a horse. I rolled my eyes.

Another numbskull, knows-nothing town. Just what I'd worked to get away from since I threw caution to the wind and moved out at eighteen. My car's breaking down made me wonder. Was it destiny, or was it fate? I couldn't be sure which, but it had a way of pulling me back towards all those things—the very things I thought I'd left in the past.

"There's a licensed Benz dealership within ten miles," I read off my phone. "Can they order for other brands as well?"

Gage laughed. A resonant tone echoed off the walls.

"The auto parts and service center on Marigold Lane East?"

"Uh-huh."

"Well, that closed years ago."

My mouth flew open and closed. "So what you are saying is that if I don't let you fix my car, I won't have a car. At all." Unbelievable.

"That about covers it," he retorted.

"Goddamn." Once the word had left my lips, I instantly regretted it.

"Did you just use the Lord's name in vain?" Gage raised a brow.

"Sorry you disapprove. You have pictures of naked women in your shop, hypocrite!"

His icy eyes twinkled. I saw mischief in them behind his serious expression. When he stepped off the platform, I watched him walk to the other parts of the garage. His chiseled, handsomely rugged features and that tanned skin made me look at him twice. Was that a smile on his lips? A lopsided grin and perfectly straight teeth.

"You got me. Let me check with Clay. He'll run an estimate and give you a better idea which day it will be ready,"

"Day? Meaning not today?" I snapped. You must be kidding. This day just kept getting better and better.

I heard Clay mumble, but then he thought better of it.

A few minutes later, Gage popped his head out of his office with an itemized list in hand.

"Looks like an easy enough fix. Unfortunately, you need some parts replaced. I can call in a request today, but they won't come until the end of the week at the earliest.

"What? End of the week?"

"Uh-huh," Gage replied.

"So, who can you call to pick you up? Your boyfriend?" Clay asked.

"No one. I'm not from around here. Guess I'll have to stay at a hotel somewhere until this is over." I looked down at my feet. Shit.

"Really? We can always give you a ride home if you like?" Gage said.

I shook my head. Home? He should only know what awaited me if I even dreamed of returning.

"Maybe there's another option," Clay interjected. "Give me a second." He disappeared into the office, then emerged with a phone in his hand and a number.

"Before we go on a wild chase, let me call."

"Good thinking." I said a silent prayer and hoped whatever he had in mind worked. I still couldn't get in touch with Lucinda. And there was no way I was sleeping in my car.

Clay cleared his throat and hung up. "Sorry to tell you this, but the B 'n' B is full. Is there anyone else we can try?"

My jaw dropped. "My cousin Lucinda. She lives in Rose Manor in Dallas. We can give her a call."

I saw them look at one another.

"That's pretty far. Are you sure?"

"What other choice do I have?" I spat. "I can't sleep here in my car." I felt the tears in my eyes.

"OK."

The phone rang and rang before going to voicemail. I looked down at the phone.

"I have a message. Thank you, God." I sighed.

*I will be on vacation until next Sunday. Please try me then. Lucinda.*

"Oh, no." I hung my head in worry.

"What's wrong, little lady?" Gage asked.

"My cousin isn't going to be home, not for a week," I whispered.

"Sorry." Clay replied.

"This damned heat is nearly frying my brains." Gage turned the air conditioner up.

"You are really going to lower the temperature? Now? I'm freezing."

My nipples agreed. They stood nice and pert under my thin top. I struggled to cover myself, but the mechanics had already seen.

"Yes, you are." Clay answered, a sexy grin on his lips.

*They are checking me out—both of them.* I gasped. *Talk about bold.*

Although I had to admit they both did have beautiful eyes and smiles to match.

"Fine. Fix my car. I give up. Besides, I'm just passing through. I have zero intention of staying here a second longer than necessary." I'd gotten this far on my own. I'd figure the rest out... somehow.

"Yes, ma'am." Clay tipped his hat.

I rolled my eyes. "I need my car today," I repeated, knowing full well that wasn't happening. The sky had turned a brilliant pink, and night would soon be upon us. Wolves howled in the distance, sending chills down my spine, which I shook off.

"Not a possibility. Can I suggest some alternatives?" Clay asked.

"A taxi service to take me to a nice hotel in the proximity?"

Gage shook his head and drummed his fingers onto the table.

"I see you're not familiar with the neighborhood. There are no hotels like that here. However, there is a very warm and very welcoming B 'n' B five minutes away," Gage smiled.

Clay frowned. "You forgot, brother. That B 'n' B went out of business too."

"Like the car dealership. Why not? What do you have here?" I sniffed.

"Besides plenty of land, cowboys." His brother smirked. "Only we left our hats at home."

"Well, speak for yourself." Clay said.

"Ha, ha, ha. Well, then I'll have to travel out of town," I replied. The car service would take some time to collect me. The sooner I called, the better.

A symbol appeared suddenly on my phone. *Low battery.* I punched in the number quickly before the phone went totally black.

"What the—?! Now what!" I screamed. I was tempted beyond measure to take the cell phone and smash it into a million pieces.

"Trouble in paradise?" Clay smirked.

"My phone is dead. And I have no place to sleep tonight," I sighed

Gage touched his chin, and a thoughtful expression played on his face. I could nearly see a light bulb going off in his head—an ah-ha moment.

"I have an idea. My sister moved out of the basement apartment. Why don't you stay with us, Ms. Riva?" Gage smiled. I watched Clay lick his lips. He stared at me in anticipation of my response.

"I… I don't know if that's such a good idea." Stay with him? My clit throbbed, and my panties felt damp. I hadn't run from one man to go stay with another. Two others. And so quickly.

"Best of all, I'll be there too. You'll have plenty of company." Clay winked at me.

"Your generous offer tempts me, but I really think I need to find a car service and get a hotel somewhere."

I began to look inside my pocketbook for my money.

"Absolutely not." Gage placed a hand on my arm.

"What?" I frowned.

"You will have a safe place to stay with a roof over your head. A comfortable bed, and we will be perfect gentlemen."

I began to choke. "If I stay with you, where will I sleep?"

"In my bed," Clay answered in a deep voice.

"I don't think so," I snapped. The image of sleeping in his arms, resting against his broad chest with his brother at my side more than made me warm. Cozy and safe.

Clay stuck his tongue out at me.

"So, what brings you to our humble little town, Miss Don't Cross Me?" He winked.

"It's Riva. And I got lost. Long story."

"I've got the time." Clay stuck his hands into his jean pockets.

I shook my head.

"Tell me, guys. Since we just met, how can I be sure you're not both serial killers?"

They were too gentlemanly and hot to be dangerous. But I couldn't risk it.

"The temperature's getting cooler so you won't roast, but I wouldn't sleep outside if I were you." Clay smiled.

"Why's that?" I crossed my arms against my chest.

"Lions and tigers and bears." He smirked.

I fought the urge to wipe that sanctimonious expression off his face.

"So, have you decided where you're staying tonight, Riva?" Gage asked, scratching his chin.

I shrugged. "Was about to just stay in my car if you bring it down from the lift. But clearly, that's not happening." I frowned in Clay's direction.

"The offer still stands," Gage reminded me.

"The apartment?" I frowned.

I sighed. "How is the basement? Is it furnished?"

Clay smirked. "Are you kidding? Do you think Little Miss Priss would stay in anything else?"

I turned my head and glared at him. "I don't know. She may have moved out a long time ago and took everything with her."

Gage shook his head. "Nope. She took what she needed. So, the bed is yours. Clean sheets. No bugs."

"Perfectly clean. Obsessively so." Clay added.

I frowned. I was staying at my new mechanics' house. This was beyond strange.

"Oh yeah. No nookie in that bed either. She went to her boyfriend's house for that, thank God." Clay smirked.

I flicked a little bloodsucker off my leg.

"All right, I'm convinced."

"The mosquitos are relentless here when they taste something sweet." Gage grinned at me, showing off his perfect smile.

I frowned.

"Still not convinced? You won't find a set of killers who keep pictures of their pets on their Androids." Gage replied, passing me his phone.

"Scroll through, and you'll see our stable. Our grandparents owned a hacienda and left it to us in their will. We have plenty of room since our sister moved out. In fact, space is all we have."

I looked through the photos of honey-colored palominos, a golden retriever, and a pre-teen on a horse.

"Who's that?"

"Oh, a neighbor's daughter. You see the snow-white horse she's sitting on? That's Jacobi. He is trained as a therapy animal."

"Nice."

The clock ticked, and I knew my chances of getting to Dallas or anywhere for that matter lessened with each passing minute. I knew if I didn't go home with the Evanses, I'd have no place to stay at all.

"You're inviting me to stay at your place?" I frowned. "You two invite all the women you just met?"

"You're not really a stranger, see. We know a little about you now. And you know about us. Besides, your car won't be ready for a few days."

I rolled my eyes.

"You don't know me. I could be a madwoman. I could creep into your beds and kill you in your sleep."

"We hope you'll do something else, but I betcha you couldn't hurt a fly," Clay drawled.

"OK, I guess I opened myself up to that one," I replied, brushing off his comments. The blush on my cheeks said otherwise.

"Come on, Riva. I promise. The place is big enough that you won't even have to see us if you don't want to. But we hope you will." Gage added.

"Well, all right. But if either one of you tries anything, I'll bury you where no one will think to look."

***

The ranch, with its sprawling green meadows, cacti, and black-eyed Susans, made me smile. I glanced over my shoulder to find a clothing line swaying with the breeze. A pair of men's underwear blew slightly in the wind next to some undershirts. Whether they belonged to Gage or Clay, I didn't know.

"Don't look," Gage said. I pretended to avert my gaze from his old drawers.

"Trust me; I've seen more than that," I flirted. A soft laugh escaped our lips.

I watched a palomino dunk its head in feed, and a duck waddle by in greeting.

I followed them into the two-story red brick home and placed my bags onto the carpet.

"Welcome to your new home. We think you'll love it here."

I raised a brow. After my terrible afternoon, all I longed for was a hot shower and a bed.

Clay coughed. "He means… just enjoy yourself." He threw his brother a dirty look. He pulled him aside, and I heard him whisper in Gage's ear.

"Way to go, bro, with the creepy comments."

"Thanks," I replied, smiling wanly.

"New home?" That meant the boys wanted me to stay here permanently? How could that even be possible when I'd only met them all of a few hours ago? Yet something about their expressions felt more than sincere. The honesty in their eyes said what words failed to.

I reached out and touched Gage's hand. The spark of electricity was unmistakable. I flinched and moved away. Had he felt it too? If he had, he didn't let on; instead, he smiled.

"You mean temporary housing," I quickly corrected him.

"Yeah," Clay said. "Might as well go see where you're staying, right, Riva?" Clay led the way to my newest digs, the basement apartment.

The walls were painted a pale pink. A vase of fresh flowers sat on the center of the dresser, making the room a pleasant contrast to the cowboy man cave.

I lifted the blossoms to my face and smiled.

"We hope you like it here. Everything's good. Clean and nice?" Gage asked.

"Yes. I really appreciate this. It's funny," I said, then caught myself. It was too soon. I'd just met them. If I told them my story now, they'd run for the hills.

"What's funny?"

"Nothing. Just that this was the very last thing I'd ever expect. That's all." I shrugged.

"OK. We're gonna freshen up. Make yourself at home. You have your own bathroom too. There's a linen closet with towels on your right-hand side," Gage added before excusing himself.

I climbed into the shower, grateful to freshen up after my long day.

"Damn, no soap." I looked around. Where does she keep everything?

I wrapped myself in a plush towel and began looking around in the bathroom cabinets.

After a few minutes, I stuck my head out and called for the brothers.

"Gage? Clay? Where's the soap?"

"Don't worry. We'll leave it for you. Just wait in the shower," I heard one of them say.

"OK." I hoped they stuck to their word. I didn't want to be unexpectedly ambushed in the nude by men I'd just met.

I heard a knock at the door a few seconds later.

"Here's your soap."

"Thanks."

I took the box from Clay's hands." I watched his sexy smile. I stood there in nothing but an oversized towel.

"Don't try anything funny. Please just pass me the soap."

The smile suddenly vanished from his face. I felt his hand on my shoulder. His expression turned somber.

"That's the reason you got lost?"

I pulled the towel closer against me. But it was too late. My bruise. He'd seen the black and blue.

I sighed. "I really need to get washed up. It's been a terrible day."

"And that's why you have a gun? Gage found it in your bag. You shouldn't leave it out like that. Could get somebody killed."

I bit my lip. There was no point in lying or trying to cover up, not now.

"You're right. That's why I left. Once he put his hands on me, I mind up my mind. I was never going back."

"If I ever find him, Gage, and I will make him farm feed."

I put my hand up. "It's really not needed. Can I take my shower now?"

Clay shook his head. Something told me this conversation wasn't over not by a long shot.

I closed the door and heard him mumble. I ignored his complaints, turning the shower on hot water and allowing the water to wash off the dust and dirt of the day.

I lathered his sister's floral shampoo into my hair and massaged my scalp. Then I watched it go down the drain with satisfaction before slipping back into the bedroom and getting dressed.

I had barely gotten dressed before I felt eyes on me. I spun around, my hand on my hip.

"Excuse me. I guess no one believes in knocking around here?"

Gage sat down on the bed and patted the spot next to him.

"I know this isn't really any of our business, but I found your gun, Riva."

I groaned. "I know. Clay told me." I avoided his gaze, instead squeezing the excess water droplets out of my hair.

"And he told me why you left your ex. I want you to know that neither one of us will ever allow anyone to hurt you. Not now. Not ever." His voice cracked with emotion.

Before I could say one word, he reached over and pulled me close. I didn't fight it. My resolve melted, and the walls came tumbling down. I felt the tears start to roll down my face.

"You need a man to protect you? Well, now you've got two," he said, kissing me softly on the cheek. He reached into his pocket and removed a handkerchief.

"Here you go," he said softly, passing it to me.

Our hands touched. I smiled, dabbing my eyes.

He stroked my cheek with his fingertips. Our eyes locked. I knew that look. That feeling. He wanted to kiss me, and I wanted him to. But how could I?

"I only just met you. It's too much. I could never—"

He silenced me, placing a finger to my lips. "I want to kiss you, Riva. But only if that's OK? Is that OK?" He stared into my eyes.

I nodded my head, giving him permission.

He lifted my face to his. Gage's soft lips covered mine.

I tasted Indian tobacco and cinnamon gum. I relaxed and kissed him back.

*** 

"You two have been more than generous, but there are things—" I began.

"We can always buy you whatever you need... within reason." Gage smiled.

I shook my head.

"Buy me? I've been on my own since I was a teenager. Whatever I wanted, I worked for. Bought myself. Besides, you and Clay have already done too much," I explained, taking a sip of juice.

"So does that mean we can't spoil you? We're not allowed?"

I dropped my shoulders and sighed.

"I appreciate the gesture, but it's really unnecessary." An idea suddenly sprang in my head. "My grandparent's furniture is still sitting in my old apartment. I have no way of getting it." I frowned.

"We'll get your stuff back," Clay replied, crushing a can of soda under his fist.

"Wish it was that easy."

The two brothers exchanged a glance.

"Oh, but it is. Just say the word, and we'll go and get your stuff back. Hell, we'll even clear out your apartment completely, your ex included if you like," Clay snapped, twirling a gun on his finger.

"Calm down, cowboy. Don't want to see you locked up."

Gage touched his hip. I saw an identical gun. I glanced in his direction.

"You either."

"No worries. If we wanted to kill him, he'd already be dead." Clay winked.

A chill went down my spine.

"I think a man that abuses a woman deserves just that," Gage interjected. "But since we both got a business to run, we gonna keep our hands clean."

I shook my head, saying a silent prayer of thanks.

Clay slipped behind me and whispered in my ear, pulling me close to him.

"Just let us know when." I could feel his hardness through his pants, and I smiled.

"To kill him or to get my furniture?"

"Both."

***

The ride to my old apartment was a tense one. I reminded the brothers over and over to be on their guard. Not act impetuously. Stay calm. I didn't know if I could do the same.

I stood outside the apartment and took a deep breath before ringing the doorbell. I saw the blinds shift. Eddie's creepy mug stared back at me from behind the peephole.

"You? Well, well, well." Eddie threw back his head and laughed. He looked so thin and dirty. His black hair looked matted and in tangles. Yuck. And the apartment stunk of stale air and fried food. What the hell had I ever seen in him?

"Look what the cat dragged in." He stood in front of the door, blocking me from entering. I could tell he was enjoying this. I'd let him have his fun, knowing full well I had not one but two men ready and waiting.

"Are you going to let me in?"

"Maybe." he looked down at his hands. "But since you left, really no need for you to come back."

"No, there is not," a woman's voice added. She sounded strangely familiar.

*The witch from my old job. Just as I suspected.*

The door slammed in my face, making me jump.

"Son of a bitch," I said, balling my hand into a fist, preparing to knock when the door flew open.

It was my old co-worker in the flesh with a sour expression on her face. She crossed her arms against her chest and her nostrils flared like a rebellious stallion.

"Come on, darlin', no need to be jealous." Eddie calmed her down, planting a kiss on her fat cheek.

"Word gets out fast when there are leftovers available," I replied, strolling across the living room. I prepared to remove one of my chairs.

Eddie slammed his hand down on the table. On instinct, I moved out of the way.

"Quite the reflexes you have there," he smirked. "Not so fast, honey. They're mine now."

I bit back an angry retort, knowing the brothers were only a whistle away.

"They belonged to my grandparents, and I'm here to take them back."

I watched his latest love plop down in the chair with a spiteful smile on her face.

"Okay, honey. If you get on your hands and knees and beg, I'll let you take them."

The anger that had been hiding deep in my body and soul began pouring out.

"You'll let me. You fucking piece—"

As if on cue, the door opened again. This time, my two cowboys stood side by side.

"What the—? I should have had the locks changed."

"And we should have called an exterminator," Gage replied. Clay looked the two of them up and down with an aggressive expression on his face.

"We can't always get what we want, can we?"

"Call the police, babe; we have two trespassers," Eddie directed. I watched the girl take out a phone, which Clay snatched from her hand.

"You're not calling anyone now; put the phone down." Clay flashed him his gun. Edward put his hands up in the air, and his girlfriend followed.

"Fine. Take what you want. Just don't shoot me."

I rolled my eyes. Typical worm. Weak. Only tough when it's directed towards a woman.

"The bed?" Gage said, pulling back a sheet inspecting it.

"Nope. I'll pass. That's already been contaminated." I glanced in the direction of my ex and his new girlfriend.

The brothers lifted the chairs and the table out of the living room into the back of their jeep.

We made several trips, taking everything that belonged to me.

At last, I watched the two of them wipe the sweat off their brows.

"Ready to go?" Gage asked. I nodded.

The gentleness they possessed floored me.

I walked over first to Gage then his brother. I kissed them both on the cheek. "Thank you."

Clay frowned.

I sat between them in the jeep.

Clay lifted his shirt off and tossed it into the back seat.

Giving in to temptation, I reached over and ran my hands over his chest.

I heard him suck in a breath.

And I knew he wanted to kiss me, because I wanted to kiss him too.

\*\*\*

The next few days went by in a blur. The boys split their time between the shop and the ranch. Although I was grateful to them, I felt something had changed in a short time. They seemed cool towards me and towards one another.

My stomach growled. It was nearly dinner time. I was in the mood for a good home-cooked meal. Since my culinary skills were lacking, I sure hoped one of them cooked.

I was about to enter the kitchen, but something held me back. The energy in the room felt like something you could cut with a knife.

"You didn't tell her, did you?" Clay asked, a hand heavy on his hip and a frown on his handsome face.

I froze. Tell her what? My heart nearly danced out of my chest, and I leaned against the wall, steadying myself. What could be the problem?

Gage threw his pen and calculator onto the table and returned his brother's sneer.

"What? That we share everything? Women included? I think I left that part out once I invited Riva to stay with us."

I sucked in a breath. They share women. Dear God. That means they want to share—me? Color flooded my cheeks. I prayed they wouldn't catch me listening, yet I couldn't sneak away. Not when they were about to confess their hottest secret. I remained, my feet nearly glued to the floor.

"How convenient."

Gage's eyes flashed.

"After Denise left, you agreed we'd never have that kind of relationship again. What's the matter, she got under your skin?"

"Yep, she did. Seeing her in the morning, in that t-shirt and shorts when I'm having coffee." A low growl emanated from his throat. "There is nothing more that I'd like to do than grab her and take her over the counter. Don't worry, brother. I'd let you have your turn. We both know I'm not greedy. I know how to share."

"Disrespectful son of a—"

Gage flew across the room, grabbing a handful of his brother's shirt and yanking him.

"I may be all those things, but hell, I get what we want. You move any slower, Riva will be out of here before you tell her how we feel."

"And how do you feel, Gage? Clay?" I interjected.

Gage released his brother. Clay adjusted his shirt, brushing him off. Now it was Gage's time to blush.

"Uhh…" Gage ran a hand through his hair and stared at me.

Clay began to laugh. His ocean-coloured eyes glittered. A devious expression showed on his face.

"I think the lady deserves an answer."

"So, which one of you is going to give it to me? Is it Mr. Gage, the strong and silent one?" I nuzzled his neck, enjoying the slight groan I heard as he pressed his body against mine. I plopped down onto the kitchen countertop and looked up at the two of them, my legs swinging out from beneath me.

"Or Clay, the wild one?"

Clay didn't respond; instead, he removed my shirt. I felt two strong sets of hands on my body, stripping me of the rest of my clothing.

"Are you sure you're ready for us?" Clay whispered, taking my nipple between his teeth.

I felt Gage's hand on my thigh, separating my legs. The look on his face. Imploring me.

"Yes," I purred.

I shifted in my spot as he slipped one finger then two inside of me. Then he removed them and licked his fingers.

"You taste so good. I can't wait to have you." He offered his finger to me, and I sucked, tasting my juices on his skin.

He lifted my face and kissed me, wrapping his mouth over mine as Clay bit lightly on my neck, sending chills down my spine.

"Let's take this to the bedroom," Clay demanded. I raced to the basement with the two at my heels.

They quickly undressed, with my help. Then I dropped to my knees. Clay held onto my head, slipping his hard cock in my mouth. I bobbed up and down until I tasted his cum on my tongue.

Gage carefully spread my legs. Catching my gaze, he kissed me softly from my ankle to my inner thigh.

I squirmed against the sensation of his lips. He opened his mouth, slowly flicking his tongue against my pearl. I was nice and wet. I wrapped my legs around his neck and rode my cowboy's face.

I orgasmed and felt ready to drop. I lay back on the bed. Gage excused himself, leaving his brother and me to enjoy ourselves.

Clay and I kissed passionately. He lifted me on top of him, and I held tight, biting my lip as he slipped inside of me. We made love for a while before the two of us collapsed sated on the bed.

I heard a knock at the door.

"Gage?"

"May I?" He glanced at Clay. Clay nodded. This time, he left us alone.

I ran my hand over Gage's chest.

"I've wanted you since the moment you set foot in my shop. Now's my turn. I want to enjoy you," he whispered, laying me onto my back

I felt his tongue hungrily suck my clit. His handsome face between my thighs made me cum quickly. We changed positions. I stroked his cock, guiding him inside me. Our bodies intertwined, and I held him between my thighs.

"Riva," he cried out. Then, he lay beside me, a serious expression on his face.

Clay entered the room, fully dressed, and cleared his throat.

"We hope you will stay with us."

I raised a brow.

"You can't get rid of me that easily," I laughed. Besides, what woman wouldn't want to be loved and protected by two men?" I reached over and stroked Gage's cheek.

Clay shook his head.

"When I think about his hands on you—"

His voice rose in anger.

"There's not a wall that I don't want to punch holes in," Gage added.

"Walls? I want to break his head. Shit, I almost did. Why'd you stop me?"

"He's not worth it, that's why," I purred.

He winced and gazed down at his feet.

"So you'll stay with us longer than one night?"

"This woman is staying as long as you two will have her. You think a lifetime is enough?" I replied, running my hands over Gage's bare chest.

He smiled and showed off his little dimples.

"Those are the words…"

"…we've been hoping for," Clay winked.

## The End

# E-Mail-Ordered Groom
## Starla Kaye

## Chapter One

"Who the hell is that?" Gwenie asked as a powerful engine caught her attention. She gaped at a massive black SUV driving across the Lazy L ranch yard. It stopped in the circle driveway to the main house she shared with her brother Thad, and a tall man climbed out.

The spunky Paint mare she'd been riding as a test after she'd changed her horseshoes took advantage of Gwenie's distraction and kicked up her back legs. Gwenie fought but lost her grip and went flying. She landed on her butt on the hard-packed earth of the corral. She glowered at the horse nickering as if laughing and merrily trotting away.

She'd noted how Thad's eyebrows had drawn together in concern until he realized the only thing damaged was her pride. As she scrambled to her feet, he was grinning his fool head off.

"You know him?" she pressed, annoyed.

"He's the answer to your dreams."

"What the heck are you talking about?" She tasted dirt as she brushed off her bottom, scooped up her hat that had fallen off, and planted it on her head. Ignoring the persnickety mare prancing around, she marched toward the white wood railing. "What dreams?"

Thad's grin stayed in place and there was an odd look in his eyes, blue like hers. "Those little scribblings you make on the pad beside the computer. When you're working on the ranch files in the office."

Gwenie rolled her eyes and strode to the iron gate. A cool breeze swept by and her long, waist-length ponytail whipped around to hit her in the face. She shoved it back over her shoulder, wishing she'd braided it instead this morning. "I scribble nonsense all the time. Always have. You know that."

Thad's gaze turned serious and he opened the gate for her. "Yeah, but they've been the same thing over and over. Even circled and underlined. Important thoughts."

"Why are you reading my notes, anyway?" Geez, she needed to be more careful with what she left lying around on the desk.

Before he could answer, the man from the expensive-looking vehicle headed in their direction with a slight limp. Her eyes widened in disbelief as she recognized the six-foot-four-inch massive bane of her existence. The boy/man she'd crushed big time over as a teenager. The one who'd basically patted her head and tolerated her as Thad's funny little kid sister whenever he came to the ranch to spend time with Thad.

"Darlin', I'm here," Drake Walters drawled in the Texas accent he'd picked up over the years. He looked pleased with himself. He tipped his pristine-looking new black Stetson at her and nodded at Thad. "Came as soon as I could."

"Why?" She stormed over to meet him. "Why are you here?"

The big oaf put his huge hands on her waist and lifted her up as if she weighed nothing. As she drew in a startled, irritated breath, he pulled her close. Their hats bumped one another and fell to the ground. He didn't notice or care as his mouth found hers. And what a wonderful mouth he had! The man kissed like he'd invented kissing. As her body savored being pressed against him, her heart did a frenzied dance. Pulling in the smell of pheromone-teasing cologne made her almost light-headed.

Thad cleared his throat, ruining the fantastical moment. "This is where I should say 'keep this private.'" He stepped closer, adding, "And remind you she *is* my sister."

"Warning noted." Drake chuckled and set Gwenie on her feet. "Couldn't resist." He winked at her with those warm, teasing brown eyes she remembered too well. Except they hadn't been warm and hinting at anything the least bit sexual in their past.

She crash-landed back in the real world, irritated that he had the gall to tease her that way. She inched back just enough to punch him in the stomach.

With his rock-hard abs, he didn't even blink and he chuckled again. "Ah, foreplay."

"Fore-foreplay?" Gwenie growled, her left eye twitching as it did when she was upset. She was so exasperated that she couldn't get any more words out. She didn't play games like this. No one had ever even tempted her with them, making it clearer that she'd only dated losers.

"Sorry about your knee," Thad said as he closed the gate and stepped toward his long-time friend. "Life-changing thing, wasn't it?"

Gwenie stared at her brother, chatting with Drake like the good buddies they'd once been. Like Drake hadn't turned his back on him and the whole town when he'd gotten his big break fourteen years ago. Like he hadn't just picked her up and kissed the hell out of her in front of him.

"It was time for me to give up the game, anyway. Getting kind of old for it." He bent to pick up his hat, grimacing. "This old body ain't what it used to be."

The man was only thirty-six, not "old." In her opinion, his "old body" looked mighty fine. Fourteen seasons playing pro-football had honed him into one outstanding physical specimen. His shoulders were far broader than they had been when she'd seen his last high school game. His biceps were so bulky they stretched the limits of his blue chambray shirt. Even his pressed jeans struggled to contain muscled thighs. The man was drool-worthy.

She grumbled under her breath, "I do *not* want him. Not, not, not." *Yes, I do. But I sure as heck don't* want *to want him.*

Both men snickered as if they'd heard her inner battle. She leveled them with a glare, vowing to kill her brother first chance she got. She didn't need this kind of distraction in her life. Wasn't it enough that she was trying to establish her career here as a farrier? No, her pesky conscience protested. *Your life is boring, boring, boring. All work and no play.*

*Which is great!* the sensible side of her pointed out.

Now her subconscious snorted, if that were possible.

Disgusted with her contrary thoughts, she shut them down. She planted her hands on her hips and pressed, "What are you doing here? How many times do I have to ask?"

Drake looked to Thad for some kind of silent male message. "I'm the answer to your dreams, according to your brother."

"*What?*" she screeched and shot another lethal glare at Thad. Older by four years, but not wiser.

Thad shrugged, as always unconcerned with her fits of temper. He raised an eyebrow at Drake's bluntness. "Well, sis, you've been writing his name dozens of times on those notepads of yours. Circling it."

Drake's entire body preened at that declaration. Those darn tempting eyes sparked with amusement. Thad's death would be a slow one, filled with lots of torture. Gwenie sucked in a breath of frustration so deep she choked. When she recovered, she hissed, "Reminders to *me*." She really needed more privacy in the house they shared, at least separate offices.

"Reminders?" he questioned, confused. "About Drake? Why?"

Reminders to get rid of the scrapbook she'd started day one of Drake's football career, beginning with his high school quarterback days to his change to being a defensive end in college and pro days. She'd started worrying that Thad would see it. He almost had one day last month when she'd been in her bedroom on a rainy night alone in the house. Or so she'd thought. He'd gone to the local dance hall with his buddies. But he'd come back at some point and surprised her by strolling into her room. She'd been adding some gossip news pieces she'd printed off the internet. She'd slammed it shut and blistered his ears for invading her privacy. Curious ever since, he pestered her about what she'd been trying to hide. His fiancée needed to set their wedding date. They'd get married and he'd stop messing with *her* life.

"About me, darlin'?" the star of her scrapbook said in a lazy drawl. He cocked a thick, dark eyebrow and looked both too damn sexy and pleased.

"Do. Not. Darlin'. Me," she gritted out. Not that she hadn't wanted to be his "darlin'" or anything else all those years ago—when she'd been young, stupid, and in lust with the popular stud quarterback of Belleville High. But he was four years older. She hadn't existed in his eyes other than as Thad's baby sister.

Pure frustration made her stomp her foot right on top of her beloved hat, making her growl and want to run screaming as far as she could from both men. The beautiful late October day had started out so nicely. Warm enough here in the Kansas Flint Hills that you didn't need a coat. Anger fired through her. Any second now flames would shoot out of her ears. *Answer to my dreams! Had he actually said that?*

"Why are you acting so crazy?" Thad asked, his handsome face mirroring bafflement. "I just wanted to help you." He nodded at Drake. "Help him, too." He studied his friend for a second and added, "Guess he's agreeable."

She gaped at her idiot brother. "Help me?" Then she zeroed in on the grinning NFL's former award-winning ex-defensive end. "Agreeable? About what?" *Do I really want to know? No.*

"You keep complaining that all your friends are getting married and having kids. That you can't find a good man of your own." Thad looked uncomfortable and added, "That your baby-making days are numbered."

*Oh, gawd!* She'd had a meltdown after her BFF's wedding last month. Thad had found her sitting in front of the great room's fireplace. She'd been drinking the wine another recently married friend had given her. She'd been mumbling to herself, dashing away the occasional tear sliding down her face. He'd looked uncomfortable as he'd sat down with her in his favorite chair. Then he'd dared to have a touchy-feely conversation with her, something he hated more than anything else in the world. But he'd done it. She hadn't remembered what she'd said, and he'd never brought it up again. Now she remembered. *Oh, gawd!*

Her heart pounded in dread. *Please, no more.*

"I've been talking to and messaging my buddy," Thad stated as if those communications solved all the world's problems, especially hers.

"About me?" What the heck had they been saying? Again, she didn't want clarification, certain it would be bad. *Answer to your dreams.* She braced herself. "Never mind. I do *not* want to know." He couldn't be playing matchmaker. *No, no, no!*

Drake flashed her the grin that brought women all over the country to their knees. At least any woman who watched football. Or followed the thousands of stories and pictures about him on every social media platform, and in magazines and newspapers. She was one of those silent groupies. Not that she'd ever intended for anyone to know her secret. She needed to get rid of that scrapbook.

"Gwendolyn," Drake began as his eyes warmed and hinted at amusement. "I'm the answer to your wishes: 'a good man of your own', aka your E-mail-ordered groom."

***

She stormed off toward the stables, giving Drake a middle finger salute over her shoulder. He chortled so loud the horse trotting around in the arena stopped and squealed in alarm. For a second, Gwenie glanced back. She put her cute little nose up in the air as she realized the Paint was okay and saw him still laughing. She saluted him again and continued striding away, grumbling with each step she took.

"She's a hell of a woman," Drake said, pleased by her attitude. It amused the heck out of him that she'd jammed her small fist into his gut. Not that he'd felt it. He didn't know a sane man who would have done that, considering his size.

"Yep." Thad watched her hurrying off. "Too much of a handful for most men. At least the men around here," he added in disgust.

Drake had come to the ranch at Thad's invitation to discuss a potential business arrangement between them. Nothing to do with his sister. In a recent phone conversation, Thad had shared about her situation with men. How she had a knack for finding losers and being disappointed. She wanted the total package: a loving husband, a happy home, and kids. She was only thirty-two, so it wasn't too late for all of that, but she believed it was. Thad worried about her. They were ranch partners, but he'd been watching out for her ever since their parents died when she was in high school. He couldn't seem to get on with his own life until he figured out hers. And that worried Drake.

*E-mail-ordered groom!* What the hell? He couldn't believe he'd said that. He had meant it more in teasing than seriously. *Answer to her wishes?* His friend had told him about her scribbles and problems with dating in confidence. It shamed him to have said that, too. Her annoyed gut punch after he'd kissed her had surprised him. Something else he didn't understand. Why had he done it? He was impulsive sometimes, but still.

"Hey, man, I didn't mean to upset her. You know me. I was just playing around."

Thad gave him another warning look but didn't yell at him like he deserved. Instead, he gave Drake a thoughtful look that puzzled him, and then his stance relaxed.

Baffled, Drake focused on the sweet, rapid sway of a perfect butt in those painted-on jeans. "When did she grow up?" *Into such a kick-me-in-the-gut beauty.* At least he had the good sense not to say that out loud.

The last he remembered she'd been a flat-chested, braces-wearing, scrawny girl. But that was what? He'd played in the NFL fourteen years and he hadn't been back to his hometown since high school. So, he hadn't seen her in person in eighteen years. She would have changed. *But damn! This much?*

She disappeared into the stable and he had an easier time putting her out of his mind. Sort of. He doubted he would soon forget how good she had felt tucked up against him. She sure wasn't flat-chested now. Not by a long way. And the braces were missing. Those lips... The way she'd sighed...

He must have groaned because Thad stepped right into his face. "My kid sister, remember? The girl who trailed after us around the ranch when you used to come here." Again, his gaze seemed to study Drake, looking for who knew what. "You tolerated her like the troublesome imp she was. That was all."

Drake nodded. "I remember. Pest."

Yet he'd been fond of the "troublesome imp" and far more tempted by the much younger girl than he should have been. Spunky, daring. He'd done his best to ignore those feelings and not let anyone know about them. Certainly not Thad, who would have beaten him to a pulp, and rightly so. He hadn't given her a lot of thought over the years, except when Thad had mentioned her. Then he'd only had a fleeting wonder about how she'd turned out.

Only moments ago, he'd almost stumbled as he'd walked toward the arena and saw the petite, spirited beauty climbing to her feet after being bucked off. *This* hadn't been the girl he remembered. Not the same now. A woman. And he'd felt drawn to her as if by a powerful magnet.

Again, he couldn't believe he'd been idiot enough to scoop her up and kiss her. A kiss she'd resisted for all of a second. Then she'd melted against him and joined right in that magical dance. *Damn. That little country miss could knock a man to his knees.*

He couldn't look Thad in the eye. "Sorry, man, it won't happen again. Messing around with Gwendolyn would be so wrong. We all know it."

*Why does doing just that appeal so much?* He could imagine that mass of long caramel-colored hair freed. He almost licked his lips at the thought of his favorite sweet treat: caramels. That beautiful hair would drape around her bare shoulders. She would show him her skills at riding. *Hell!* His damn jeans felt tight. He hoped his friend wouldn't notice.

Thad mumbled something that sounded like, "You're a fool if you believe that."

Before Drake could question him, Thad started walking toward the house. "Let's go to my office. We should talk about your idea. When you first mentioned using part of the ranch as a retraining place for injured football players, I had serious doubts. But I've been thinking. Maybe it might work."

Drake shoved all thoughts of Gwendolyn aside. This potential business was why he'd come to the Lazy L. He needed to restart his life now that playing pro ball was in his past. There were many places he could try it, but he was ready to come home. His parents no longer lived here, having followed him to Dallas to be near him. He'd built them a house there, and his dad managed his business investments. Now that he wouldn't play for the Dallas Mustangs, he wasn't excited about staying there. And the women who had played around with him while he'd been at the top of his game had deserted him. They'd only wanted his money and reputation. Their current focus was his new, young, healthy replacement. Truth was, he didn't care. They'd never been a challenge—not like Gwendolyn could be.

*What the hell?* Why couldn't he get past thinking about her? Because he'd kissed her, and she'd resisted but then kissed him back. And then she'd slugged him and "saluted" him as she'd stormed away.

As they headed for the large, two-story log house that had been the Lassiter home for three generations, Thad asked, "Gwendolyn? Why not 'Gwenie'?"

"That fit her as a kid," Drake said, smiling. "*Gwendolyn* fits her as a woman."

Thad chuckled. "Just so you know, she hates that name."

Drake grinned and knew he'd be calling her that for sure.

## Chapter Two

Gwenie had had no peace since Drake had exploded out of nowhere into her world nearly three months ago. Thad couldn't stop talking about Drake's new business plan. Yes, it sounded like an interesting idea and she hoped it worked out for him. With all she'd been going through since deciding to become a farrier, she understood the excitement and the endless headaches of getting a business started. She was struggling with her career choice. Being a female farrier and proving to alpha male ranchers that you could do the job wasn't easy. *Men. Stubborn to the core.*

She was darn tired of hearing her brother saying Drake this, Drake that.

Sweat rolled off Gwenie's forehead. It might be freezing outside this mid-January day, but in here near her forge it was hot as hell.

She lifted the hammer high above the anvil for what seemed like the hundredth time. She'd already spent over an hour molding and shaping two new horseshoes for Beelzebub. Thad's stallion had been limping yesterday, meaning his hind hooves had issues. Most days she enjoyed her work. But you had to concentrate hard, or you suffered the consequences, which she was doing after being careless with the sharp knife she used working on Bee's front hooves. Because of that big, ex-football player who spent far too much time in her thoughts.

She pounded the piece of steel with enough force to rattle her teeth. Even though Drake had left the ranch after his week-long stay and his meetings with Thad, she felt like he shadowed her everywhen she went. He was there in the kitchen grabbing another beer from the fridge while she snagged an apple for a quick snack. He sat in *her* spot on the leather sofa in the great room watching a football game with Thad. His spicy, memorable scent lingered in the downstairs bathroom. And he covered most of her bed as he stretched out and gave her a come-to-me look.

He had done none of those things. Her imagination could be way over-productive.

"Darn you, Drake Walters," she grumbled and slammed the hammer down again. The thudding sound echoed around the building but didn't disturb the six horses stabled here. Thad and two ranch hands had taken them out earlier. They'd decided to check fences on horseback today. Except Bee was outside in the corral because he needed the new shoes she was working on.

"Leave. Me. Alone." The hammer banged down once more and the muscles in her arm throbbed. The bandage wrapping around her left hand showed signs of blood from the cut on her palm. His fault! She'd been crazy distracted again with Bee. She got that way too darn often, every time her mind replayed how Drake had pronounced himself her "E-mail-ordered groom."

What man would want *her* for a bride? She stepped away from her workbench in the back of the stable. She was a disaster. Her long hair hung in a limp, messy ponytail. Sweat beaded over her dirt-smudged face, trickled between her breasts and down her back. Her jeans were stained, ripped at the knees, and her tank top—not worth thinking about.

She set the hammer down and studied the shoe she'd just finished. It looked like it would work. She was a darn good farrier and proud of that. It hadn't been easy getting to this point. Thad had encouraged her as she'd gone to a shoeing school to learn the basics of equine foot care along with equine anatomy, physiology, and behavior. A lot of it she'd known from growing up on a ranch. Then she'd apprenticed with a wonderful, gruff farrier in Oklahoma before coming home here in June to start her own farrier business.

She glanced around her working part of the stable with the forge, the anvil on a short bench, and her many tools. Not the most feminine of worlds, but hers. She could cook, but nothing fancy. No interest in it other than filling a hungry belly. Keeping the house nice and tidy wasn't her specialty either, but it wasn't a pig sty.

Her bedroom held her secret feminine side. There she was all "girly." She had delicate lacy curtains, a plush floral-patterned rug beside her canopied bed, and red satin sheets. Girly with a bit of sexy added.

What would Drake think of her bedroom? Not that he would ever see it. Except in her naughty dreams, which had started during that week he'd slept in a guest room down the hall from her. And got worse, or better, with each new day.

Her lifestyle was so different from Drake's that they might as well be from different planets. He had gazillions in the bank and investments from all those years as a prized defensive end. And he had at least three houses scattered across the country. Mansions decorated by top-notch designers. He had a warehouse full of luxurious cars, too, like that fancy red luxury SUV he'd driven here. Closets filled with clothes and shoes. She'd seen a tell-all photo layout once that described his life and possessions. The man was a serious clotheshorse and collector of expensive "toys."

While she didn't have his wealth, she and Thad weren't suffering. The Lazy L had a solid reputation for cattle breeding, and they ran five hundred head of Angus and Hereford cattle on eleven thousand acres of prime land in the Kansas Flint Hills. They shared the not-too-shabby log home that their ancestors had built. But Thad was building a house for him and Aimee, leaving her with the family home. She drove a ten-year-old pickup truck with more than a few dents and scratches. And her wardrobe was comprised of well-worn jeans, tank tops and western shirts, a couple skirts for when she went dancing, various boots, and a pair of stilettos she had bought on a whim but never worn.

She sighed. They fit together like that square peg in a round hole thing. But, dang it, when they locked lips…

"So, how is my darlin' today?"

Startled, Gwenie knocked against the workbench and the hammer fell off. It landed on her already sore foot, which Bee had stepped on earlier. She hissed in pain and glowered in annoyance at Drake.

"When did you get here?" Hands on hips, she snapped, "I'm *not* your darlin'!" Although she enjoyed hearing him call her that. Not that she would ever admit it.

With that sexy-as-hell grin, he ambled toward her on those long, muscled legs. Straight toward her. His chocolate brown eyes looked intent. Her heart hammered and she couldn't seem to move, waiting for what she didn't know.

He stopped right in front of her, close enough that she smelled his woodsy scent, felt the heat coming off his hard-muscled body. With a gentleness that contrasted to his size, he fingered some stray hairs that had escaped the ponytail and shifted them behind her ear. She shivered as his fingers brushed her sensitive ear.

His grin grew when he toyed with one delicate, short dangling earring. "A horse." His deep voice that never failed to make her insides quiver sounded amused. "Fitting."

She gulped, torn between wanting to shove him away or grab hold of his skin-tight, black t-shirt and pull him to her. "If you're looking for Thad, he's—"

"Already talked to him. He'll be out on the range for most of the day," Drake said, cutting her off. He thumbed some beads of sweat away from her forehead.

"Eeww," she said, stunned he would do such a thing.

The strange man chuckled and did it again. "I've been around a lot of sweaty men in my life. This doesn't even compare." His nostrils flared. "Fact is, darlin', on you it's like an aphrodisiac. Irresistible."

Gwenie snorted, although charmed by his ridiculousness. She'd seen pictures of him working out in the team's gym, shirtless. Okay, she looked at those photos now and then. Whenever she did, all those acres of pecs and abs and tan skin made her want to touch every inch. His workout shorts had ridden low and she'd wanted to sneak a peek…

"Stop it!" she snapped, more to stop her wandering thoughts than to make him stop touching her.

His eyes lit up as if accepting a challenge. In the next second, he cupped the sides of her dirty face and lowered his mouth to hers. She didn't move, couldn't breathe. They fit perfectly together. There wasn't any of the awkwardness she'd felt with other men. Men who had no clue how to kiss a woman. But this man did. *Oh yeah, this man did!*

His tongue slipped along her lips and she opened them enough that it slid into her mouth. He tasted of coffee and cinnamon. Cinnamon rolls? The questioning thought disappeared as she threw herself into the wondrous moment.

Those big hands lowered to cup her buttocks, drawing her into intimate contact with—*Oh lordy, lordy!*—with an impressive, rigid cock pressed between them. She ground her hips against the hard length, prying a hungry growl from him.

Unable to resist, she did it again and his erection seemed to double in size. Who knew she was so talented? Some of what she'd read in those romances she devoured must have sunk into her mind.

Still making love to her with his talented mouth, he lifted her off her feet. His heart pounded against her chest, against her swelling, aching breasts. Just like those "heaving breasts" she'd read about.

This had to be the most unromantic place to do this. With all her grime and sweat, she must look like the least sexy woman ever. How could he want her? *Oh, yeah. Man.* That said it all, according to her brother.

None of that mattered. If he was into this, she sure as hell was.

She curled her legs around him and clutched his shoulders. Again, her brain seemed to pull the ideas from all those stored sexual fantasies. She silently thanked those talented authors. This was uncharted territory with her limited experience and those losers she'd been with. They hadn't awakened any of these needs or sensations in her.

The next steps were up to Drake. She had faith that he knew whatever needed to be done. In her too-boring life, she'd never have another chance like this. This would be something to carry in her memories forever, long after he came to his senses and went chasing after a woman who would fit him far better. A man like him didn't fit her either. He might have joked about settling down, marrying. But he wouldn't. And she could never be merely another of his "play toys."

She wriggled again in encouragement. Every woman part of her tingled in anticipation and she gave a small whimper. For now, he could be *hers* to enjoy.

***

He had to have her. Right damn now.

Drake held her to him, her sweet ass rubbing against the part of him demanding attention. He'd only intended to find Gwendolyn and talk to her about him moving into the big house for a while with her and Thad. Thad had suggested it. He needed to be on the ranch as he got the plans for his new business going. There was a lot to do and he was ready to start. This new challenge was what he needed to fill the hole in his life that retiring from football had created.

The instant he'd seen her, all dirty and glistening with sweat, his brain had fogged up. Hunger had taken charge and he'd gone to her determined to satisfy it with kissing her again. He'd thought a lot about their kiss the last time he was here. Which was crazy. He must have kissed hundreds of women over the years. She shouldn't have been anything special, but, dammit, she was. He'd tried to keep his secret feelings for her buried all these years. She was his best friend's kid sister, too young for him to pay attention to back then. Everything was different now. She was different, and so was he.

Gwendolyn wriggled against him, that sweet ass nestled against his throbbing erection. He groaned and they unlocked lips. He fought to steady his breathing, stop his heart rate from going off the scales. *Take a chance.* Could he? Dare he?

She rubbed again and gave a shivery whimper. Hell, she was turned on, too. As with football and focusing on his goal of taking down a ball carrier, he was goal-minded now. *Must. Have. Her.*

"Where?" he asked, hearing the desperation in his voice. "You're killing me."

"There's a storage room." She pointed to the back corner.

He clutched her tighter and took off running. Her light weight was nothing compared to barreling through two-hundred-plus-pound men. He wasn't even winded when they sped into the small room lit by a dusty window. All kinds of saddles, bridles, and more stuff than he could name sat on shelves and hung on wall pegs. A waist-high bench held only a bridle being repaired on it. *Perfect!*

He set her on her feet, used his forearm to brush off the bench. When he glanced at her, he noticed the dirty, blood-dotted bandage wrapped around her left hand. "You're hurt." Bad enough to stop them now? *Please no.*

"It's fine," she said, seeing his worried look.

Relieved, he growled, "Strip. Now."

She blinked at him and he realized what a horny idiot he'd sounded like. But instead of telling him, "Go to hell" like she should have said, she countered with, "Back at you, Football Boy."

"I'm a full-grown man, darlin'," he teased back.

Again, she surprised him. "Prove it."

\*\*\*

Had she really dared him like that? Was she going to take this thing farther? Gwenie stood in front of the bench, breathing so hard it was a wonder she didn't pass out. She'd fantasized about him for so many years. What if they did this and he fell far short of the dream lover she'd believed he would be? She certainly wasn't any man's idea of a "dream lover."

"Are we doing this or not?" He studied her from a few feet away, his eyes intense with purpose, chest puffing out with each deep breath he took. One strong hand was ready to unzip his jeans. But she sensed he would back down if she'd changed her mind.

"Are you protected? I've got a condom in my wallet." He patted his back pocket, looked panicked. "Hell. My wallet is in my car." He turned away.

She snagged his arm. "I'm on the pill," she admitted, debating for a half-second about telling him to go get the condom.

Instead, she tilted up her chin in determination, released him, and unbuttoned the top button on her jeans. "Bet I can beat you." With that she went to work and had her jeans undone and pushed down in a flash. But she'd failed to think about her boots.

He hadn't thought that far ahead, either. When she looked at him, he was frowning in irritation. "Damn," he muttered, attempting to toe one boot heel.

She giggled, ridiculous as that was. "Think we can manage half-undressed? With our boots on? I'm game if you are."

His grin was his answer. He took a second to shut the door, then he shuffled toward her, doing his best with his jeans and boxers strangling his calves. A long, rigid cock swayed from side to side like a pendulum swinging as he got closer. Her mouth watered and she licked her lips. *Oh lordy, lordy!*

He caught her reaction and grinned even more. "Ready to see what *he* can do?"

Her lower lips quivered in a wild, happy dance, and she felt moisture beading between her legs. "Other tricks? I can already see *he* stands up and begs." *Did I really say that?*

With a chuckle, he gripped the length, moving his fist up and down just once. Her fingers trembled with the need to reach out and touch it, too. But he picked her up around the waist and plopped her down on the workbench. It was cold and rough against her bare skin. Arousing. She hoped she didn't get splinters in her butt.

"How about you lie back? Keep that sweet ass of yours right on the edge." His drawl was thick, commanding. When she didn't move, he nudged her backward. "How about we play hide and seek? You're flexible, right?"

*Flexible?* Gwenie had trouble concentrating on anything. *Breathe in, out. In, out. Oh, lordy, that wasn't helping.* Not when a completely different experience came to mind. Somehow, she asked in a confused tone, "What?"

Drake tugged off one of her boots and then the other, tossing them across the small space. She lay there watching him, wondering, uncertain, until he took hold of her legs hampered by rumpled clothing and pushed them up, up, up. Her face heated at the image she must have made. But that thought fled when he scooted closer and announced, "I'm going to *hide* my big boy inside you." He panted and held his "big boy."

It wasn't easy, but she craned her head up enough that she could see his face. "Seek?"

His determined grin was back. "I'm going after your secret treasure."

She stared at the rounded head of his "big boy" with a drop of cum beaded on top. As her heart raced again, he put the cockhead at the entrance to her frantic and needing body. Grimacing, he slid his cock inside, out again. Then inside a little deeper. Teasing her until she whimpered.

"Secret treasure?" she gasped, trying to ignore the strain in her thighs to maintain this awkward position, wishing he'd stop teasing and dive deep inside her.

"That famous G-spot," he ground out and drove to what felt like was her core. "Oh, damn, darlin'!"

Her head fell backward, and she squeezed her eyes shut. "Not. Your. Darlin'," she mumbled. She hadn't been sure he would even fit, but he darn sure did!

Unconcerned with her protest, he got straight to the business of proving he was in fact fantasy-worthy. He rammed over and over, grunting from the effort.

Her fingers clutched the edge of the wooden bench and her injured palm caught her attention. For a bare second. Ignoring it, she shoved upward to meet his thrusts.

He cupped her butt, held her up, and continued pounding, deeper and deeper. His face contorted with strain, but he was dogged determined to reach his goal of torturing her until…

"Oh, yeah!" she gasped. "There! Right there!" She screamed in agonized pleasure.

Was he done with her? Hell, no. The man was relentless. He'd reached the place she'd only heard about and swore she'd never forget again. She couldn't seem to find enough air to breathe.

Panting, he released her butt and she felt boneless. She started to lower her hackled legs, but his big body was still in the way. And he wasn't done with her. He leaned forward, pressing her legs high again, and drove on and on. Fuzzy-brained, she noted sweat beading on his forehead and upper lip. His eyes went out of focus and he sucked in ragged breaths.

There it was again! That frantic, shivering need within her. With each thrust she arched upward, whimpered. Until she couldn't focus. Until another orgasm tore through her and she screamed even louder, "Drake! Oh, Drake!"

Before she could catch her breath, he rammed deep one last time and roared out with his release. For just a second, he held himself above her. His chest heaved with his effort to come back to the present. Finally, he lowered his forehead against hers, sighing in satisfaction.

Gwenie was more than fulfilled too. But her thighs begged for relief. She could only be this limber for so long. Yet she couldn't resist fingering his thick, sweaty hair. What happened now? A quick, wild romp in the hay, so to speak, meant nothing. Couldn't mean anything. In her heart, she wanted a forever kind of guy. Drake was an enjoy-the-moment kind of guy.

"Gwenie? Drake? You in here?" Thad called out from somewhere in the stable.

## Chapter Three

"Damn." Drake disentangled from Gwenie as fast as a lightning strike. He jerked up his boxers and jeans and tucked in his T-shirt equally fast. "He's supposed to be gone all day," he snarled.

"You'll have to stall him," Gwenie said, sliding off the bench and getting tangled in the mess of clothing shoved low on her legs. "He can't catch us like this." She didn't even want to think about how humiliating that would be.

"Gwenie? Drake?" Thad called out again, sounding closer.

Drake strode to the closed door, grumbling under his breath about people with piss-poor timing. As he reached for the doorknob, he glanced back at her. "I've got this." He hesitated and added, "Next time we won't be so stupid."

She struggled to slide her panties and jeans back into place, glowering at him. "There *won't* be a next time. We both know it." Which was true, but so sad. Her body was still recovering and wanted a lot more of his explorations. In a less awkward position, on a more comfortable surface. Something soft.

His sweat-covered brow creased with a scowl. "There will be."

If only... *No.* She wasn't naïve. There was no way a simple country woman like her could ever tame a playboy like him. They might have shared a hot moment, but it had been a fluke. She'd lost her good sense. He'd been... well, a man. He'd taken advantage of her slip.

Filled with regret but grim determination, she shook her head. "Not up for discussion." She breathed a sigh of relief after fastening the jean's button.

"It sure as hell is!" He straightened, thrusting those massive shoulders up, that impressive chest out.

Before either of them could continue the argument, footsteps came even closer. "Gwenie, Drake?"

Gwenie hated that she hadn't cleaned up. But then none of this should have happened. She'd lost her mind. Let her years of lusting after a man so wrong for her blindside her. She deserved this discomfort.

"What's going on?" Thad had reached the closed door and sounded upset.

"Why aren't you out on the range?" she bit out, frustrated with everyone.

The doorknob turned, and Drake grabbed hold of it. He refused to let it move again. His gaze slid to her. "Hurry up," he hissed.

She dived for her boots, wincing from her sore foot, which had swollen some. "I'm trying," she hissed back. She was tempted to just not put them on.

Thad let loose a string of curses and worked harder to open the door. "I will pound the hell out of you, *buddy!*"

Drake stiffened. "You can try."

Jamming her feet into the boots, Gwenie blew out an irritated breath. "Seriously, you two?"

Thad tugged on the doorknob again; Drake held tighter; his face strained. "I warned him not to—"

"Not to screw me?" she demanded and stomped to the door. She elbowed Drake in the gut. Surprised, he staggered back a few inches and gaped at her in shock. When she turned the knob, she discovered Thad had released it. Probably stunned, too.

She pulled the door open, met her brother's poleaxed gaze, and snapped, "I'm *not* a child any longer. I'm a grown woman."

"But—"

"Uh-uh, no *but* to it."

She felt Drake moving behind her, felt his tension. She sensed Thad's defend-his-sister instincts mounting. She put a hand on each of their chests to hold them apart. "Take it down a notch, boys. *I* made the decision here. *Me, me, me*. Got that."

Neither man was listening to her. They both stepped forward, squishing her between them. "Fine. Play your I'm-tougher-than-you game. I'm out of here."

She wiggled free and stormed away. It didn't take more than a second before she heard shoving, then fists connecting with flesh. One determined brother defending his sister for a ridiculous reason. One much buffer man determined to... what? Save face because he'd gotten caught stepping over a line the two of them had drawn?

"I want you off this ranch. Today!" Thad raged, landing a punch that forced a grunt of pain from his friend.

Another punch landed, followed by another grunt of pain. "No. I'm staying."

"Start your business somewhere else." A smash into the door sent it slamming against the wall.

A shove sent Thad crashing into the wall and sent bridles flying off the pegs, thudding to the floor. "No. But I'm staying because I'm going to marry Gwendolyn."

She'd slowed her departure, straining to hear their argument. At his announcement, she spun on her heel. One side of Thad's mouth had blood dripping down, but he looked pleased by what he'd heard.

Drake swiped at blood beside his mouth, too. He blinked as if what he'd said surprised him. No doubt it had been a spur-of-the-moment bluster.

Gwenie stepped closer and, with hands on her hips, snapped, "Stay. Go. I don't care." She focused on Drake as her heart pounded. "We are *not* getting married. And *stop* calling me Gwendolyn."

The idiot man grinned and she realized she'd given him a challenge. Drake had lived for challenges on the football field for years. He was already reveling in the challenge of starting a new business. Now she'd given him a new challenge. *Darn him!* She wasn't a prize to win, another stat to add to his record.

"Get that gleam out of your eye, Drake Walters. It isn't happening." She spun away again, stumbling, but marching toward the front of the stable to the sound of two dumb men laughing.

One of them with a Texas drawl telling her dimwit brother, "Think we can pull off a Valentine's Day weddin'?"

\*\*\*

Drake couldn't believe what a hailstorm he'd unleashed by allowing his dick to rule his brain. Since those hot minutes of pure craziness, his body kept bombarding him with demands to do it again. Only making actual *love* this time to the irresistible Gwendolyn instead of just f—

No, he wouldn't apply that disgusting word to anything he ever did with her.

He rolled from one side to the other, tangling his feet in the sheets. The bedside clock announced in big, red, glowing numbers that it was two thirty-eight. He wasn't getting a lick of sleep tonight. But he was doing a lot of Pilates, of sorts. Rolling over and over and over. Interspersing that with sitting up and punching his pillow into submission. Or standing up to pace the room hoping to tire himself out. None of it was working.

A full moon shone brightly through the uncovered window across the big guest room and drew him. He climbed out of the rumpled king-sized bed and strode across the wood floor to look at the golden globe. The lyrics to "That's Amore" hit him like another hailstone. *What the hell?*

He groaned and braced his hands on the sides of the window. Ever since he'd teased Gwendolyn about being her E-mail-ordered groom, he'd become a mess. Yes, he'd been drawn to her when she was too young for him, too innocent. Now she wasn't either of those things. Four years difference wasn't any big deal anymore. And innocent? If she was before he'd dived for her G-spot, she sure wasn't now.

His cock hardened in an instant just remembering what they'd done, how she'd responded. He scowled down at it. "Buddy, you've already gotten me into big trouble with her." Except he thought maybe she'd over-reacted a tad when she'd stormed out of the stable. He'd seen the longing in her eyes even as she'd told him they were not getting married.

*Getting married? Were they really going to?* Again, he'd been half-teasing when he'd questioned Thad about a Valentine's Day wedding. Right?

Another hailstone of reality hit him in the gut. He wanted to do it. She wasn't anything like the women he normally dated or took as lovers. And that was damn fine. She was her own person and always had been. Gwendolyn had never put on airs to impress anyone. What you saw was what you got with her. What he'd gotten from her was proof that she had the potential to be one seriously passionate lover. But he wanted more than that. He wanted her to be one seriously hot *wife*.

Pleased that he'd made the best decision for both of them, he strode out of his bedroom and down the hall. He didn't stop until he stood in front of her bedroom door. He was thankful Thad had gone to town to spend the night with his fiancée.

Pulling in a breath, Drake knocked on the door. It was time to get her on the same page he was. "Gwendolyn."

He waited a second and knocked again. "Gwendolyn, we need to talk."

He was about to try again when the door was jerked open. Her narrowed eyes sparked with annoyance and then she looked down his length, shook her head, and slammed the door. "You are such an idiot."

"I'm in love with you," he muttered, but doubted she'd heard him. "Not an idiot." Then he glanced down and realized he was bare-ass-and-everything-else naked. Okay, maybe he was an idiot.

***

*In love with you.* Gwenie felt her eyes burn; her lower lip trembled. It wasn't possible. He was still caught up in a state of lust. It just couldn't be more than that.

She leaned against the door, wondering if he would try to open it or even knock again. He didn't. His footsteps headed back down the hallway.

Naked. He'd come to talk to her all bad-ass-naked. Who did that? Okay, a man very at home in his skin. A man hoping for another round or two of hot sex.

Beneath her over-sized Denver Mustangs t-shirt that she'd worn to bed for so long it was almost threadbare, her body screamed at her to go for that round or two. Her breasts had swollen, and the nipples were hard nobs. He hadn't touched them when they'd made love—had raunchy sex—in the storage room. She'd wanted him to, but everything had gone from zero to a thousand miles per hour in seconds.

Disappointed and depressed, she climbed back into her warm bed. Almost without thinking, she cupped her begging breasts and massaged them, just as she would have wanted him to do. She couldn't put her mouth to them and suckle them like he would have done. *Darn him.*

Her heart two-stepped as she continued massaging her breasts. Between her legs, her clit wanted attention, too. She could get Mr. Handy Dandy out of the bedside table's drawer. But she didn't feel up to making that much effort.

Had he gotten back to his room yet? Had he turned around to come back and try again?

She strained to hear. A door closed down the hall. *Wuss. You gave up so easily.*

Fine. Who needed him anyway? She tugged the t-shirt over her head and threw it to the floor. She didn't wear panties to bed so there was nothing else to keep her from taking out her frustration with some pleasuring.

After lying back, she pulled her legs up and spread them wide. It wasn't quite the same as when she'd lain on the bench, legs hampered by her clothes and shoved back to her shoulders. Her inner thighs felt a twinge of strain leftover from before. At least wood wasn't threatening to put splinters in her butt.

Holding four fingers together, she rubbed them back and forth over her clit. Up and down. Side to side. Until she moaned from the sensations building up within her.

She tensed, needed more. Much more. She needed Drake sliding that excellent cock of his deep inside her.

Moisture had already beaded beneath her fingers and she coated them with it. *Inside. Now.*

Just as two fingers danced at the entrance to her vagina, the door opened.

"Oh, darlin', that's one hell of a sight!" Drake said on a tortured groan. His eyes were heated, huge, focused. His chest drew in one deep, shuddering breath after another.

Gwenie started to pull her hand away, but he slammed the door and yelled, "No! Don't stop. I beg of you."

She blinked at him, blushing, but kept her hand in place. "This turns you on?" She'd read about that somewhere in one of her romance novels. But she'd thought it just made up. Guess not.

He was still deliciously naked. As he crossed the floor as if hypnotized, he took his long, stiff cock in one hand and stroked up and down. His gaze met hers and he ordered gruffly, "Work it, darlin'."

The rebellious side of her wanted to refuse. What was the point? So, she eased the fingers into her moist and eager body.

He stopped next to the bed and, watching each other, they played. Her fingers driving in and out. His hand moving up and down.

Until she arched upward, squeezing her eyes shut, and crying out with a release that exhausted her.

Until he groaned out, "Damn, that's beautiful!"

A second later as she watched him, he stiffened from head to toe, grimacing as if in pain. And then cum shot all over his hand.

He sank onto the side of her bed, sucking in air. It took him several minutes to come back to the moment, and when he did, he fingered her red satin sheets. Grinning, he studied the rest of her room. "You're a constant surprise, Gwendolyn."

No other man besides her brother had seen her room. She felt defensive, as if he would judge her in some weird way for the contrast between the determined female farrier and the secret, more feminine and sexy side of her.

And then he faced her, and his gaze landed on the large yellow sunflower tattoo on her upper left hip. He grinned again and stood up to turn around. He pointed to his muscled butt and a tattoo of a bucking mustang.

She blinked in surprise. "I thought you said once in an interview that you wouldn't ever get a tattoo."

He shrugged his massive shoulders. "Well, there was this one night… a little too much tequila."

Oh, how she loved this man. She had loved him since he was a rowdy boy. Then as a full-of-himself teenage football jock. And as an I'm-going-to-own-the-game college football star. Then as…

The reason no other man had appealed to her was because they couldn't. They weren't Drake Walters.

She sobered, heart pinching. "I can't play your teasing game anymore. I can't let you break my heart and I know you will."

***

The sadness in her beautiful blue eyes tore at Drake. Her words hurt even more. She wasn't talking about the hot-damn-time they'd had in the stable. Or even just now when they'd both masturbated like dueling banjos. She believed his E-mail-ordered groom announcement had been a joke. And his declaration that they were getting married, too. They had been at first, but then he'd changed his mind. He was dead serious.

He'd faced down men the size of Mack trucks determined to level him. He'd dealt with photographers and news reporters and a hell of a lot of social media hype over the years. He'd watched women who'd never really cared about him come in and out of his life. None of that had been easy.

But *this* was the hardest moment of them all. His stomach knotted and wasn't sure he could do it.

"Drake, I can't—"

When he saw a tear trickling down her cheek, he found his strength again. He strode toward her, thumbed the tear away, and held her troubled gaze with his. "I'm not playing games with you, Gwendolyn Lassiter."

She worried her lower lip.

*Now or never.* He went down to his knees beside the bed, reaching out to hold her hand. "I've told women a lot of crap over the years. Never lied to them. Just said what they wanted to hear to get them into my bed."

One corner of her mouth tipped up. "I don't doubt any of that for a second." The smile faded. "But I don't want to hear that crap. Although I sure haven't shown you it, I'm *not* that kind of woman."

He squeezed her hand. "No, darlin', you're not. You're the kind of woman I want to spend the rest of my life with. The *only* woman I want."

New tears trickled down her face, but she gazed at him with such hope. "We're nothing alike. I—"

All he could think to do to stop her doubts was kiss her. Show her how much he loved her. As he pulled her to him and did just that, he knew he'd made the best choice in his life.

When they inched apart, she teased, "Did I hear you telling Thad something about Valentine's Day?"

"That's only a few weeks off," he sat back on his heels, ignoring the twinge in his bad knee. "You pick the date. I'll make it happen." He sighed. "Maybe I should live somewhere else until then."

She pretended to pout. "Is that what you want?"

"Do I have a choice?"

"There is always the guest room you're already using." She patted the bed and nodded around the room. "Or there's here with me. I'll share."

He nudged her to the middle of the bed and crawled in next to her, frowning. "I don't mind sharing, but I need a lot bigger bed."

"Can I still have red satin sheets?" She fingered the beard stubble on his square jaw.

"Absolutely." He took her hand and nibbled on the finger.

"Okay, we'll figure it out." She slid a leg over his, rubbed her knee against his growing erection. "Interested in—"

"Hell yes!" He reached over and lifted her up to straddle him. "How about some ride 'em, cowgirl?"

She lifted until she could drop down on just the tip of his cock, which he obligingly held up. "You do love a game."

"Only with you." He arched up, trying to encourage her to slide down.

Stubborn woman resisted. With a laugh, she sucked him inside and said, "Valentine's Day works for me."

The End

# Pearl, Ben and REO
### Alan Souter

## Chapter One

### White Springs, Wyoming – Gold Buckle Rodeo, June 1909

### Ben and Pearl

The crowd in the seats circling the rough-hewn arena knew this next event would be a dilly. At the far end of the whitewood plank enclosure, Ben Hodges was in the saddle aboard Fred, his big roan horse, coiled rope in one hand, the other grabbing a loose rein and a fist full of the stallion's mane. Next door to Ben, a penned-up big bull calf had his eyes fixed on the far fence and his home with the other calves. He was motivated to get there. The silence was so thick, the local newspaper claimed, "you could hear a field mouse fart" waiting for the timer to start the action. What Ben couldn't hear was the deep sonic hum resonating from the barrel race teens and twenties girls on the fence, staring with wet lips and loose buttons at that big sexy hunk straddling that big horse. Then… the timer struck his bell and started the clock.

Chute cowboys heaved open the wooden gate. That big bull calf didn't waste a second. He rushed from his pen into the wide-open arena, short legs churning the dirt, ears back and nose snorting as he sucked in freedom and big-sky air.

Ben and Fred watched the calf's charge toward home, until he crossed the line that set Fred free with a huge lunge and Ben hanging on with steel thighs and that handful of mane. In two strides, Fred was halfway to the calf. By the third gallop, Ben had built his lariat loop. The calf never heard that loop reach out from horse and rider, arc through the air… and drop over his head. By that time, Fred had skidded to a stop on four braced hooves. Ben cleared leather and hit the dirt on the run. The bull calf, jerked to a stop by the lariat, spun around and now faced

Ben, that big galoot, big in the shoulders, big in the chest, and frightful in the face, with a loop of pigging string clamped in his teeth.

The rest was a test of strength and will. Ben was all knees, long arms and relentless hands flanking the animal to the ground, grabbing up three of the calf's legs and wrapping the pigging string once, twice, three times and tying it off. All the time, Fred kept the rope taut, and the calf lost his steam.

The crowd roared as Ben backed away from the helpless animal and threw his arms in the air with a whoop. He strode back to Fred, vaulted into the saddle and waited out the seconds ticking by as the calf gave a little struggle but stayed on his side, legs tied secure. The crowd clapped again. Fred relaxed the lariat.

Ben wiped his arm across his forehead as the arena crowd hushed again, waiting for the ride's score. The judges puttered and chatted for a maddeningly long time while the arena helpers freed the calf and gathered Ben's lariat. Finally, the head judge picked up the big shellac-stiff paper megaphone and hollered into the small end.

"Ladies and gentlemen, we have a winner with a record-breaking score..."

The number of seconds the effort had taken was immaterial to the crowd. Everyone knew and loved the perennial Ben Hodges, the big man on the big roan horse. He quietly paused in coiling his lariat to raise his Stetson in response to the crowd's adulation. His white shirt tucked into faded Levi Strauss blue denims was sweat-stained, but his mind was drifting to the long ride home and the ritual greeting waiting for him from the love of his life, his wife, Pearl.

She was a half-breed Lakota Sioux. Her American half came from a captured white woman of great beauty who died of smallpox a year after giving birth. Her father had been a Sioux warrior, hunter, and tracker. Pearl had inherited her mother's beauty and her father's intensity. Ben knew he had an armful on their wedding night, when she'd left him bruised, abused and with a smile on his face that would take two strong men to remove. Pearl shared Ben's problem: her no-nonsense, let's-get-it-on intensity had scared away suiters, as had his size—the muscular build of a gentle giant. Together, they fit like two pieces of a jigsaw puzzle.

Ben looked forward to the long ride home just to get his energy back. He had his extra shirt and a frying pan, and a slab of fatback, a tin of U.S. Army powdered eggs plus a sack of corn dodgers which would suit him for breakfast on the trail. Two bags of oats and freshly mowed alfalfa plus a half dozen apples would take care of Fred for the overnight ride. He knew the size of the feast Pearl prepared for his homecomings.

Ben let his thoughts drift as Fred's monotonous clip-clop lulled his senses that the flat scenery did nothing to excite. Only warblers and finches zipped across the approaching hills of grass. Ben tired quickly of picking out the perky yellow goldfinches from the speedy but less perky Kentucky warblers.

No sooner had he ridden a mile or so that the old aches and twinges started to become annoying. Fred's rocking chair gate was easy enough, but age was creeping up on the massive steed. He could still haul Ben around and still run down those calves that got faster and more devious every year, but his blowing came from deep in his lungs. Ben knew that by the time he reached his favorite camping spot, a stand of willows and birches about a quarter-mile off the main trail, both horse and rider would be ready to call it a day. For Ben, thirty years of rodeo and ten years of Pearl didn't leave much for the crows to pick over.

***

Almost through half of the next day, he'd followed his own fence line, and for the past half-mile he'd seen her standing on the porch of their low-slung ranch house. A brick wall sealed one end, with a stone chimney above a large fireplace where—he knew—she had aired out the woven rugs that gathered in front of the hearth, thick, soft and durable. Those rugs had seen a lot of action. He had to chuckle.

 Smoke curled up from the chimney, and around back he knew she'd have one of three big clawfoot bathtubs filled to halfway with hot water. He'd have to use it to gain entry into her domain through the bathhouse that would soon be busy with hired hands for summer work bringing the horse herd down to auction from the fat grass in the hills. He knew he smelled of horses and calves, bad socks that she'd burn, and summer sweat. Fred had to be turned out and brushed down and his tack put up in the livery stalls.

Pearl, in her buckskin jacket she wore against the dusk chill, had taken up station next to the side corral fence where they lunged new horses to judge their gait. Pearl always waited there in the rocking chair he'd made to her specifications. She liked to watch Ben wave and go through his homecoming chores before he—her imagination at work here—stripped naked and stepped into that big tub with a block of yellow soap and his back brush.

Pearl liked to watch Ben move. He had grace to his stride for all his size. Every ounce and every pound, every bone and every muscle seemed to have its own place. She knew that he knew she was watching him for her own pleasure, like he'd observed her when she fed out the lunge line to a new and nervous addition to their sale-horse remuda. She'd been calm and had spoken softly to the animal, letting out more lariat as the horse circled her in the corral. A casual observer would never guess the smoldering thunder packed into her slender whipcord frame beneath a head of glossy black hair. That soft mouth had whispered sing-song Lakota Sioux to the hammerhead Cayuse she totally controlled. Now she was doing the same thing to Ben. The rituals had their purpose. Nothing like a good hot bath and the atonal wail of the Lakota Death Song to stir sluggish blood.

Pearl got up from her chair to put biscuits in the warming oven, poke the roast with a fork and figure one hour until dinner seemed about right. She could feel the stirring inside those tight jeans, feel the catch in her throat when she heard him singing loud in the bathhouse. After ten years, she could recognize the impatience in his manner that predicated good news—even with a slight limp favoring his right knee. Pearl covered the roast and closed the oven door.

She shucked out of her buckskin jacket and crossed from the kitchen to the main room, and the aroma of cooking meat followed her, blending with the kindled lick of firewood. The log fire that burned in the great hearth warmed the rugs and blankets her grandmother had woven. The logs added their light to the freshly lit candles on the bisected slab of oak which served as their dining table.

Her jeans peeled off with relative ease revealing only her skin, and her gift to him, which she had shaved clean with her cut-throat razor. The heat from the hearth kissed her flesh with a feathery tingle as she scuffed off her moccasins. Then she waited in her chair that faced the fireplace next to his into which, each evening, he dropped with a satisfied baritone rumble, to read or smoke the long Indian pipe she had given him for his last birthday. The tobacco jar sat on the sideboard next to a bottle of Old Crow whiskey from which he sipped in moderation.

She heard the kitchen door open and close, the soft tread of bare feet on the wood floor and he was there, a dark, sculptured silhouette just out of the firelight, holding the towel in front of him in his shy way.

"Hello."

"Hello to you," answered Pearl. "Did you have good fortune in White Springs?"

"Fred did his best. We won first prize." Ben looked down at his feet. "I think he's ready to retire. He's almost twenty. I think he would enjoy stud service."

Pearl laughed that no-holds-barred bark. "Yes! The dun mare, or the bay. He has shown interest in the bay." She uncrossed her legs. "All this talk of stud service has awakened a memory." She uncoiled from the chair into the flamelight. Her denim shirt slipped from her shoulders and that glimmer from the fireplace touched her hard-nipple breasts, the soft slope of her stomach and sculpted thighs as her feet disappeared into the tumble of down-soft rugs. The firelight flickered as her high-cheekboned face regarded him through heavy eyelids and parted lips that curled into a smile which bathed away all the petty hurts from his body.

He came to her and she met him, her head against his chest, his chin gliding through her black hair, her breasts against his lower ribs, and her thighs, strong thighs, crushed against his. Pearl's lips and teeth and then tongue found his neck, the hot pulse of his carotid artery, the aliveness of him. She wanted to climb him like a tree... and then she cried out with a grin as both his hands found her buttocks and lifted her mouth to his. Their first kiss was a soft brush of lips, and then she gently chewed his lower lip and ran her tongue across it. The kiss became more insistent as his large hands swayed her body across his lean torso. And then he discovered her gift, smooth to the touch.

In the moving shadows and flamelight that touched his rugged features, she saw the smile first in his eyes, and then on his lips, and finally she felt the flat of his palm and wedge of his fingers on bare skin between her legs. Pearl wrapped her arms around his neck and her legs around his thighs, shinnying up his oak tree physique, her breath hot in her throat until she felt the first touch of his cock and lowered herself onto its impalement. A low growl filled her chest as he let her down onto the rugs and rolled onto his back. Her black hair gleamed in the heat and light of the hearth. Within that dark nest of unbraided, tousled hair, her eyes appeared as a pair of highlights that extinguished as the lids slowly closed.

With her eyes closed and her head rocking slowly back and forth, Pearl began a gentle, teasing motion with her circling hips as she rose and settled on his cock. Another ancient song and rhythm played in her head, her body responding with a sway and a lunge of its own until Ben grabbed her waist and she clutched at his wrists

"Hola!" she cried, fell forward on his torso and kicked her legs out behind her as the first orgasm rippled through her. There would be more.

## Chapter Two

## REO

Pearl came out onto the porch sipping from a tin cup of beer. It had gone frosty when she came up from the cold cellar where the keg was kept, and the warm sunrise breeze kissed the metal. She dropped into Her Chair that was next to His Chair where he had collapsed in his usual heap. He bestowed a raised eyebrow. She returned it. The two eyebrows spoke a dictionary full of not-necessary words about the brisk and lusty homecoming and lumberjack dinner that had followed last night and finished up in the bedroom. Ben turned his attention back to his mug of black boiled coffee and spoke.

"I been thinkin'," he said.

Pearl took a long swig of lager. "Every time I've heard that our lives have made a big swing from the well-traveled road."

"I ever let you down? Remember, we started out with everything we owned in a wagon bed hauled by two drays and that sad-eyed ropin' pony—"

"Rex," Pearl interrupted.

"Yeah, Rex. He could fall asleep in the chute, but at the bell—bam! He was on that poor calf, I was off his back, and the calf's legs were all wrapped up. Whooee!"

"You were skinnier back then." Pearl nodded. "But that cayuse won us our first rodeo season."

"And we never looked back. I won a half dozen times that first season. You took three barrel race wins, you and old Rex. He could do everything but cook breakfast."

Pearl gave Ben a soft look and stretched in Her Chair like a contented pussycat. "He was a half-and-half like me, only half Arabian and half quarter horse, with that one droopy eye." She paused as a few crows rose up from the cornfield across the road and then asked, "Okay, what's your thought?"

"Not too many rodeos left in me, or old Fred. He's goin' on twenty. I think he would enjoy stud service."

Pearl unleashed one of her knowing chuckles. "I bet you would too. Where is this goin'?"

"It ain't goin'; that's the problem," Ben grumped. "We built this place on our horse sales and our rodeo winnings. Monday morning, we got four hands comin' in to round up the herd and drive 'em to fresh grass an' water at the creek. Then they bring 'em down here t' the stalls and the turnouts. All that time costs money, and so far we got more goin' out than comin' in. "You know we lost the Diamond-K horse contract since ol' Red, the foreman, sold off those nags of his to the dog food company. We were goin' to replace them with fresh stock. He bought three steam automobiles and a gasoline station-hack to pick up his dude tourists at the Grant City Depot and take 'em up to the Three Peso Mountain tent camp. After two-inch slabs of prime steak an' taters, Red hired four blanket Indians, real fierce lookin', t' tell scary stories of massacres and such around the campfire. A singin' cowboy signed on who couldn't sit a saddle if ya' roped him onto it. Next mornin', Red's cook, that Chinee fellah, fills them dudes up with eggs, beans an' sidemeat for the mule ride down to the abandoned gold mine. You get my drift?"

Pearl finished her beer, reached across to Ben and laid her hand on his forehead. "Nope, you ain't got a fever. I love you like crazy, so it ain't like you've turned loco, but I sense by your roundabout story that you want to look elsewhere less strenuous for our declinin' years. I'll warn ya right now, I don't look scary in a blanket. I don't know of any massacres worth talkin' about. And as for my singin'—well, you've heard my singin'."

Ben took her hand and kissed it. "You're the most terrifyin' female I know, darlin'. Tell you what. I'm goin' into Grant City today, while you talk with some fellahs I met at the White Springs Rodeo who want to come here an' look at our horses with a squinty eye an' pockets full of cash." He sat forward on His Chair all awake and eager.

Pearl said, "You're way ahead of me on this." She looked up at him as he stood and started toward the ranch house front door with his mug of cooled coffee.

"Don't wait up for me, darlin'."

With a creaking slam, the ranch door shut, and Pearl felt a small chill run up her backbone.

It was dark when she gave up her vigil and finally turned in.

***

The sun was up when Pearl awoke, alone in her half of the huge bed. She groped her way into her denim shirt, jeans and buckskin jacket, tugged on her boots and opened the bedroom door to the scents of his Bay Rum shaving lotion and boiled coffee. Biscuit crumbs led to the kitchen back door. Ben was nowhere in sight, but Fred nickered and turned his head in her direction from the oat bucket hanging on the lunging corral fence. Pearl couldn't stand it any longer.

"Ben?"

He returned her shout from behind the horse barn stalls. "Back here, darlin'."

Pearl set off at a slow trot until she turned the corner of the barn. There was Ben, all smiles, sitting in His Chair, which he had lugged from the porch, his legs stretched out and boots crossed in front of him, elbows up and fingers locked behind his head and beneath the back brim of his tipped-forward Stetson. After taking in contented Ben, Pearl realized they were not alone. She focused on the thing sharing the lunging corral and puckered up twice before the words came out.

"Wh-wh-what is it?"

"'It' is all ours. This is a REO Runabout automobile."

Pearl made her way unsteadily to Her Chair, thoughtfully placed next to his, and caved into it. Her normally bronzed color had paled considerably. How had she missed it? What happened that she let it get this far along? Slowly she turned her head from the cherry red spectacle in front of her to poor Ben, poor addled Ben. For sure and certainly he had lost his mind.

"Ain't she beautiful?" Ben grinned. "See the way the sun sparkles off her brass headlamps? And the yellow paint on her wood wheel spokes—that's a classy touch."

Pearl collected herself and tried to do what usually worked every time Ben had "surprised" her in the past. For instance, that dress he saw in the Grant City General Store and Select Merchandise Emporium. He thought it would add some color to her otherwise drab wardrobe. She just went along and wore it for two weeks. Eventually, he came to her and suggested maybe she didn't need so much color—with her natural healthy beauty and all. She hung it from crossed sticks and stuck it into the cornfield. They didn't see a crow out there for six months.

"Ben, how'd that thing get out here? You didn't drive it."

"Nope, the fellah that sold it to me drove it here with his horse tied on behind to ride back t' Grant City. He suggested we do the same—tie ol' Fred on the back end for a while until we get the hang of her."

Pearl swiveled her eyes on Ben like a gun turret on a battleship. "Did I hear a 'we' in there someplace?"

"Sure thing. She's for both of us. That's part of my plan. People see you drivin' her, perched up behind the steerin' wheel like the Queen of Hungary, and they'll think 'If a woman can bring that contraption to heel, anybody can handle the critter.'"

By now, Pearl was as limp as a leaf of week-old lettuce. Ben kept sayin' "she" this and "she" that, like that heap of tin and bolts was a person. If "she"—if this "REO"—was another woman, like that waitress at Doherty's Saloon who made no secret that her aim in life was to get Ben into bed, or into a hayloft, or out back behind the saloon's chicken coop, or even those barrel race girls at the rodeo who purred like kittens and low-buttoned their shirt fronts when he was around... Pearl shook her head. No, he'd sailed through all them female wiles like they were just buddies added to his long list of Grant City pards. Even so, Pearl stewed, she could handle them phillies; they were flesh and blood. This REO critter was tin and gasoline.

Ben stood up and tugged at her sleeve. "Com'on, let me show you around ol' Miss REO." He brandished a slim booklet. "That fellah gave me this instruction book, two extra rubber tires, and a tank full of stove gas t' get us goin'."

Pearl shook his hand free. "Don't drag me. I can walk."

She entered the lunging corral, giving the four-wheeled, two-seated, two-eyed critter—now kissed full on its flanks by the early morning sun—a wide berth and focused her most critical squinty eye. Like anyone raised with horses, she circled Miss REO, checking out her conformation.

She saw some wear on the tufted leather seats and paint applied over boot scrapes on the driver's side running board. She thumbed each half-curved fender and they seemed sound. Each wheel had the same number of wooden spokes, and REO had been shod with what appeared to be good rubber. Pearl kicked a tire. She had seen a fellow do that once to an old Locomobile that had been towed into town by a span of big-shouldered German plow horses after it broke down on the road. The farmer got two dollars for the hauling job from the dude who piloted or captained the thing. Pearl remembered the man's long canvas duster, gauntlets and bug-eyed goggles. The layabouts sitting on the saloon steps had had a good laugh that day. No way would she ever wear such a getup.

Pearl inspected the hatch on top of the metal cowling that sat out front between the headlamps. She'd seen "automobilists" with their heads down inside that box, working on the motor. Might as well check out REO's teeth. She raised the hatch and moaned.

"Ben?" she whined.

"Yeah, sweetheart," Ben answered, not looking up from his instruction book page.

"No wonder that shifty gent towed your 'Miss REO' out here. You been hornswoggled."

"How's that?"

"There ain't no motor, that's what."

Ben looked up at Pearl and then at Miss REO. "It's underneath," he said. "The motor is under the seat—says right here."

Pearl shrugged and looked down at the two filler caps beneath the hatch. "What kind of gas buggy has the motor under the seat?"

"Accordin' to this book," Ben said with annoying patience, "what you're lookin' at is where the gasoline an' water for the rad-iator goes. The motor has two cylinders that"—he squinted at the type and read—"produces ten horsepower and a top speed of thirty miles an hour. The REO Runabout can travel fifty miles using only one gallon of gasoline."

Pearl bent down trying to see the motor. She straightened up and scratched her head. "Ten horsepower? Is that a fact? How much does gasoline cost?"

"Stove gas from the general store?" Ben scratched his chin. "If you filter out the bugs and such from the store's keg, about ten cents a gallon. If the storekeeper gets rid of the bugs and such, add two cents a gallon."

Pearl did some math on her fingers. "That's cheaper than oats. If Miss REO lives up t' that book, we come out about four horses t' the good."

Ben nodded. "See, I told you. In that box behind the seat is a two-gallon gasoline can. Fill that up an' we can go a hundred miles before we have t' fill 'er up again. Then there's oil an' grease t' keep topped up an' five dry-cell batteries. I figger we can go that one hundred miles for about a dollar." Absently, he stroked one of REO's fenders. "A dollar fifty, tops."

"What if she throws a shoe?" Pearl felt she was losing her arguments. Was she also losing Ben to this tin hussy? She scowled and folded her arms across her chest.

Ben knew he had gained ground. "That salesman fellah put an extra tire tube on top of that box. See it there? It's right next to the air pump."

Pearl felt light-headed from sniffing the gasoline that seemed to be the critter's natural scent. She decided to follow her Sioux father's teaching.

"When not sure, charge the Yengeese. Take many scalps!"

Pearl stepped up out of the prairie grass onto the passenger side running board and gingerly settled into the left side bucket seat to ponder.

She and Ben had been married and pards for more than ten years. They'd sided each other a lot of times when one or the other had gotten in a scrape or done something stupid. Now, Ben had himself in a real scrape. He believed this bucket of bolts was his future. He really thought this red-painted harlot had punched his ticket. Ben had lost his mind of course, but over those years, Pearl had always sided him against whatever might come. She loved him with all her heart, and that was all there was to it.

"An' no more saddle sores," said Ben and returned to the book.

"Let me really get this straight," Pearl said. "I sit here like some eastern potentate while you drive with this wheel an' these pedals an' levers."

"Yep."

"You figgered out yet how t' put the spurs to her?"

"Yep. Well, sort'a. I figger I'll learn as I do it."

"You gonna turn 'er loose?"

Ben made his "situation resolved" face and closed the book. "You get down from your perch there, walk around t' the other side and find the crank handle stickin' out."

Pearl muttered, "I knew there had t' be more to it." She climbed down and found the crank handle while Ben hauled his big frame up and took his seat behind the steering wheel.

Ben fiddled about with levers and peddles. "You give the crank a turn an' let go. If I don't set this spark thing right, Miss REO'll backfire an' maybe that crank might whip around and break your arm."

Pearl stood upright looking at Ben. "That's a fine thing t' know. You do somethin' wrong and I get the broke arm." Oh, Ben, she thought to herself, are you cuttin' me out?

"I got it set right," Ben said. "Let 'er rip."

"A fine thing t' know," Pearl muttered, bending down and grasping the crank handle. She dug her boots into the soft dirt and heaved on the crank handle. It didn't budge.

Ben opened the book again and read using his finger to find the words. "T'other way," he said.

"Oh, Lord." Pearl shifted her grip and spun the crank again. There came a sputter and a pop, a sputter and a pop, and then silence.

Ben read further. He reached down through a hole in the floor and adjusted the carburetor float a quarter turn.

"She'll go now," Ben said.

Pearl took a deep breath, brushed her hair from her face and grasped the crank handle once more. With a tug, the REO's flywheel spun, the starter buzzed with battery current, the pistons moved in their sleeves and went sputter-pop, sputter-pop, and silent.

Ben grinned. "You almost got it that time. Turn 'er loose!"

Pearl wiped sweat mixed with tears from her eyes, gave the crank another spin, and the sputter-pop, sputter-pop kept sputtering until the sound smoothed out to a sputter, sputter, sputter and finally settled into a bapeta-bapeta-bapeta and an exhalation of exhaust smoke burst from beneath the auto.

"She's cookin'!" shouted Ben. "Climb aboard!"

Pearl ran around the back of the car and climbed up into the passenger seat again, this time wide-eyed as the Red Beast shook and breathed out smoke. The little car vibrated, and the bapeta-bapeta-bapeta came up through the floorboards, through the soles of her boots and rattled her teeth until she closed her mouth.

Ben held the book and the steering wheel in one hand, eased the spark control back toward him and pressed his foot down on the throttle pedal. The bapetas smoothed out even more into a steady bipeta-bipeta-bipeta. Ben grabbed the brake handle that jutted from the right side of his seat and pushed it forward. Miss REO swayed a bit on her four slender tires and began to creep ahead. Pearl braced her boot on the low dashboard, grabbed the back of the seat behind Ben and gripped her door with her free hand.

Ben moved the spark control forward and Miss REO picked up speed. They motored out the gate and onto flat prairie. She bumped over the grass in a circle and then, as the ground sloped down, she picked up more speed. Ben felt uneasy and moved his hand to the brake lever. He hauled back on it and stomped on the reverse pedal for good measure. Miss REO bucked and bounced high in and out of a prairie dog hole. Ben came unglued from the seat and his Stetson flew off. The car bucked once more, the engine died and it came to a halt, rocking on its springs.

Ben sat in silence for a few moments, gripping the steering wheel and trying to regain his breath. When it appeared that all action had stopped, he looked over at Pearl. But she had disappeared. Ben half stood in the seat and looked back along their short path. Pearl sat disheveled in the prairie grass, a few yards the other side of that prairie dog hole.

"What you doin' back there?" Ben asked, trying desperately not to laugh.

"I am where you can always find me around a rank horse. That 'lady' of yours tossed me teakettle over tar bucket into the long grass an' I am thinkin' of stayin' right her until you sort that critter out."

The odor of unburned gasoline hung around them.

"I admit, that didn't go too well," Ben said. "The pedal and lever business is gonna take some work."

Pearl looked up at Ben. "Want me t' throw a blanket over her lamps t' gentle her an' keep her steady?" she asked.

Ben smiled and then started a deep rolling chuckle. "Damned if we ain't a real pair of 'automobilists'," he wheezed.

Covering her face with her hands, Pearl started to laugh and sniffle back her tears. Her ribs hurt, stressed from the tumble, but she couldn't stop.

"Whooee, Pearl! When I get this critter broke, I'm gonna buy us an aeroplane next! No more bumpy roads! Just us up there with the birds!"

They laughed until they could hardly catch a breath, and then Pearl climbed to her feet and made her way warily around Miss REO and took her position at the crank. As they had done with horses and with any trouble they had found themselves in over the years, each knew their place. The only way to get the job done was to get on with it, no matter how many times they found themselves sitting high in the middle of the air.

A half-hour passed and finally Miss REO was making her way in a wide circle, leaving concentric tire ruts in the grass. The purple cloud of curses that hung above their efforts began to dissipate. Miss REO's elliptical springs caused her to sway over small bumps, but some came harder than others, making Pearl and Ben's teeth clack together.

"This is like sittin' aboard a spring wagon full of brick!" Ben shouted. "I keep lookin' ahead and there ain't no horse's ass lookin' back! It ain't natural!"

"Kinda makes y' feel like you can go anywhere y' want, don't it?" Pearl shouted as he steered. "It's like everythin' out front of us is wide open!"

"I reckon that's our future out there, sweetheart!"

Ben steered out of the rutted circle. Miss REO climbed the slope and topped the rise onto the oiled gravel road to Grant City.

"What 'future' you got in mind for the three of us?" Pearl slipped her arm through his and leaned against his broad shoulder. "Sounds unnatural to me."

"Oh, yeah." Ben brightened. "All the autos in Grant City and near about come here aboard the Santa Fe Railroad with a shipping charge tacked on. I'm goin' partners with the fellah that sold me Miss REO and set up a shop here t' sell these horseless critters—and bigger ones too for families an' haulin' freight. We'll make a sellin' deal with the folks who build these gas buggies. Maybe put together an automobile blacksmith; they take a lot of fixin' to keep 'em on the road."

Pearl looked over her shoulder. "Weren't you supposed t' tie Fred on behind in case of a mishap?"

Ben slapped his forehead. "Damn! Woman, what would I do without you?" He hugged his big arm around her shoulders.

Pearl chuckled as Miss REO swept into a U-turn on the wide wagon road. She smiled up at his craggy face set in a wide grin.

"Find someone else t' sort your socks, I suppose."

"Haw! Haw! Haw!" He busted loose with his big laugh.

The chuckle on Pearl's lips turned down just a bit on the ends.

Back home, Pearl finished her ranch and horse chores and sat down on the back porch to peel some potatoes for dinner. Ben came sailing out the kitchen door with an empty sack, and for the first time, Pearl noticed Fred was saddled at the lunge corral.

"Where're you goin'?' she asked.

Ben mounted. "Goin' into Grant City t' get some beeswax, rags an' cleanin' alcohol to spiff up Miss REO."

She shouted at his back, "Don't you be late for dinner!"

Ben just lifted his Stetson and spurred Fred from a high lope into a stretched-out canter.

Pearl paused, holding two small potatoes in her hand with half a curl of potato skin carved from one. She had shaded those pretty chicks in town from layin' snares for her fellah, but Ben had that bright look of a frisky yearling colt feeling his oats. She glanced at Miss REO, parked in the corral, gleaming cherry red and brass, and finished the potato peel until it dropped into the bucket at her feet. From those two small, red potatoes in her hand, and one having a peel sliced from it, came an idea.

\*\*\*

"Bean stew?" Ben pouted over the steaming bowl next to a stack of salty crackers. "This is what we feed the hired hands on Friday nights."

Pearl glanced over her shoulder. "I got busy with my chores. There's lots of work I do aroun' here you got no idea of. Eat your stew."

Ben dragged his spoon through the pinto beans, corn, potatoes and gravy. "Injun food," he muttered. "You can't tell me the meat locker's empty."

She faced him, her hands on her hips. "You want me t' chicken-fry a steak for you? And when you're done tryin' to chaw it down, you can fix that hole in your boot with what's left. You got time t' fool with that Miss REO, then some poor kitchen maid has t' do what you're not doin'. And don't call me Injun. I'm only half, an' proud of it, *Yengee*."

Ben mopped a dab of stew from his chin. "T'ain't fair, woman. What I'm doin' with Miss REO, makin' her look pretty an' sound pretty, is called Advertising. We got to sell a whole herd of REOs t' equal our horse money."

Pearl folded her arms as Ben swept up the last of the stew with the last of the bread. His eyes widened. "Is that why my three-day-old work socks found their way into my fresh-washed shirt drawer?"

She looked away. "Accidents happen when you're doin' the work of two!"

"I'd agree with that." He stood and pointed at her. "If my long johns didn't have so much starch in 'em, I stood 'em in a corner!"

She faced his pointy finger. "Who helped offload our summer sweet hay delivery? I had mealworms and fungus beetles on me and in my clothes when I finished!" She turned to the kitchen door. "See if you can get that Miss REO to warm your feet in bed next Saturday night!"

Ben looked along his pointy finger at an empty doorway.

Pearl stomped out onto the front porch and dropped into Her Chair. Dusk had claimed most of the sky, with the sun showing only as a deep red streak across the horizon. She looked up past the porch overhang at the first of the pin-prick stars. The main road about a quarter of a mile away was empty. No, it wasn't. A wagon pulled by two spans of horses was making its way up the incline and was almost at their gate. The driver raised his hat. He was the son of their neighbor who owned the ranch about four miles down the road. Slater. Bob Slater. Pearl waved back. She watched the wagon for a long time as the sky darkened and the moon took over.

The thought popped into her head. *I bet Ben could sell a REO motor car to the Slaters. Look how much time Bob would save coverin' that stretch of road at twenty miles an hour. How much studyin' or how many chores could he do in the time he is wastin' right now.*

Pearl sat and she thought. She raked up a crop of ideas to sell REO motor cars. That's how she could side Ben. They both knew horses, an' she knew people—their neighbors to start with. He was learnin' about tinkerin' with the machine. She knew about tinkerin' with folks.

She got up from Her Chair, straightened her back and went inside.

\*\*\*

Ben had stopped snorting out back by the tack barn. He'd plowed up the dirt along the lunge corral where Miss REO shone like a jewel in the half dusk, half moonlight. He leaned against the four-rail fence. Pearl was unreasonable. Pearl didn't understand business. Pearl couldn't see the future. She was letting her Lakota Sioux half do her thinking. He looked at the bales of sweet hay just inside the tack barn door and made a face. But she was no fool. She ran the ranch when he was away rodeoing. There was a wise side to her nature—a side that read folks pretty good. He studied Miss REO—a beautiful example of modern machinery. Folks around Grant City didn't have a lot of spare cash to take a chance on "investing"—that's the word Ben's new partner threw around—in a gas buggy automobile. That's a big word to corn and wheat farmers, horse and cattle herders. They had to see a need, a need that wasn't a pig in a poke. That half-Indian lady did have a silver tongue.

Ben turned around and looked at the ranch house. The rooms were dark except for a glow from the front room.

\*\*\*

Pearl had lugged His Chair and Her Chair into the living room and the fireplace was glowing with the fire she had built. She dropped into Her Chair wearing her decorated Sioux shift. Her hair was tied back into an extended tail, showing the long amethyst earrings Ben had given her.

She didn't hear Ben enter, because he was carrying his boots.

"Hello?" she asked from just out of the firelight.

"Hello," he replied from the other side of the hearth's banked flames. He cleared his throat and then said, "I've been thinking."

Pearl's voice had a smile in it. "So have I."

"We should do it more often," his husky baritone said.

She stood into the firelight. "I have many ideas about how we can adopt Miss REO."

As he stepped into the firelight, she saw he was wearing his Levis and an open work shirt, and had bare feet.

"A visiting sister," he said, shrugging off his shirt.

Pearl ran her tongue over her lips. "A big-city sister with city manners who must learn the ways of our people."

"*Ta-yá- yahí,*" Ben said,

Pearl nodded. "And welcome to you." She held up her open arms. He stepped forward and undid the tie behind her neck. She let the shift slide off her shoulders to drop around her ankles. She undid the buttons to his Levis and gravity obeyed.

"Our lives are one," Pearl said in Lakota Sioux.

Ben answered in Lakota Sioux. "Now and forever, as the seasons change."

They came together in the firelight. His large, calloused hands had a gentle stroke. She slid her cheek up the tanned expanse of his chest to kiss his chin and then his lips, and his forearms lifted her on up until her firm breasts reached his mouth and tongue. In her mind, the drum circle began its steady beat. Pearl closed her eyes as he cradled her weightless and her chin pillowed in his hair. The first thin wail of Pearl's Lakota Death Song conjured their love that would never die, and as he entered her, she shouted his Sioux greeting "*Ta-yá- yahí!*"

The End

# Bullets and Bustles
## Suzanne Smith

## Chapter One

It was high noon, the worst time of the day for a shootout. Especially since I was the one standing in the middle of the street with the tumbleweeds dancing under my feet, compromising my balance. Even with the wide, flat brim of my brown felt hat pulled down low on my forehead, the glaring rays of the sun were blinding me. I was squinting so hard my eye muscles were getting tired.

"Did you hear me, Slim Gallagher?" I shouted aggressively to the portly, scruffy-bearded, ginger-haired man who stood twenty-five yards away from me. "I am a servant of the court with a warrant in my pocket signed by Circuit Court Judge Glenn Tomas of Arizona for the arrest of you, Little Roy Simms, Billy Ray Jones, and Frank Carson. Come peacefully, and there won't be any trouble. Be advised, I'm authorized to use deadly force."

I expected him to laugh and tell me that I belonged in the kitchen and not on the battlefield, like the others I had gunned down before him had, but he didn't. I watched as he turned his head to Roy on the right, then to Billy and Frank on the left. The men fanned out around him in a straight line.

"I've heard about you. Emma Tombs, isn't that your name?" Slim asked. "The pretty, blue-eyed, blonde-haired bitch that carries a gun almost as big as she is. They say that you and your Colt Navy revolver never miss the target. That you're so fast you can put down four men before the first one even gets his gun out of his holster. Got a nickname for you too, don't they?"

"They call her the undisputed Angel of Death," Billy Ray chimed in, spitting a wad of spent chewing tobacco on the ground next to him. "She don't look like much to me. Probably looks a lot better laying flat on her back."

"Well, there's four of us here now, missy. I say we put those rumors to a test," Slim said impudently as he dropped his arms to his sides, keeping his elbows stiff, but slightly bent, the five fingers on each hand spread. Like puppets on a string, the men standing on both sides of him did the same.

My hands started to sweat. My heart beat triple time. "Last chance, Slim." The dryness of my mouth made it hard to even get those few words out. He responded with nothing. No speech or motion. Only total stillness, the stillness that comes with focusing every ounce of energy into the placement of the bullet to be fired. He drew first. The others quickly followed. In less than two seconds, all four men lay on the dusty ground, belly up and bloodied.

***

Mild nausea filtered through my body as I sat in Marshal Jeremy Tate's rickety wooden office chair, sipping his musty tasting, stale coffee and watching him thumb through the stack of green bills on the desk in front of him.

"There you go, Emma," he said, as he slid the money in front of me. "Eight hundred, as agreed."

I wadded up the cash and shoved it in my sturdy, black leather saddlebag. He was looking at me with the oddest, concerned expression on his face. "Something wrong, Marshal?"

"You look a little out of sorts. Kinda peaked. You feeling OK?"

"I'm fine. I just didn't get much sleep last night."

"That all it is?"

"Yeah." That was only a half-truth. The full truth was that I hadn't gotten more than three hours sleep a night for the last three months. I had started to have nightmares, disturbing, grotesque images of every man that I had hunted and killed that were so terrible I had woken up almost every night in a cold sweat. Last night, it was the young sidewinder Curley Thomas I had seen in my dream, with liquidy chunks of his yellow brain matter leaking out of the bullet hole I had put in his head like a runny scrambled egg. Right now, I was wondering if the four men I had gunned down today would be joining Curley and the others in their tortuous nighttime merriment. It bought me no comfort to think that they would.

"I know it pains you some to talk about this, but I gotta ask."

"Yes?"

"Have you given any more thought to going after Johnny Romma? I'm only mentioning it because the bounty just went up to ten thousand, the highest I ever seen. You could do a lot with that money. Maybe even buy yourself a cute little house, like the one you used to have."

I clenched my jaw. The name Johnny Romma held more meaning for me than any other. He wasn't just another bounty. He was the man that had changed my life. He had set into motion a tragic chain of events when he had murdered my abusive, but financially supportive husband, Gregory. If it weren't for Johnny, I would never have lost my home and been destitute and sleeping in my neighbor's barn. Nor would I have shot the man in the barn who'd tried to steal my horse, Blazie, collected my first bounty on that same compulsive horse thief's head, or been inducted into the lucrative world of hunting wanted outlaws for money.

While my new life as a bounty hunter had been manageable in the beginning, and to some degree had made me feel like a useful member of society who piously meted out a harsh justice to those that deserved it, it seemed to me now that this path, the path that Johnny Romma's lawless behavior had compelled me to take, had become my undoing. The unstoppable, ghoulish nightmares that had recently affixed themselves to me from my mercenary kills wiped out any sense of essentiality that I had previously enjoyed and wounded me far deeper than any superficial bodily injury my deceased husband Gregory had ever perpetrated on me. So deep, I had begun to wonder if I'd be able to survive another night without going insane.

As badly as I may have wanted to go after Johnny and punish him for my misery, I knew it was time to get out of the killing business, try to lead a normal life, or as normal a life as a ruthless killer in a petticoat could.

"That's a lot of money, but I think I'll pass on Johnny. I was considering leaving Yuma County for a while. Take a little break, maybe a long break."

"If that's how you feel, I'm glad." Marshal Tate said, with a knowing, fatherly smile. "If you have a single doubt about what you do, it's time to move on. In this line of work, you hesitate to pull the trigger for split second and you're done for. I think we both know that."

"I do. But I also know that if you had a hand in bringing Johnny Romma to justice, you'd be a famous man in these parts."

"True. But if I get a hankering to make a name for myself, I can always put Snub Nose Mike and his brother Smiley on his trail."

"I have no love for Romma, but even he doesn't deserve their brand of justice," I said through curled lips, remembering the sinister smile on the faces of both these deputized thugs the day I'd watched them string up baby-faced cattle thief Timmy Fallon after he had thrown his gun to the ground and surrendered.

"I know you don't like them. Truth be told, I don't like them much either. But, they do get the job done, although their methods leave a lot to be desired."

"It's a moot point anyway. He's so slippery, they'll never catch him. Pinkerton's best detectives haven't been able to find him, and they've been looking for him for the last year. No one but the men he rides with know what he looks like without his scarf on his face, much less where he hangs his hat."

"Turns out that last week Smiley caught up with one of the men that used to ride with him. Creasy, I think they call him."

"What'd they find out?"

"Nothing. Nada. Zero. If he knows where Johnny is, he ain't talking. He was offered amnesty. Still, he gave up nothing. That kind of says something about Johnny."

"Like what?"

"Trust and loyalty are hard to come by. A man that inspires both is not your run-of-the-mill cutthroat."

"I disagree. What he did to Gregory shows him as just that."

"Yeah. That has me stumped." He scratched his bald head. "Gutting a man and leaving him to bleed out isn't his style. He always goes for the quick kill. A bullet in the heart or in the head. He's a consummate professional. Neat and tidy. Purposeful. Him gutting Gregory seemed, I don't know, angry and personal."

"You think someone else killed Gregory?"

"No. Before Gregory died, he told me he'd never met the man who butchered him, but that man told him his name was Johnny Romma. Seems that was the one time Romma didn't try to hide his identity. There would have been no point in Gregory lying. I just wonder why he did it.

Anyway, I think we've talked enough about ghosts of the past. We should be celebrating. You're starting a new life. Where you plan on going?"

"I'm staying in Arizona, but I thought I'd head on up to Mohave County. A little town called Oatman."

"Oatman?" He stared out into space. "Ain't that the town they named after the little girl that was kidnapped and released by the Indians? They marked up her face some, didn't they?"

"The Mohave tribe marked her chin in blue ink to show she belonged to them. It was their way of protecting her."

"I didn't think there was anything much going on in that area. Some mining maybe."

"Yes. Some mining. But nothing other than. Property is cheap there and it's quiet. I think that maybe what I need now. A little peace and quiet. I've saved some money. I'm gonna open up a diner."

He raised a brow. "You sure about that?"

While I was a crack shot with a pistol, everybody in town knew I couldn't cook a decent meal. But career options were limited for a young, independent woman trying to keep her head above water. "OK. I know I'm not the best cook."

"That's an understatement. I had to use a hacksaw to cut the biscuits you made."

"I'll practice," I said, with a smile. "I'll get better."

"I believe you will. When you plan on leaving?"

"This Sunday."

"Come by Saturday night. I'll have Irma make some of her famous mutton stew for you. Extra carrots, just like you like."

"How can I say no?" I stood up to leave.

Marshal Tate walked over to me. The spiky blades of his unruly gray beard tickled my forehead as he leaned forward and kissed it. "I'm gonna miss you, Emma Tombs. Even if you can't cook."

My eyes began to water. I was losing my best friend. I thought about all the times he had comforted me in the wake of Gregory's violence. Wiped my bloody nose. Wrapped my cracked rib. Sat with me all night and hummed a cheerful bedtime lullaby with a cold towel pressed against my swollen head. He had gone to all that trouble knowing that I would return to Gregory as soon as I could walk. He never once treated me like I was a simpleton for continually putting myself in harm's way or asked me the question that I had asked myself over and over. Why did

I always go back to Gregory? Maybe it was because he knew I didn't have the answer.

## Chapter Two

Pride swelled in my bosom as I watched Max hang the wooden sign with the ornate and sinuous white lettering above the screen door. Emma's Tasty Diner. It was more than a sign he was putting up. It was tangible proof of my new beginning,

"Like it, Emma?"

I'd been in Oatman, Arizona for a month now. When I'd first arrived, I was overwhelmed by the strange locale. The whole town was surrounded by mountains. Enormous, ragged, gray-green and brown hills that sprouted all the way from the foot of the earth to the apex of heaven. These marvels of nature had made me feel as if I were so small that one day they would just come to life and swallow me whole. But the more I had studied their savage beauty, the more I began to think of them as close friends. Impenetrable protectors that were there to keep this tucked-away, underdeveloped community safe and separate from the rest of the world.

"I love it," I said, handing Max a soggy greenback. "See you for breakfast?"

"Yup. Be back in about one hour."

I was still standing on the wooden deck of stairs and admiring my new sign when I heard the footsteps behind me.

"Do you know if Emma's is open yet?" asked the stranger with the deep, silky voice.

I turned around. One glance at the comely, long, lean man dressed in black from head to toe, with the sun-kissed, bronze face made my pulse accelerate. He reminded me of a black leopard. Sleek and strong. "Sure," I answered, gazing into his vibrant brown eyes. "I'm Emma. Nice to meet you…?"

"I'm JD." He extended his hand.

A jolt of electricity shot through me as our fingers touched. "Come on in." I ushered him to the open screen door and brushed the imaginary dust off the table closest to the entrance. "This table OK?"

He nodded, then sat down.

"Can I get you a menu?"

"No. I know what I want." He laid his black linen Panama hat on the empty chair next to him. I loved the way his thick, disheveled, dark curls sparkled in the sunlight. Like diamond infused waves of black ocean water. "Four softly scrambled eggs, with plenty of grits and a side of sausage. I'd also like a stack of hot cakes, doused with butter and extra maple syrup. Maybe a cup of that delicious smelling coffee to start. If that isn't too much trouble."

Where he was going to put all that food, I couldn't guess. His shoulders were broad, but there was not an ounce of fat on him. "Not at all."

I felt his eyes burning into my backside as I walked away. Some women would have been insulted by his bold flirtatiousness. But I liked the attention. I had never felt this wanted or desired. When I was married, I had been little more than Gregory's toy, to be played with when it suited him and boxed away when it didn't. I began to sway my hips from side to side, hoping the exaggerated movement of my body under my baggy blue dungarees wouldn't go without his notice.

I took my time clearing away the dirty breakfast dishes from JD's table, stealing quick glimpses at him out of the corner of my eye. He had devoured every morsel of food on his plate. I felt myself blush as I entertained the thought that maybe his voracious appetite extended to the bedroom as well. I laid the dishes on the edge of the counter then came back to where he was sitting.

"Would you like some more coffee?" I asked, barely making eye contact.

"Please." He held the empty china cup in his hand out.

"How was your meal?" Of course, I already knew any meal I cooked was a bad one. It was hard not to notice how strained his face had looked every time he had taken a bite of a charred hotcake or shoveled a fork full of lard-soaked fried potatoes in his mouth.

"It was—"

He paused. "Great."

We both laughed. "You're a terrible liar. I know I can't cook worth a damn."

"Why did you open a diner if you can't cook?"

I shrugged my shoulders. "It seemed like a good idea at the time. You new in town?"

"Been here about one month. You?"

"Same."

"Where'd you come from?'

"Yuma. You?"

"Nowhere in particular," he said, fidgeting with his napkin. "I'm more or less a drifter."

I stared at his expensive-looking black waistcoat and slacks. They had to be tailor-made. There were no gaps in the waist of the slacks and no bubbles of bulky material around the top of the shoulders of the waistcoat, like you sometimes find with store-bought clothing. He looked sharp, like a man of means. A banker perhaps. "You don't look like a drifter."

"Well, I did just invest in a small ranch on the outskirts of town. So, I guess I'm a rancher now. I'll buy me a few cattle and I'm good to go."

"How many head you got now?"

"None. I know as little about ranching as you do about cooking. Figured I'd read a book. Might help me some."

We laughed again. "Quite a pair we are. The diner owner that don't know how to cook and the rancher that don't know how to ranch."

"Emma's Tasty Diner might not have the best food in town, but it has other attractions," he said, with a mischievous grin.

As much as I liked his flattery, it was distracting me from my duties and throwing me off schedule. It was difficult to try to ascertain if I had enough jars of raspberry jam on the counter or enough loaves of cornbread on the shelves to accommodate the early morning breakfast crowd when all I could think about was how good JD would look without those fancy black britches on. I was almost glad when old man Tucker walked through the door and took his usual seat at the table next to us, breaking up our amorous tête-à-tête. "I have to go now. It was nice talking to you, JD.""Likewise. What time do you open tomorrow?"

"We open at six."

He put his hat on, and laid money enough to cover five meals on the table. "See you tomorrow at six," he said, giving me a wink as he walked out.

I'd known JD only a little more than an hour. I was thoroughly smitten. He was uncommonly handsome, with a good sense of humor and the best manners I'd ever seen. He had the confidence and elegance of a city born gent, blended with the warm, laid back approachability of a down-home country boy. But he had another quality about him that

I wasn't sure if I liked or disliked. He seemed to be a man of mystery, never really giving me any concrete details of where he'd come from before he came to Oatman, though I had asked him that specific question. I supposed he'd tell me in his own good time. All I had to do was wait.

## Chapter Three

The last of the day's register receipts had been tallied up. Emma's Tasty Diner had been open for eight weeks now. Business wise, today had been my most profitable day. All the sweetcakes on the shelves were sold out, and my supply of beans and taters was so low, I would have to head over to Clyde's General Store four days ahead of schedule to replenish them. But on a personal level, my day had been disastrous. JD had come in for breakfast, but I had been so busy I had barely gotten a chance to say hi to him. While I had been slicing bread and chopping onions, pretty, young, tawny-haired, blue-eyed Philomena Casha had joined him at his table. They had eaten breakfast together. They had left together. That was almost seven hours ago. By now, she had probably used her irresistible feminine wiles to lure him to her bed. Before long, she'd lure him to the alter.

I ran my thumb across the thin, red, raised scar over my left temple, compliments of Gregory ramming my head into a wall when I didn't have dinner on the table on time. I felt ridiculous. Why would I think, even for a second, that an intelligent, good-looking man like JD would be interested in used goods like me when he could have a fresh, vivacious woman like Philomena? Sure, we'd chatted about the weather, the mountains, food and other trivialities, but he was only being polite. He was probably bored to death.

I wearily walked to the window and flipped the open sign over to closed. No sooner had I flipped the sign when I heard the door creak open. "We're clos—"

I tried to hide my surprise. It was JD. He was standing at my door, not lying in Philomena's bed. "What are you doing here?"

"I've been trying to talk to you all week," he said, sounding slightly irritated. "But you are so damn busy all the time. I insist you sit down with me right now."

"I'm not sure your new girlfriend would like us sitting together," I blurted out, a little embarrassed at how childish and jealous I sounded.

"If you are referring to Philomena Casha, I have no interest in her. She asked me to escort her home and I obliged. That's all."

"It's none of my business anyway," I said nonchalantly, covering up the expansive relief I felt.

JD pulled out the chair next to him. "Please sit down."

"OK." I sat down. "What do you want to talk about?"

"Old man Tucker is having a celebration Sunday. He just had his first grandson. It's nothing too fancy, just some folks gathering in his house, eating good food, drinking ale, and dancing. I'd like you to come with me."

"You want to court me?"

"Yes."

"Why?"

He slid his hand in mine. "You're smart and beautiful. All I know about you is that you can't cook. I'd like to know more."

How I wished being a bad cook was my only flaw. But there was the little matter of me killing men for money. In the eyes of most decent people, I was a monster. A primped and perfumed anomaly in a skirt worthy of loathing, but not of love. The town folk had tolerated me because I was useful, kept them safe from the menacing riffraff that came their way. Other than Marshal Tate, there wasn't one person in Yuma or anywhere else I had plied my trade that had any fondness for me. Who would? Certainly not the genteel, well-mannered man sitting in front of me. I slid my hand out of his. "Once you know me better you may not like me very much," I said, disappointed in myself.

"Let me be the judge of that. For now, all I want is for you go to the dance with me. If you don't want to talk, you don't have to. If you're not comfortable, we'll leave. Come on, what do you say? I think we could both stand to have a bit of fun."

My heart melted as his gaze met mine. All this time, I had been looking at him as if he was no more than a mannequin. His thick, wavy black hair; his high, chiseled cheekbones; the earthy deep tint of his wide, brown eyes; his tall, toned and tan body. I had seen only the outline of a handsome, colorful canvas. But right now, when I took a second, better-anchored look at him, I saw more. I saw a man touched by melancholia, who carried the weight of the world in the girth of those beautiful, explosive brown eyes. It was almost as if he was trapped in his own body, desperately reaching out to me from the inside. He needed to be saved from himself, just like I needed to be saved from myself. Did he have nightmares too? Maybe not. But I felt certain that he was plagued by his own demons and had even less inner peace than I did. There might be hope for me after all.

"Yes." I once again slid my hand in his. "I'll go."

***

Round and round the center of old man Tucker's lofty living room JD spun me. As I tapped my heels on the bare wood floor to the twang of the banjo and the fiddle, I started to feel like a kid again. Worry free. Living in the moment. I had forgotten how much I loved to dance. It didn't hurt that JD had an excellent sense of rhythm and was light on his feet, probably the best dancer I had ever seen. When the music finally stopped, I was breathing like a winded mule.

"Let's go outside and get some air." JD was huffing and puffing, a mist of sweat glistening on his handsome face.

He took my arm in his and we walked to the porch. I smoothed out the back ruffle of my dress and took my seat on the garden bench. He sat next to me.

"Sure is a beautiful night. I don't think I've ever seen so many stars."

JD was right. The stars were plentiful and breathtaking in their design, with vivid polar white centers and points, and a fiery twinkle that demanded attention. "It sure is."

"I'm glad you came tonight, Emma."

"Me too. Where'd you learn to dance like that?"

"I had a sister, Sally, who was two years younger than me. Every Sunday, she took a dance lesson from old Mrs. Withers. When she came home, she insisted on practicing her new steps with me. If my lead wasn't to her liking, or if I turned at the wrong time, or if I stepped on her feet, she slapped me upside the head. I had to do my best if I didn't want to get the tar beat out of me." He laughed quietly. "Sally was a bit of a tyrant, but a lovable one."

"Do you still see each other?'

"No," he answered poignantly. "She passed away awhile back."

"I'm sorry."

"I miss her every day. She was my world. Ma and Pa were both sickly and died when I was five. Sally and me went to live with my Uncle Pete. Neither of us ever really got on with Uncle Pete. He had no affection for us. Seemed like a day didn't go by without him reminding us of what a burden we were to him. Know what I mean?"

"Yes," I said sincerely, remembering the similarly cold treatment I had received from my Uncle Shamus. But Uncle Shamus had done one good thing for me. He'd bought me my first Colt Paterson revolver. While the other girls had learned how to bake a cake, I had practiced shooting bottles and cans off the tree stump in his backyard. The only time I was happy was when I had my long-nosed, steel-bodied, six-chambered pal and protector in my hand.

Uncle Shamus had never seemed to object to my obsession with this dangerous weapon. I suppose that was because he hoped I'd accidently shoot myself and he'd be rid of me. He had been less than thrilled when I had won the first-place medal for superior speed and marksmanship at our annual County Fair, beating out some twenty grown men, though I was barely fourteen.

"What about you?"

"What about me?"

"Any kin?"

"No. My ma and pa passed away a long time ago," I said, not really knowing or caring if this was true. "My Uncle Shamus took me in, but he passed away too."

"No other family?"

I looked at the ground, stalling for time, debating whether or not I should tell him about Gregory. Not only because that part of my life was over and done with, but also because I didn't want him to think of me as a widow. I knew that in the minds of many men the label was a negative one. One that inspired a sort of begrudging pity, as if the man's death was tragic but being asked to extend a helping hand to his surviving widow was an imposition. I didn't want his pity. I wanted his respect.

"I was married once. My husband's name was Gregory. He's dead now." I waited for his reaction with bated breath.

"Was Gregory a good man?"

My mouth dropped open. I hadn't anticipated him asking this strange and intimate question. I had expected him to say he was sorry to hear that. Maybe even that he was glad that I was free to court him. This question made it clear that he didn't pity me, but it was far too personal. It went right to the heart of my relationship with Gregory. How did I answer it? Did I say, yes, he was a good man? He provided me with food, clothing, and shelter. Or did I say no, he was an animal? A man who was so selfish and cruel that he spent our second and third wedding anniversary in the bed of his sultry, raven-haired mistress.

"No. He wasn't a good man. I'm glad he's dead," I said, with a bluntness in my voice that stunned me.

"Why'd you stay with a man like that, when you have so much to offer?"

I couldn't explain my puzzling behavior when it came to staying with Gregory to JD any better than I could explain it to myself. I wasn't dim-witted or weak-willed. I deserved better than Gregory and I knew it.

"I don't know," I said, lamely.

"I'm sorry." He raised my gaze to his. "I didn't mean to pry. It's just that you are a fascinating woman, but a hard one to get to know." He cupped my chin in his hands.

I saw the hungry, wanton look in his eyes that Pastor Green had preached against at every Sunday sermon. The look that said abandon your reason and logic, and your clothes. He drew me closer and pressed his moist lips to mine. It was as if this was the kiss I had been waiting for for years. The kiss that felt like the first rain after a long drought. The kiss that I would never have regrets about. Every part of me was on fire. I may have been married before, but I had never once felt the unfamiliar throbbing that I felt between my legs now. Or the heavy pounding in my heart. I wanted him to touch me, to never stop touching me. I felt my nipples swell underneath my cotton corset as he ran his hands up and down the small of my back.

"I've wanted you since the first time I saw you," he whispered seductively. "Come home with me tonight."

"I can't wait that long," I panted. "Let's go across the street to my diner. I have a cot in back." He gently swept me off my feet. I wrapped my arms around his neck and laid my head on his chest, breathing in the intoxicating, musky scent of his thick skin as he walked.

After he set me down, I was in such a hurry to get inside I dropped the keys twice. "Damn it!" I muttered.

JD picked up the keys and unlocked the door. I closed it behind us. Once we were face to face, he kissed me again. But this time, more ferociously. More demanding. There was no space between us, but I pulled him closer, digging my fingernails into his back.

"Don't stop," I moaned, as he suckled on my breast. He raised my skirt and petticoat over my hips. My body began to buck wildly as he slid his hot fingers inside me. In and out, over and over. Harder. Faster. I couldn't control myself. I didn't want to. Pastor Green was right. This felt too good not to be a mortal sin.

"Where's the cot?" he asked, his voice dripping with want.

"Later for the cot." I pushed him backward on the dusty floor until his body lay flat and flush against the planks of wood beneath him. I kneeled beside him. My fingers quivered as I pulled his pants down and took his swollen cock in my hand. The more I stroked his bare flesh, the harder it got. "I need you inside me. Now."

He gripped my fleshy buttocks and lifted me on top of him. He sunk his engorged organ into me, deeper and deeper until I screamed his name and he screamed mine. As we lay in each other's arms, still partially clothed, I realized this was the first time I had ever made love. Been with a man that gave as much as he took. I was glad that I was a woman, soft and pliable in his strong hands. I relished the raw, primal, possessive feel of him holding me so tight I could scarcely draw breath. I wanted more.

"Let's go find that cot now," I said as I started to rub his growing shaft again.

## Chapter Four

Half awake and half asleep on the small, lumpy cot in my storeroom, I heard the hissing, popping sizzle of bacon frying. I wondered what time it was. There wasn't much light coming from the teeny, overhead porthole window, but by the grayness of the room, I guessed it had to be dawn. No matter how tired I was, it was time to get my ass in gear.

I stood up and wrapped the cotton blanket at the foot of the cot around my naked body, holding it in place with one hand and folding the flimsy mattress and collapsible metal frame in half and latching it shut with the other. I grinned as I looked at the fancy blue silk dress I had worn last night, bunched up in a ball in the middle of the floor. The frilly bodice was going to need some serious mending. JD had practically ripped it off me when he grew tired of fumbling with the delicate pearl buttons.

Lazily strolling over to the footlocker by the door, I dropped the blanket and slipped into a freshly laundered pair of jeans and a white button-down shirt. I smoothed my tousled blond curls down with my hand and walked around the corner and into the main dining area.

When I saw JD standing by the stove, I let out a soft giggle. He was flipping the fatty strips of bacon in the pan with a fork, one by one, with his white shirt sleeves rolled up to his elbow. He had my flowered pink apron tied around his waist. Though frying bacon was hardly an intimate act, this told me something about who he was. He was a man who was comfortable in his manhood, secure enough to do whatever he pleased, even if he looked ridiculous doing it. It was the most endearing sight I had ever seen.

"I thought you were kidding about making breakfast," I said, as I walked up behind him and wrapped my arms around his waist.

He lay the pan on the counter and turned around to face me. "I promised I would." He slipped his hand under the back of my untucked shirt, his fingers leaving a hot trail from the tip of my spine to the nape of my neck. "Hope you don't mind me borrowing your apron. I'm a good cook, but a sloppy one. How do you like your eggs?" he asked, his manly southern drawl so teasing and sexy it made the moisture between my legs resurface.

"Sunnyside up."

"Go sit down." He playfully slapped my bottom. "I'll bring your food over in a minute."

JD washed, dried, and put away every pot and pan he had used and the last of the breakfast plates. He smiled as he untied the apron and laid it on the empty table next to me. "Well?" He pulled up a chair and sat down.

"The meal was delicious." I sipped his perfectly blended, not too strong, not too weak coffee. "You cook, you clean, and you dance like the dickens. If you knew how to sew, you'd be perfect."

"I sew. Quite well too."

"Showoff," I cooed. "You'll make some woman a wonderful husband one day."

"Maybe that woman will be you. Would you like that?" He had such an intense look on his face that I knew he was serious.

I started to squirm in my chair. It was a bold, ill-timed proposal that made me feel uncomfortable. He was moving too fast. It was obvious the physical attraction between us was strong. But beyond that, I knew nothing about him. It wasn't that I was opposed to marriage, but after my disastrous alliance with Gregory, I could not afford to act like some googly-eyed schoolgirl and throw caution to the wind. "I don't know you well enough to answer that question."

"You know exactly who I am, Emma." His sensitive, yet penetrating stare caressed every inch of me. "I'm the man who wants to know every line of your face, every curve of your flesh. I want to hear your voice, share your thoughts, monopolize your heart. I'm the man that adores you. What more do you need to know?"

When he put it that way, so direct and simple, breaking down strands of complex feelings and bundling them together like they were no more complicated than links of sausage, what more did I need to know? Even if I didn't need to know anything more about him, he needed to know more about me.

"I treasure your sentiment, I really do. But I don't think you have any idea who you are pledging your heart to," I said, past a lump growing in my throat. "I've made some bad mistakes in my past; mistakes I can't undo."

"Like what?"

"You wouldn't understand."

"Try me."

"I—"

My words froze in my throat. I couldn't bear to see the horrified look on his face when I told him his sweet little Emma, who slaved over a stove all day and went to bed as early as the chickens every night, had once been a hunter and killer of men.

"We all have a past." He locked his fingers in mine. "I'm afraid mine is catching up with me a lot sooner than I thought it would."

"What do you mean?" I asked, uneasy with the subtle edginess in his voice.

"I'd love to court you proper, take you dancing, enjoy a Sunday stroll in the park. But I can't. I'm running out of time." He stared me dead in the eye. "I—"

The bell over the door tinkered as old man Tucker limped in. "Morning, JD. Emma. You left your pretty shawl in my house last night. Guess you two young'uns had other things on your mind," he said, a sly grin plastered on his face. "Anyhow, I was picking up some supplies at Clyde's and thought I'd drop it off."

"That was nice of you."

"'Tweren't no big deal." He laid the black, knitted shawl on the back of the chair closest to him. "Smells mighty good in here, Miss Emma. You open for breakfast yet?"

"Uh, well, sure."

"Ain't making a pest of myself, am I?"

"No sir, Mr. Tucker. Take a seat. I was just heading out." JD rolled down his shirt sleeves. He leaned forward and kissed me on the cheek. "Come to my ranch at seven o'clock Friday night," he whispered in my ear. "Just head straight west. I'm less than a half-mile past the Oatman sign that marks the edge of town. It's a small place with big windows in the front and lots of flowers. I will tell you everything."

I tried to focus on getting the lumps out of old man Curtis's overcooked brown gravy and the hard crunch out of the undercooked grits. But it was no use. All I could think of was JD's strange behavior and him telling me he was running out of time. There were only two types of young men that had a reduced shelf life. One type was those that were terminally ill. The other, those that were wanted by the law and about to be apprehended. Even if he hadn't been the picture of health, in my gut, I already knew which type he was.

## Chapter Five

Friday was here. Despite my despairing mood and Blazie's intolerably slow arthritic gait down the trail that led to JD's cabin, I couldn't ignore the beauty around me. The green mountains were charcoal gray now, with a bodacious sky above them that proudly displayed wispy patches of faded, pink clouds nestled cozily against a pronounced royal blue and purple backsplash. Even the scraggly cactus plants that lined both sides of the road looked fat and fluffy in the disappearing light of day. Like they were wearing fuzzy black sweaters. It was the kind of scene you'd read about in a romance book. Two young lovers, meeting in the wide, open range, riding off into the sunset to live happily ever after.

But this was no romance book. After what JD had said to me about running out of time, I doubted if I'd be riding off into the sunset or anywhere else with him. I felt like such a fool. All the telltale signs of him being on the run were there. The way he'd always nervously looked over his shoulder as he'd eaten his breakfast, politely excused himself and walked out of the diner every time a stranger had tried to engage him in small talk, cracked his knuckles whenever Sheriff Jones and his deputy had come in. It was obvious that he had been anxious. But I was so caught up in his soulful brown eyes I had never thought to ask him why. All I knew about him was what he had wanted me to see. He was a good cook, a fantastic dancer, and a warm and tender lover.

Maybe he was so good at loving because practice had made him that way. Was that what I was to him? A conquest to be made before he moved on to greener pastures? But if that were all he wanted me for, why didn't he just cut and run once he bedded me? If the law were hot on his trail, he was taking a big risk by staying around to explain his behavior to me. Still, I was taking a big risk by coming here too. I suspected he was a wanted man, but wanted for what, I didn't know. I shuddered to think that he could have been a crazed killer that had just murdered his whole family and was making plans to do the same to me.

"Whoa, Blazie," I said as I steered her over to the rustic building that five minutes ago had been little more than a dot in the distance. JD's cabin was just as he had described it. Small and boxy, with square, frameless, broad windows took up most of the front of the building. Row after row of muted red and orange flower petals peeked out of the terracotta flower pots that sat along the wide window ledge. It was charming, or would have been, had I been here under different circumstances. The soft glow of the amber candlelight on the table in the center of the room gave me a clear visual of JD's long, lean silhouette. He was pacing back and forth. I guessed he was as nervous as me.

I dismounted Blazie and tied her rawhide rein to the hitching post. My adrenaline spiked as I walked up the two steep deck stairs and knocked on the door, tightening the strap of my Colt revolver around my leg.

The door squeaked open. "Come in, Emma," JD said without any hint of surprise as his eyes dropped to the gun strapped to my leg. I gave him the same once over, relieved that he was not wearing his gun belt under his waistcoat, at least not as far as I could see.

I sat down at the table, keeping my left hand on the arm of the ladderback chair, but my right hand close to the gun in my holster. JD sat down and pulled his chair next to mine. I scooted back in my seat.

"Please don't treat me as if I had the plague."

"How should I treat you, JD? You lied to me." I felt the tears well up in my eyes. "You used me."

"No. I never used you, Emma. But I did lie. About who I was. I bought you here so that I could make that right. Ask me anything you want."

"Who are you?"

His pregnant pause added to my angst.

"I'm the most wanted outlaw in the state." He said in a barely audible, boyish voice. "My name is Johnny David Romma. My friends call me JD."

I felt as if I had been punched in the gut, the wind knocked out of me. Here I was sitting face to face with the same man who'd murdered my husband and turned me into a killer for hire. Every time I saw my victims' faces in my nightmares, I thought of Johnny Romma. I drew my gun and pointed it at his temple. This kill was one I wouldn't have any nightmares about.

"You murdered my husband," I shouted in a heated tone, cocking the trigger.

'No. I killed the man who murdered my baby sister."

"Liar!"

"I'm unarmed." He drew back the edge of his waistcoat. He was telling the truth. He didn't have a gun belt on. "I can prove what I say. I have something to show you. It's in my vest pocket."

I moved the barrel of the gun closer to his forehead. "Move nice and slow, or I swear I'll blow your head off."

He reached in his trim vest pocket and pulled out a coin-shaped locket. The clasp on the short, tattered, silver chain was broken off. He slid it across the table and in front of me. "Does this look familiar?"

I flipped the locket open with my free hand. I gasped when I saw the portrait of the square-jawed, green-eyed, mustached man and the pixie-nosed, pink-cheeked, blond girl with the floppy curls inside.

"Recognize the two people in the portrait? You should. One is you. The other is your husband."

"I gave this locket to Gregory on our wedding day," I uttered, befuddled. "He told me he lost it. How did you get it?"

"He lost it alright," Johnny said bitterly. "It was on the floor next to my sister's dead body. I guess when you're gutting a young woman you don't have time to worry about such trinkets falling out of your pocket."

"Why would he murder a woman he didn't even know?"

"He knew her. They met when she went to Yuma to settle our late Aunt Irma's affairs. He handed her the deed to the parcel of land that Aunt Irma had bequeathed her. She said Gregory was sweet and obliging.

He helped her navigate all the legalities when she sold the land. I was laying low with my friend Creasy at the time of my Aunt's death, staying up on his farm in Utah, when she sent me a telegram saying she had fallen in love.

"Less than ten weeks later, I got another telegram from her telling me that she had found out the man that she had given her heart to was married. She wrote that she had ended the affair and he was furious with her. I went home to try to console her. But I was too late. The bastard had already killed her. I did the same thing to Gregory that he did to my sister. Gutted him and left him to bleed out." His eyes bore into mine. "I'm sorry, but I won't apologize for what I did to Gregory."

My head started to ache. Gregory was a violent bully. I had known that firsthand. But a murderer? Why hadn't he killed me? He'd had plenty of opportunities. He could have pushed me off a cliff, thrown me into the river, or bludgeoned me to death and buried me in the backyard. Maybe it was because he had no feeling for me one way or the other. He neither hated me nor loved me. I was inconsequential. A brainless, heartless shell of a thing. Like a rock on the street. He beat me simply because he could. He rode me out of habit or boredom or both, with no emotion attached. I was so relieved when it was over, I never asked what his pitiless indifference to me had meant. Now I knew. Having a monster like Gregory truly love you was a death sentence.

Try as I may, I could no longer hate Johnny for what he had done to Gregory. If I had been in his shoes and had seen the person I loved most in the world slaughtered like a pig, I would've done the same thing. Revenge was a concept that was easy to understand. What was harder to grasp was why he had inserted himself into my life, why he was here with me now. I uncocked the trigger, but kept the gun pointed at his temple.

"I understand why you did what you did to Gregory now. I know who he was to you. But what I don't know is who am I to you?"

"At first, you were nothing more than Gregory's widow. As word spread of how good you were with your pistol, you became the woman I sought out to satisfy my professional curiosity. I had to meet the female that was said to be as quick as I was on the draw."

"Now?"

"You are now the woman I love." He took a step closer. "The woman I love to hold in my arms and comfort. Period."

As pathetic as it was, I wanted to believe him, to think that the passionate, loving connection we had shared was genuine. But our relationship was built on a lie. And that meant our love was too. I tightened my hand on my gun. I was not going to let him make a fool of me again.

"I don't believe you. Why would you love me when you know I'm obliged to take you in?"

"Because I know who you really are. I understand you."

"You couldn't possibly understand me."

"That's where you're wrong. You are just like me."

"I'm nothing like you. You rob banks. You kill for money."

"We both kill for the same reason, and it's not the money. It's to fill that void we have" —he touched his hand to his heart—"in here."

"That's not true. I kill men that are a threat to society. Guilty men. My work is sanctioned by the court."

"But not by God," he said sadly. "If you believe what you do is so righteous, why do you have nightmares?" he asked, his glare razor sharp.

My body trembled. I had never mentioned my nightmares to anyone. They were far too ugly. Johnny probing the darkest recesses of my mind made me feel like an insect on display.

"How-how did you know about the nightmares?" I stuttered.

"I have them too. Every night when I close my eyes, I see the faces of the men I have shot down. I replay the terrified look I saw in their eyes when they realized their next breath would be their last. I hear their pleas for mercy, so loud I feel as if I may go deaf. Some of the things I see in my dreams border on ridiculous, like Deputy Jack Ortiz with his head blown clean off his shoulders and lying next to my feet, smiling at me with his toothless grin and saying hello in Spanish. It's a terrible, unshakable feeling, knowing you've taken away everything a man ever was and everything he would have been, that he died because you are damaged. Make no mistake about it," he said, as he brushed my stiff cheek, "we are both damaged."

I hated that he saw me as damaged, even if he was putting himself in the same category. But on some level, I had to concede that maybe he was right. I was damaged. Maybe the degradation and humiliation of Gregory's beatings had left me with internal scars. Maybe I was punishing Slim and my other bounties for what Gregory had done to me and not for their true crimes. If my motives for killing were impure and vindictive, unjust, that might explain the reason I was having nightmares. I felt guilty. Riddled with remorse.

Now that I understood the reason for the nightmares, maybe I could figure out how to lessen my guilt, or what to do to stop them altogether. I slowly lowered and holstered my gun. I didn't embrace Johnny's damage theory, but I reluctantly accepted it. My steady stare met his.

"What you just said about me being damaged makes a lot of sense. I was oblivious to it before, but now I realize how badly Gregory's abuse has affected me. I don't think I hunted down my bounties because of who they were or what they had done," I said sheepishly. "I hunted them down because I was acting on the anger I felt towards Gregory. I've gotten that out of my system now. I think I can stop the nightmares."

He took a deep breath. "It's not that easy, Emma. The nightmares go way beyond Gregory," he said in a strained voice, his eyes wracked with exasperation. "Before you can stop them, you have to interpret their reason and their meaning. To do that, you have to go deep inside of yourself, search your soul. You have to see yourself as you really are. I can help you do that. Are you willing to let me, even if you don't like what you see?"

I felt a pinch of irritation. It was presumptuous of Johnny to imply that he knew me better than I knew myself. Like he could see some dark, obscure layer of my person that I was blind to. Still, I was curious to see what he had to say, even if it was bullshit.

"Yes," I answered in a rigid, vexed voice.

"When we were sitting on old man Tucker's porch, I asked you why you stayed with Gregory and you never answered me. I need you to answer that question now."

"I don't know."

"Did you stay because of his money?"

"No."

"Love?"

"No."

"Did he immobilize you physically?"

"No. I guess I was just too cowardly to run," I said, ashamed.

He took a step closer. "Look at me."

I raised my gaze to his.

"I think you stayed with Gregory because you were using him."

Johnny insinuating that Gregory was the victim in our marriage jarred me. "Using him for what? His boxing skills?"

"In a sense, yes."

My blood started to boil. "Are you saying I liked to be beat like a dog?"

"No. You didn't like to be beat. But you did like the attention it bought. At the time, that was the only way you knew how to get it."

"That's ridiculous!" I shouted, incensed.

He tried to wrap his arms around me, but I pulled away.

"How did you feel after he beat you?"

"Sick and sore."

"No. I mean how did you feel"—he touched his hand to my heart—"in here. When the stuffy shopkeepers and prissy teachers, who'd never said a word to you before, rallied around you and offered you support? When you went to the marshal and he nursed your wounds and fed you, like you were a child? You were the center of attention. An important, valuable person. Don't tell me you didn't love that feeling."

Shock kept me silent. Of course, I loved that feeling, but not because I was desperate for affection. Or out of some deranged need for attention. It was because—

My mind drew a blank. He was rearranging my thoughts in my head like pieces of furniture, trying to make them fit into his perverted assessment of me. I didn't know what went where anymore. It was frustrating not to be able to explain my own behavior.

He took my shaky hand in his, his grip firm. "I know what your biggest fear is, Emma. I saw it when I looked into your sad eyes the first time we met. I felt it when I made love to you. The desperation in your body, the need to have your existence validated. Your biggest fear isn't getting hit. It's not even dying. It's the same as mine. The fear of being invisible. We'd do anything to escape that isolating feeling of inferiority and worthlessness. Steal. Kill. Allow ourselves to be hit. Anything," he reiterated.

"That's not who I am," I said in a huff, not liking the grim picture he was painting of me.

"It's precisely who you are," he retorted. "Who we both are. Our need to be seen at any cost is like a disease. It festers inside of us, unrelenting and progressive. I don't know if we can conquer it, but if we want to control it, we need to understand it, to go back to the origin."

"You've lost me. You keep saying we, like I know what you are talking about. We need to understand the disease that we have. If we want to conquer it, we need to go back to the origin. What does that even mean, the origin?"

"The beginning. The point in our lives when we first realized how lousy we felt and who was responsible for making us feel that way. My devastating, life-altering sense of invisibility began to take shape when I was five, when Sally and I went to live with my Uncle Pete after we were orphaned. From the moment I set foot in his house, he went out of his way to snub me. It started off with little things, like him never remembering my name and sometimes forgetting to set a place at the dinner table for me. After a few years, it got much worse. Uncle Pete stopped talking to me altogether and refused to even look at me. There were days I had to pinch myself to make sure I was flesh and blood, not just a puff of smoke. I was so unhappy I ran away from home the day I turned fifteen. I had no money and nowhere to go. I ended up sleeping in the gutter, starving. That's when I had robbed my first bank."

His smile was the most moving one I had ever seen. Both sorrowful and blissful. Like he was reminiscing his birth and his death at the same time.

"The sheriff sent a posse after me. There were five men on horseback, all riding as fast as they could, kicking up dust and firing their rifles at my head. Astonishingly, I didn't feel scared. I felt alive. After years of being nonexistent, someone had finally seen me. That was all I cared about. Not killing or dying. The glory of being seen. Being seen meant being real. Being real meant being loved. It's twisted, but that's the truth. Once I had experienced that high, I knew there was no way I could go back to being Uncle Pete's nameless boy."

He pulled me close.

"You may have stayed with Gregory because of the attention his barbarity afforded you. But it wasn't Gregory that initiated that pathological, all-consuming need to be noticed inside you. Your illness originated long before that. Who was it?" he asked, his tone hypnotic and coaxing. "Who was your Uncle Pete?"

I wanted to protest, to keep my guard up and tell him he was wrong. I didn't stay with Gregory because I had an obsessive need for attention. Nor did I have an Uncle Pete that had made me feel invisible. But the truth was, he wasn't wrong. I had known for a long time that I hadn't stayed with Gregory for love or money, or out of fear. If I had stayed with him for any other reason than the one that Johnny suggesting now,

I would've figured it out already. Johnny's explanation was the only one that fit my bizarre behavior.

And I did have an Uncle Pete. As the matter of fact, I had two. Two people in my past life that should have loved and cherished me, but had instead taken every opportunity to belittle me, to cripple me emotionally. In spite of everything Johnny was, or maybe because of everything he was, I trusted him. He was the only one in the world that wouldn't judge me.

Johnny had introduced himself to me. It was time for me to introduce myself to Johnny. My real self. That sullen, insecure, abandoned child who felt as if she inspired even less love than a rat. I felt my heart break as the painful memories of a traumatic childhood once again took center stage in my mind.

"My mother and father. They were my Uncle Pete," I said, in a nervous hush. "They initiated that all-consuming need in me to be noticed."

"What did they do?"

"When I was nine, they sent me to the store to get a sack of cornmeal. I came back and they were gone. They had taken everything we owned, even the cat, Mittens. I never saw them again."

"I'm sorry," he said, empathetically.

"It shouldn't have surprised me. They never remembered anything about me. My birthday, my favorite color, what kind of candy I liked to eat, what kind of games I liked to play. Nothing. I was there, but I was a ghost they couldn't see. They left me behind to die," I sobbed, unable to hold back my tears. "You were right. About me loving the sympathy and pity I got from everyone in town when Gregory beat me. About me feeling invisible. About the void I have in my heart. I didn't want to admit it, but I knew there was something off about me the first time I shot a man when he'd tried to steal my horse. When I saw his dead body on the ground, I felt sick. Not only because his flesh was covered in blood from head to toe and had a pungent ammonia scent that burned my nostrils, but because I realized I had done the unthinkable. I had taken a precious human life. Deep down inside, it felt wrong. I didn't think I'd ever be able to move past that horror. Yet, the minute Marshal Tate had handed me the bounty money, that sick feeling miraculously went away. I was on cloud nine. I told myself I was so happy because it was a lot of money he had given me and I needed it badly, but that wasn't the reason. The real reason was that when he paid me, I had felt recognized, like I was the star of my own show."

"He saw you," Johnny said, in a caring voice.

"Yes." I looked into his eyes. "No one can understand how good that felt, or what someone like me would do to hang onto that feeling. Every time I gunned a man down and collected a bounty, it was like I was spitting in Ma and Pa's face, letting them know I was somebody, that they'd made the wrong decision by cutting me loose. I felt that way up until the time I started having nightmares, when it seemed the devil had come to collect his due. Tonight, I tried to blame Gregory for my nightmares. Before that, I blamed you. The only person I should have blamed was myself. I'm sorry." I meant it with all my heart.

"Don't be."

"For better or worse, I know who I am now, Johnny. I've searched my soul and gone deep inside of myself, like you told me to. But I still don't understand the nightmares. If I am so bad, and if you are so bad, why should either of us lose any sleep over what we have done? We should revel and gloat in our evil, not have nightmares."

"The nightmares are a blessing."

"It doesn't feel that way."

"I know. But the pain they bring are God's way of reminding us that we have a conscience, that we are still worthy of forgiveness."

"Forgiveness," I said, in a defeated voice. "How would we get that? After all the harm that we have done?"

"We need to earn it. Before we can be forgiven, we have to learn how to forgive. We can start with those who have wronged us the most. I need to let go of my anger towards my Uncle Pete, and you need to let go of your anger towards your ma and pa. Maybe we can try to look at them as flawed human beings who've made mistakes, just as we have. I think once we've gotten all that stagnating hatred out of our system, we can move forward, commit all our energy to loving each other. If we can forge new memories built on love and not on hate, create rather than destroy, maybe we can balance the scales. Salvage our souls."

I wished I felt as confident as Johnny sounded, but I didn't. "What if I can't forgive Ma and Pa?"

"You can try. So can I. It's the only chance we have. "Come with me." He touched his forehead to mine. "Help me heal. Help yourself heal. Stop the nightmares for both of us."

"I'll be hunted for the rest of my life." I held his stare. "I don't know if I can live like that."

"My darling Emma," he murmured, tracing the outline of my lips with his finger. "You are so new at this game, so innocent. Don't you know you're already hunted? Those men you killed had family and friends who loved them. They want to even the score. They will seek you out. I found you with very little effort. You have a reputation now. That will always follow you, just like mine will follow me."

"It's ironic." I hung my head, letting the knowledge that I'd gone from being the hunter to being the hunted sink in. "I always wanted to make a name for myself. Now that I have, it's destroying me."

"Don't think like that," he said, encouragingly. "If we go far enough away, and if enough time passes, maybe they'll forget about us. Overseas. Perhaps Spain. We can swim, lie in the sun, and eat all day. I can bake you *pan de leche* for breakfast, some *paella de marisco* for lunch, *arroz cubano* for dinner. Would you like that?"

"I have no idea what you just said, but yes," I smiled. "If you cooked it, I'd like it."

"We can go wherever you want. But we have to leave soon. Time is a luxury neither of us has."

Johnny had faith in me. But did I have faith in myself? "I don't know what to do."

"Follow your heart." He whispered, as his lips met mine.

I was lost in his deep, moist, passionate kiss when I heard Blazie's high-pitched, nervous neigh.

"Someone's here!" Alarmed, I whipped my body around and faced the front door. The door flew off the hinges, landing on the hooked rug by the entryway with a muffled thud. On the other side of the threshold stood Snub Nose Mike and his brother Smiley. Both had their guns drawn and pointed directly at Johnny.

"No tricks, Romma," Mike said as he cocked the trigger of his gun. "Get those hands in the air where I can see them." He angled his head to the left. "Emma? I thought you'd retired."

"I did, for a while." I said, in a small voice.

"I smelled you coming a week ago, bounty hunter. How'd you find me?" Johnny asked, disdainfully.

"Creasy gave you up. Took some doing, but a man will say anything when you dip his feet in a bucket of kerosene and set them on fire."

"Damn animal!"

"And then some," Mike replied, sadistically. "Move out of the way, Emma. I aim to shoot me a killer."

I stepped in front of Johnny, shielding his body with mine. "He's unarmed."

"Good," he said, whistling for the men shuffling on the deck outside to come in. "Cos if he wasn't, we'd be in deep shit. Last summer, Johnny Romma here shot six men at once up in Colorado. Men quick on the draw, that made their living with their pistols." His eyes zoned in on Johnny's face. "That's quite a feat. There's only five of us here tonight so it should be easy for you to repeat the same thing. Maybe not, seeing as how you don't have a gun. Move, Emma," he said a second time, the impatience in his voice obvious.

"No," I roared stubbornly. "I won't let you kill a man in cold blood."

"Ain't like you to give so much consideration to the finer points of the law." His brow tightened as he studied Johnny's face, then mine. "What a hoot." Mike chuckled. "You're partial to this murdering scum, ain't you? That simpering look on your face says it all. You know something? I'm almost glad this happened. I never liked you much. Something about you didn't add up. One day you were Gregory's punching bag, the biggest scaredy cat I ever met, the next you were the most fearless bounty killer in the state. It's like you got two different people inside you. Who the hell are you really, Emma Tombs?"

"I'm an abominable person who has led a wasted and sterile life," I answered, without pride. "But I want to be someone better. Help me do that," I pleaded. "Let Johnny and me go."

"Not a chance." He closed his left eye and steadied his arm. "Goodnight, Romma."

I felt a hard shove to my shoulder and my gun being lifted out of its holster. I was on the floor in the blink of an eye. Five shots were fired so fast that the sound of one seemed to overlap the other. An eerie silence permeated the room. I tried to stand but became dizzy and fell. I felt the trail of warm blood begin to trickle from my forehead to my cheek. Panic started to set in. Had I been shot? Had Johnny been shot?

"Johnny," I screamed, my throat raspy.

"I'm here," he said, in a taut, attentive voice. He dropped my gun on the floor and kneeled down next to me, cradling my aching head and back in his arms.

"Are you OK?"

"Yes."

I touched my hand to my sticky forehead. "Am I shot?"

"No. You hit your head when I knocked you down." He undid his black bandana and gently wiped the blood off my face. "I'm sorry I hurt you. I didn't know any other way to get you out of the line of fire."

"Mike and the others, are they dead?"

"Yes." He faced the floor.

I raised my head off his lap and looked around the room. There were five crumpled bodies, all lying next to each other. Each had a single, straight line of bright red blood that ran from that gaping, black, powdery bullet hole between his eyes, down the bridge of his nose, past the cleft of his chin, and disappeared beneath the top of his shirt collar. Marshal Tate was right. Johnny was a neat and tidy killer. A gifted child that hadn't drawn outside the lines.

"You should've let me pull the trigger," I said, hating death, but wanting to assume the responsibility I felt for the men being shot with my gun. "I could've taken them."

"I know."

"Why didn't you let me?"

"Because that'll be five less faces you'll have to see in your nightmares," he said, his voice clear. "I don't ever want to see you suffer. I love you. If you don't feel the same about me, tell me now." The tears hung suspended on his long, dark lashes. "If all I am to you is a low-down murdering scum like Mike said, then take me in. I won't resist."

My heart went out to the humble, gaunt-faced man holding me in his arms. If I acted on the letter of the law, the only course of action I had would be to take him in. To see him strung up for what he had done to Mike and his cohorts. There was no question of his guilt. I had witnessed all five murders firsthand. Yet, he'd acted as he had to save me. He had eaten my sins, choked on them, risked his own sanity so I wouldn't have to risk mine. He had accepted my depravity without reservation.

He saw me, and I saw him. We hadn't bonded together over the exchange of sweet chocolates and fragrant flowers. We had bonded together over the profanity and bitterness of death. I might have been crazy, but I wanted to believe that would make a stable foundation, one that was stronger than any vow taken in church or any signed legal paper.

"I'm not taking you in Johnny." I lay my head on his chest. "I love you too much to do that."

He stood up and held out his trembling hand. "Then let the men in this room be the last we ever hurt. Will you come with me?" he asked, in a vulnerable voice. "Leave behind Emma the undisputed Angel of Death, start a new life as my wife?"

A sweet picture enveloped my mind as I looked into his warm brown eyes. I saw myself, dressed in faded dungarees and a plain white cotton shirt, just as I was now, sitting in a worn-out wicker rocking chair, with a fluffy, orange kitten stretched out across my lap and a floppy-eared, big-footed black puppy curled up in a ball at my feet. My cheeks were plump, and my belly was swollen, as if I had just swallowed a whole watermelon. What I didn't see anywhere in the picture was my Colt revolver or a dead body.

The name Johnny Romma still held more meaning for me than any other. But he was no longer just the man that changed my life. He was the man that saved my life. The dark knight in tarnished armor that had lassoed my heart and given me the inner peace that had eluded me for so long. For the first time ever, I was a whole human being.

"Yes, I will come with you," I said, as I took his hand in mine and felt the divine hope of those given a second chance at life blossom inside me.

## The End

# About the authors

## Zia Westfield

Zia Westfield has a penchant for the quirky and the zany, qualities which often show up in her paranormal romantic suspense stories. Her contemporary romantic suspense tales follow a more traditional path, but there's always room for a dose of humor or a little snark. She makes her home in Tokyo with her husband and sons. She holds a full-time job, volunteers too much because she doesn't know how to say "no," and generally finds peace between the pages of a book or when she's writing out the stories in her head.

## Callie Carmen

Callie started in the book business as a bookstore manager, which was the perfect place for her since she was an avid reader. After two years, she moved to the corporate office as a buyer and eventually became a senior book buyer. This was a rewarding career she loved.

Along the way, Callie decided to become a stay home mom, but couldn't give up working around books altogether. She volunteered to run the book fairs in her small town, six per year. At the same time, Callie started and ran A Child Oasis Company, with the sole purpose of placing a small book library in the homes of all the needy children in the nearby city.

As her children became teens, Callie found she needed more in her personal life than being the volunteer mom for the schools. She sat down at the computer one day and Patrick, Book One of the Risking Love series was born. Since then she has completed five of the six novels in the series. Michael, the final book in the series is in edits and should be out by winter 2021. All can be read as standalone stories. She also wrote Dream Catcher, published by Black Velvet Seductions as part of the Mystic Desire anthology and a mobster romance, The Enemy I Know, in the Craving Loyalty Anthology. If you enjoyed reading Ava's story, pick up a copy of Joshua, Book Five of the Risking Love series where Ava's story began.

Callie is married to her soul mate and best friend. Like her characters, she is a firm believer in true love and love at first sight.

## Virginia Wallace

Virginia Wallace is a native of the Chesapeake Bay region, on the Southeast coast of the United States. Nomadic by nature, Virginia has lived all over, from the mountains of New England to the rolling hills of the American Heartland.

She began her creative career during her late teens and early twenties, working as a freelance portrait and commercial artist. She slowly transitioned into writing, eventually self-publishing three novels for the indie book market.

As a writer, Virginia Wallace has always worked at meshing modern stories with a lush style reminiscent of 19th Century American and European literature.

## Jan Selbourne

Jan Selbourne was born and educated in Melbourne, Australia and her love of literature and history began as soon as she learned to read and hold a pen. After graduating from a Melbourne business college her career began in the dusty world of ledgers and accounting, working in Victoria, Queensland and the United Kingdom. On the point of retiring she changed course to work as secretary of a large New South Wales historical society. Now retired, Jan is enjoying her love of traveling and literature. She has two children, a stray live-in cat and lives near Maitland, New South Wales.

## Alice Renaud

Alice lives in London, UK with her husband and son. By day she works full time as a compliance specialist for a pharmaceutical company. On Sundays she's a lay assistant in her local church. By night she writes fantasy and paranormal romance about shape-shifting mermen, lovelorn demons and thieving angels. A Merman's Choice is the first book in a trilogy inspired by the landscapes of Brittany (where she was raised) and Wales (her mother's homeland). She never completely grew up.

# Estelle Pettersen

Estelle Pettersen is an Australian author and former journalist whose romance stories explore empowerment, freedom, and finding one's strength. She has a Bachelor of Arts degree, majoring in Journalism and Psychology, from the University of Queensland, Australia. Her second degree is an MBA from Queensland University of Technology, Australia. She is a member of Romance Writers of Australia and is passionate about history, languages, cultures, traveling, food, and wine. She is happily married and living in Norway these days.

# Eileen Troemel

Author of Moon Affirmations as well as poetry, novels, and short stories, Eileen enjoys telling a good story or expressing a heartfelt emotion. She's been published in The American Tarot Association's Quarterly Journal, What's Cooking America, Children, Churches and Daddies, and many other publications. In addition to her work, she loves to read, crochet, craft, research genealogy, and spend time with family. She has three adult daughters and has been married to her husband for 40 years.

# Nancy Golinski

Nancy is married and lives on the outskirts of Amish country in the great state of Ohio. When she's not writing, you can usually find her hiking, crafting, traveling, or attending the theatre. She is also a part-time college professor and has written two nonfiction books on women's health.

# Patricia Elliott

Patricia Elliott lives in beautiful British Columbia with her family. Now that her four kids are more independent, being 16+ years old, she has chosen to actively pursue her passion for the written word. When she was a youngster, she spent the majority of her time writing fanfiction and poetry to avoid the harsh reality of bullying. Writing allowed her to escape into another world, even if temporarily; a world in which she could be anyone or anything, even a mermaid. Dreams really can come true. If you believe it, you can achieve it!

## Dee S. Knight

A few years ago, Dee S. Knight began writing, making getting up in the morning fun. During the day, her characters killed people, fell in love, became drunk with power, or sober with responsibility. And they had sex, lots of sex. Writing was so much fun Dee decided to keep at it. That's how she spends her days. Her nights? Well, she's lucky that her dream man, childhood sweetheart, and long-time hubby are all the same guy, and nights are their secret. Dee loves writing erotic romance and sharing her stories with you. She hopes you enjoy!

## R.M. Olivia

R.M. Olivia writes sexy romance. She doesn't discriminate in her choice of characters or stories. As long as the characters speak to her, she will continue to write. She enjoys rainy evenings, sunsets, and strawberry cheesecake truffles. Is chocolate better than sex? She thinks so.

Writing is her creative outlet and favorite escape. She hopes her writing transports readers to a place without limits and causes them to shed their inhibitions at the first click of the page.

## Starla Kaye

Starla wears many hats professionally and as a writer. She is the community coordinator for a Midwestern accounting firm, a gerontologist who volunteers with an active group of senior adults, a mentor/teacher of writing, and a multi-published author. She dabbles in writing romances of many sub-genres: contemporary, historical Western, medieval, sci-fi, fantasy, paranormal, and Regency. To date, she has published 20 novels, 37 novellas, 7 anthologies, and 15 short stories.

## Alan Souter

Alan is the author and co-author of more than 50 traditionally published U.S. histories, military histories, biographies, fine arts and auto racing titles. He graduated from the School of the Chicago Art Institute and the University of Chicago with a Bachelor Degree and graduate honors in photography. As a photojournalist, he has covered assignments in most of the world from the Arctic to sailing up the Nile and across the Egyptian Sahara on camelback, documented stories in the

British Isles, South America, China, the Caribbean, and North America. His articles and columns have appeared in dozens of magazines and newspapers. Alan's background also includes the U.S. Merchant Marine, parachuting, and certified expert marksman. With his co-author wife, Janet, he founded the Avril 1 Group, Inc. in 1997 and has produced lectures on their books and adventures. They have three grown children in the arts and communications.

## Suzanne Smith

Suzanne grew up in Bucktown, a bustling community on the Northwest side of Chicago. She attended North Park College and earned a Bachelor's degree in Liberal Arts. Currently, she works full time as the manager of a dental office located in the Gold Coast area of Chicago. When she's not working, she likes to curl up on the sofa and watch a good movie or read a good book with her two rescue cats.

# More Black Velvet Seductions titles

Their Lady Gloriana by Starla Kaye
Cowboys in Charge by Starla Kaye
Her Cowboy's Way by Starla Kaye
Punished by Richard Savage, Nadia Nautalia & Starla Kaye
Accidental Affair by Leslie McKelvey
Right Place, Right Time by Leslie McKelvey
Her Sister's Keeper by Leslie McKelvey
Playing for Keeps by Glenda Horsfall
Playing By His Rules by Glenda Horsfall
The Stir of Echo by Susan Gabriel
Rally Fever by Crea Jones
Behind The Clouds by Jan Selbourne
Trusting Love Again by Starla Kaye
Runaway Heart by Leslie McKelvey
The Otherling by Heather M. Walker
First Submission - Anthology
These Eyes So Green by Deborah Kelsey
Dark Awakening by Karlene Cameron
The Reclaiming of Charlotte Moss by Heather M. Walker
Ryann's Revenge by Rai Karr & Breanna Hayse
The Postman's Daughter by Sally Anne Palmer
Final Kill by Leslie McKelvey
Killer Secrets by Zia Westfield
Crossover, Texas by Freia Hooper-Bradford
The Caretaker by Carol Schoenig
The King's Blade by L.J. Dare
Uniform Desire - Anthology
Safe by Keren Hughes
Finishing the Game by M.K. Smith
Out of the Shadows by Gabriella Hewitt
A Woman's Secret by C.L. Koch
Her Lover's Face by Patricia Elliott
Naval Maneuvers by Dee S. Knight
Perilous Love by Jan Selbourne
Patrick by Callie Carmen
The Brute and I by Suzanne Smith
Home by Keren Hughes
Only A Good Man Will Do by Dee S. Knight

Secret Santa by Keren Hughes
Killer Lies by Zia Westfield
A Merman's Choice by Alice Renaud
All She Ever Needed by Lora Logan
Nicolas by Callie Carmen
Paging Dr. Turov by Gibby Campbell
Out of the Ashes by Keren Hughes
A Thread of Sand by Alan Souter
Stolen Beauty by Piper St. James
Mystic Desire - Anthology
Killer Deceptions by Zia Westfield
Edgeplay by Annabel Allan
Music for a Merman by Alice Renaud
Joseph by Callie Carmen
Not You Again! by Patricia Elliott
The Unveiling of Amber by Viola Russell
Husband Material by Keren Hughes
Never Have I Ever by Julia McBryant
Hard Limits by Annabel Allan
Anthony by Callie Carmen
Paper Hearts by Keren Hughes
The King's Spy by L.J. Dare
More Than Words by Keren Hughes & Jodie Harrold
Lessons on Seduction by Estelle Pettersen
Rigged by Annabel Allan
Desire Me Again - Anthology
Mermaids Marry in Green by Alice Renaud
Holy Matchmaker by Nancy Golinski
Joshua by Callie Carmen
Whiskey Lullaby by Keren Hughes
Forgiveness by Starla Kaye
When the White Knight Falls by Virginia Wallace

Our back catalog is being released on Kindle Unlimited
You can find us on:
Twitter: BVSBooks
Facebook: Black Velvet Seductions
See our bookshelf on Amazon now! Search "BVS Black Velvet
Seductions Publishing Company"